NIGHT
CANDY

NIGHT CANDY

A COLLEEN HAYES MYSTERY

MAX TOMLINSON

OCEANVIEW (PUBLISHING
SARASOTA, FLORIDA

ISBN 978-1-60809-621-3

Published in the United States of America by Oceanview Publishing

Sarasota, Florida

www.oceanviewpub.com

10 9 8 7 6 5 4 3 2

In memory of my father, Alfred Earl Tomlinson,
the man who gave me the writing bug

JUSTICE COMES IN MANY FORMS

DIANE CHAMBERLAIN

NIGHT
CANDY

NIGHT
CANDY

CHAPTER ONE

The end of the decade hung with winter cold as Colleen Hayes drove over to Chinatown to serve papers on a restaurant owner who'd stiffed forty-three illegals. A Friday night, the day after Thanksgiving. Boom, her associate, filled the Torino's passenger seat with a bulk that would have done a wrestler proud. His USMC field jacket was showing its age. So was Colleen's Torino, audibly sucking gas as it chugged up Leavenworth, leaving twin puffs of smoke in the rearview mirror when she down-shifted. Sister Sledge were on the radio, and they were family.

But Colleen's heart was too heavy with the news of her daughter to worry about the price of gas.

"Everything OK, Chief?" Boom asked, pushing his thick-framed glasses up his nose and flipping a page in the textbook in his lap. Boom was a Vietnam vet with dark brown skin and a calm voice. He supplemented his GI Bill by assisting Colleen on jobs where muscle might be required. Not being an ex-felon like Colleen, and having a gun permit, he was also able to legally carry a firearm.

Colleen said that everything *was* OK. There was no need to share her problems.

"You sure?"

"God, I hate to see that," she said, changing the subject.

On the next corner underneath a 1920s apartment building that had once been grand but now was not, three young women hunkered down in the cold. An Asian woman, in her thirties perhaps, wore a shortie black raincoat that showed off legs encased in black nylon. Her collar was up high around her ears. The girl in the middle was white, tall and lanky, with a dark mod hat pulled down over her long, shiny blonde hair, and knobby knees peeking above black platform boots. She wore a big Giants varsity jacket. Skinny white thighs ended in snug denim hot pants. She shivered as she stood next to a fireplug of a Black woman with a stylish Afro, smoking a long cigarette in terse puffs. None of the three women were smiling. There wasn't a reason to. It was a miserable night. If all went well, they'd collect twenty dollars a pop from anonymous clients who hopefully wouldn't mistreat them, give half to some pimp who might, and do it all again tomorrow.

"Hate to see it too," Boom said.

Night Candy hadn't struck for a while. But even so.

She couldn't just drive by.

Colleen blew a hard sigh, shifted the Torino down, pulled up in front of the ladies on the corner. Came to a stop, engine rumbling in idle. She yanked the handbrake, got out of the car. In her chamois-soft bell-bottom denims and black leather coat, she wasn't competition for the three, who were dolled up to attract business. Her long, dark hair was pulled back in a no-nonsense ponytail and looped through the back of a Giants ball cap.

"Evening, ladies," she said.

The Black woman blew a puff of crystalline smoke and shook her head.

"Go Giants," the tall blondie said in a twang, nodding at Colleen's hat. She had a sizable nose and lots of makeup to hide the black eye she was sporting. Reminded Colleen of herself when she was still young, married to a guy she eventually put an end to, spending the better part of a decade in prison for it. "How you doin' yourself, Officer?"

"I'm no cop," Colleen said. "Just another citizen."

"One looking for a party?" the Asian woman said with a curious look.

"Nope," Colleen said.

"How about your friend there?" the Black woman said, indicating Boom in the car. "He's a bruiser."

"Nope, and nope," Colleen said.

"We don't need competition or representation," she said in a cool voice, sipping her cigarette. "Already spoken for."

"Does he make sure you use rubbers?" Colleen said. "There's some scary shit going around."

"You might just find out how scary, you don't mind your own damn business and mosey on. He won't like it, he sees you interrupting commerce."

"If you don't buy," Blondie said, fluttering her long fingers, adorned with rings. "Then you must fly."

"I can't imagine you three haven't seen the news," Colleen said.

"Night Candy," the Asian woman said. "Yes, we know. But it's been months since anything happened."

"Even so," Colleen said, "it's not a concern?"

"The ozone layer concerns me," Blondie said. "But what can *I* do about it?" She gave a taut grin, and a small inlaid diamond sparkled on a canine tooth.

"My dang rent concerns me," said the Asian woman.

"Well," Colleen said, handing out business cards, "if you three ever want to think about a career change, give me a call. No charge."

The blonde woman read her card, the Asian woman stuck hers in her pocket, and the Black woman handed hers back.

"Hayes Confidential," Blondie said, looking up. "Private Investigator."

"You guys must've heard of COYOTE," Colleen continued. *Call Off Your Old Tired Ethics* was a sex worker's coalition founded a few years back. "An organization for working girls. I know the woman who runs it. If someone is giving you a bad time"—she eyed Blondie, who someone had given a bad time to—"or is taking too much of your hard-earned cash, or making you work when you don't want to, like a freezing cold night after Thanksgiving, she can tell you about your options. And, believe it or not, there are some."

"This has been a public service announcement," the Black woman said, smoking.

"We got it," the Asian woman said.

But the blonde woman was watching, listening. One out of three was better than none.

"You already know my name," Colleen said. "Colleen."

"Traci. With an *i*."

Colleen looked at the Asian woman with a questioning smile.

"Fia," she said.

Colleen turned to the Black woman, raised her eyebrows.

"None of your damn business," she said.

Two out of three.

"Well, nice to meet you all," Colleen said.

A car pulled up, a new BMW 6 series with a few rowdy guys in suits. The kind who made thirty K a year selling stock. An electric window whirred down, and a young face with a slick-back haircut gave Traci a leer and a come-hither finger.

"Prince Charming awaits." She strutted over with an exaggerated swagger. "*You* look like you like to live life on the edge," she said to the man at the wheel.

"How many times a night does she say that?" Colleen asked the others.

"Just go, already," the Black woman said, flicking her cigarette out past Colleen, just missing her, into the street where it spit embers.

"I can take a hint," Colleen said. "Well, I said my bit. Stay safe, ladies."

She went back to the car, got in.

"That looks like it went over like a lead balloon," Boom said.

"Just spreading joy wherever I go," Colleen said.

The radio was now playing "Funky Christmas."

"I don't frigging believe it," she said. "One day after Thanksgiving."

"It's called 'Christmas Creep,'" Boom said. "Gets worse every year."

"Pretty soon it'll be before T-day," Colleen said, stepping on the clutch, putting the car into gear. "Let's go serve some papers on Mr. Fan and get into the holiday spirit."

Before she took off, she glanced over at the frozen trio on the corner. Traci was negotiating with a suit and looked up long enough to catch her eye. She brushed a long strand of blonde hair out of her face and gave Colleen a wistful smile. Colleen returned it, thinking of her own daughter, Pam, out there on her own again, somewhere, who knew where.

CHAPTER TWO

Sitting in his car, Ray watched her from the corner of Polk and Pine. Tall, slender, long blonde hair. She looked like a real blonde. Just like Alice. She was lurking in the shadows under the awning of a camera store, its windows emblazoned with XMAS SALE ads, across the street from the Palms Café club. Guitars chopped the frozen air like buzz saws. Kids were hanging out in front of the Palms in spray-painted leather, ripped jeans, chains, spiky hair. A stiff Mohawk bobbed up and down. Cigarettes glowed and feet were stomped.

Ray saw her staying out of plain sight. A street hustler playing it low key. Black mini, torn fishnets, platform boots. Big black leather jacket, zipped up against the bone-chilling cold.

Get rid of the outfit, and a few other things, she could pass for Alice.

Just what he was looking for.

And she was alone. That was important.

Ray started up the Riviera, the big 455 growling to life, put the Buick into Drive, drove slowly past her doorway. She gave him a furtive little look as he trolled by, followed by raised eyebrows. She was open for business. A pretty oval face.

He drove down to the intersection, spun a U-ey, came back just as slow. A calm excitement overcame him. A new conquest.

He came to a stop in front of the awning across from the Palms. Hit the passenger-side electric window. Guitar noise bounced off the windows of the camera store and into the car, along with a blast of cold. He cranked the heater, double time.

She emerged from the shadows. Meeting his gaze. Her shiny long blonde hair was real, not a dye job. Crucial. Not much up top. But that was cool. Alice wasn't exactly buxom either.

She sashayed over to the car in her platforms. Leaned on the sill. Bracelets rattling. Gave him a wicked smile. Wide lips, painted pink.

"Hey, handsome," she said in a husky voice. "Nice car."

"How do you handle this cold?"

"A girl's gotta eat."

He smiled. "Which is what?"

She winked. "Just about everything."

He patted the passenger seat. "In that case you better get in."

"Whoa," she said. "It's forty."

Forty. High for street. But she was just what he needed.

"Cool. Get in."

She did and he could smell the patchouli oil as her window went up. Not his favorite scent.

They set off.

She flipped down the sun visor, adjusted her bangs. Lots of eye makeup. "Go down Polk," she said. "Turn left on Bush. There's a parking lot by the hospital."

"I was hoping for somewhere more private."

"This is plenty private," she said. "I know the guard. And your forty only buys you fifteen minutes." She consulted a big chunky watch. "Make that fourteen."

He acquiesced.

Down the street from St. Francisco Memorial, they parked in the back of the small doctor's lot, high brick walls of old SF Tenderloin on three sides. A hospital van on one side of the Riviera, a Mercedes on the other made it private, provided no one came along. It was dark.

"And you're sure about this?" Ray said.

"Like I said, I know the night security guard at the hospital. Trust me."

Trust a street hooker.

She turned, smiled.

"You're a good-looking guy," she said, touching his leg.

He knew that. In his prime, over six foot, toned at the gym daily, nice, neat chestnut hair, combed back, square jaw. Women liked him. And he took full advantage.

She pulled a condom from her jacket pocket.

And then he saw it. The Adam's apple.

"Oh, for fuck's sake," he said, exhaling.

"What is it, handsome?"

He nodded at her. *Him?* Smirked. "Talk about your false advertising."

She/he turned, perplexed. "What? Not what you wanted, sweetheart?"

"Not in the slightest."

"You sure about that?"

"Look," he said. "This isn't going to work. Just get out."

She/he reached for his crotch. "Don't knock it until you've tried it."

He smacked the hand away and saw now it was rougher than a woman's. That's what he got for being in a hurry. "Let's not and just say we did."

"Your loss." He put his hand out, palm up. "But there's still a little matter of forty bucks."

"Forty bucks, my ass. Get out."

"Seems you might be a tad confused about a couple of things," he said. "A deal's a deal."

Ray gripped the steering wheel with two fists. "I'm not confused about a damn thing. Especially what happens next if you don't get out of my fucking car." He turned, smiled, raised his eyebrows. "This is the last time I'm going to ask you nicely."

He/she muttered, hit the door handle, climbed out in the clompy platform boots. Slammed the door.

"Damn twinkie!"

"Have a nice day." Ray twisted the ignition key. Threw the car into Drive, pulled out of the tight spot.

And as he did, he heard the scrape. Metal on metal. Rear panel.

The guy or whatever he was had just keyed his fucking car.

Motherfucker!

Ray hated to lose his temper.

He slammed on the brakes with a screech, smashed the Riviera into Park, left it running, got out, marched back to the sham woman standing in the gap where they had parked.

Grinning, a screwdriver dangling in his hand.

"You have any idea how much that paint job cost?" Ray said between his teeth. His fists were flexing and unflexing.

His opponent tilted his head to examine the rear of the car, a boat tail which made the Buick the classy ride that it was, then he looked at the pretty midnight blue paint, now with a wild white scrawl across it. Like graffiti on the Sistine Chapel. And then he looked back at Ray.

"Lot more than forty bucks, I'd say. And whose fault is that?"

Ray's neck vibrated. Tension that knotted up. Vision that blurred.

"I'd say yours." He walked toward the hooker, fists so tight they hurt.

The hooker's face dropped. He held up the screwdriver in defiance.

"I'd think twice if I were you, sweetheart."

"Thinking's overrated, *sweetheart*," Ray said.

And came in at him.

And when he was done, panting, sweating, the man in fishnets lay splayed before him, head propped up against the brick wall between the van and Mercedes at an unnatural angle. Not a living one. Lips cut and bloody.

"Get up," Ray said, bending over, resting his hands on his knees, catching his breath.

No response. No movement.

"Get up already."

Nothing. Just the whir of traffic on Pine Street.

"Crap."

As Ray's head began to clear, he heard his car, still chugging away behind him.

He looked at his dead victim.

Well, it was too late now.

Things didn't always work out the way you planned.

He felt strangely calm. As he always did.

What to do with him?

He bent down, grabbed the ankles of his black platform boots. Dragged him, the man's head sliding down the brick wall, hitting the asphalt with an unpleasant crack. Arms twisted around on the ground.

Straightened him out in between the two vehicles. Dead weight. Ray was puffing. Then he went around to the man's head, straightened it.

Arranged the arms like wings. Pushed them down just a little.

Like an angel.

Ray stood up, admired his handiwork for a moment, realized the back of his hand was bleeding where he'd been slashed with the screwdriver.

Screwdriver. He hunted for it. Found it, by the wheel of a van. Picked it up. He'd get rid of it later.

He strolled back to the car, puffs of exhaust in the cold winter night. Opened the trunk. Tossed in the screwdriver, got out a pink shop rag near the spare tire, wrapped it around his hand. He still had work to do.

The movement of a figure threw a shadow across the entrance of the lot.

Ray stood back behind the trunk. His blazing headlights helped mask him from view.

It was a security guard, staring into the parking lot from California Street. An old Mexican dude with a weather-beaten face, '50s ducktail, in a polyester jacket with one of those big clocks hanging over his shoulder, the ones where they punched keys hanging on chains for their patrols. A guard at the hospital. The tranny had mentioned they patrolled this lot, that she had one looking out for her. Him. Whatever.

He'd been watching. But for how long?

Did he see the body?

Damn.

Ray reached into the trunk, pulled the screwdriver. He stuck his arm out of the shadows, held the screwdriver up, showed it to the guard.

"Speedy Gonzales," Ray sang mockingly in a low voice, along with the old song, "why don't 'cha go home?"

The guard's face dropped. He turned. Took off.

Ray tossed the screwdriver back into the trunk, slammed it shut, got back in the car, threw the car into Drive, hit the gas.

Flipped the headlights off as he swerved out onto California, the car bouncing.

He disliked unfinished business. But these things happened.

Supertramp were on the radio, singing about taking the long way home. But Ray wasn't going home. There was no time like the present. He still needed the real thing.

CHAPTER THREE

Less than an hour later, Ray turned a corner, heading up Leavenworth for the umpteenth time. It was late, well past midnight. And it seemed colder—if that was possible. The car heater was blowing on high. The back of his hand was bandaged—he'd dashed into a late-night store to buy Band-Aids after the transvestite got him with the screwdriver. Soon to be something that never happened. It wasn't Ray's fault the tranny picked the wrong person to mess with. Unfortunate, yes, but he—she—*it*—should have known better. The way of the world.

But there she was now—a *real* she—coming out of a corner liquor store in her boots and miniskirt, long white legs, thin. He needed her thin. She was wearing a big black Giants jacket and a retro black mod hat over her long blonde hair. A real blonde. Perfect. Prominent nose, but that worked too.

Close to Alice.

Definitely female. It showed in her walk. He wouldn't make that mistake again.

She was on her own, good. Her two friends—the little Asian one with the chunky legs, and the Black chick with the Afro, looked like she'd chew you up and spit you out—were either with customers or had gone home.

The blonde took her position on the corner, opening up a pack of smokes. She lit one, stamping her platformed feet while she puffed.

He put the Riviera into Drive, drove up, pulled over to the curb, rolled down the window.

Gave her a big smile, the kind women liked.

She returned it, along with a squint. She puffed on her smoke, came sauntering over to the car, hip movement galore. Putting on a show.

"*You* look like you like to live life on the edge," she said.

"You got that right," he said.

CHAPTER FOUR

Owens pulled up in front of the white stucco house with the pink trim on Wawona, the house he had paid for. Was still paying for, to be more precise. And hadn't lived in for over a year.

It was late afternoon, and the early fog was pulling into West Portal from the ocean.

He wouldn't go up, ring the doorbell. It didn't feel right, no longer living there. Up until recently Alice had had that restraining order out against him.

He honked the horn, two light taps.

The porch light went on upstairs, and the door opened and out she came, blonde hair flipping.

And there she was, Alice, wearing a light coat, one he didn't recognize, but, as always, a glimpse of her was enough to soften him. It was impossible to hate her even though she'd done a pretty good job on him and he'd managed a reasonable facsimile on occasion. But never for long.

She came down the stairs, high heels, long willowy legs. She was carrying her overnight bag. Hope welled.

She gave him a cool smile, but it *was* a smile. First one he believed he'd seen since the divorce.

She came across the street as he got out and hurried around the car to open the passenger door, take her bag.

He put her bag in the trunk next to his, and the gift he had ready, and went back, got in. The car was full of her. Not just her fragrance. But her. *Her.*

"It's cold out there," he said.

Small talk. Something he was lousy at.

"It is December."

"You look nice," he said.

Another smile, polite. Distant? Well, they'd been through hell in the last year. He reminded himself not to push things. He had gotten this far, beaten the odds. Was he a fool? Maybe he was a lucky one.

She blinked as she looked him over. They didn't touch. A kiss would have been out of the question, even a peck.

"Nice jacket," she said. "Blue always suited you."

"Thanks."

"You've lost weight."

"Twenty-two pounds." Maybe he should have just said thanks again.

Don't get your hopes up.

"But you look tired," she said, pulling down the visor, primping, not looking at him.

He'd been up since the wee hours, investigating a 187 out by St. Francis Memorial. A dead transvestite. But he never brought work home when they were married, and he wasn't about to start now.

"Just the same old grind," he said, pushing a smile. "Are we all set?"

"Reservation at the Joshua Inn," she said. "The Redwood."

The cabin where they had spent their honeymoon. She liked the llamas on the property, farther up the hill. He liked the idea that he might be getting a second chance. As an inspector with SFPD, he thought about the old saw, returning to the scene of the crime.

He almost asked, *Are you sure about this, Alice?* But caught himself.

"Great," was all he said, putting the car into gear. "I made a dinner res at Triple S." Where they had eaten more than once on their honeymoon. Steaks and a salad bar.

He wanted to ask her so many things. Say so many things. But he didn't.

In a relationship, the one who cared the least had the most power. And that was Alice.

"Let's try to beat traffic," she said. "Berkeley will be a parking lot already."

CHAPTER FIVE

NIGHT CANDY STRIKES AGAIN

The newspaper in front of Colleen's office door on Pier 26 was folded up with a rubber band around it. Even so, the headline was clearly visible along the top.

Colleen picked up the *Chronicle*, found herself reading it right there in front of her office, formerly a marine maintenance shop. The sounds of the bay sloshing beneath the thick boards of the pier below punctuated her thoughts.

"The suspected killer who goes by the name of 'Night Candy' may have struck again after a three-month hiatus as a fourth victim was found, this time in the doctors' parking lot of Saint Francis Memorial Hospital early Saturday morning.

SFPD were alerted to the body of a man apparently found posed in the crucifixion position characteristic to previous Night Candy murders. The man, whose details are being withheld pending further investigation and notification of kin, is reported to be of a similar background to other victims."

Meaning he was a prostitute, Colleen concluded.

"The body was found in the rear of a parking lot by a security guard from Saint Francis Memorial Hospital on patrol. A positive identification will not be confirmed until an autopsy is performed.

Until the autopsy, no further details on the condition of the body, or speculations on the cause of death, will be released. Any new information should still be directed to Inspector Owens of SFPD."

Colleen realized she needed to touch base with Owens. It had been a while. Too long. But he would ask her about Pam, and she wasn't ready to talk about that.

She let herself into her office. Turned on the overhead, filling the tall, dark room with harsh fluorescence from high in the unfinished ceiling. Colleen went around and sat at her battered green metal desk, appropriated from her stint guarding an empty paint factory in Hunter's Point. The San Francisco Bay was choppy and grey through the window behind her.

Over the last year, three other victims had been killed in ceremonial fashion until the killings had seemingly stopped: a woman in St. Cecilia's church out in the Sunset, found in front of the confessional booth with her hands spread out crucifixion style; the second, a transvestite splayed before the cement cross on Mt. Davidson, a rosary in one hand; and a third, a woman on Baker Beach, posed in a snow angel position in the sand.

The three had been sprayed with a teen fragrance known as Night Candy. None of them had been sexually violated.

Colleen couldn't help but think about Traci with an "i" and her two partners in the Tenderloin, and the risk they were taking.

Meanwhile, she had a divorce case to get started on. Yet another divorce case. Staying busy was the only way she could see to getting past life without Pam and the grandson that might have been.

CHAPTER SIX

"Alice is *dead?*" Colleen said.

She couldn't believe it.

Matt Dwight returned a somber nod, took a sip of his Irish coffee.

They were sitting, Sgt. Matt Dwight and Colleen, in the bar at Pier 23, not far from Colleen's office. In the corner a jazz trio played a smooth bossa nova. Not a lot of people yet, still early evening.

Matt's tie was loosened an inch from his high collar. His normally coiffed dark-brown hair was a little asunder after a day full of surprises at SFPD. Matt was a good-looking guy in his late thirties, with defined cheekbones and eyes that were darker blue than most blue eyes. He and Colleen had been an item for some time, although it went in fits and starts. Tonight was another start.

Colleen wore her soft denim flares, Frye boots, nothing dressy apart from the cream top with a long bow. She kept a few things on hangers in her office for post-work dates.

She still couldn't resolve herself to accepting the news about Alice Owens.

"How?" Her gin and tonic, with the plastic swizzle stick that looked like a paddle, sat untouched on the bar. "Tell me."

"Alice's body was found in Calistoga Sunday," Matt said. "Two days ago." Calistoga was a town in the wine country, popular with well-heeled tourists and retirees. Mud baths and Merlot. "The Joshua Inn."

"I know they were thinking of going for the weekend," Colleen said. "Owens' last-ditch effort to win Alice back." Colleen had thought it a bad idea. Now this. "What the hell happened?"

"The cabin they were staying in caught fire. Looks like Owens got out alive. Alice wasn't so lucky."

Colleen stirred her drink with her paddle stick. None of this seemed real. "Owens wouldn't abandon Alice. He was crazy about her."

Matt sipped his Irish coffee. "Crazy being the operative word?"

"What is that supposed to mean?"

"Just that matters of life and death can change a man's values."

Colleen returned a narrow-eyed look. "Not Owens."

Matt exhaled a sigh. "Oh, right, I forgot: the man's a saint."

Colleen's anger popped. Matt had always been jealous of her relationship with Owens, even though it was purely platonic. "You just accused him of saving his skin at her expense."

"Then you're definitely not going to like the next part."

"Get it over with."

Matt set his drink down. "They arrested him."

A bolt of alarm jolted her upright.

"Owens arrested? For murder?" The realizations came in waves, faster than she could process them. "They think he *murdered* Alice? What kind of proof do they have? That the two of them might have had an argument? That she died in a fire? That's not enough."

Matt took a breath, picked up his drink, sipped. "They found a bullet. Back of her head. Looked like the fire might have been intended to cover all of that up."

"No," Colleen said. "Never."

"You've said it yourself, Colleen, Owens was crazy about her. Maybe things didn't go his way."

"He was in love with her."

"Right, but there's love, and there's a whole lot which tries to pass itself off as the same thing. By some accounts he was stalking her."

"I don't buy it." Even so, her thoughts wavered. Owens *was* preoccupied with his ex. He had plenty of company though. But he was one of the few cops she respected and could depend on.

"Where is Owens now?" she asked.

"Santa Rosa. He was questioned by Calistoga PD with SFPD present and arrested by Sonoma County Sheriffs. This morning."

Now she knew why Owens hadn't returned her recent call about Night Candy. "And you didn't tell me?"

"What was I supposed to do? Call you up from work and say 'hey, the guy you think walks on water just got arrested for killing his ex'?"

"That would have been one way."

"I'm telling you now, Colleen: in person."

"I would have wanted to know."

Matt shrugged defensively. "It's not like you and I have exactly been doing a lot of talking lately. You're the one who wanted a break from things. I thought Owens could wait until we sat down. Besides, I honestly didn't know how much you might already know."

She had to admit, she'd been distant from everyone lately because of Pam. Keeping Matt at arm's length too.

She took a deep breath, let it out slowly. "I know," she said. "This is on me. I just wish I'd known sooner."

"You need to get your head around the fact he might have done it, Colleen," Matt said quietly. "Sonoma County sure thinks so."

She picked up her untouched drink, took a sip. Willed herself to calm down.

"All I'm saying," Matt said, "is that when push comes to shove, true character is revealed."

"*Your* true character, perhaps. Admit it, Matt, you never liked the guy."

"Owens might have interfered with a couple of cases, but I don't hold it against him."

She sipped her drink, eyed him. "Sure, you don't."

"Well, SFPD might."

"Don't tell me they think he actually had something to do with Alice too?"

"You'll have to ask IA."

"Internal Affairs? Who's heading up the case?"

"Ryan."

"Ryan!" She almost spit. The man was a supreme ass. He'd done his best to nail Colleen in the past, and now he had Owens, another person he disliked with fervor. "When did Ryan move to IA?"

"Earlier this year."

"Jesus H. Poor Owens."

"Poor *Owens*? Owens didn't get burned to a crisp, Colleen. He got out unscathed. He might have even set the damn fire. After he shot his ex. You need to leave an open mind."

Colleen stopped herself. She wasn't in the mood for an argument with Matt tonight.

And then she realized she was sitting across from an SFPD cop she had been to bed with on a fairly regular basis, even with the time-outs. Yet Owens came first in the trust department. What did that say?

Whatever it said, she had to reach out to Owens. She was one of his CIs—a Confidential Informant. He'd gone to bat for her on multiple occasions, an ex-con on parole trying to navigate the PI business without a license. She dug out her purse, put a ten-dollar bill down by her unfinished drink. "I have to run."

Matt's eyes rounded in surprise. "Seriously? You're going to go see Owens? *Now?*"

"Why not? I can't think about anything else."

"Because he's in the Sonoma County slammer, for one thing. It's almost eight p.m. And mainly because we have a date. We haven't seen each other for weeks. As you might recall."

"We both agreed we needed some time off."

"No, *you* agreed we needed some time off."

"So did you, if you're being honest with yourself."

"If I'm being honest, Coll, I'd say I feel like I'm being jerked around. What the hell do you want anyway?"

What she wanted, needed, for the last few weeks, was some time to process Pam. Pam's sudden departure had blindsided her emotionally. After years of trying to win her daughter back, unable to truly connect while Pam was a girl and Colleen was in prison, she thought she had finally succeeded, following Pam out to California. And they had finally reached a closeness—hadn't they?

But what did she know?

And now she needed to process Owens.

She gave a repentant smile. "I'm sorry, Matt. Hearing about Alice just killed the mood." She winced inside at her word choice.

"Shit," Matt said, setting his drink down with a clunk. "You haven't even told me how Pam's doing."

No, she hadn't. "Another time."

"Meaning?"

Colleen shrugged.

"Well, when is she going to have that baby anyway?" he said.

Sometimes he could be obtuse.

"Immaculate conception," Colleen said, standing up. The baby's father was a cult leader who had almost persuaded a couple of hundred of his followers to leap into an active volcano, Pam included. Colleen had managed to prevent that. It had also meant a reunion with Pam that was the original reason Colleen had come out to California after her release from prison in Colorado over a year ago. Pam had a habit of falling in with a bad crowd.

And now Pam was gone again. The baby never made it.

Matt scrutinized her. "Is Pam OK, Colleen?"

Colleen collapsed into a sigh. "She lost the baby, Matt. I didn't know how to tell you. I'm sorry. I didn't know how to tell anybody."

Matt sat back, open-mouthed. "Jesus, Colleen. *I'm* sorry. Really. I really am. Is Pam OK? Otherwise, I mean?"

"Who knows?" Colleen exhaled. "She took off on me again."

Matt slumped in his chair. A lot of drama when all he wanted was a night with her. "I know I've said a few things about Pam, how I thought she was taking advantage of you, but no one deserves that."

"Thanks," Colleen said. "Let's take a rain check, Matt. I'm lousy company tonight."

"Hey, I'm used to it." He smiled.

"Ha ha. Very funny."

Colleen leaned over, gave Matt a juicy peck on the lips.

She left, Matt staying behind to finish his drink. Last time she left him he bumped into a couple of stewardesses, even though, supposedly, nothing happened. Well, she only had herself to blame. But it was still the '70s. For a few more weeks. She couldn't wait until this decade was dead and gone.

She walked outside, cars whooshing along Embarcadero by the bay, the freezing cold actually refreshing after all she'd just heard.

She walked to her car, keys in hand.

She'd find a way to see Owens tomorrow. Sonoma County was an hour or more north, and that's when the traffic was cooperating.

And as she got to the Torino, a part of her, a part of her she didn't like, said, *What if?*

What if Owens had gone off the deep end?

No, she thought, *no*. Not Owens.

CHAPTER SEVEN

"Bring Back the Death Penalty!"

Half a dozen protesters waved signs and blocked the beige stone entrance to the Sonoma County Main Adult Detention Facility in Santa Rosa, chanting for the news camera and anchor with the big hair poised in front of a microphone. She had an appropriately solemn look on her face. Behind her the morning sun was losing a battle with grey clouds that hung over the mountains. Colleen had driven up from San Francisco, a good hour plus and sixty miles of morning travel.

"No killer cops in our county!"

Bad news traveled fast. Colleen parked and got out of the Torino, donning her tapered blue sport jacket that went with the grey flared polyester slacks, crisp white cotton blouse, and sensible heels, better for getting past people than jeans and sneakers.

She walked around the protesters, giving them a wide berth, and on through the glass doors.

It took almost two hours for her to see Owens.

* * *

"I came as soon as I could," Colleen said into the wall phone as she sat down.

Owens sat down on the other side of the wire-reinforced glass in an orange jumpsuit, which was jarring for Colleen to see—not just a cop as prisoner, but a cop she held in high regard. Owens was middle-aged, close to six feet, and had lost weight during the last year, since the divorce, with jowls that hung on a slackened face and a gaunt stare that was no doubt worsened by his current situation. His dark eyes were heavily ringed, from lack of sleep she suspected, and more. His dark hair, grey at the temples, had grown out from the crew cut he'd sported after the divorce and hadn't been combed in some time.

But the crowning glory was the bruised nose, purple-yellow on one side, spreading across his left cheek, complemented by a bloody bandage above one eyebrow.

"Sweet Jesus," Colleen said after she got a good look.

Owens held the phone to his ear. They both knew these calls could be monitored.

"A welcoming party," he said. "Most inmates don't like cops."

"They didn't move you to isolation?" she said.

"Working on it, I'm told."

She shook her head.

"I appreciate you coming, Colleen. No one else has checked in. IA has no doubt warned everyone at SFPD to keep their distance during the investigation."

"Your buddy Ryan has a hand in it," she said.

"A big one. Never liked me to begin with and now he's got his opportunity."

"Give it time," she said, not knowing what else to say. She didn't mention the fan club outside chanting for the TV cameras. Hopefully Owens didn't know.

"I'm so sorry about Alice," she said.

"Thanks," he said, slumping forward, phone to his ear. A heavy sigh crackled over the line.

"What the hell happened?"

Owens looked up, staring desolately at a spot somewhere over her head. "We went up to the Joshua Inn for the weekend," he said, sounding battle fatigued.

"Calistoga. You said you were thinking of it."

"Things went south early on. I took her to dinner at the Triple S, and you could cut the air with a knife. Cold, formal. A washout. Then I took Alice back to the Joshua Inn. As we pull into the place, before we even get out of the car, she tells me she can't go through with it. She'd made a mistake. It wasn't that big of a surprise after the way things had gone. I knew halfway through dinner. But even so . . ."

Owens had been carrying a torch for his ex, even with the divorce.

"So, you didn't go into the cabin?" she said.

"I came home."

"You left her there? How was she supposed to get back to SF?"

"I guess I wasn't thinking about Alice. I figured she'd call a cab, sleep it off, whatever. It was late. She didn't want to come back to San Francisco with me, so I let her use the room. Why not? It was already paid for. And it would have been one awkward drive home together."

"And the fire?"

Owens shook his head. "Calistoga Fire Department says a space heater was plugged in, next to the bed apparently. The comforter caught. The place went up." For the first time he cupped his eyes in his big hand. "Why in hell did I think we could patch things up? We never should have gone up there. Now she's dead."

Colleen let the emotional wave pass.

The subject of Alice being shot hadn't come up yet.

"And the cops think you had something to do with the fire?"

All Owens could seem to muster up was a forsaken nod.

"Because Alice was shot," she said quietly.

She saw Owens swallow, look away for a moment. "That's what they say."

"How do you explain that?"

"I can't." He shrugged. "Suicide? No, she was shot in the back of the head. The gun was Alice's. But registered in my name."

"Jesus. How on earth did that happen?"

Owens grimaced, phone to his ear. "I bought it for her, back when we were married. I was working all hours and she wanted it for protection."

Some protection.

"And the gun was found in the cabin?"

"In the fire rubble apparently. One shot fired."

"How convenient for the police that the gun was left there." They looked at each other through the wire glass for a moment, Colleen's mind flying with so many thoughts she couldn't hold onto all of them.

Owens was hard to read. Their professional connection was solid though they had started off as adversaries. But she still didn't really know him on a personal level. Owens, like many cops, kept his feelings barricaded. She knew the divorce had been brutal on him. He'd married a woman half his age, gone through the humiliation of trying to keep her: clothes, hair dye, and other things that, when Alice finally dumped him for a man her own age, changed him. Colleen had never met Alice in person, only spoken to her on the phone, but thought her a witch for the way she'd treated Owens, alive or not.

"So," she said, "Alice dumps you, you shoot her in a fit of jealous passion, leave the gun at the crime scene, try to cover it all up by setting the place on fire with a comforter cover left next to a space heater."

"Yeah, I did all that—even though there are far easier ways to get rid of your ex."

"Run me by the timeline. What time did the fire take place?"

Owens took a deep breath. "Calistoga Fire Department showed up around four a.m. Sunday morning, I'm told. So, it all happened between sometime Saturday night or thereafter."

"And when did you cross the bridge back into San Francisco?"

"Around midnight."

"And the police got involved when?"

"Along with the fire department. Sunday morning. Some detective named Sanderlin from Calistoga PD stopped by the motel where I live on Sunday, questioned me informally. Then, yesterday at work, 850 Bryant, I get called in to see the chief. Ryan was there with Detective Sanderlin and a couple of uniforms, like I might try to make a run for it. They arrested me, right there, brought me up here. Then the case was transferred to Sonoma County."

"Nice guy," she said. Meaning Ryan.

"Ryan could barely contain his joy. He's been waiting for something like this. When he moved to Internal Affairs, I thought I was free of him. Then this thing fell into his lap."

Colleen knew Ryan's hostility firsthand. Ryan and his partner had driven Colleen down to the Farmers Market in the middle of the night once and tried to intimidate her in the hopes of her backing off a case she was working. Not just intimidate—*threaten*.

"Alice's death wasn't your fault," she said. But as soon as she said it, she realized she might be saying it more for herself than Owens. She didn't like that thought.

Owens stared into the crisscrossed glass, eyes out of focus, his face in two halves by the bruise on one side, giving him a split appearance. "I told this Detective Sanderlin in my statement that Alice used to use sleeping pills. She could have popped one or two before going to bed. On top of the booze at dinner, she'd never notice the space heater lighting the place up."

They looked at each other through the wired glass for a moment, Colleen's mind rapid with so many thoughts.

"That doesn't explain how she got shot," she said.

"No, I realize that. Unless she was shot afterwards."

"Any more thoughts?"

Owens shook his head. "Someone broke into the cabin? While she was sleeping? It's pretty remote up there."

"Run me by the timeline one more time."

Owens returned a tense smile. Standard investigating procedure: keep asking the same questions over and over. If something's not right, it shakes out. Owens was being questioned for a change. By someone he'd never expected to be questioned by.

"I didn't do it, Colleen."

"Humor me."

Owens let out another deep sigh. "I left Alice at the Joshua Inn around eleven p.m. Calistoga Fire supposedly responded about four a.m. after a call. A part of the cabin was burnt down by then and her body . . ." Owens grimaced, blinking away the gloom. "You get the picture."

Hours in the flames would have done a lot of damage. But it wouldn't have been complete. Human bodies, particularly the meatier parts, took up to half a day to burn.

"Where is she now?" Colleen asked quietly.

"My guess is here in Napa County or one of the local coroners."

"Any other suspects?"

"Not that I know. But they wouldn't tell me."

"Anyone who might have had a grudge against Alice?"

"Ray Quick," Owens said. "Alice's ex-boyfriend. They'd just split up."

"Alice told you that?"

"Not exactly."

"And what does 'not exactly' mean?"

Owens looked away. "It means I found out."

"Found out *how*?"

Owens looked at Colleen. "I was keeping an eye on Alice, OK? I saw them arguing. Not long after, Ray moved a bunch of his stuff out."

That Owens was stalking his ex wouldn't look good if it came to light. "How long had you been keeping tabs on Alice?"

Owens didn't respond.

"How long?" she said again.

"A while. Ever since the separation."

"Over a year?"

Owens looked sheepish. Shadowing his ex for over a year.

"Whose idea was it to go for a weekend getaway?" she asked.

"Mine. When I saw Ray was on the outs, I thought I might have a shot to get back with her."

"Who picked the Joshua Inn?"

"She did. We went there for our honeymoon. She loved the place."

"So, Alice and her guy break up," she said. "And then you ask her to go up to Calistoga with you. "

"And then she got cold feet. Classic Alice. Well, I did push. I pushed too hard."

"This Ray, did he know where you two were headed for the weekend?"

"Who knows? But he's got an alibi. He was at work."

"Where's that?"

"He's a bartender at The Claddagh."

An Irish bar on Clement.

"Bars close at two," she said. "He could have made it up to Calistoga." An hour's drive, that time of night.

"Not enough time for the body to burn . . . as much as it did. They're estimating time of death at before midnight, around the time I left."

"Maybe this Ray left work early."

"The cops think his alibi is solid."

"Who's in charge of the investigation?"

"Here in Sonoma, Detective Kikuyama. They moved me here where they have a homicide team. In Calistoga that detective named Sanderlin took the initial call after Calistoga Fire found the body."

"You've got everybody and his brother piling on."

"Don't forget SFPD Internal Affairs."

"Your buddy Ryan. When it rains, it pours."

"They don't get many homicides up this way. Everybody wants in."

A free-for-all wouldn't work in Owens' favor. He had no allies and there was already a rush to judgement based on the TV crew outside.

Colleen had gone to prison for close to a decade for killing her own husband back in '67.

"I know what it's like to lose it with a spouse," she said quietly.

"I loved Alice, as crazy as that sounds."

It was the *crazy* part that bothered Colleen. Matt had thought the same thing.

"And if I was going to kill her," Owens said, "I'd do a better job of it."

Not if you went off the rails and lost it, the way I did all those years ago. It happened. She pushed the thought to one side again. She'd have to trust him.

"Maybe Alice had somebody else," she said. "Besides Ray."

"Possibly. Alice liked attention. And it was plentiful."

Colleen didn't know what to think. "What did you two fight about? In general?"

He gave a sardonic laugh. "The toilet seat left up? My breathing too loudly? But often it was money—Alice spent like a sailor on shore leave. The bottom line was that the world owed her more than some middle-aged cop and a full five in West Portal."

"Anybody see you leave the Joshua Inn at eleven p.m.?"

"The cabin is out in the woods. Secluded."

"Have you been officially arraigned yet?" she asked.

"Murder one."

"How much is bail?"

"Fifty K. Might as well be five million."

"Do you have a lawyer?"

"All I've got is the divorce lawyer. Who let Alice walk off with everything: house, alimony. I'll check out the court-assigned attorney here and take it from there."

"Some local court-appointed attorney in a part of the state that gets no homicides? I'll ask Gus to help out."

"Your hippie surfer lawyer? Helping out a fascist cop?"

"He owes me," she said. "And he's good. If you don't want him, and the court-appointed defense doesn't work out, he can find you someone you like. At least talk to him."

"I'll figure something out."

"Why don't you want my help?"

"I don't want you to get your neck caught in a mangle, Colleen. Your popularity at SFPD is zip to begin with."

The thought occurred to her that he didn't want her prying.

"I couldn't care less."

"Then you've got it nailed. Ryan will take you down if he catches you interfering. You're still on parole."

"I'm OK with that."

"Well, I'm not," he said. "Don't you have some juicy divorce cases to work on? While Pam gets bigger?"

"This isn't the time to be noble," she said. "This thing can snowball. Right on top of you. I'm going to help whether you like it or not."

Owens rubbed his forehead with his free hand.

Then he looked her in the eye. "Then I thank you. Really."

"You still have keys to your old house in West Portal? Alice's house now?"

Owens stared at her. Maybe he didn't want to say anything in case the cops were eavesdropping. Maybe he didn't want her to think stalking Alice was worse than he'd let on.

He sighed. "I had a court order to stay away from the house. Even though I had the privilege of paying for the place."

She didn't know that. But a lot of divorces went that way. Most of her investigations were divorce, and people got ugly.

"What does this Ray Quick look like?"

"Big, good-looking specimen. Knows it too. A gym rat. And you should stay away from him, along with everyone else connected to this."

"You keep saying that."

"I know," Owens said. "How are *you* doing?"

"OK," she said. "And you're changing the subject."

"I think we beat the other one to death for the time being. I don't want you impacted by this."

"Your concern is heartwarming but I'm not your little sister. Anything you need short-term?"

"A time machine. So I go back one week and rethink about booking that damn geodesic dome Alice thought was so California cool."

She heard that. "I'll make sure Gus Pedersen—my lawyer—gets hold of you as soon as possible."

He was too preoccupied to ask about Pam. And that was fine.

Still, she didn't like Owens pushing back so much. You'd think he'd be chomping at the bit to find Alice's killer.

She also didn't like the niggling little doubt she had about a guy she thought so highly of.

CHAPTER EIGHT

The Sonoma County Sheriff's Office was only about two blocks away from the Main Adult Detention Facility, so Colleen drove over after visiting Owens. Detective Kikuyama was apparently the one heading up Owens' case.

She asked for the detective at the front desk, said it was about Owens, gave the duty officer dressed in tan and green her business card. She was told to wait. She did, standing by the notice board while Christmas music oozed from a radio on the desk at low volume.

A few minutes later, Detective Kikuyama appeared, a slender, youngish Japanese American with the frown of an older man. He wore grey slacks and a white shirt with a blue tie, everything too big for him. His white T-shirt showed prominently under the shirt. His badge was clipped to his belt. He lifted Colleen's card from the desk and read it so quickly she wondered if he read it at all.

When she told him she was an acquaintance of Owens, his eyes narrowed. She asked if they could speak privately.

"You've got about a minute," he said, tapping her card on the back of his hand. "It'll have to be here or nowhere."

"My visit is informal," she said. "I was just hoping you can bring me up to speed with the investigation."

"Owens has been charged. Murder One. Now you're up to speed."

"I just visited him," she said. "He was beaten up by some of the inmates, by the way. He should be isolated."

"You'll have to talk to the MADF staff."

"Can you tell me what time you investigated the crime scene at the Joshua Inn?"

"No."

"Who did you speak to there?" she asked.

"Nothing I can share."

"Nothing? I've worked with Owens, and I know he isn't guilty."

"Do you know how many times I've heard that?" he said. He tried to hand her card back.

"Please," she said, "hang onto it. In case you have any questions I can help with."

"I won't be needing your help—" he read her card—"Miss Hayes. Let me make one thing clear: we're busy. I met you as a courtesy today, but that's all the time I'm going to have for you."

"And I appreciate it, Detective. Have you looked into the possibility that someone set Owens up? I think I might have a lead."

"I don't want to waste your time. And I don't want you wasting mine either." He pushed her card back on her.

He left her there, holding her card, while on the radio, chestnuts were roasting on an open fire.

*　*　*

Colleen decided to drive over to Calistoga on the way home. She could try Calistoga PD, where the investigation began. It couldn't be any less helpful than Kikuyama.

Taking the Petrified Forest Road through parkland, Northern California countryside rarely failed to calm one's inner spirit, but today everything seemed tinged with the death of a woman who'd been murdered and burnt up in a fire. Late afternoon, a cool, clear winter evening was beginning to descend.

Half an hour later, Colleen drove into Calistoga, a town of a few thousand people that was home to wineries and mud baths. She passed the Joshua Inn along 29, a big, rambling, shingle-sided bed-and-breakfast amidst the pines at the beginning of the foothills. Where Alice had died. She decided to pull off.

Up the hill, two geodesic dome cabins were located past the main house. A pair of curious llamas stopped grazing to watch Colleen get out of the car. A hard, sunless chill bit through her jacket.

On the wraparound porch of the big house, wind chimes tinkled, punctuated by the chopping of wood in the distance. The wind shifted, and the smell of the recent cabin fire drifted her way. Colleen's imagination let her imagine other things burnt, knowing the grim outcome of that fire.

She followed the scent through the pines to a clearing where the shell of the third dome was cordoned off with yellow crime scene tape that fluttered in the breeze. The fire had consumed a good section of the cabin and the top of the domed roof. Black scorch marks emphasized where the flames had licked the surfaces.

Off toward the back, through more trees, she saw a tall, lean man splitting wood with an ax. An old German shepherd lay on the ground next to him by the relic of a pale blue pickup truck with an over-the-hood camper shell, circa 1950.

She headed over.

He was an old longhair bound together by sinew. A sweat-stained blue paisley bandanna around his head kept a long grey mane somewhat in place. A grey hillbilly beard hung on a face that was worn and wrinkled, with sunken cheeks and a prominent nose that had been broken at one time. A Grateful Dead skull hovered over the breast pocket of a faded denim jacket, a lightning bolt down the center. *All who wander are not lost.* A pile of unchopped wood lay on one side of a fat upright log that served as a chopping block. An equal pile of split wood lay on the other.

He stood up straight, the long ax gripped in a bony hand.

Colleen introduced herself. Being a female, she knew she was good for a few questions at least. He didn't give his name, but his eyes scanned her body in her slacks. Smiling wasn't in his repertoire.

"You must work here," she said, nodding at the main house.

"Now and then."

"That looks like it was quite a fire," she said, indicating the dome now. "Good thing it didn't start a forest fire."

He set his ax down next to the log, stood, crossed his arms.

"What's this about, exactly?"

She got out one of her sham business cards, listing her as Carol Aird, investigator, and handed it to him.

He put the card in the back pocket of his tattered jeans without reading it. He didn't speak or move. No wasted effort.

"Did you happen to be here the night the fire took place?" she asked. He looked like he might live in that truck. Handyman about town.

"Check with the Fire Department. Or the Police. Washington Street."

"My friend's ex-wife was killed in that fire," she said.

He nodded sagely. "Some might say your 'friend' might just be a little bit guilty then."

Bad news did travel fast. "I'm not one of them."

He squinted. "Your friend is a cop."

"One of the good ones. Were you here that night? Sleeping in your truck maybe? Looks like a handy little setup."

"Check with Donna," he said, gesturing at the house. He picked up a log, set it on the block. He spit on his palm, rubbed his hands together, picked up his ax, studied her for a moment. Then he heaved the ax over his head in a practiced swing, let it fall, splitting the log evenly in two. A section of log shot by her leg, and she did her best not to flinch.

"I'm just trying to get some info," she said. "I'm not Rockefeller but I can pay for confidential information. And that's how it stays."

He picked up another log, ignoring her.

"Give me a call if you think of anything," Colleen said.

No response. The chopping of wood resumed.

She headed to the house.

Inside the open downstairs of the big, messy, lodge-style hotel, with a moose head over the staircase, a woman was on the phone at a desk in back, arguing with someone. She was a blousy type in her early forties with a short, dark bob that needed a brush run through it. Her white blouse was damp in spots, and the sleeves were rolled up. A film of perspiration sheened her face and neck. She looked like a poor man's Elizabeth Taylor. Colleen stood by while she continued her conversation.

"I can't give you what I don't have, Sam," she said. "Check back first of the month." She tapped a filterless Pall Mall out of a pack and stuck it between her lips while Sam on the other end of the line protested. She looked up at Colleen with dark eyes and gave a little shake of her head, sisters commiserating.

"And people in hell want ice water, Sam," she said. "Sorry, first of the month is the best I can do." She hung up, hunted for matches on a desk cluttered with bills, a wrench, a toilet valve. Colleen waited while she tore a paper match out of a book, lit her cigarette, sat back in a squeaky office chair. She was wearing faded black Capri pants and beat-up flats.

She beamed an official smile.

"You must be Donna," Colleen said.

"I am she," she said brightly. "Need a room?"

"I'm actually looking into the death of Alice Owens," Colleen said, putting another Carol Aird card on her desk.

The smile disappeared. Donna took a drag on the cigarette, blew smoke to one side. Tapped ash into a full ashtray on the corner of her desk. She picked up the card and read it.

"What kind of investigator?" she asked.

"Private. I'm actually working for my client's lawyer."

"Uh-huh. And who's your client?"

"Edmund Owens."

"The guy who booked the room?" She did a double stare. "Wasn't he the one arrested?"

"He was, but he's innocent until proven guilty."

"Oh, and you were here, while they were yelling their damn heads off."

Owens had told Colleen that he hadn't gone in the cabin.

"They were in the cabin?"

"That's kind of where you go when you book one, babe."

"And they were fighting? Inside? What time was that?"

"You know what? You really need to leave." She stood up, smashed her cigarette out. It smoldered in the heaped ashtray. "I've got beds to make."

"I was hoping I could take a quick look at the fire damage in the cabin," Colleen said.

She stopped. "I guess you didn't notice that crime scene tape."

"I can pay for a quick look in that cabin," Colleen said. "Twenty bucks. I'll be in and out in five minutes. No one will know. And I won't have to come back here."

Donna gave a plastic smile, adjusted her basket. "Don't come back here at all. Leave."

"Fifty." Colleen got out her money clip so Donna could see it. She didn't even know if she had that much on her, and if she did, it would clean her out. But she was curious how long a woman who appeared pressed for money would keep turning it down.

Donna walked out the open french door, onto the deck with the laundry basket.

"Anders!" she shouted. "If this woman isn't gone in one minute, help her find her way out."

"Got it, Donna!" Anders shouted back.

Colleen put her money clip away, went out to the Torino, started it up, did a quick three-point turn in the dirt driveway. Anders was standing to one side, ax over his shoulder, watching her with vacant eyes that seemed focused all the same. Donna was walking up the path toward one of the domes with the laundry basket. She stopped halfway, turned around, watched Colleen complete her turn and leave.

Colleen pulled out onto the narrow Highway 29 and heard the air snap with blows of the ax.

She was going to be burning some gas going back and forth from San Francisco as this investigation proceeded. But she knew one thing. Donna, and quite possibly her helper, Anders, had something to hide.

She needed a look inside that cabin where Alice Owens had met her end.

CHAPTER NINE

It was getting late as Colleen pulled up in front of the Calistoga Police Department, a Spanish colonial–style building with arched colonnades and a barrel tile roof that looked pleasant with the last of the day's light on it. Nothing like the powerhouse Hall of Justice in San Francisco.

She parked out front and went inside where a middle-aged female desk officer in glasses and a dark blue uniform with a few extra well-placed pounds and a Laura Petrie flip sat behind an information counter with a miniature Christmas tree on it with tiny ornaments. Colleen, still in her sensible grey flared slacks and blue jacket, asked for Detective Sanderlin.

"He's out on a call," the desk officer said.

"So, he's coming back?"

She checked the time. "Can't confirm that." It was getting late.

Colleen didn't want to make unnecessary trips to and from San Francisco, so she left a business card. A real business card. "I'll check back in a little while. I'll go get a cup of coffee. Any recommendations?"

"Zack's. By the river."

"Can you please ask Detective Sanderlin to call me there if he gets back soon?"

The desk officer said that she would.

Colleen thanked her, headed out, drank watery coffee in an empty diner, thought of Owens sitting in a cell with a bruised face while she listened to Christmas music that made the time crawl. An hour later she returned to Calistoga PD. No sign of Detective Sanderlin. She left, knowing frustration was a part of many cases, especially early on. But the day had pretty much been a washout.

Just as she walked out of the station, a black LTD pulled up, screaming "unmarked vehicle" with its plain hubcaps and no-frills appearance. A short, swarthy man got out, pushing fifty, in brown flared slacks, shiny brown leather jacket, and high-heeled brown boots to compensate for his height. She took a guess and approached.

"Detective Sanderlin?"

"Yes?" He furrowed his thick brows as she introduced herself and handed him a card.

"I'm working on behalf of Inspector Owens. I was hoping I could ask a few quick questions."

Sanderlin looked at his watch. "It's Sonoma County's case now."

"But you were the first detective at the scene," she said. "I'd really like to hear what you saw."

"I'm not sure I can tell you anything."

"I drove up from San Francisco," she said. "I've been running around all day. Owens is a good friend. I'm doing this pro bono. I know he didn't do what he's accused of. I'm just trying to get a handle on things so I can help him out."

Sanderlin nodded. "I went in right after the fire department put the fire out. They got there about four a.m. I got a look about forty-five minutes after that. Just before five. The Doe was in bed, about 30–50 percent burnt. If you've ever seen anything like that, you know what I'm talking about. Her face was gone. Nothing to identify. Her bag hadn't been unpacked. The space heater was by the bed, what was left of it. Was it an accident?" He shrugged. "I don't know. I don't think so. Neither did the Sonoma County DA. Especially after it turned out she'd been shot."

"From what I heard they had a disagreement in the car and Inspector Owens left after that. That she went into the cabin alone."

"That's not what a witness told me."

"Which witness was that?" she asked. "Donna? The manager at the Joshua Inn? Anders? Her handyman?"

Sanderlin shook his head. "Witness testimony isn't something I share."

"You found the gun?" she asked

"Later that day, when I went back to look around some more, when it was light. Smith and Wesson 38 revolver."

Thorough. She had to reevaluate her opinion of small-town police. "Where did you find it?"

"Under the bed, which was partially burnt up. There were five shots left. Forensics at Sonoma has it."

"I'm surprised none of the remaining shots had gone off in the fire."

"They might have if the fire hadn't been put out and the place burnt down. But it was protected enough and far enough away from the source of the fire. He probably thought he was in the clear."

"Whereabouts was it under the bed?"

"Toward the head of the bed."

"Which side?"

He thought. "Toward the upper left."

"Away from the space heater?"

He nodded. "Other side of the bed, kitty corner."

Where it might be likely to easily survive a fire and be incriminating evidence.

"Any prints on the gun?"

"Partials. His. The gun was registered in his name too."

"Wouldn't a gun burnt in a fire be hard to analyze?"

"Not always. The polymer frame was burnt but the steel parts—the barrel and such—were still intact. Recovering prints can be tough, but as I said, the gun was somewhat protected from that fire. The serial number was intact. The partial latent prints survived where the residue darkened. They were baked in, if you know what I mean."

She thanked him for his explanation. "Sounds pretty convenient if someone set him up."

Sanderlin returned a sardonic smile. "I think we got the right guy."

"Who called it in? The fire?"

"Anonymous call from a phone booth. Male, older. Around three forty-five a.m."

She thought about Anders. He could have called in the fire so that enough evidence would survive to implicate Owens.

"Did you question the handyman?"

"You already asked me that." Sanderlin checked his watch again. "No comment."

"I know Owens pretty well," she said. "And I just can't see it. But I can see a staged shooting and fire to set him up."

Sanderlin squeezed the bridge of his nose. "A distraught ex, not thinking clearly? Acting out of anger? I'm not homicide and if we get one murder a year up here, that's news. But this isn't out of reach. He pretty much clammed up when I interviewed him."

"Maybe Owens was in shock. Maybe he was being careful not to incriminate himself."

"Sometimes cops think they're exempt. Like they're going to get a pass. He could have easily shot her on impulse, started the fire to cover it up."

"Then why on earth would he leave the gun behind?"

"Yeah, I agree. But he was pretty upset, not thinking. And maybe he thought there would be nothing left. He got unlucky in that respect."

"That still seems like a big gamble."

"Again, people in that state of mind don't think straight. Guys do desperate things sometimes when they get tossed aside, especially after a punishing divorce. I heard she was out of his league to begin with. I almost feel sorry for him."

Almost.

He must have been reading her face. "Maybe he didn't do it, but the evidence says otherwise. The trial will confirm it." He handed her card back. "I won't need this."

She was beginning to feel like a leper. "Please keep it. I'm hoping you might touch base if anything comes up."

He put the card in his jacket pocket. "Check with Sonoma County Sheriffs for any new developments."

He left her, headed into the station in a short, rapid gait. Colleen was left with more than a feeling of dissatisfaction.

Who could have argued with Alice Owens in the cabin before she died if it wasn't Owens? Owens had said he hadn't gone in.

If Owens was telling the truth.

*   *   *

Colleen swung by the Joshua Inn again on her way home, stopped on Highway 29, peered in from the tree-lined road. Late evening. A couple of cars were parked in front of the lodge, the place lit up. Anders' 1950s pickup with the camper shell sat not far from the burnt-out cabin off to the rear by the side. The crime scene tape fluttered in the breeze in the glow of a light emanating from the back of the camper shell, its door open.

Not the time to try and investigate the fire scene.

She had paid work to catch up on in SF, a report to a client due tomorrow. She was falling behind on an investigation for an elderly couple who were getting bilked by their contractor. Before she went home, she needed to swing by the house he was working on and see what work was, or wasn't, being done.

She wondered what Pam was doing. She wondered how Owens was doing. She bet no one was having a great day.

She'd have to get back up here another time. Soon.

CHAPTER TEN

Colleen got home late, thanks to a long drive back to the Bay Area and checking out the stalled construction project for her elderly clients by City College. The house was in deep deconstruction mode, down to joists and studs, no sign of recent activity. The contractor was holding the couple's house for ransom until they coughed up more cash. With her flashlight she had seen a gas meter had been moved and was now hanging in the middle of a bedroom. Why? To skirt inspections while they worked on the rest of the house? Not too kosher.

She made notes in her penny notebook, headed home.

She parked in the rear of her building on the west side of Potrero Hill, where a small, outdoor yard was reserved for tenant cars. She climbed the wooden stairs up to her back porch on the third floor. The whir of freeway traffic wafted from 101 over the top of the building, white noise to her now, welcome after a long day. She opened the door to the kitchen to an empty, dark, silent flat. No TV blasting, no Pam playing the stereo, no cigarette smoke. Things that once drove Colleen nuts, she now missed and knew she would for some time.

She hoped it wasn't forever. That there would be a reunion.

She turned, looked out at a foggy Bay Bridge for a moment, try-ing to savor a view that was worth savoring. Delayed shutting the kitchen door. No rush to remind herself what the flat held. Silence and emptiness.

The note Pam had left was still on the 1940s red-and-white tile counter, pinned under the sugar bowl.

Mom—

I'm leaving. Please try to understand.

Love,
Pamela

Colleen took a deep breath and did try to understand. Again. Understand Pam losing the baby, the burden of guilt too much for her. She wanted to tell Pam that she had nothing to feel guilty for. That she would be there for her. But Pam didn't want that. Colleen was always pushing herself on her daughter, it seemed, who had been running from her ever since she got out of prison.

She did understand. She just couldn't explain it to Pam.

Maybe if she never touched the note, left it where it was, all of it would magically disappear, be gone one morning, like a bad dream.

In the living room nothing had changed from that morning. No ashtray full of cigarette butts. No coffee cups or wine glasses strewn across the glass coffee table.

She ignored the Christmas tree in the corner, dry needles on the hardwood floor, packages underneath for her grandchild who would never be, never see them opened. A Paddington bear with a yellow Christmas bow on his red hat and a label from Santa around his neck. It was about the most miserable thing she could imagine.

Just to torment herself, get it all out of the way, she went to Pam's room, pushed open the door one more time.

Pam's single bed stripped. Little Lambert's cot in silence on the other side, a stuffed shark lying on its back, alone.

A birth that ended in heartbreak after hours in Delivery at SF General.

And the child's mother, Colleen's only child, gone too.

She looked over at the nightstand, at the picture of Pam when she was fourteen or so, before her Goth phase, a pretty girl with freckles and a rare smile, her long red hair tousled by the wind or something. She had been through so much. Her father and his abuse. Colleen's decade in prison. Living with a grandmother not easy to live with. Pam taking off when Colleen got out of prison, coming to California. Colleen coming after her. And last year, they had finally reconnected, Pam returning to the pretty girl who smiled again, her red hair lighting up her face again.

And then this.

Colleen wasn't going to chase after Pam again. Pam had her reasons to leave. Colleen had been too hard on her. She just hoped Pam was safe wherever she was. She pulled the door shut, vowed never to look inside again. Until tomorrow.

The phone rang.

She grabbed the phone off the kitchen wall. Hoping it might be Pam. Always hoping.

"Colleen Hayes?" a reedy voice said. Not Pam's. Her spirits dropped.

With a grimace, she recognized the voice. It belonged to the weasel who'd been with Inspector Ryan last year, when Ryan had threatened her, not in so many words, exactly, but clear enough. She'd had to demand they let her out of the car, had to walk home from the farmers market on Alemany in the middle of the night. She recalled the guy staring at her in the rearview mirror. He'd looked like Heinrich Himmler without the charisma.

"How lovely to hear from you, Detective Stoll," she said with sarcasm.

"Whatever it is you think you're doing in Santa Rosa—stop."

SFPD must have got wind of her visit to see Owens. And Detective Kikuyama. That was quick.

"Did Kikuyama call you?" she said. "Simply because I asked a few questions?"

"You're unlicensed to practice in this state. You have no business getting involved in a sensitive investigation."

"*Sensitive*? I know Ryan has it in for Owens, but this is utter bullshit. It's not even SFPD's case."

"Take this seriously."

"Tell Inspector Ryan and the rest of those spineless bastards you should be ashamed of yourselves for looking the other way while Owens gets set up for a murder he didn't commit. He also got the crap beat out of him in jail."

"Consider yourself warned."

"Can you give me the number for SFPD citizen complaints? And the correct spelling of your name?"

The phone clicked off.

They were done. For now.

She went to the front window, looked down at Vermont three floors below.

Owens deserved a lot more.

She went into the kitchen and grabbed a wine glass, only to discover that she'd drunk the last of the wine two nights ago. She wasn't about to go back out and find a liquor store. That might mean she had some kind of drinking problem. But, with Pam gone, and Owens sitting in a cell up in Santa Rosa, beat to a pulp, and Alice lying dead in a stainless-steel drawer somewhere, she had the blues. Something reached deeper tonight, something that made her more than simply discouraged.

Under the kitchen sink she found a dusty bottle of cheap brandy she used for cooking, three-quarters full. She didn't own a snifter. She found a Tom and Jerry glass the gas station had given her for a fill-up. She poured a finger of dark brown liquor into it. Two.

She drank it down, standing there in the dark kitchen. Savored the afterburn.

Rummaging around in the junk drawer she found a partial pack of Virginia Slims she hadn't thrown out. She lit one up and it was dry and acrid and tasted like shit and that suited her mood just fine. She poured more brandy into her glass, took it, along with the bottle, into the living room where she sat on the sleek leather sofa in the dark, kicked off her shoes, put her feet up on the coffee table, sat in the dark, smoked and drank.

And, in the darkness, everything she'd just tried to shake off came back. Trying to get into her head. Owens. Would he really? Kill Alice? If you had asked her a week ago, she would have said not only *no*, but, *hell no*. But now she wasn't sure what she'd say. She wasn't sure about a lot of things.

If she was going to get through this month, without Pam, and little Lambert, and Owens, then getting to the bottom of this was vital. She owed it to Owens. It meant something to be loyal to someone, even when you weren't sure.

She owed it to herself to prove that Owens was innocent.

*   *   *

Middle of the night she awoke, asleep on the sofa.

Someone was coming through her front door.

CHAPTER ELEVEN

Colleen sat up, blinking away sleep. Squinting into the hallway. Murky shadows. She stood up, unsteady from brandy and comatose slumber, staggered toward the hall closet where her sawed-off shotgun was bolted to the wall behind the coats.

She saw a somewhat familiar sight standing in the doorway to her flat.

"Hello, stranger," the shadow said.

"Alex," Colleen said, her shoulders relaxing. She turned on the hall light.

Alex was dressed to the nines, as per usual, tonight in an oversized camel hair coat over a beige knit dress and pants combo, the cost of which would most likely cover Colleen's rent for a month. Her blonde hair had been recently curled and hung long. Alex was always an eyeful.

Even better was the fact that her blue eyes were clear tonight and she seemed to be sober, especially this late. No telltale bottle of champagne in a paper bag either, normally a late-night accessory when she came visiting after the bars shut.

"What time is it?" Colleen said, rubbing her eyes.

"Obviously past someone's bedtime," Alex said.

"Come on in. Grab a seat."

Alex came in, her chic black Italian shoes with the buckles clicking on the hardwood floor. She picked up the bottle of brandy on the coffee table by the neck, now half-full, held it up, examined the label, shook her head with a *tsk*.

"Can I borrow this, Coll? I think the lawn mower needs refueling." She set it down on the glass coffee table, sat in the Scandinavian leather recliner opposite, still in her coat.

"Safeway's finest," Colleen said, fishing out a cigarette, smoothing her hair, sitting back down. "I think I bought it to bake a cheesecake. That's my excuse anyway." She was feeling decidedly bleary.

Alex gave her a rueful smile. Normally it was she who was in her cups and Colleen administering the lectures.

"I know," Colleen said. "Spare me the irony." She lit up a stale cigarette with a paper match, shook out the match, tossed it toward the ashtray. It missed, landing on a magazine. "And I also know I look like shit."

"I would never say that," Alex said. "A little rough and ready perhaps."

"Unlike you." Colleen nodded at the runway-worthy outfit.

There had been a time when Alex and Colleen had considered taking their friendship one step further. It had failed to happen. But it had been close.

"I'm more concerned about your state of mind," Alex said.

Colleen checked her watch. Two thirty in the morning. "I admit I had a couple of drinks."

"A couple."

Colleen puffed. "Can't help but notice how clear-eyed and bushy-tailed you are, madam, especially since the bars have just shut. Kudos."

Alex reached into her coat pocket, came out with a bronze plastic chip on a little chain. Held it up.

"Thirty days," she said.

"Seriously?" Colleen said. "You haven't had a drink for thirty days?"

"It only feels like three hundred," Alex said, giving the chip a kiss before slipping it back in her pocket.

"I'm more than a little proud of you," Colleen said. And she was. Alex was one of the last people she'd thought would climb on the wagon and stay there for any length of time. "You didn't say anything about it."

"I wanted to make it first, not tell anyone."

"I like it." Colleen nodded. Their eyes met. "To what do I owe the pleasure?" Frequently Alex, who lived in a mansion that her father left her in Half Moon Bay, would party in the city and then drive down the coast along a sinuous Highway 1, and Colleen had given her a key with instructions to stay over rather than dodge guardrails and combat two highways through double-vision. But tonight, that wasn't an issue.

"You stood me up," Alex said.

"Say what?"

"Late dinner at Hamburger Mary's?" Alex raised her eyebrows.

"Shit on a stick!" Colleen said. "I'm so sorry, Alex! I completely forgot."

"I figured," she said. "So, I thought I'd better check in . . ." She left the sentence unfinished.

Since Pam left, Colleen had been a basket case. She thought she was handling things better than she had been. But obviously not.

"Thanks," Colleen said, reddening. "I promise to pull myself together."

"Any word from Pam?"

Colleen smoked harsh smoke, blew it out. Shook her head, fighting a sniff.

"No," she croaked.

"I'm a little worried about you."

"I'm a little worried about Pam," Colleen said.

"She just needs space."

"I hope that's it."

"She'll be back."

Colleen showed crossed fingers as she took a final puff, smashed out her cigarette, stood up. "Well, I blew off dinner and I can't offer you a drink. Want some tea?"

"Sure," Alex said.

Colleen padded into the kitchen, put the kettle on the stove. Lit it up. "What did you do when I didn't show up at Hamburger Mary's?"

"Left a couple of messages on your answering machine." Which Colleen hadn't checked.

"I was too busy getting hammered and feeling sorry for myself."

"Then I went down to Peg's Place for a Calistoga water. Which doesn't taste anything like champagne, by the way."

"I'm glad you didn't succumb."

Alex smiled. "Not just yet. I'm going to give it some time. Clear my head. Figure out what the heck was going on with my old man . . . and Margaret's murder."

Alex's sister, Margaret, had been murdered when Alex was young. It was Colleen's first case. But there was a truckload of emotional baggage left behind for Alex to carry. Her father had been a domineering man who made it clear that his favorite daughter was not the one who had lived.

"Everything else OK?" Alex said.

"Not really."

"Oh?"

"Owens," Colleen sighed.

"I thought you two were strictly friends."

"Oh, nothing like that." Colleen told Alex about Owens' situation.

Alex was open-mouthed.

"That's why I blew you off," Colleen said. "I've been running around Sonoma County to no avail." She didn't bother to mention the threat from Detective Stoll that had distracted her.

It was a long silence before Alex spoke.

"Well, that's awful," Alex said before looking at her. "You don't think he . . ." She stopped.

"No," Colleen said, shaking her head. "No. Not Owens."

CHAPTER TWELVE

Next morning, gazing out the back window of her home office while she drank extra-strength, fresh-brewed coffee, Colleen called her answering machine at work. Dark grey fog had the east part of town socked in. But it was still early. It might burn off. Hopefully, along with the muddiness in her head. Too much brandy last night. Cheap brandy at that.

The machine answered in two rings, meaning there were voice messages waiting. She knew there would be. Alex said she had left two last night when Colleen forgot about their dinner date.

But there was a third.

Maybe it was new business. One could hope.

"This is Rhonda," the voice said. "I need to talk to you." Rhonda, the Black fireplug with the Afro that could get her on *Soul Train*. Friend of Traci, the tall blonde working girl with the nose of character, whom Colleen had spoken with the other night in the Loin, warning the ladies about Night Candy.

Rhonda's voice had a solemn tone to it.

Colleen called the number. An older man with a raspy voice answered. Rhonda wasn't home. The TV was on at volume to a morning show.

"She's taken her son to school," he said. "Then she comes home and gets some sleep. She works nights."

That kind of blew Colleen's mind. But many working girls were just like anyone else, leading "normal" lives outside of "work," just trying to make ends meet. The man on the phone was probably her father and did not have a clue what kind of work Rhonda actually did.

"Her message sounded important," Colleen said. "She can call me before she turns in if she likes."

The gentleman took the message.

Colleen went to work, sorting through some photos of a man kissing another man in a bar on Castro. His wife was going to get a surprise.

Talk about a grubby job to make ends meet.

Not long after she got a call from Rhonda.

"I'm at Kerry's," she said. "Army and South Van Ness." In the background Colleen heard the clanking of dishes, people talking. A waitress shouted out an order for eggs and hash browns.

"I can't talk at home," Rhonda added.

Rhonda lived with family. "I'll be there," Colleen said. "Fifteen minutes."

Shortly after, Colleen parked in the lot behind a diner that was open twenty-four hours, a San Francisco mainstay with its 1960s sign high above a semi-industrial thoroughfare that cut the city off from the part the tourists would never see. Blue collar. Old San Francisco, the working people slowly getting squeezed out.

Rhonda was sitting at a counter, pink sweatpants showing below a puffy, white down coat with a faux fur collar. White platform tennies rested on the chrome footrest of her stool. She had on big round sunglasses and sipped an orange juice, smoking a menthol cigarette. The overhead speakers were chirping with the Captain and Tennille.

Love will keep us together. If only, Colleen thought. It seemed to do the opposite often enough.

Colleen felt less colorful in her jeans, sneaks, sweater, and leather car coat. She sat down on the stool next to Rhonda and ordered black coffee.

"Something tells me your call wasn't good news," Colleen said.

Rhonda tapped ash and turned to Colleen. Even with the sunglasses Colleen saw her face drawn, anxious.

"Traci's gone," she said. She turned back, looked straight ahead, took a puff.

There it was.

"How long?" Colleen said.

"Saw her last Friday," Rhonda said.

Night Candy crossed Colleen's mind.

"Five days," she said. "I take it that's not normal."

"We check in with each other most days," Rhonda said, puffing on her cigarette. "In this line of work, you have to."

Colleen nodded. "And you saw her last Friday?"

"Around midnight. On our corner on Leavenworth. I was off with a client. Fia was freezing and went home. So, Traci was left on her own. No one else."

No one up to any good anyway.

"Could she have gone off with a client on a jaunt somewhere?" Colleen asked.

Rhonda smoked. "She would have let Billy know." She tapped some ash into a Budweiser ashtray.

"Billy's your pimp?"

Rhonda nodded.

"I don't suppose you called the police?"

Rhonda gave Colleen a wry smile. "And upset Billy?"

The police were the last people Rhonda's pimp would want involved.

"Would Traci have taken some business off to the side? Without Billy knowing?"

Rhonda shook her head. "Not worth it. Billy doesn't go for that, as you might imagine, and the one thing he does provide is protection. He's a pimp but he's no gorilla." A gorilla was a pimp who got rough with his girls.

"I'm sure he's a wonderful guy."

"I've called her place a couple times. Her landlady hasn't seen her since last week."

Colleen sipped coffee. What she was thinking was clear. And then Rhonda said it.

"Traci was worried about this Night Candy," Rhonda said. "We all were. *Are.*"

Colleen took a deep breath. "Do you have a picture of Traci?"

Rhonda set her cigarette on the lip of the ashtray, reached into the pocket of her coat, came out with a Polaroid, rings and bracelets jangling.

She set it down on the counter.

A photo of the three working women in a street, all smiles, Traci holding up a bottle of what appeared to be champagne. She wore a paper top hat that read "Welcome 1979" in glitter. New Year's. People all around them, a lot of men. It looked like the Castro.

Colleen felt a momentary pang as she looked at the photo, hoping it wasn't going to be one of the last of Traci, then pocketed it.

"Does Traci have any family?"

"Somewhere. But she never went into details. Always clammed up when that subject reared its head."

Many working girls were estranged from their families.

"Time to put your money where your mouth is," Rhonda said. "You wanted to help. Traci needs help."

"Has Billy been looking for her?"

"The usual stuff. No one has seen her."

"Where do I find this Billy?" Colleen said.

Rhonda turned, looked at her again. "You don't."

"If you want my help," Colleen said, "that's the way this works."

"You can imagine how thrilled he's going to be to have you involved."

"I'll keep your name out of it."

"He's not stupid."

"Neither am I," Colleen said. "I know how to handle people like Billy."

Rhonda obviously thought that all over, picked up her cigarette from the ashtray, took a puff.

"Billy Shen. His crew hangs out at the Jade Palace. On Washington."

The Jade Palace. Chinatown. She knew the place. It was one of the restaurants owned by the man she'd served papers on for failing to pay forty-three employees. Illegal employees. Easy to stiff.

"I'll need Traci's phone number and address, too," Colleen said.

Rhonda told her. A flop hotel in the Mission.

"You gave my business card back to me that night when I stopped to chat with you three on Leavenworth. About Night Candy. How'd you get hold of me?"

"Fia."

"What about that transvestite who was killed nearby? Saint Francis Memorial doctors' parking lot. It would have been the same night Traci disappeared."

"Some loner on Polk," Rhonda said. "Don't know him. But it fits. No one to look out for him. Easy pickings."

Colleen cleared her throat. "Do people think it was Night Candy?"

Rhonda grimaced. They were getting into uncomfortable territory now, Night Candy and Traci in the same conversation. But it couldn't be denied.

Rhonda took a deep breath. "NC's done one other demiboy. He likes working girls so, yeah, obviously."

"He has," Colleen said. She got out another business card, jotted another phone number on the back. "That's my home number. In case you get any new info." She set it in front of Rhonda's orange juice glass.

Rhonda smashed her cigarette out.

"Want a ride home?" Colleen said.

Rhonda shook her head, no. "No thanks."

Colleen hoped she was wrong about Traci. But her instincts said otherwise.

CHAPTER THIRTEEN

Colleen had to circle 16th and Valencia several times before she found parking in an alley a block away from Traci's apartment building. The Mission was always a challenging parking experience and getting to be more so.

"Apartment building" was one way to put it; residence hotel was another. Signs advertised by-the-week—Section 8 accepted. The bedraggled structure, with bare wood showing where paint was badly needed, had been a grand Victorian back in the day. Now it was carved up into small units. Stoop dwellers kicked back and lingered, drinking beer before noon.

Colleen asked about Traci.

Nobody had seen her since last week.

"Can you tell me anything about her?"

"She's nice," an aging Latino said, wearing a red paisley do-rag and dark sunglasses in the fog. The guy had been around awhile. "Always says hello."

And Colleen bet he was always around on his stoop so he would know.

"Know where she might be?"

"I know she works nights."

"Anyone stop by to see her? Family? Boyfriend?"

Do-rag looked up at Colleen. Even with the murky shades she saw the squint of suspicion. "And who are you, exactly?" he said.

She handed him a business card. "Just a casual friend. People are starting to get concerned. So, I'm making enquiries. Don't worry, none of this will get her into trouble. Hopefully the opposite."

Colleen thanked him, went up the stairs, rang the bell for the manager.

No answer.

On her way back down, Colleen stood on the sidewalk, one leg cocked up on the step above. "So, if you see anything, hear anything..." She raised her eyebrows.

He took a swig from his can of beer. "I could let you know."

*   *   *

It was too early in the day to start looking for Billy Shen, Traci's pimp. The Jade Palace, where Billy apparently hung out, wouldn't be open until lunch. And besides, any self-respecting pimp didn't show up for work until the sun went down.

So Colleen drove over to Wawona Street in West Portal, where Owens had once lived with Alice. Alice had gotten the house in the divorce. It was another grey day, where the fog beaded the car and left splotches of grime when it dried. Colleen flipped on the windshield wipers to see where she was going.

It was just around nine a.m. when Colleen motored down Wawona, past Alice's white '40s stucco house with the pink trim. No car in the narrow driveway, no lights. No signs of life. She circled the block, parked across from the branch library by the Muni Metro station, slipped on a pair of shades, pulled on her floppy black hat with the wide brim to hide her face, got her set of lock-picking tools and various B&E instruments, slipped them into her shoulder bag, headed down to 41. A streetcar echoed into the West Portal tunnel behind her.

Wawona was one street off West Portal Avenue, busy for a residential street, the odd person looking for a parking spot, a few stragglers walking briskly in the direction of the station to head downtown to work. An old codger in a blue bucket hat was walking a white poodle at a leisurely pace, letting the dog sniff every tree.

She strolled past 41. There was a stairway with stucco walls leading up to the porch and the front door. The house was one step up from a basic San Francisco junior five built during the war when the ship workers were moving into the city.

Colleen stopped, checked around. A couple of people walking but no one paying attention. She climbed the steps, which were painted light brown, in good shape, like the rest of the place. Owens had said Alice was house proud.

Up on the porch several newspapers were piled on the welcome mat. She rang the doorbell, waited. Reached into her shoulder bag, felt for the leather case with the lock-picking tools. Looking around.

Down on the street, the white poodle was checking out a car tire. The old fellow in the hat was looking up at Colleen. Dang.

She returned a polite smile, tucked her lock-picking set back, rang the bell again so the old guy could see her. She waited, checked her watch so he could see that, too, and turned to head back down the stairs.

"Looking for someone?" the old guy said.

"I'm a friend of Alice's," she said.

"Oh. So, you're not aware of what happened?"

Nosy old guy, wanting to be first with the bad news.

"Of course I am," she said in an admonishing tone.

"Sorry for your loss," he said dutifully.

She'd have to find a better time when the street wasn't so busy.

Up by the library she got back into the Torino, started it up, and drove back down Wawona where it took a while to find a spot with a view of Alice's house. She parked, turned on the radio, turned it off when "Rockin' Around the Christmas Tree" came on. She waited.

The mailman wandered up Wawona with a full sack, delivering mail.

She turned on the radio again, switched to news talk. The December mayoral runoff was in full swing after a tight election and it was looking like Dianne Feinstein was going to be the first female mayor of San Francisco, after the tragic murder of Mayor Moscone last year. But Jello Biafra, singer with the Dead Kennedys, had gotten almost four percent of the vote on the promise that he would reopen Playland, the bedraggled but beloved amusement park by the beach, and give everybody over the age of ten a hit of LSD.

Colleen was fighting the urge for a cigarette when she heard the throaty rumble of an American V8. A midnight blue Buick Riviera with flashy wheels trolled by and disappeared around the corner on Ulloa.

Not long after, a big good-looking guy came marching down the street, hands in the pockets of a black leather jacket. He was lantern-jawed with sculpted dark hair and wore dark sunglasses.

At 41 Wawona he went up the steps, where he appeared to collect the newspapers—it was hard to see with the stucco wall blocking the view. Ray Quick, Alice's ex-boyfriend? What was he doing there? He let himself in with a key, which was interesting, since Ray and Alice had apparently split before Alice's fateful weekend with Owens.

Minutes later, the big good-looking guy appeared empty-handed, skipped down the steps, went striding back up Wawona.

Colleen waited until he turned the corner, started up the Torino, followed him from a distance around the block to the main drag.

On West Portal Avenue she saw him get into the midnight blue Buick Riviera. He backed out of the angled parking spot, and she caught a glimpse of the rear passenger side of his car where the paintwork had been keyed or something similar. A serious gouge on a pretty car. Recent? Someone with a car like that kept it up.

He headed off. She followed for several blocks. She saw him check his rearview mirror from time to time before he turned right on Sloat, the wide thoroughfare that stretched out to the beach. She held back in the hopes he wouldn't spot her.

When she finally turned right on Sloat, the lanes were busy with morning traffic. The blue Riviera was nowhere. She'd lost him. But she'd seen part of his license plate and was reciting it to herself.

She headed down to Embarcadero to get some paid work done. In her office on Pier 26, with the view of the Bay Bridge out her back window, she called Matt Dwight, her on-and-off flame and a sergeant at SFPD.

He was glad to hear from her. She apologized for bailing on him the other night. They set up a date for tomorrow night. She asked how the Alice Owens investigation was going.

"It's not," he said. "Not here, anyway. Sonoma County's case."

"Any chance you can run a plate for me?"

Matt gave a polite sigh. She was always asking for favors. But she had agreed to meet him for a date.

"This better not be related to the Owens thing," he said. "That's off limits with the IA investigation pending. No one here can talk about it."

"It's not," she said, crossing her fingers because she wasn't quite telling the truth. She gave Matt the partial plate for the Riviera. "It looks like an early '70s," she said. "Big-ass boattail. Custom paint so who knows what color it's listed under."

"I'll get back to you," he said. "Looking forward to you-know-what."

"Me too," she said.

She went back to paid work. Which meant calling the woman whose husband liked to hang out in the Castro and dance with other guys. The woman took it hard.

"At least it's not another woman," Colleen offered.

* * *

She swung by the Jade Palace in Chinatown, just opening up pre-lunch. Billy Shen, Traci's pimp, supposedly hung out here and Colleen was curious what he might know about Traci's disappearance. The restaurant faced down into the financial district where the white Transamerica Pyramid stood against a grey winter sky, the bay looming beyond. The Jade Palace was situated in an old San Francisco three-story brick building, packed in with a chaotic assortment of other structures old and new, but mostly old. The restaurant signs on Washington were garish, English and Hanzi text, the latter foreign to the Western eye.

The Jade Palace had been in the news last year. Five dead, eleven wounded after a gang shooting. The Paper Sons were on one side of it, one of the oldest tongs in San Francisco. She wondered if Billy Shen was connected to them.

Two Asian youths in fashioned hair and sharp clothes stood out front, smoking cigarettes in snappish, cool puffs, giving Colleen the eye as she double-parked, got out, approached them.

"I'm looking for Billy," she asked.

Neither one of them was Billy apparently, but they looked like the kind of punks who might work for a pimp who worked for a tong. Neither responded beyond staring at her.

"When do you expect him?" she asked.

"Why?" one said.

"It's business," was all she said. "I've got a payment."

That seemed to be enough. "Not until tonight."

"OK," she said, thanking them.

Back at Pier 26, she parked the Torino on the old, covered deck, went back to her office, the water sloshing below the thick planks. It was never warm and this winter it was anything but. The phone light was blinking.

A message from Matt.

"Raymond B. Quick," he said. "1971 Buick Riviera. His address is 41 Wawona, in the city. See you tomorrow."

The guy Owens had mentioned. Who had broken up with Alice, providing Owens the opportunity for a reconciliation weekend up in Calistoga.

Who had a car registered at Alice's address. So, a long-term boyfriend at one time. And still had a key to Alice's house. And was still using it. Even though he was an ex.

Why?

But these days, arrangements between consenting adults took all shapes. On her next trip up to Santa Rosa to see Owens, she'd get more info. But she had enough to know Ray was worth watching.

Owens had told her that Ray worked in an Irish bar on Clement Street. The Claddagh.

She went back to her paperwork, going over the details of another philandering case in progress. Where would she be without cheaters and louses?

CHAPTER FOURTEEN

"You sure you don't want me to come with you, Chief?" Boom said.

"I'm sure," Colleen said, tapping her cigarette in the Torino's ashtray below the dash. She had broken down and bought a pack. At over sixty cents it was pure foolishness. "We're going to try low key first. Who knows? Maybe Billy Shen is a reasonable guy."

"A pimp with the Paper Sons?" Boom said, peering through the windshield. Down Washington the night street was alight with neon restaurant signs. "One of the oldest tongs in the city?" Under his USMC field jacket, he wore a heavy green sweater against the cold. "Sorry, my money's not on 'reasonable.'" Boom pushed his glasses up his nose. "If you're not out in five, I'm coming in after you."

"The Piña Colada Song" came on the radio, about as awful as it got. "That's my queue to move," she said.

"I'm hip." Boom hit the radio 'off' button.

Colleen got out, dressed in her soft bell-bottom jeans, Pony Topstars, wide-stripe pink-and-white sweater under her black leather coat. She tucked her cigarette in the corner of her mouth while she buttoned up against the winter chill. Headed down Washington to the Jade Palace. She tossed the cigarette and pushed open the glass door, the tantalizing scent of garlic and spices mingled with fresh seafood assaulting her nose. The volume of chatter was high, customers vying to be heard amidst the clank of dishes.

The lights were up to match the noise level, bright enough to make one squint. Big round tables were packed with diners; Lazy Susans were loaded down with exotic fare; crabs in big blue-and-white bowls occupied most tables. The clatter of dishes from the kitchen in back punctuated the conversations in Cantonese. Cardboard Christmas decorations were stuck up with Scotch tape here and there.

"Table for one?" a Chinese waiter in a white cotton bus coat said, standing by a host stand.

"I'm here to see Billy."

He narrowed his eyes. "Is Mr. Shen expecting you?"

"No."

He grimaced. "Who do I say is here?"

Good question. Billy didn't know her from Adam.

"A friend of Traci's," she said. "Traci with an 'i.'"

"Wait here."

The waiter went back into the narrow restaurant. Colleen peered around the corner where white double doors fronted a noisy kitchen. To one side a group of hip, young Asians took up a large round table by a wall of fish tanks swarming with live crab. Three young men were attempting to one-up each other in clothes and hair styles. A couple of girlfriends in magazine-worthy outfits were outdoing the men, with the addition of makeup and jewelry. Cigarette smoke haze hung over the table.

Colleen saw the waiter lean over and speak to a tall, slender man in a skinny black tie and shiny grey double-breasted suit that likely cost a small fortune but still managed to look the opposite. He had a carved duck's ass hairdo that probably took up a fair amount of time, replete with a curl over his tall forehead.

He gave the waiter a shake of the head at the man's question, picked up a small cup without a handle with both hands, sipped. He had a serious, grave face.

The waiter returned as Colleen resumed her position by the host stand.

"Mr. Shen is not available."

"Yes, I can see how busy he is with his tea."

The waiter's eyes became even less humorless. "You will have to leave."

Colleen pushed past him, to the rear of the restaurant to Billy and his crew.

Billy looked up coolly. He was probably in his early thirties although the expressionless look in his eyes made him seem older.

He sipped tea, blinked at Colleen as if she weren't there. His friends dropped their conversation, one or two glancing at her as well.

"Do I know you?" He had a deep voice. His two male companions had bulges under their arms, one on the right side of his jacket, the other on the left.

"As I mentioned to the host, I'm a friend of Traci," she said.

He drank more tea. "And why is that important?"

"Because she's been missing for almost a week." Colleen got out a business card, set it on the table. Billy Shen cocked his head, read the card sideways without picking it up. Looked back up at her.

"A rent-a-cop."

"I prefer 'security consultant.'"

"And looking for Traci."

"Looking *out* for her."

He took a sip of tea. "She doesn't need you for that."

"Well, you're obviously not doing a very good job. Otherwise, she wouldn't have vanished into thin air."

He set his cup down, rubbed his face. Studied his cup.

"This is where I tell you to mind your own business," he said.

"That's fine," she said. "Because I've made Traci my business. Now, we can talk in private, or here in front of your crew."

He consulted his wristwatch, a chunky gold Rolex. It wasn't a fake. He didn't look at Colleen.

"Traci is free to go where she pleases," he said.

"I wonder," Colleen said. "You take half of what she makes, run her life. Last time I saw her someone had given her a black eye. Chances are it could have been you or one of your fine employees. So, the least you can do is help me find her. You know as well as I do that Night Candy is out on the streets."

Billy frowned as he turned his teacup on the tabletop.

"Show her out," he said quietly to the two young men in suits.

The two got up from the table amidst a squeaking of chairs, one putting hands on hips. He had the start of a paunch. He was losing his hair and tufting it up with hair product.

"Out," he said in a heavy accent.

"What are you going to do if I don't leave?" Colleen said. "Beat me up in front of the customers? That's Christmassy."

"You have ten seconds before we take you out into the street."

"You know, I've got a good hairdresser if you want to do something about that hair."

His eyes narrowed and he and his partner moved quickly, grabbed Colleen, hauled her out of the restaurant. Even she was surprised at their speed.

Outside the thinning-hair guy tossed her against a parked Chevy Vega. It rocked and the alarm went off, whooping up and down Washington. It didn't really hurt but it didn't feel particularly good either.

"Don't come back," Thinning Hair said. The two turned and went back inside the restaurant, Colleen straightening herself up amidst the shrieking alarm.

Boom had gotten out of the Torino and was already crossing Washington with a baseball bat in his hand.

"You OK, Chief?"

"Yes. I'm just perplexed at who would put an alarm on a Chevy Vega."

"I take it Billy Shen wasn't receptive."

"You would be correct."

"I see." Boom went up to the glass door of the Jade Palace, held it open.

"After you, Chief."

"Thank you."

Colleen walked back into the noise factory, Boom behind her.

"You can't come in here," the waiter in the white jacket said, standing by the host station.

"I think we just did," Boom said.

The waiter flinched at a large Black man in a camouflage jacket with a baseball bat. Boom headed to the back of the restaurant where the Paper Sons were laughing now.

They saw Boom coming and the guy with the thinning hair stood up, his mouth dropping just as Boom reached back into a full swing with the bat. Before the man could get a gun out of his jacket, Boom connected the bat to his shoulder. There was a painful grunt, and the man flew back into the fish tanks against the wall, making them rock precariously. He gripped onto the rim of one to steady himself. Boom got his other shoulder, and he tumbled back toward the table, the fish tanks coming down with him, crashing over onto the table with a flood of water and sprawling crabs. One of the young women leapt up, screaming.

The second Paper Son was up now, a big automatic coming out of his jacket. Boom knocked it out of his hand with another swing of the bat that culminated in a crack of bone and the gun smacking another fish tank, where it bounced off, spinning in the air until it landed on the floor. Patrons were shouting and jumping up, one or two headed for the door.

Crabs were crawling over the table and water ran down the sides, drenching the occupants.

Billy Shen stood up, tall, his pants soaked, his face a calm fury. He stared at Colleen.

"When you're ready to talk about Traci," Colleen said, "give me a call."

Colleen and Boom left the restaurant, the bat down by Boom's side. They headed over to the Torino.

"That crab with garlic noodles smelled damn good," Boom said.

"Didn't it?" Colleen said, getting her keys out.

CHAPTER FIFTEEN

Colleen dropped Boom off in the Fillmore at the Pink Projects, a forbidding public housing complex of two towers where he lived with his grandmother, and then headed out to Clement Street. She wanted a closer look at Ray Quick, ex-fling of Alice Owens. What was he doing in her house after she died? After they had apparently broken up?

Eleven p.m. Colleen sat down on a barstool in The Claddagh. The bar was dark and low lit and smelled of beer, both fresh and spilled. A goodly crowd had gathered as a Celtic band played a jaunty version of "All Around My Hat" on a small corner stage. Much of the clientele were from the Emerald Isle, some still in construction clothes from the workday. The Bay Area's Irish presence went back to the Gold Rush. On the bar a huge pickle jar, half full of change and bills, bore a label: BELFAST VACATION FUND. IRA donations. Strings of silver tinsel were draped from the mirrors. A small tree by the register hung with green Irish-themed ornaments, three-leaf clovers, trinity knots, Celtic crosses, green Santas.

A well-preserved fifty-something redhead with red, red hair and lipstick to match served Colleen half a pint of freshly pulled Guinness. But the drink was a work prop. Colleen paid, left a dollar tip on a dollar beer.

"Ray working tonight?" she asked casually.

"Getting a fresh keg as we speak," the redhead said.

"Do you know if he worked last Saturday night?"

The woman shot her a look. "Who wants to know?"

"Just little old me," Colleen said, taking a play sip of thick dark beer. It was what one called an acquired taste.

"And why might that be?"

"He stood me up," Colleen said. "I waited all night."

The woman took the money, threw the extra dollar into the Belfast Vacation Fund. "Well, now you know what you're dealing with."

It was a little catty and that's when Colleen knew this woman had a thing for Ray. Probably had a thing *with* Ray. Ray seemed to get around.

"Tell me about it," Colleen said. "Did he go anywhere after work?"

The woman returned a wry smile. "Actually, he was here with the rest of us after hours. A private send-off for Bobby, who was leaving. We were here until late." She smiled in an unpleasant way.

"How late was that?"

"Three? Three thirty? No one was feeling any pain. And when Ray left, he didn't leave alone." She raised her eyebrows. "Hate to be the one to break the news to you."

Sure, she was. "Ah," Colleen said, acting suitably hurt. But Ray probably couldn't have made it up to Calistoga unless he was driving ninety the whole way. Interesting that he had a solid alibi nailed down for the time when Alice was murdered, though.

Almost as if he'd need it.

"But the boys in blue already asked him all that," the barmaid said.

"Really?" Colleen said, playing along. Owens had already told her as much. "Why is that?"

"My, my, you really are in the dark. His old girlfriend was killed in a fire that night."

"No!" Colleen said.

"Afraid so." She wiped down the bar. "Up in Calistoga."

"Wow," Colleen said, shaking her head. "I guess she really is an old flame now, huh?"

The woman reared back. "That's awful!"

"I know." Colleen sipped. She put her glass down, pushed it away. "How on earth do people drink this stuff?"

A big guy came out of the back of the bar in a tight black Izod shirt, revealing arms that spent time at the gym. It was the same guy she'd seen at 41 Wawona that morning, owner of the Riviera that Matt had run a check on for her. Ray Quick. Square jaw and chiseled face. His short, dark hair was perfect. For a certain type of female, he was irresistible. Even though she was no more, Colleen thought less of Alice for stooping so low when she'd once had Owens.

Ray came over, wiped his hands on a bar towel. "Keg's changed, Mary," he said to the redhead. Then he gave Colleen sleepy eyes and a twisted half smile that was probably meant to make her slide off her barstool. He looked like he should be bilking widows in Palm Springs.

"Hi there," he said. "I'm Ray."

Mary did a double take, eyed Colleen, then Ray, then Colleen again, squinting at her.

"Funny thing, Ray," Mary said, fixing a stare on Colleen. "She claims you stood her up the other night. When Alice died. But you don't seem to know her."

"What?" Ray said, confused at first. Then his eyes narrowed on Colleen as well. "Who are you?"

"Don't you remember, Ray?" Colleen said. "You were going to come over to my place with a can of whip cream. What happened? Did you get started without me and eat it all yourself? How did you reach the hard parts?"

"What the hell? Who *are* you?"

"I think I left a faucet running." Colleen hopped off the barstool, made for the door.

Outside, in the cold, she dashed for the Torino parked around the corner. Never park too close when a hasty foot retreat might be needed.

She heard the door to The Claddagh open as the Celtic music floated out onto Clement.

Then, Ray shouting: "What is your game?"

As much as Colleen hated to run from a situation, she did just that. But she'd lit a fuse and that would do for now.

CHAPTER SIXTEEN

Just before one a.m., Colleen motored down Wawona back to the white house with the pink trim that Alice Owens once owned, having just left The Claddagh and a confused Ray Quick behind. All was dark. No landing light on. Ray should still be at work. She figured she had a little time if he was going to stop by.

She parked down the block, got out of the Torino, pulling her black ball cap down for cover. She went to the trunk, dug around in her bag of tricks, got her lock-pick set in its leather case, which also contained a small ring of bump keys and doctor's reflex hammer that functioned as a striker. She recalled the lock being a Schlage. Not any harder to pick than anything else. But all locks could be stubborn. She hoped this one was older and looser, belonging to an older house.

She also retrieved the extending baton she had picked up last year. Not being able to carry a firearm without violating parole, the baton was an option that would get her into less trouble if she were caught with it. She stuck it in the pocket of her coat. She got a small flashlight out, plastic gloves, tucked them in a coat pocket as well.

She strolled up Wawona. No activity. She approached Alice's house, then up the stairs to the front door.

Looking around surreptitiously, Colleen got her bump keys and reflex hammer out, selected the Schlage master. Slid the key into the lock all the way, then pulled it out, slowly, teasing the lock until she felt it catch. Then she smacked the bump key lightly with the hammer. And again. The lock popped open, and she let herself in, leaving the lights off. Once inside, she pulled on her plastic gloves and got her flashlight out.

The house was your classic 1940s San Francisco full five, as opposed to a junior five, a step up from the average house for its time. Five rooms, but with a formal dining room as opposed to a dining area off the kitchen, all on one level over a long garage. An earthquake special—vulnerable to collapse in a big shaker. The living room had crown molding and a fireplace and hardwood floors leading into the dining room, all classic period details. The woodwork shone off the flashlight; the mirror over the fireplace sparkled. House-proud Alice.

The flashlight beam floated over a picture frame with a photograph of Alice Owens in a black glamour dress, tall, slender, young, and blonde. A stunner. But she had the mouth, a hard, straight line. You could see she was trouble. Or had been.

Into the kitchen, neat as a pin. Colleen saw no evidence that the police had been here.

With her flashlight, Colleen ventured into the main bedroom. Big dark panel headboard bed with posts and a white duvet and an abundance of pillows. Alice had been a pillows woman. Lace tissue box cover. Another photo of Alice Owens in a bathing suit, hands behind her neck in a bombshell pose, leaning back against a big rock by a river. It was no mystery why Owens fell so hard.

Colleen checked the mahogany side tables. One had a *McCall* magazine on it, so that was probably Alice's side. Colleen checked the drawer. There had theoretically been a pistol at one time, a 38 used to shoot Alice. Now nothing out of the ordinary. She checked the other nightstand. Same.

Quickly she went through closets and dressers. High-end stuff a young woman like Alice Owens would wear, and shoes to keep them company. Owens said Alice kept Macy's and I. Magnin's in business all by herself. One of the things they fought about.

The makeup table seemed fairly barren for a woman who seemed to think so highly of herself. But then again, Alice had makeup-free looks.

Colleen scoured the rest of the house, found nothing of real interest.

The bathroom medicine cabinet had few bottles. No prescriptions. No expensive creams.

Colleen went down into the garage where a late model lemon yellow AMC Hornet was parked. Owens had picked Alice up for her fateful date, so her vehicle was still here.

The workbench was a clutter of tools and junk. The pegboard on the wall behind had many empty slots where tools were to be hung by size—outlined in blue—but that practice had obviously been abandoned. Ray probably didn't heed Owens' organizational habits.

Colleen fished around amidst the tools and cans and such, noticed a bottle of Clorox pool purification tablets. You could count on one hand the number of houses in San Francisco that had swimming pools. And they weren't middle-class houses in West Portal that had postage-stamp backyards. Alice might have had a pool boy and no pool, but purification tablets seemed like a stretch. Colleen left the bottle where she'd found it, next to a can of Prestone heavy duty brake fluid.

Under the front stairs, Colleen found a big, dark cubbyhole with a section of raised foundation across the front of the house under the porch. She peered in through the studs. Damp, musty, cold wind blowing through gaps but neat. A box of empty bottles. A stack of newspapers, tied up.

By the old-style side-hinged garage doors Colleen found what she was looking for, the mail slot. She went over, pointed her flashlight into the wooden box under it.

Empty.

Alice had been dead since Saturday. Five days. Colleen would have expected some mail by now. Where was it?

She went over to the garbage can, pulled the metal lid off gently.

No garbage but a couple of piles of mail. Several days' worth. She reached down, without letting the garbage can touch her coat, grabbed a handful. Unopened. Went through it with her flashlight.

Junk mail or mail for Alice. A PG&E bill. Unopened.

Then it came to her: Ray was checking the mail and if it wasn't something he was interested in, he simply tossed it. Colleen recalled him showing up earlier that morning shortly after the mailman arrived. Leaving soon after.

Ray was expecting a letter.

She knew where she'd be tomorrow morning when the mail arrived.

CHAPTER SEVENTEEN

Next morning, ten a.m., Colleen was parked down Wawona again, listening to Dr. Don Rose on KFRC.

She was tapping her fingers on the steering wheel to "My Sharona" when the mailman slid mail into the slot at number 41.

Bingo.

She got out of the car, wearing jeans and sneaks and a denim shirt over a polo neck. Her tools in her shoulder bag were at the ready. If her theory was correct, Ray would be stopping by any moment. She needed to beat him to the punch. There were one or two people heading toward the Muni station, but it was a risk she'd have to take. She pulled her black floppy hat down on her head, scooted up the street and up the stairs of number 41.

With her Schlage bump key she jiggled her way into 41 again, locked the door behind her. Donned plastic gloves.

Downstairs to the garage.

She checked the box by the mail slot. Fresh mail.

Come to mama.

She went through it quickly. A phone bill from Pac Bell, this month's *Cosmopolitan.* Alice was liberated before she died. An article on Ted Kennedy: "The Facts, The Fiction, The Fantasies." Ugh.

But look at *this*.

An official letter from All Indemnity Insurance of California. Addressed to Mr. Raymond Quick.

She could tear it open here. Or take it with her, open it later—carefully—make a copy, seal it back up, return it, cover her tracks. And get out of here pronto.

That's what she'd do.

She wasn't a mail thief. She was a mail borrower.

She pocketed Ray's letter, put everything else back in the box just as footsteps outside approached the front stairs.

She froze.

The footsteps stepped up the stairs to the front door.

Ray.

Her heart went into overdrive.

She looked around.

Under the front stairs, where there was that unfinished space.

Through the joists she climbed, quietly, into the giant cubbyhole of sorts, hugging her shoulder bag. She lay down on the cement, hunkered up against the foundation to conceal herself.

A key slid into the lock upstairs. A pair of self-assured feet marched into the kitchen, through the back door and down the steps, getting louder as they descended into the garage. Around the AMC Hornet. Her heart was thumping along with the footsteps, and she measured her breaths.

She stayed low.

The person went over to the mailbox, went through what was left of the day's mail.

"Fuck," Ray said.

The garbage can lid squealed as he pulled it off, tossed the mail in the garbage can, slammed the lid back into place.

Stood there for a moment.

A long moment. Colleen held her breath, the pressure building.

Ray swore again, then crossed the garage, went back upstairs, across the house, out the front door, locked it, came down the steps right over her head.

And then he was gone.

She waited for the pounding in her chest to subside and for him to go away.

Back upstairs, she checked that things were as she'd found them, let herself out, locked the front door.

She leaned out on the porch and checked Wawona up and down. And here came Bucket Hat with his damn poodle, both of them in no rush. She ducked back, squatted down behind the stucco wall of the porch to let them pass. The dog stopped out front, sniffed for what seemed like forever as Colleen's pulse accelerated again. *Come on,* she said telepathically to the dog. Finally, with relief, she heard Bucket Hat say "let's go, girl," and then the two strollers pottered up Wawona.

She gave it another minute, raised herself up, hurried down the steps.

And there was Bucket Hat, turning, seeing her, eying her. Recognizing her? They had spoken. She lowered her head, headed off into the opposite direction. *Damn.*

CHAPTER EIGHTEEN

"Two hundred and fifty thousand dollars," Colleen said into the phone, sitting in front of the wire reinforced glass up at Sonoma County Jail. "No prize for guessing who the sole beneficiary is."

Owens, in his orange jumpsuit, phone to his ear, blinked, dumbfounded as he absorbed Colleen's news. The bruise on his cheek from his shower beating was more yellow than purple now. He was unshaven, a few days growth of stubble, something she'd never seen on him before. His hair hadn't been combed. It didn't suit a guy who was always put together. She worried about him slipping. Although he had every reason to.

It was afternoon. Weekend traffic out of town had been sluggish from SF. The rest of the visitor slots on either side of her were full. She'd had to wait two hours for a visit.

"Are you sure, Colleen?" Owens finally said in a faltering voice.

She wasn't going to go into detail about her mail theft over a call that could be monitored.

"There's no doubt," she said. "The insurance company is in the process of arbitrating the claim."

Owens returned a tense frown, took a deep breath, exhaled, leaned forward, phone to one ear, then folded his free hand over his eyes. Was he weeping? She'd never seen him anything but resolute and determined and she didn't like it. But he was dealing with the fact that Ray Quick must have had a hand in Alice's death—if he wasn't the architect of it. With access to Alice's house, he'd also have access to the gun that killed her, a gun registered to Owens.

There might have been uncertainty before, but now it was clear.

"My god," he croaked, hand still over his eyes.

"You were set up," she said quietly. "Worse than."

He took another deep breath, rubbed his face. Looked at her. His eyes were glistening.

"Ray killed her," he said in a clotted voice.

She took a deep breath herself. "It sure looks that way."

If there was any good at all to come out of this, it was that, in that moment, her doubts about Owens killing Alice evaporated. He was more heartbroken over the fact that his ex—a woman who had dragged him across the emotional coals during a humiliating, year-long divorce—had been murdered rather than the fact that he'd been set up for it. That was the Owens she knew.

"But Ray has an alibi," she said. "He was working the night of Alice's murder. And he was. I double-checked."

"A quarter million can easily pay for an accomplice or two."

Just what she'd been thinking.

And then she saw his face stiffen into silent anger. "And Ray's out there," he said. "While I'm here. And he put me here."

"I'm out here, too," she said. "And I'm on your side. We're going to fix this."

Owens nodded stiffly. His grief was turning quickly to anger.

"There are a lot of dots that have to be connected," she said. "A lot of dots."

"Looks like Alice picked the wrong guy to fool around with," he said, shaking his head. "Who else knows about this?"

"All Indemnity Insurance of California. And Ray. He keeps checking his mailbox."

"Seems like the police should know."

"I agree," she said. "I'll take care of it. But I'm not confident in the police arresting him right away. They've already got you. And if Ray's tipped off, questioned, he might well have a contingency plan. I don't want him to take off."

"Me neither."

"What about SFPD?" she said. "There's no crime scene tape on the door at 41 or any indication that they've even been there." She raised her eyebrows. "I didn't see any evidence of them being there either." Meaning when she had cased the place.

Owens nodded at her inference. "It's not SFPD's case. If Sonoma County Sheriffs didn't request a search, SFPD wouldn't have done it. And in the event of a homicide, there's not always a reason to check the victim's residence."

"Is there anyone at SFPD I can talk to?"

Owens frowned. "I don't know who my friends are. Enemies, no shortage. But Ryan's IA investigation is going to make sure everyone on the force stands back. No one will be allowed to get involved."

"I can ask Matt."

"You think so?"

"Who knows?" Matt hadn't been as supportive as she would have liked. She shrugged. "How about your new partner?"

"Fos? He's a good kid. But that's what he is. He's new. Green. And he doesn't need to be caught up in this mess."

Fos. "Maybe he and I can compare notes. Off the record."

"You are determined to get yourself into trouble. With the IA investigation Fos can't talk to you about me either. You risk getting him into trouble with IA. And he's new."

"What if we just chat about the 49ers?"

Owens shook his head. "Stay. Away."

"SFPD Internal Affairs is happy to stand by and watch you spend the next twenty years in prison. I don't want to mess anything up either. Let me feel him out. I can approach him about something else."

Owens rubbed his hand over his eyes, obviously thinking. He looked up. "Not a good idea."

"Stop being so damn noble and look out for yourself for once."

Another deep breath and sigh from Owens. "OK. But tread warily."

"Thinking back on when you picked Alice up that night, does anything come to mind?" she asked. "About Ray?"

He shook his head. "All I knew was that the two of them were on the outs. Supposedly."

"OK," she said. "I'm on it. But it means you're stuck in here in the meantime. Until I make some progress."

"I can handle it."

Could he? His face had been clenched into a shiny grimace since he'd gotten the news about the death benefit.

"You have a lawyer yet?" she asked.

"Public defender up here. We met once. Not inspiring."

"What about Gus?"

"I told him to hold off. I'm trying to make the public defender work."

Did he want to be found guilty? Pay for Alice's death somehow? See it as his fault somehow?

"Screw that," she said. "Use Gus."

"The surfer dude? Can I afford him?"

"I don't see how you can*not* afford him. Even with the latest news, this could turn ugly on you in a heartbeat. I'm calling him again and telling him to get involved. Don't push back this time. We'll work something out."

There was a pause.

"OK, thanks. Thanks, Colleen. I mean it."

That was a relief, if a minor one. "*De nada.*"

"How are things otherwise?" he asked.

She wasn't in the mood to talk about Pam. "One of my girls disappeared."

"What girls?'

"The three who hang around Leavenworth. Working girls I've adopted. But one's been gone more than a week. I don't like it. I can't help but think of Night Candy. Her name is Traci."

Owens gave a deep sigh that resonated over the phone. "Fos might be able to help with that. I was bringing him up to speed on Night Candy. But he might have been reassigned. And, remember, he can't talk about anything else."

"Got it," she said. It would give her an opportunity to feel Fos out.

The guard who'd been standing in the back of the room staring at nothing came forward, tapped his wristwatch, showed Colleen.

She acknowledged with a nod, then said to Owens, "Well, the good news is we got something to go on."

He looked at her, their eyes connecting. "The good news for me is that now you know I didn't do it."

She blushed. She couldn't deny it. The doubt had been there.

But she still didn't care for the look on Owens' face. The tautness of his cold stare. Here was a man full of rage. And who could blame him? But maybe it was better he was here for the time being, where he couldn't go off the deep end and find Ray.

"Hang in there," she said.

Outside, the protesters holding signs about killer cops were down to two as Colleen walked to her car. Maybe that was more good news. Such as it was.

But it didn't seem like much.

CHAPTER NINETEEN

Colleen arrived in Calistoga just after rush hour, or what passed for rush hour there. The winter sun had descended, a heavy dusk filtering through the trees as she drove by. She needed a look at the fire damage in the cabin where Alice Owens had died. Anders, the handyman, and Donna, the manager, had prevented her the other day. Something didn't smell right, especially now, with the revelation about the life insurance claim on Alice Owens.

A laundry service van and two extra cars were parked in front of the rambling house. That meant guests—people on the premises. Up the hill, she saw Donna showing a couple into one of the two remaining geodesic dome cabins. Down in the pines, not far from the burnt-out dome, the light blue 1950s pickup with the camper shell was parked off to one side. Anders was walking toward the main house with a toolbox.

Not a good time. Colleen would come back later when there was less activity.

At Zack's diner in Calistoga, she ordered a salad although she wasn't hungry. She hadn't been eating, not since Pam left. Her clothes were loose. She could tell herself that was a good thing, but it didn't feel very good. Alice's death didn't help. Owens sitting in a cell didn't help. Ray Quick as a murderer didn't help.

Traci missing didn't help.

She needed something that helped.

So, she picked at her salad, killing time. When she was done, she nursed a cup of coffee. "Jingle Bells" on the radio didn't help.

* * *

Later she drove back out to the Joshua Inn. Through the trees she saw the battered Chevy pickup with the camper shell still parked. She bet Anders lived in his vehicle.

She stopped down the road, pulled over, got her copy of *Pride and Prejudice* from the glove compartment, the book that had been hollowed out to stash her Bersa Piccola 22, an automatic that fit in the palm of her hand, not very legal but handy when needed.

Getting out of the car she flipped the safety off, slipped the gun in the back pocket of her Levi's. Opened the trunk and retrieved her shoulder bag. Tucked her hair under her ball cap pulled down low for anonymity, found her smaller flashlight, less obvious when prowling around, and her collapsible baton. Threw the bag over her shoulder, pulled on thin gloves. She walked down along the two-lane road to the entrance of the B&B. Off in the distance she heard a car.

The house was partially lit downstairs but quiet now. One additional car was parked in front. One of the cabins up the hill had lights on.

No one around, she ducked across the dirt road into the trees, heading back to the burnt-out cabin. The camper shell had a light on in the back and music drifted out. Some old Quicksilver Messenger Service: "Pride of Man." Anders was still living in the '60s. Noise cover, but she'd still have to be dead quiet. She knew he had a German shepherd.

Ducking under the crime scene tape, she made her way back, avoiding piles of pine needles that might broadcast her footsteps.

At the recessed entrance to the dome cabin the fire smell was pungent. She looked either way, checking the house and the camper. The front door to the cabin was unlocked, barely pulled shut, having been smashed in, no doubt when the fire department had responded.

Inside she pulled the door quietly shut behind her and lit up the flashlight, keeping the beam low. Everything had been drenched, and the reek of dead, wet smoke hung in the air, despite the broken windows where the fire department had plied their trade, making it good and cold. Shivering, she lit up the lower part of a room. Much of the center was charred and burnt, especially around the bed, which had collapsed and tilted to one side. The shell of a space heater sat next to the foot, the apparent cause of the fire. Remnants of furniture—a dresser, a chair—were partially burnt. The drapes closest to the bed hung in shreds, like dead skin drying on a rack.

On the scorched mattress, burnt through to springs in places, was a contour of fabric where Alice's body had lain, her corpse having preserved a grisly silhouette. Along with the waterlogged fire stench, it was enough to turn Colleen's stomach. She fought to keep her salad down.

She guided the flashlight around the room, looking for anything that stood out in the grim mess. At the head of the bed where the frame had collapsed, a carbonized nightstand sat tilted to one side. Much of the nightstand had burned away. The metal lamp that had been on top was burnt and lying on the floor next to it. She walked over to the head of the bed, keeping her flashlight low, waving it across the ashy wreckage. In theory the space heater had made the bed catch fire and the fire spread along the bed up to the nightstand. It certainly looked that way at first glance. But the nightstand had obviously burnt with some strength. Curious. Multiple sites of ignition were a sign of arson. The arsonist may not have trusted the space heater to do the job. From a fire science class she'd taken at City College, Colleen had learned that there were four questions to ask yourself when investigating a fire. 1. Fire behavior. Initially, the space heater, but the nightstand was looking like another possible source. 2. Suspicious behavior—already established—someone trying to pin a murder on Owens. 3. Environmental modification, oily rags and the like. That remained to be seen but the nightstand was standing out—to her anyway. 4. Incendiary devices. Those, too, remained to be seen.

The nightstand had once had a door that had partially burnt away.

She went over, got on her haunches, trying to avoid the ash, pointed the flashlight into the burnt gap of the nightstand door. She got her collapsible baton out of her shoulder bag, shook it, extending it halfway, about a foot in length.

She pulled open what was left of the door, slowly, which began to collapse. She stopped, peered around inside with the flashlight and baton. Why so much ash? Books? Magazines? Papers? She brushed some ash away with the tip of the baton, lighting up the interior of the nightstand with her flashlight.

Something tinny clanked against the baton.

She brushed more ash aside with the tip of her flashlight, the light swirling in the dead cinders.

Something reflected in the cloudy beam of light.

Squatting, she poked around some more with the baton.

A metal can, a few inches across. A silver bottom.

She hooked it with the tip of the thin baton, picked it up, examined it. Didn't look like much.

But she was thinking it might be a Sterno can, an easy way to start a fire. But detectable. This can had the feint burnt words "Rio Mare" on the side, alongside the picture of a fish. A tuna fish can, of all things. The inside bottom of the can shone in the beam; the sides were scorched. It had quite possibly been that hot to burn the bottom clean.

A memory flashed in her mind as she looked it over.

The bottle of Clorox pool purification tablets and can of brake fluid she had seen on the workbench at 41 Wawona two nights ago. She had wondered about them. If both were poured into a can such as this, and left inside the nightstand, the perfect fire starter. No match required. A delay before it caught. Just shut the door to the nightstand and leave. And, once burnt, undetectable. A can like this on its own could easily be dismissed as innocuous.

Ray Quick had $250,000 worth of motive. He'd been spurned by Alice, probably never had any great love for Owens. He had access to Alice's house, where the gun used to shoot Alice would have been, a gun registered in Owens' name. So, get rid of Alice, frame Owens. Make it look like a botched cover-up. Collect.

Her head buzzed with the realization.

This can was evidence. Easy to miss by a small local fire department, struggling to put a fire out in the middle of the night. They wouldn't have a dedicated arson investigation team. And the space heater would look like the culprit.

She couldn't take the can, as much as she would have liked to have it dusted for prints. From what Detective Sanderlin had said, prints could survive a fire.

She put it back where she found it with the tip of her baton. She'd have to report it. As soon as possible.

Colleen stood up, reexamined the possible trail of fire along the nightstand to the bed. Now that she had found the can, it was looking more and more like the source.

She took in a deep breath of burnt, cold air, thinking.

Suddenly, the bark of a dog broke her concentration, a big bark, a single warning yelp. From the camper. Anders' dog. Her nerves tensed up.

Opening the door quietly and pulling it just as quietly shut behind her, she hurried outside under the pines, saw movement in the camper shell. She ducked under the crime scene tape, headed for the trees away from the house, keeping herself in darkness, holding her shoulder bag to her side with one arm to keep it from banging. Anxious wasn't the word. The rear door of the camper squawked open, and she heard a good eighty to ninety pounds of German shepherd hit the ground as the animal began to snarl. It broke into a gallop toward her, its paws beating the ground.

"Who is it, Roscoe?" she heard Anders say, his voice following the action.

She stretched her legs into a full run, but it felt like the slow motion of a nightmare, the dog gaining ground steadily behind her, growling in anticipation. Her effort to outrun him wouldn't be enough. The thought of a big dog attacking her filled her with nothing less than terror.

Her breath was coming in painful gasps as she headed for thick growth separating her from the road. The cold night air burned her throat.

"Sic 'im, Roscoe!" Anders shouted.

The dog barreled down on her as she reached a tall thicket.

The animal gnashed the lower part of her calf in a razorblade of pain, and she spun, frantically ripping her flesh loose of its jaws. But even that brief bite made her leg sing with agony as the dog latched onto the hem of her jeans now, growling and shaking her leg like a toy.

"Good boy, Roscoe!" Anders was strolling through the shadows in long johns, a shotgun casually over one shoulder.

"Who goes there?"

Head down, she pulled the Bersa from her back pocket and, as much as she disliked the idea, pointed the gun at the dog. She could feel the warm blood running into her sock amidst a stinging of hurt. Roscoe growled and held onto the leg of her bell-bottoms. She didn't want to speak, give her sex away, give her identity away, if it wasn't too late.

She pointed the gun alongside the dog's head, the barrel pointed away from it directly, but close enough to get the point across. Then she fired.

The small shot was enough to make the dog's eyes light up with fear, followed by anger. It flinched and squealed but didn't let go of her jeans.

"Stop it right there!" Anders shouted. He unslung the shotgun.

The hem of her bell-bottoms in the dog's teeth ripped, her leg jerked around, and she pointed the Bersa directly at the dog.

Roscoe stood, growling.

A standoff. She couldn't see herself shooting a dog, but Anders didn't know that.

He stopped where he was, grimacing.

"Get him off of me," she said in a low voice. "Now."

He hesitated.

She fired another shot, away from the dog's head. Roscoe flinched, let go.

Finally, Anders spoke. "Down, Roscoe."

The dog stood back. A sliver of relief.

She pointed the Bersa at Anders.

"Drop it," she said, motioning at the shotgun.

Anders lay the shotgun down on the ground.

She gestured for him to put his hands up, back away. He did.

She moved forward slowly, the dog watching her, a low rumble in its throat.

She picked up the shotgun, broke it, dumped the shells.

She backed away, her gun still up, ready to fire at Anders or the dog. Every backstep sliced into the spot above her ankle.

She pushed through the brush, dumping the shotgun, kept pushing through the remaining hedge, the branches thrashing her every step of the way. Once onto the dark road, she gasped with relief. She dashed for the Torino, every step on her wounded leg a numbing effort. Checking back, she saw no sign of Anders. She climbed into the car, tossed her pistol on the passenger seat, started up the car with shaking fingers, leaving the lights off. The dog bite rushed with pain as she stepped down on the clutch, threw the car into gear, took off. No lights.

In the rearview she saw nothing. She had darkness on her side. But Anders had gotten a partial look at her. And heard her speak. Thank God she had left bogus business cards.

But now they had been alerted.

She'd have to get the evidence in that cabin looked at, sooner rather than later. If it didn't disappear.

CHAPTER TWENTY

On the way to the Calistoga Police Department, Colleen stopped at a 76 station, gassed up the Torino, and used the restroom. Rolling up her jeans, she examined the dog bite. It probably wasn't as bad as it felt, but it felt pretty damn bad: a serious gash at the bottom of her calf that blossomed with bloody, pulpy tissue. She shuddered. The only bonus was that Fido could have bit her ankle and broken bone. Small mercies. But for a brief attack, he'd done plenty of damage. Wincing with pain, she bathed the cut gingerly with freezing cold water, her foot poised over the grimy sink. Mayhem yoga. No hot water and no soap. She wrapped her ankle and lower calf with paper towels, pulled her sock up delicately around it. Her prized Pony Topstars were trashed, this one a bloody mess. She took off her denim shirt, which was smudged with soot and ash, rinsed her face, and ran a brush through her hair. She swept off the fire ash residue from the rest of her jeans as best as possible. One cheek was lacerated where a branch had smacked her.

She limped to the phone booth in the gas station, called CPD. An older officer answered. She asked for Detective Sanderlin. He was off duty.

"Any way I can get hold of him now?" she asked. "It's related to the homicide at the Joshua Inn."

The officer put her on hold while she made a call. Got back on her line. "I'll have to take a message," she said.

She left a message, stressed the importance. "I'll be back in San Francisco in about an hour. Please tell him to call me any time, no matter how late it is."

She shambled out into the station and back to her car. The pain in her leg was a nice, steady throb. She had never realized how many steps one took in a day.

On the way back to SF, she stopped by the Joshua Inn on Highway 29 briefly, doused the headlights, left the car running while she got out and peered through the trees.

She saw a light bouncing around inside the cabin. *Damn it.*

Someone was in there, after her visit. Her mood worsened.

She'd done all she could for now. She limped back to her car, frustrated. Back to SF.

*   *   *

Ten fifteen, she sat in the emergency room at SF General on Potrero, her leg up on a plastic chair. It throbbed but had stopped bleeding freely. The lower right leg of her treasured soft flared jeans was ripped and bloodstained. Another wardrobe write-off. Saturday, so there was a line of people ahead of her. She was going to be here for a while, but she needed stitches.

But she knew one thing: Anders, and possibly the manager, were somehow connected to Alice's slaying. And hence, with Ray Quick.

CHAPTER TWENTY-ONE

The next morning in her office, while Colleen was slipping the letter from All Indemnity Insurance listing Ray Quick as the sole beneficiary of a $250,000 death benefit for Alice Owens into the safe, the phone rang. She shut the safe door, spun the tumbler, went over, and answered the phone. Her calf was raw from the stitches she'd received in the middle of the night at SF General and freshly bandaged. She'd popped aspirin for breakfast, along with plenty of coffee to keep her going on little sleep. She'd live.

It was Detective Sanderlin.

She thanked him for calling and told him what she'd found in the cabin up at Joshua Inn.

There was a pause before he answered.

"Are you saying you actually entered that site?"

"I didn't take the can," she said. "If you locate it, there's a good chance you'll identify your arsonist."

"This is all highly improper," he said.

"I know," she admitted. "But things looked suspicious. And, as it turns out, things *were* suspicious."

"Suspicious how?"

"After I left that note for you last night, I stopped back at the Joshua Inn on my way home. Someone was in that cabin. With a flashlight."

She heard Sanderlin take a deep breath. "But you didn't see who?"

"No, but I'm leaning toward the handyman—Anders. He's the one who chased me off the property with his dog." She didn't mention the gun play. "I've also come across some other evidence that points to another individual with a strong motive to murder Alice Owens." Colleen told him who.

"Ray Quick?" Sanderlin said. "Her ex-boyfriend? He's got an alibi."

"It's too solid. He's made sure people can vouch for him. He could also have an accomplice. Like Anders. Ray's got a huge financial motive. And he still has access to Alice Owens' house. Where he comes and goes at will. He could have easily had access to her gun too, which belonged to Owens."

"How do you know he has access to her house?"

"Been staking the place out." She wasn't going to admit to entering 41 Wawona herself.

"What's Ray's financial motive?"

She told him about the death benefit.

"And how do you know that?"

"I just know," she said. "I was hoping you'd try to gather that tuna can from the fire, check it for fingerprints, but I suspect the thing has grown legs by now."

"You said the handyman chased you off the property?"

"I've got a dog bite with eighteen stitches to prove it. Did anyone at Joshua Inn report my visit last night?"

"Hang on." He covered the phone, and she heard a muffled conversation in the background.

He came back on the line. "No."

"Kind of odd, don't you think?"

"People up here mind their own business."

"Especially when they're up to no good," she said. "How hard would it be to take a quick look in that cabin's nightstand? Just for yuks?"

"You do know this case was transferred to Sonoma County."

"Detective Kikuyama won't work with me."

"Sounds like he might have reason. Maybe you should heed Detective Kikuyama's words. Stay off the property. It's called 'trespassing.' And entering a crime scene is a chargeable offense."

"I know what it must sound like," she said. "Some meddlesome private investigator sticking her nose where it didn't belong, right? But Owens didn't kill Alice. He was set up. Everything I find supports that. You're my only shot right now. I figure you want this case done right. It was yours to begin with."

There was another pause. At least he didn't hang up on her. "OK," he said. "I'll go out to the inn, take a look around. But I'm warning you again: stay off the property."

"Got it," she said. "I appreciate it." But her gut instinct told her it would be too late. She wondered about the pool purification tablets and brake fluid. She hadn't mentioned them to Sanderlin because, again, it would mean admitting she'd been inside 41 Wawona.

"I've got to go," Detective Sanderlin said.

"Please keep me in the loop." But he had already hung up.

CHAPTER TWENTY-TWO

Next morning Colleen took care of some paid work, meeting with the woman whose husband liked to dance with men in the Castro. She felt for the woman and strongly suggested, against her own financial interests, that she find a way to talk to her spouse. Give him room, if she was open to that, and come to some kind of friendly resolution. Hayes Confidential, advice columnist in training. Fortunately, for every lousy marriage looking for a spouse to blame, there were two more waiting, and she had another one lined up, this time a husband who wanted to know why his wife was spending so much time working late. The wife worked for a railroad company at One Market Plaza, which was close to Pier 26, so the job could almost work itself. Camera at the ready, Colleen headed down along the Embarcadero. A grey cold winter day, with plenty of cold bay breezes that chilled the cheeks. When she got to Market Street, it was bustling.

She caught the woman, a pretty, young Filipina, going out to lunch with a young, good-looking white guy in a trendy burgundy suit with flares and platform shoes to match. The two seemed awfully chummy as they walked out together. She got a picture of them brushing hands once they left One Market Plaza, slinked back to her office, feeling grubby.

Her message light was blinking.

It was Detective Sanderlin again. She called him right back.

He had stopped by the Joshua Inn to take another look at the cabin.

"And?" she asked.

"They told me to come back with a warrant."

"Not exactly forthcoming," she said.

"Not exactly. But, like you say, it'll be too late. It's not even our case anymore so I can't call in a warrant. But the fact that they pushed back letting me search the place tells me something isn't right."

At least he believed her.

"When you say 'they,'" she asked, "you mean the manager too? Donna?"

"And her helper. The old longhair."

"So, both of them are in on hiding the evidence."

"It's possible that she just doesn't want the bad publicity."

"But not too probable."

"I hear you," he said. "I'm going to be contacting Sonoma County where they have access to a warrant and an arson investigation team. I can suggest they try the state fire marshall."

"It sounds like all of that all takes time."

"It does."

While Owens sits in a cell. "I appreciate it."

"Keep me posted if you hear anything new," Sanderlin said. "But don't go looking for it. Stay away from the Joshua Inn. No more interfering."

"Got it," she said, even though it was her "interfering" that raised this issue in the first place. She thanked him and got off the phone.

But now she knew for sure Ray Quick had allies up at Joshua Inn.

* * *

On the way to pick up her photos of the pretty young wife and her paramour, Colleen swung by 850 Bryant, the Hall of Justice, called SFPD Homicide from a pay phone in the marble lobby, asked for Fos Alvarez, Owens' new partner. The high-ceilinged entrance boomed with people and noise, and she had to cover her non-phone ear.

"Detective Alvarez." He had a deep young voice.

"I'm a close acquaintance of Owens," she said. "I'm also his CI." Confidential Informant. There was a long pause while the hum of conversations droned in the background upstairs on the fifth floor. "We've worked together on a few things."

"Then you know I can't talk about him," Fos said. He was about to hang up.

She needed his help. "What if it was about Night Candy? Can you talk about that?"

Fos stopped. "Night Candy?"

"Possibly."

"Because with the IA investigation I can't talk about Owens."

"I know."

"So, what have you got?"

"Downstairs," she said. "I'll meet you out front."

She heard him inhale while he seemed to think about it. "Five minutes."

Colleen exited the Hall of Justice to a grey, ice-cold San Francisco afternoon, stood at the bottom of the wide steps. Her breath was visible in puffs. Shortly afterwards a tall, slender Latino appeared through the doors. He wore a brown suit along with a skinny black tie on a black shirt. His hair was parted in the middle accentuating a long brooding face. Not a wrinkle in his smooth, dark skin. If he was over thirty, she would have been surprised.

She gave him a nod of acknowledgment, and he stepped down the dozen or so stairs that fronted the grey monolith. They moved over to one side, away from the heavy foot traffic going in and out of 850.

"I hope you're not wasting my time," he said in a deep baritone. "You've got a rep around here."

"Well, at least I don't have to worry about you speaking your mind."

"Owens spoke highly of you. But he's about the only one."

"I notice that you speak about Owens in the past tense, as if he's no longer a part of the Homicide team."

"Night Candy?" Fos said, raising his eyebrows. "I believe that's how this conversation started."

She told him about Traci. She had swung by the girls on Leavenworth. Still no sign.

"Who hasn't even been reported missing," he said.

"Sex workers and their bosses don't tend to deal with the police."

He shrugged. "No body. No obvious link to Night Candy."

"She's been missing for over a week. Not far from where the transvestite hooker was found dead at St. Francis Memorial. Both sex workers."

"OK."

"I think she might have been killed."

"Why?"

"Maybe we can go somewhere. It's a long story."

"And we're not talking about Owens, right?"

What a hard ass. "Owens investigated the St. Francis Memorial murder—the transvestite—first, before he got arrested—so his name might come up in that respect. And I do have a question about Alice Owens. All off the record, of course."

"And I just told you I can't talk about Owens. That includes his ex."

"Look, I really need your help. Owens really needs your help."

He squinted, obviously aggravated. "We're back to Owens. You don't listen."

"Why don't *you* lighten up for five minutes and just hear me out?"

"Your five minutes are already up."

"Owens is your damn partner. And you're just going to let him rot in a freaking cell? While your bosses play their games upstairs? Owens didn't kill Alice. I bet money you know that. And I'm pretty sure *I* know who did. His name is Ray Quick. Alice's ex. He's the guy you want to look at."

"That case is out of our jurisdiction." Fos checked his watch. "We're done here." He turned, walked back up the stairs, taking them two at a time. He pushed through the glass door.

One step forward. One step back. Fos was a big step back.

CHAPTER TWENTY-THREE

Back in her office on Pier 26, Colleen examined a grainy photo of a man with a younger man in the darkness of a street corner in the Castro.

This was one seedy job when you got right down to it.

She put on her black leather coat, ready to call it a day. Headed to her car on the covered pier. Past the new architect's office, who was working late, lights on. Chan Imports had a fresh pallet of Hello Kitty merchandise. Mr. Chan, a big friendly guy in a green apron, gave her a smile as he humped boxes into his storage area. She waved back, got into the Torino, headed home. Kiss were on KFOG with some disco-tinged rock.

There had been a bottle of pool purification tablets along with a can of brake fluid on the workbench in Alice Owens' garage. Pool purification tablets were chlorine. Chlorine mixed with brake fluid would create a spontaneous fire ball that would burn itself away. Just like what seemed to be the case up at Joshua Inn.

And Ray Quick had a key to Alice's house.

She wondered if those pool purification pills and brake fluid were still on the workbench.

Twenty minutes later she drove by The Claddagh on Clement where Ray Quick's midnight blue Buick Riviera with the telltale key scrape on the right rear fender was parked at an angle alongside the other cars on the street. Ray was at work. All she needed to know.

She took Arguello through Golden Gate Park over to West Portal. Dark shadows of the tree branches moved in the wind, whipping up more winter cold. At 41 Wawona she had to wait until the street was clear before she let herself in with her bump key and hammer.

Downstairs on the workbench, no bottle of Clorox pool purification tablets. No can of brake fluid.

As before, she didn't have enough real evidence. Even though she knew. There was only one thing to do. Follow Ray until he showed his hand.

* * *

Colleen went home, skipped dinner one more time, took a shower with a plastic bag over her bandaged leg, which was feeling tender as the day wore on. She set the alarm for 1:00 a.m., five hours from now, and lay on the heated waterbed. Despite the throbbing in her leg, she felt warm and tired after days of almost no rest. Pamela's sudden departure after losing the baby was more manageable, but it would always be with her. Although she was more than ready for Pam to show up again. But that wasn't the way Pam worked. When Pam left, she left.

She wished Pam would at least call.

And stacked on top of everything was Traci with an "i."

Colleen had to stay busy to stay sane. She had to help Owens, one of the few people she had left in her life.

She let the warm waves of her waterbed lull her to sleep.

At two in the morning, bundled up in a sweater and a three-quarter-length, narrow-waisted sheepskin coat with soft white unshorn edging and collar, armed with a thermos of coffee, she sat in the shadows parked down Wawona. The bars were just shutting. Ray might show.

Not long afterwards, a familiar rumble came up the street. Colleen slumped down in her seat until the car went by, then raised herself up just enough to see the taillights of Ray Quick's Riviera over the steering wheel. The taillights went down to the end of the block where the car took a right and disappeared from view. Then she saw Ray come walking down Wawona and go up into the house of the woman he had murdered for a quarter of a million bucks.

He left again, minutes later.

Waiting for that insurance letter. The one in Colleen's safe. Poor baby.

It took several tries to start the Torino, cold weather and bad rings, and a car that had seen better days.

She followed Ray down Sloat. Was he heading out toward the beach? Colleen kept her distance, paramount this time of night when tailing someone.

Just past Stern Grove, Ray pulled into a driveway at a house across from the reservoir. That's where he must've gone the other day when she'd followed him down Sloat and lost him.

He got out of the car, walked to the front door. Colleen pulled into the far lane, ambled down Sloat, spun a U-ey.

Came back in the far lane.

Ray was at the front door, which had opened.

A woman in a white robe let him in, gave him a long kiss.

The middle-aged redhead who worked the bar at The Claddagh. Mary.

Ray Quick didn't seem to have suffered Alice's absence for long.

CHAPTER TWENTY-FOUR

Waiting was something Colleen could do. Nine-plus years in Denver Women's Correctional Facility said as much.

But following Ray Quick around for two days was beginning to wear. Her finances were suffering. But Ray was staying cool. Coming home to Mary the redhead after working in the pub and checking Alice Owens's house in West Portal for that letter that Colleen had diverted.

It was time to kick it up a notch.

That evening, after Ray had gone into The Claddagh to work, she dropped his precious letter from All Indemnity Insurance, of which she'd carefully steamed open and resealed after making a copy, into the mail slot at 41 Wawona. That should get him to move.

And tonight, past two a.m. down the street from Alice Owens's house one more time, the windshield began to blur with droplets of accumulating late-night fog. The radio was on low; Meat Loaf had just started singing "Bat Out of Hell" when Colleen heard the distinctive sound of Ray's car coming up the street. She ducked down low in her seat again as the car motored past, and a few minutes later, she saw Ray go up the stairs of number 41.

Only this time, when he left, he was tapping a letter against his thigh. And damn if there wasn't a smirk on his face.

Not so glum tonight.

She gave it a minute, started up the car, followed. Staying behind a distance, thinking about trading cars with someone because she'd been following Ray for a while now.

Down along Sloat. Only tonight Ray didn't stop at the redhead's love nest. He kept going. That surprised her.

Down to Ocean Beach, the moon breaking through the clouds over a calm Pacific Ocean. She had to keep her distance. It was slightly warmer tonight, but that was due to the wind dying.

And on down Highway 1 along the coast to Daly City, Pacifica, the town giving away to stretches of coastline. The Riviera's brake lights glowed red before the car turned off at a motel, an unassuming place, easy to miss. A dozen sun-bleached units were tucked away in the dunes.

She slowed down as she drove by, craning her neck to see over the tall coastal grass blowing lazily to one side. Ray's Riviera was pulling around the back of the Shorebird Motel.

She drove down to the next turnoff, pulled over on Highway 1. Grabbed her extendible baton, got out of the car. A harsh breeze tinted with salt from the ocean had picked up and the cold returned. She headed back along the road, with her sheepskin coat buttoned. The stitches from the dog bite on her calf pulled, making her wince.

At the Shorebird she approached cautiously, the weed-strewn asphalt of the parking area showing only two other vehicles. Not too many people staying at a run-down motel along the California coast in winter.

She headed around the back, where she saw Ray's car parked in front of a room number 7, the only one lit.

She tiptoed over. Close enough to hear.

Two people were making love, going at it like gangbusters. You'd think her line of work would have toughened her up, but there were things she didn't need to hear. Like Ray talking dirty. He was celebrating his quarter mil. He certainly wasn't grieving Alice.

Enough. She turned around, headed back to her car.

CHAPTER TWENTY-FIVE

Next morning Colleen's office phone was ringing as she was unlocking the door. Her leg smarted as she ran to answer it, but it did feel better than yesterday. She was able to answer before the call rolled over to her answering machine.

"Hey," Matt said. "Up for lunch?"

"Kind of a busy day," she said. She had to catch up on her paid cases, wrap up the week.

"I've got some news."

News. She wasn't sure if that sounded good or bad. But Matt had been trying harder of late.

"In that case . . ." she said.

"Rudy's at noon." Rudy's was a cop bar near the Hall of Justice.

She called the San Francisco Medical Examiner-Coroner's Office at 850 Bryant and asked for Alistair Laurie, her ME contact. It was time to take Owens' situation up a notch as well.

Alistair answered in his soft Scottish accent.

"Buy you a drink when you get off work tonight?" she asked.

"Asking a Scotsman if he wants a drink, Colleen?"

She threw her black leather coat on over her jeans and sweater, went out to the Permit Office on South Van Ness where she stood in a very slow line, favoring her good leg, to verify a job where the contractor had left her clients—a genteel elderly couple—without gas for close to a month, abandoning the job until they coughed up more cash. To her surprise, she found the job was listed as a simple water heater replacement. The actual work was far more extensive, and the contractor was skirting permit issues—unbeknownst to the owners, while he fleeced them for time and materials, which was essentially a license to steal. Colleen searched for the inspector who had signed off on various stages of work, suspicious considering the water heater permit. It wouldn't be the first time an inspector colluded with a contractor. Colleen finally found her, a woman who said she would take care of it when Colleen threatened to file a complaint and take the case to the *Chronicle*. With any luck that would be enough to get the contactor to drop the blackmail routine and finish the job.

By the time Colleen got to Rudy's, it was well after noon.

Matt was standing at the bar, turning a glass of beer on the counter with forced patience, looking coiffed and slightly miffed at the same time. He checked his watch theatrically when she pushed her way up to the bar. The place was packed, cops of all shapes and sizes, uniformed and not, drinking and eating, eating and drinking. Glittery Christmas decorations hung around the place, and the jukebox was playing "Time Passages" by Al Stewart, and it made Colleen sadder than usual. Pam and the grandbaby that hadn't made it would be with her for many Christmases to come.

"Must be payday," she said, nodding at the boozing cops.

"I had a table but had to give it up," Matt said.

"Sorry, Matt," she said. "The SF Permit office is not a model of efficiency."

Matt must have detected her mood because his softened.

"Hey," he said, squeezing her arm affectionately. "The food here isn't that great anyway. You probably did us a favor." He waved the bartender down.

"Just coffee," she said. She wasn't going to start drinking so early in the day, and she had to meet Alistair tonight at another bar. Her coffee showed up, and she could smell the hours on the hotplate. "I'll just have to upgrade your lunch to a free dinner," she said, winking. "Followed by dessert."

Matt beamed. "Someone pinch me." Then he set his beer down. "You doing OK?"

She said that she was.

"I did some digging," he said. "About Owens."

She hadn't wanted to ask and appreciated that he'd brought it up. She took a sip of burnt coffee, winced, set the mug down.

"I was reminded once again that the case isn't ours," Matt continued. "And with Ryan's pending IA investigation, it's off limits."

"So, while Owens sits in a cell, Ray can collect on a quarter-million life insurance policy on Alice."

Matt's eyes opened wide. "You're kidding."

"I wish."

"How did you find that out?"

"It wasn't tough." Then she told him about the suspicious fire.

Matt sighed. "The important thing, as I see it, is that Owens gets out of jail."

"Eventually," she said. "*Maybe*. It's not a done deal. Sonoma County won't give me the time of day."

"It's going to cost me, but let me talk to the Deputy Chief."

A small ripple of encouragement flowed through her. "You're a prince, Matt."

"Not quite," Matt said. "I should have gotten involved sooner. You were right. It's chickenshit the way Owens is being treated."

Yes, it was but she was just glad he was coming around. "What is it with Ryan and Owens anyway?" Inspector Ryan had been transferred to Internal Affairs, where he was putting Owens through hell by ignoring his case and refusing to lift a finger to help.

"Apart from the fact that Ryan was born with the 'dickhead' gene?" Matt set his beer down. "He's always been resentful of Owens. But the case last year—the one you worked on in Italy—was what pushed him over the edge."

She had helped Owens solve a murder that led to the arrest of a suspect Ryan had figured for a case he was working on with Matt. Matt had been bent out of shape too, at the time, but had gotten over it. Ryan, not so much.

"Enough about me," she said. "You said you had some news."

Matt's face grew serious. "I've been accepted for final interviews with the CIA."

She was more than surprised. She knew he'd applied but had forgotten about it, assumed it was a wash. "Final interviews?"

"Langley."

She took a deep breath, put on a smile. "But that's great, Matt. I didn't know."

"I didn't want to say anything until it looked like a lock. The written tests and first round of interviews were done here, down at the Federal building."

That would mean he was leaving, at least for a while, if not for much longer. "So, when do you leave for Langley?"

"Day after tomorrow. Six a.m. flight."

Sunday. Another shock.

She cleared her throat, composed herself. "Well, I guess I only have myself to blame for ignoring you all this time."

Matt returned a sad smile. "You've got a lot on your mind, Coll. And some distance won't hurt us, right?" His look turned pensive. "Isn't that what you want? Some space?"

What she wanted didn't seem important. Was that why he was being sweet, trying to help her out with Owens after he'd initially resisted? She forced another smile.

"Well, you better be up for a goodbye date tomorrow," she said. "I'm going to send you off in style. Hopefully you'll still be able to walk when I'm done with you."

"Hmm. I might not leave after all . . ."

Then, "Speak of the devil," Matt said, nodding at the door.

Colleen turned to see Inspector Ryan enter, the bar door swinging shut behind him. Shy of medium height, he was heavy, wearing an ill-fitting jacket and a poorly knotted tie. He needed a haircut. He looked like Fred Flintstone with a hangover.

Ryan walked by without seeing them, it seemed, down to the end of the bar where he stood to one side of the serving hatch. He raised a finger and the barman poured him a shot of something brown. He downed it, pointed at the empty shot glass. It was refilled.

"Back in a sec," Colleen said to Matt.

"Please be careful," Matt said behind her.

She approached Ryan just as he was lifting the shot glass to his lips. He was shorter than her. He gave her a sideways glance full of suspicion, realizing who she was.

"Last time we talked," she said, "you and your little helper Stoll threatened me," she said. "Down by the farmers market—remember? I had to walk home in the middle of the night—once you finally let me out of the car. You were trying to scare me off a case. It didn't work, by the way."

Ryan set his glass down, untouched. Set his hands on the bar. "What do you want?"

"Ray Quick—Alice's ex. He's still got a key to her house, where he comes and goes at will. He stands to collect a quarter-million-dollar life insurance policy on her. And he's got something funky going on with Joshua Inn—where Alice died. Hundred-to-one he set Owens up."

"Why are you telling me? That's Sonoma County's case."

"Because you're making sure SFPD drags their feet. You know Owens is innocent."

"In that case, Sonoma County will confirm that."

"What have you got against Owens?"

"You are one pushy broad, you know that?"

"'*Broad?* Is it really 1979?"

"Oh, I'm sorry," he said. "*Bitch*. One pushy *bitch*."

She let her temper subside. "Tell your little gopher Stoll not to call me up anymore. It's called harassment. Keep it up and you'll both find out what a *bitch* I can be."

She returned to Matt.

"A wild hunch tells me you and Ryan didn't trade yuletide wishes of joy," Matt said.

"If he thinks I'm going to sit around and let the fates decide what happens to Owens while Ray Quick gets away with his shit, he's got another thing coming."

Matt looked at her broodingly. "As I said, please be careful."

"I know," she said. "I know."

A syrupy Christmas song by John Denver and the Muppets came on the jukebox. "A Baby Just Like You." It reminded her of Pam. Everything seemed to. She didn't need to hear a song about a baby right now.

CHAPTER TWENTY-SIX

Cold evening drizzle settled on Colleen's face as she stepped across
Geary Street, dodging traffic that continued past rush hour. Her leg
was slowly healing. Bordering downtown in the shadow of Nob
Hill, the Tenderloin had become one of San Francisco's grittier
neighborhoods, with influxes of refugees from Southeast Asia and
a population of inner-city poor. Mom-and-Pop stores and neighborhood bars rubbed shoulders with welfare hotels and run-down
apartment buildings built during the early 1900s.

She pushed open the door to the Edinburgh Castle Pub where a
warm glow prevailed. The old tavern was an institution, attested to
by its once-grand tile floor and wood panels.

She found Alistair Laurie standing at the bar, a cigarette smolder-
ing from his fingers as he cradled a half-empty pint. A middle-aged
man with thinning grey hair and glasses, Alistair was still in his ME
uniform: black pants, narrow black tie, white shirt, black jacket with
the gold buttons and gold stripes around the cuffs. He greeted
Colleen with a friendly hello in his soft brogue, his eyes intensified
by his years working as a San Francisco Medical Examiner
Investigator. In spite of his profession, Alistair was a positive force.
He'd been a wanderer before settling down at the city's morgue,

even living on the streets and in flop hotels for a stint before landing a job that didn't require a degree or prior medical training, just a willingness to deal with death on a clear-eyed basis.

She set a ten-dollar bill on the countertop made up of coins embedded in Plexiglas and signaled for the barwoman.

"Twisting my arm," Alistair said, draining his beer. Colleen ordered a wine spritzer for herself. Alcohol and working cases didn't mix.

"So," Alistair said, sipping the foam off a fresh pint of bitter. "Why does the fair lady detective need the services of a lowly ME investigator this time?"

"Who do you know in the coroner's office in Sonoma County?"

Alistair took a drink of beer, licked foam off his lip, set his glass down.

"Up there they report to the sherriff. Napa County Coroner's."

Alistair knew about Owens and his ex. She gave him an update.

"But why so interested, Colleen? It's a tragedy to be sure. But what's done is done."

"This fire had a little help."

He sipped beer. "It must be terribly stressful to have a suspicious mind."

"Fifty percent of fires are thought to be arson."

"Do you think Owens is in that fifty percent?"

"Not in the slightest," she said. "But others do. Their version is that Owens shot Alice in a remote little bed-and-breakfast, and the space heater did the rest. But that makes less sense the more I dig."

"Well, Owens was quite . . . ah . . . attached to Alice," Alistair said.

"Not so attached he'd kill her."

Alistair gave her a sideways squint. "Defending your old pal is honorable, Colleen, but it might be affecting your vision a tad. You'd be surprised what a person—even someone like Owens—is capable of in the heat of passion. I've seen it. Many times."

"A smart cop like Owens wouldn't try to cover up a shooting with a fire that wouldn't hide a bullet in the skull. But someone who doesn't know the ins-and-outs of forensic pathology might."

Alistair took a drink of bitter. "Someone like who?"

"Alice's former boyfriend, Ray Quick, is due to receive a quarter of a million bucks as a death benefit."

"Well, that's certainly interesting."

"Kind of what I thought."

Alistair's beer was running low. Colleen signaled the barwoman for a refill. A minute later Alistair supped the top off a fresh pint.

"He comes and goes at her house—still." Colleen went on to tell him about the disappearing evidence at Joshua Inn. "Ten to one Ray's got a helper. Or two." She told him about the manager and the ax man.

When she was done, Alistair set his half-empty pint down.

"And SFPD isn't involved?" he asked.

"Not in a good way. Ryan has been wanting to see Owens take a fall ever since Owens stepped on a case of his. Now Ryan is Internal Affairs, and a case has been opened on Owens while Sonoma County works the murder case."

Alistair shook his head. "Poor man is definitely getting the shaft."

"What does it take to get a copy of Alice Owens' autopsy report?"

"They're not always a matter of public record to begin with," he said. "And with an active homicide investigation, hers is sure to be restricted."

Colleen cleared her throat: "How hard would it be to take a look at Alice's body?"

Alistair turned his drink on a coaster, gave Colleen a shrewd look. "I don't know anyone up there. I'd need a reason."

"Being as this is a murder investigation on someone who reports to SFPD, and the report is restricted, you could be doing your due diligence."

"Without authorization?" Alistair drank an inch of beer. "A bit of a stretch. You've got my curiosity, though. But whatever we did would have to fly under the radar. Well under."

"My favorite flight path."

"If I get any pushback, we have to stop. No questions. You realize that, Colleen?"

"If anything happens, you blame everything on me."

"Not sure if that gets me off any hooks." Alistair took a drink of beer, set his glass down. "But let me make a call or two."

CHAPTER TWENTY-SEVEN

Next morning Colleen and Alistair sped across the Golden Gate Bridge through Marin, the Torino's pipes punching noise into the fog. Past San Quentin, the flat bay shined the last of the moonlight. Past Petaluma, countryside finally rose out of darkness. Colleen shaved a good fifteen minutes off the hour-and-fifteen drive.

They pulled up at Napa County Coroner's by the quiet county airport early, past the old town along the river. The small building was a far cry from the ME's office in San Francisco's Hall of Justice.

They sat in the car for a moment as Alistair read some paperwork he had on Napa County Coroner's.

"No homicides so far this year," Alistair said. "Only twelve unnatural deaths."

"And the year is almost over," Colleen said. "You've got to wonder how much experience they have." Maybe one of the reasons the murder might have been committed up here.

Alistair nodded in agreement, got out of the car, dressed in his SF City ME investigator outfit for officialdom's sake. Colleen joined him, wearing a formal blue pantssuit and heels. She'd dressed her wound, now a week old, in a new, less bulky bandage. The tenderness was minimal. She had her leather bag of tricks over one shoulder.

They checked in with the front desk, Alistair presenting his request to examine case C79-512, one Alice Owens. Colleen showed no ID, letting the officer think she was some sort of official.

The duty officer, a sheriff's deputy in a crisp khaki uniform with a wary frown, took Alistair's form, read it. A small plastic Christmas tree with tiny ornaments on the counter looked surreal in the current surroundings.

"On a Saturday?" the clerk asked, looking up in surprise.

"We're in a bit of a hurry," Alistair said.

The deputy stood up, disappeared behind a white door. He returned, said someone would be out, sat down, returned to his paperwork.

Colleen and Alistair waited before a diener—a morgue worker—in a white coat came out holding Alistair's request. He had an unruly thatch of dark hair and had cut himself shaving. His name tag read: MORRIS.

He handed Alistair a report, gave Colleen a quick glance, possibly wondering how she fit into all of this. Over Alistair's shoulder, Colleen read the autopsy report. Cause of death was listed as "Gunshot wound to head (Gunshot Wound 'A'), close range, entering left parietal scalp, without exit." Perforation of skull and brain, lots of medical info Colleen didn't understand, and a note that the projectile was recovered from the left base of the skull. The bullet linked the gun to Owens.

Alistair gave the rest of the report a quick perusal before he looked up at Morris. "So, the actual autopsy was done in Calistoga?"

Morris confirmed that it was.

"We'd like to have a look at her," Alistair said.

"What?" Morris's eyes opened in surprise.

"An SFPD inspector is involved," Colleen said. "We need to verify for our records, since the autopsy was done elsewhere. Just a formality. It's SOP."

"I can't do that without Coroner Campbell's OK. And he's not here on the weekend."

One of the reasons they'd picked Saturday.

"Then we need to speak with Coroner Campbell," Colleen said.

Morris swallowed, blinking in hesitation. After taking a breath, he made a phone call. No answer. He hung up, looking uncertain.

"I don't know what to tell you," he said.

Colleen exhaled. "We drove up from the Bay Area. As you can imagine there's a mountain of pressure to get this taken care of soon. It's all over the news. The accused is an SFPD homicide inspector."

"I know." Morris grimaced. Not the kind of guy to make decisions on his own. "But the remains are scheduled to be transferred to Jacobsen's funeral home this afternoon."

"You can't be serious," Colleen said. "For someone who's dead, she's moving around an awful lot. Who requested the remains? The family?"

"That would be confidential."

"In that case," Alistair said, "we definitely need to take a look before the remains are moved. Then we can file our paperwork and be done with it."

"I'm sorry," Morris said. "You'll have to get Campbell's OK."

Alistair gave Colleen an almost imperceptible nod. Plan B.

"I've got the release of remains form here," Colleen said, opening her shoulder bag. "We'll have the remains sent to San Francisco for inspection." She produced a California Release of Remains form, signed off with a scribble she had fashioned. If anyone complained, it wouldn't be Alistair's handiwork and she could take responsibility for the ruse.

Morris read the form.

"But the autopsy is completed," he said. "I've just given you a copy of the report."

"And we do appreciate that," she said. "But an SFPD inspector has been charged with murder," she said again.

Morris attempted to brush his hair into place with his fingers, looking uncomfortable. He took a deep shaky breath. "Do you have the means to transport the remains?"

"No," she said, "but while you're getting them ready, I'll call and request an ME wagon. Worse comes to worse, we can always have someone drive one up from San Francisco."

She watched Morris' face tighten as he weighed things up. The day could end up being an ordeal for him, with possible recriminations for not being cooperative in a murder case.

"Look," Colleen said to Morris. "All we want is a quick look to confirm that all is in order—which I'm sure it is—and then we'll be on our way."

Morris thought about that.

"I'd need to be there with you," he said.

"We wouldn't want it any other way," she said.

*   *   *

Behind the door the autopsy room held an autopsy "suite," a stainless-steel unit affixed to the wall containing sinks, shelves, instruments, bottles of liquids, a large hanging scale for weighing organs and such. The room was brightly lit and cool and smelled of ammonia. An empty gurney stood by. A chart on the wall showed the basic human body, one side of it without skin.

Morris donned plastic gloves, offered Alistair a gown, face mask, and gloves as well. Alistair declined the mask and gown, took the gloves. Colleen was presented only a face mask, perhaps assuming she was not taking an active part in the exam. Morris went and pulled the latch on a substantial stainless-steel door, rolled out another gurney with a black cadaver bag on it. The bag had handles. The contents were shorter than a tall woman and thin, raised on one side, like an adolescent or elderly body that had rolled over on one side and gone to sleep, and Colleen realized with a start that a corpse retrieved from a fire would be smaller and lighter than a "normal" one, and likely misshapen by the blaze. She fought a shudder as Morris moved the gurney into place at the workstation while Alistair moved to one side.

Morris lined the gurney up.

"Ready?" He seemed to be talking more to Colleen than Alistair, noting the mask dangling in her hand, which she had not donned, not wanting to be seen as an amateur since Morris and Alistair were going without.

Morris unzipped the bag and the sight of the woman's roasted face, with the top of her head removed and replaced as a result of the autopsy, followed by the stench of burnt hair and what smelled like burnt liver, even after refrigeration, made Colleen's stomach turn.

She slipped her mask on, stood back, waited for her insides to settle.

Alistair examined the corpse. Morris pointed out the key characteristics.

"Triple flexion of the limbs due to muscle thermal retraction. Pugilistic attitude consisting of an anteromedial flexion of the humerus, flexion of the forearm on the arm and flexion of the wrist on the forearm . . ."

All Colleen could see was a mummified woman who appeared to have shrunk. As if from fear? What had been in her mind? She'd been shot. Wouldn't being burned alive in a fire have been something she had mercifully been spared?

Colleen said as much.

Alistair said there were many factors involved, asked Morris about the contents of the trachea.

He was told there were milligrams of soot in her throat.

He and Colleen traded looks. Colleen got it. For soot to be in the trachea, Alice might still have been breathing. Another rush of revulsion overcame her. Had this poor woman possibly been alive *after* the fire had started?

That would mean she had been shot after she'd been killed.

Colleen had never met Alice Owens in real life, having only seen photos, and this body was similar—slender and tallish—or had been before the ravages of the fire had shrunken and disfigured her. The woman's head was shriveled and brown, like an empty leather bottle. Her charred lips were curled back.

Colleen surreptitiously got her Polaroid camera out of her bag.

While Morris and Alistair were talking, she got off a quick shot, during which time she thought she saw something flash in the woman's mouth. She caught the Polaroid as it was ejected.

"I really must protest!" Morris said to Colleen.

"My apologies." Colleen put her camera away. "I didn't mean to upset anyone. It's just for our records." She slid the photo in her jacket pocket.

She squinted at the twisted burnt upper lip. Alice's teeth were covered with charred matter, no doubt from the fire, but something had stood out for just a moment. The flash.

"What's that?" she said to Alistair.

Alistair bent down, inspected.

"The right cuspid," he said. "The 'eye tooth' we called it, where I grew up."

"The canine," Colleen said.

"That's right."

Something triggered Colleen's memory. "Can you take a closer look, please? It looks like there might be something on her tooth."

"Do you have a probe?" Alistair asked Morris. "I've got one if you don't have one handy."

"There." Morris pointed at a tray of instruments on the stainless-steel shelf.

Alistair selected what looked like something a dentist would use to poke around in your mouth. He bent over the cadaver's head and slowly pushed back the upper lip, which looked as tough as an old shoe.

Alistair scraped at the eye tooth. The glint showed.

"It's a small stone," he said, his back to Colleen. "A diamond possibly. A dental inlay."

Another recollection nudged Colleen's memory, a realization so powerful it made her shiver. "May I?"

She leaned forward as Alistair held the lip back with the probe.

The tip of a small diamond on the canine tooth.

She got her camera out again.

"No!" Morris said. "No more photos."

"This is important," Colleen said.

"She's right," Alistair said. "The dental inlay isn't mentioned in the autopsy report."

"No! Not until Doctor Campbell authorizes it. In fact, I think this whole examination is going to have to wait. I made a mistake in letting you do this."

"But this is an active murder investigation," Colleen said. "And the inlay is new evidence."

"Well, it will simply have to wait," Morris said, reaching over, carefully zipping the bag back over the cadaver's head. "You've had your look. And now you're going to have to leave."

Colleen fought a burst of frustration. But she had seen what she had seen. A film of nauseous sweat collected on her forehead. Her stomach roiled with disgust.

*   *   *

Outside, in the car, Alistair rolled down the window, lit up a ciga-rette. Colleen bummed one from him and lit it off his, rolling her window down as well. It occurred to her that the woman in the body bag might have died from smoke inhalation and here she was, with more of the same going directly into her own lungs. She blew smoke out the window and put the car in gear while Alistair leafed through the autopsy report.

"What does it say about a dental exam?" she asked.

Alistair turned a page, reading, cigarette hanging from the corner of his mouth. "The dental exam was outsourced," he said. "Not un-usual for a smaller coroner's office like Calistoga."

"Well, whoever did it missed the diamond implant."

"Sloppy work," Alistair said. He held up the paperwork, squinted. "Rita Zielinski, DDS."

Deliberately sloppy? Colleen said: "A pint of bitter says Alice never had a dental implant."

Alistair gave Colleen a piercing look. "What are you saying, Colleen?"

"We'll find out," she said, pulling over at a phone booth. "Be right back." She let the engine idle, slipped into the phone booth, dropped a dime into the slot, and called directory inquiries. She asked for Rita Zielinski, DDS.

"Calistoga Dental," the operator said. "Do you want to transfer the call, ma'am?"

Colleen said no, she just needed the phone number and address. She had a pen and her penny notebook ready.

She jotted down the information.

Back in the car, she said: "I need to make a quick detour."

"A quick detour where, Colleen?"

"Calistoga."

"That's not exactly 'quick.'"

"While we're up here."

Alistair frowned. Colleen got to Calistoga in under half an hour, stopped at a 76 station, asked the gas attendant where Grant Street was. He pointed into town, gave her directions.

In town, not far from the high school, she found a rustic building from the last century that had been gussied up, the brick painted white, contrasting with vines crawling up the side. CALISTOGA DENTAL was written in classic script on an antiqued sign. It all looked very high end.

She pulled over, stopped, turned off the ignition.

"How long is this going to take?" Alistair asked, checking his watch.

"I just want to get a look at Dr. Zielinski. Who writes flaky dental reports for the coroner's office? I'll buy you lunch." Even though Colleen didn't want much in the way of food after her morning.

She got out and went in where a bell tinkled. Everything was spic and span; everything was white. The art on the walls was primarily white, abstract, soft and pleasant. The sheer curtains were white. The music coming out of the sound system sounded white, silky and ephemeral. Waves on a beach crashed behind supple flutes. The place was too stylish for Christmas decorations. Several clients waited in white chairs.

Through the back were the dental offices. She could hear a drill whirring.

At the desk an attractive young brunette with hoop earrings and a white lab coat met her with a dazzling smile.

"I've got one heck of a toothache," Colleen said, holding her jaw. "Any chance Dr. Zielinski could take a look at it?"

"I'm sorry but Dr. Zielinski's booked," she said, scanning a full appointment book. "I can fit you next Friday afternoon."

"Not sure I'll make it to next Friday," Colleen said, "but thanks. I'll call back." She took a business card from a white holder on the desk. "Oh. May I please use your restroom?"

The assistant pointed her to the back through a hallway.

In the hallway Colleen nosed around, pretending to look for the bathroom. In an office, a fat man was lying flat on a dental chair, gripping its arms tightly while an attractive woman in her fifties, white coat, white bell-bottom slacks, light beige shoes, with a shiny blonde bouffant, was engrossed in the man's mouth with a dental drill. The window behind her had curlicue bars on it, painted white, climbing with bougainvillea.

The dentist looked up as Colleen walked by. Her tanned face bore a hint of crow's feet. She wore pink lipstick. She was battling the ebbing of her youth and doing a good job of it.

"Hi, Dr. Zielinski," Colleen said.

"Can I help you?" she said in a nasal voice, one that seemed suspicious by nature.

"Just looking for the restroom."

"To your right. The one that says 'restroom'?" She shook her head and went back to work.

The restroom had no window. Back in the hallway, Colleen passed an office where a young man with a bodybuilder frame in white slacks and silk white T was pulling a file from a filing cabinet.

He turned as Colleen stopped, studied the window. White bars, natch.

"Hi there," he said with a firm, confident smile full of even, white teeth. No woman was safe from his charms, and he knew it. "How can I help you out?"

"I'm fine, thanks." Colleen gave him a warm smile because that's what a lot of women did with a guy who looked like that.

Then she left.

Back in the car, Alistair was smoking another cigarette, looking at his watch. She thanked him for waiting.

"Anything of interest?" he asked.

"The dentist that turned in a less-than-stellar dental exam on 'Alice Owens' seems to have a very thriving practice. And an obsession for white. I think it signifies that she might be struggling with her sense of integrity."

"Food for thought," he said, tapping ash out the window.

They set off in search of a restaurant for lunch.

She didn't want to say she knew who the woman in the body bag was and complicate things right now. But all she could think of was Traci with an "i." Traci was close to Alice's age, build, and hair color. A very good stand-in—except for Traci's inlaid tooth.

And Traci had been missing. Since the night before Alice died.

Colleen couldn't shake the repulsion she felt, the sickening feeling that made her feel weak and clammy as she drove.

But she was on the right track. She needed to stay focused.

But she also had to wonder: Whatever happened to Alice Owens?

CHAPTER TWENTY-EIGHT

"Little diamond on the canine tooth." Colleen forced a big toothy smile, tapped her own canine with a fingertip.

Owens sat on the other side of the wire reinforced glass, stunned.

The bruises on the side of his face still bore a hint of yellow. His hair was uncombed. His orange jumpsuit was rumpled, contrasting the cop he was, or once was. He was now being kept in Ad Seg—Administration Segregation—for his own safety, after the beating by fellow prisoners. He looked as calm as a man framed for the murder of his wife—who might not be dead—could be, but the implications were playing havoc with him.

As they were with Colleen.

"Not the last time I saw Alice," Owens said in a halting voice. "I don't think so, anyway."

"You're not sure?"

"I can't be sure of anything that happened that night. Not anymore."

"This isn't a good time to lose it on me," she said. "Focus." She repeated the word with more emphasis. "*Focus.*"

Owens squeezed his eyes shut for a few seconds, reopened them. Repeated the process.

He shook his head. "Truth is, I didn't get a good look at Alice's mouth that night, now that I think about it. I can't remember her smiling once. Smiling wasn't really her thing to begin with."

Colleen took a deep breath. "I was really hoping for 'yes' or 'no.'"

"Alice was pretty conservative," he added. "*Is*, I should say—if she's alive. Conservative unless it comes to fooling around with other men."

Owens was at the point where he was growing less guarded with his comments.

"That's kind of what I was thinking, even though I've never met her."

"You know what this means," he said listlessly.

"I do," Colleen said. "I do."

Ray killed her. Or, somehow, she was still alive.

"Bottom line," Colleen said, "is that you were set up. That's what we need to move on. Get you out of here."

Owens nodded, blinking again, off in the ozone. Disturbing looks of tension and anger crossed his face periodically.

"Who's Alice's dentist?" Colleen said.

"Dr. Kenworth," Owens said. "West Portal Dental. Paid for the last cleaning not too long ago. Alice still let me do that," he said. "Pay her bills. Since I had coverage."

"Well, as the one who paid her dental bills, you should have a right to request her dental records. Call on Monday and have them ready at the counter and authorize me to pick them up."

Owens shook his head again in a mixture of suppressed rage and confusion. On the one hand, his ex, someone he had held a torch for, might still be alive. Or her new beau had killed her. Or she and her new beau might be pulling a fast one. And had committed murder and framed him.

Colleen shared those thoughts.

Owens' eyes saddened before they resumed a piercing fury. "I can't see Alice being part of something like that. Infidelity is one thing. Committing murder is another. I think Ray could just as easily have gotten rid of her too."

"One thing's certain," Colleen said. "Ray Quick is a lot more than anyone bargained for."

"That's the understatement of the year."

"I'll be in touch," she said. "The good news is that this will throw your arrest into question. So, hopefully you're sprung sooner rather than later. Is Gus taking good care of you?" Gus, her lawyer.

"He is," Owens said. "I'm lucky as hell to have you on my side, Colleen." But again, his voice was apathetic. "You're the only friend I've got right now."

"Same here," she said.

"When I get out of here . . ." he said between his teeth, looking away, then stopped.

He was starting to scare her.

"No," she said, shaking her head. "I don't want to hear about it." Revenge.

"Seems it was just fine for you."

"And I served close to ten years for it," she said. "And it wasn't worth it. In fact, it was just the opposite."

She saw him draw a deep breath, fighting to control himself. His temple was pulsing. He'd been in here close to two weeks, living with the hell of his situation.

Finally, he said, "Yeah. You're right."

She shouldn't be having this conversation with a man who believed in law and order.

"Hang in there," she said. "Call your dentist."

He gave a curt nod, made a fist of solidarity.

They hung up their respective phones. She stood up, pressed her fist against the glass. He did the same.

"Don't touch the glass," the guard behind her said.

*　*　*

Outside in the parking lot, the skies were darkening. Late afternoon. Colleen got into the Torino, which was feeling all too familiar with the constant driving back and forth from San Francisco. She stopped for gas, and while she filled an empty tank once again, she called Gus in Stinson Beach from the pay phone. Gus had just come in from surfing. By her calculations, it had to be forty degrees. Probably a lot less at the beach. There was no deterring some.

She brought him up to speed.

"How long before you get an answer back from West Portal Dental?" he asked.

"I'm hoping in the next couple of days. But Owens was almost sure Alice never had a dental implant."

"*Almost*," Gus stressed. "Not the best word when it comes to a crucial piece of evidence."

"Let's assume *never*."

"She could have had an implant done somewhere else since the divorce."

Colleen sighed at the pushback. "Throw in the disappearing can used as a fire starter—which Sanderlin said was funky when Joshua Inn kept him at arm's length—and the quarter mil benefit Ray Quick stands to get. Add in his fishy behavior, I know Owens was set up."

"Your visit with Alistair to Santa Rosa Morgue is probably going to get shot down in a courtroom."

"What exactly am I supposed to do, Gus? Stand by while Owens rots in a cell? I need to get him out of there one way or another. Rita

Zielinski, DDS: that implant isn't on the dental exam she wrote which was used to identify the corpse. That alone should get Owens out of jail. I can't call Detective Kikuyama since he shooed me off in no uncertain terms. Sanderlin listened, but it's not his case. With Ryan and the SFPD IA investigation, SFPD is a no-go. But someone should pull Ray Quick in for questioning again."

"I'll call the Sonoma County DA again, but I suspect he's going to want more."

"Then I'll get you more."

"Just do it without stepping on any toes, Colleen: that means don't harass Kikuyama until the DA talks to him. *If* he talks to him. And you know better than to approach Ryan again."

"I know."

"I'll call the DA first thing tomorrow." It was Sunday.

"OK," she said with a sigh. "Leave me a message on my work machine, please. I'm heading back to SF now." It might be the weekend, but she had regular work that was backing up. And she needed to get paid.

And she needed to stay busy.

She hung up, frustrated, walked back to her car where the pump read over twenty bucks. Jesus. The hood was up. The pump attendant held the dipstick out for her to read. The oil on the stick was dark and grainy.

"She's down a quart," he said. He rubbed his thumb on the gritty oil. "And she needs work."

"She needs a ring job," Colleen said. "Go ahead and throw a quart of 10-30 in. A can of STP too, if you got one handy."

"Yes, ma'am."

Things had to break in Owens' favor soon—for her pocketbook if nothing else.

CHAPTER TWENTY-NINE

That evening, as Colleen was getting dressed to go out to dinner with Matt, who'd be on his way to Langley the next morning, her phone rang.

It was Gus.

"The Sonoma County prosecutor is going to ask for your evidence to be reviewed."

A bump of encouragement. "You spoke to him on a Sunday?"

"I have my ways."

"But no charges dropped for Owens?"

"Not yet," Gus said. "He stays in jail until the evidence is reviewed."

"What is wrong with these people?"

"Nothing. You don't know how often defense attorneys bring the prosecutor exculpatory evidence that's been manufactured, bought, bribed, paid for, or whatnot. So, the lead investigator is going to investigate and report back to the DA with a recommendation. Then, with any luck, Owens is a free man."

"And that lead investigator would be Detective Kikuyama?" she asked. Sonoma County Sheriffs.

"You got it, Toyota."

Her enthusiasm waned.

"Does he have all the latest dirt?" she asked.

"I passed on what you gave me. Hopefully he heard from your guy Sanderlin about the possible missing evidence. Make sure all your sources are legit and can support what you say, or Owens might get shot down. Sanderlin is key. And that dental implant is a biggie."

"I can only go so far with Alistair. I can't implicate him too much."

"Well, if he cares about Owens, he needs to bend."

Meanwhile, Owens sits in a cell.

"Got it." She thanked Gus, got off the phone.

Sanderlin should not be a problem. But she had to make sure Alistair would back her up.

The doorbell rang. Matt.

She hit the intercom. "Meet you downstairs."

"What's the rush? Dinner isn't until eight. We can have a drink. I bought champagne."

"I need to make a quick stop."

"You're kidding, right? Is this about work?"

"It won't take long." She signed off, threw her coat on over her red dress and perfumery and trotted downstairs in her white hose and black platform boots to meet Matt at the door. The bandage on her leg had been downsized and was feeling much better. But Matt was going to get a shock. In more ways than one.

*　*　*

She found Alistair at the bar in the Edinburgh Castle in his civvies, jeans and a plaid shirt, supping a pint.

He looked at her in surprise as she approached the bar, dressed to the nines as she was.

"I think they have a dress code here, Colleen. Nothing as classy as that is allowed."

"It's OK," she said. "I'm low rent at heart."

He drained his pint, set the empty pot on the bar. "What is the lady drinking?"

"I can't stay," she said. "Matt's waiting in the car."

"Something important?"

She told him about the investigation into Owens being reopened. The possibility Owens would be released.

"Well, that's great news, Colleen."

"Yes and no. The charges won't be dropped unless things line up." She looked Alistair in the eye. "I know we said the visit to Santa Rosa Morgue was hush-hush, but Detective Kikuyama from Sonoma County Sheriff's is very likely to call you about it."

Alistair took a deep breath through his nostrils, rubbed his grey beard.

"I know, I know," Colleen said. "But the implant is crucial. And your word carries a lot more weight than mine."

"It means quite possibly stepping on SFPD's toes."

"The ME's office is allowed to make their own decisions, aren't they? Open their own cases?"

"But I need authorization from above. Which I didn't have. You knew that."

"It would mean a lot to me, Alistair. And it would mean a whole lot more to Owens."

Alistair blinked, obviously turning that over. He looked at his watch. "Guess I better get back into work and open a case, then. Before I get caught with my trousers down."

"I am forever in your debt, Alistair. Can I buy you one for the road?"

Alistair shook his head. She'd lost some points. "No," he said. "Owens needs all the help he can get."

* * *

The phone ringing in the living room pulled Colleen from a deep sleep, a rare event of late.

Pleasantly groggy, she lifted her head from the warmth of her waterbed, suddenly realizing Matt was no longer lying next to her.

He'd left early for his flight to Langley.

She didn't remember him saying goodbye.

The bed sloshed as she threw off the rainbow quilt, climbed out naked, pulled on her kimono, the belt trailing into the living room where the white princess phone sat on the glass coffee table.

She always held out hope that it might be Pam.

She answered, rubbing sleep from her eyes. Fog swirled out the windows over Potrero. The bite healing on her calf was itching.

"Hello?"

No response.

She waited.

A crackle of static.

She'd give it one more shot. You never knew. It might be Pam.

"Who is this?"

Nothing. Just more pops on the line.

Someone not happy with her ongoing investigation into Owens?

"Go to hell," she said. "And have a nice day."

She hung up.

She made coffee, noting that Matt hadn't left a note, and it felt as if they were already separated. He'd get the job, of course, and move back east until he was posted somewhere, which wouldn't be San Francisco. San Francisco was choice duty and new hires didn't rate. He'd been pushing for Colleen to marry him, and she'd resisted, and she wondered if that was a deal-breaker. But she was no longer the marrying kind. For all their bumps and hiccups, he meant something to her, more than she had thought, especially now that he was gone.

She showered, got ready for work. She needed income. Moving languidly after a night with Matt, something she always savored, even more precious now knowing those nights would be few and far between from now on. At least her calf was lower priority. Ugly to look at, it was healing. Matt had given it a soft kiss. Yeah, she might be missing him already.

She'd parked on the street last night when she came home yesterday so Matt could park in her slot in the back lot. He had a new Ford Capri and worried about break-ins.

In new black jeans—her favorite bell-bottoms were goners after the dog attack—Frye boots, winter sweater, and sheepskin coat for extra warmth, she threw on her shoulder bag, headed downstairs, feeling just a little blue.

She pulled the beveled glass front door shut behind her and headed up Vermont. The dark grey morning felt more like a late afternoon that had gone wrong, and the dim light was oppressive on the eyes and spirit. She blinked away the strangeness of this last winter of the decade: Pam, Owens, Matt. Traci.

The Torino was up the street, just below McKinley Square, a green space with a playground that basked in the noise from the freeway above it. Deserted. Too early and too cold.

She had spent so much time pushing Matt away and now he was gone.

She dug in her coat pocket for her car key as she crossed over, when the whine of a large engine behind her broke her thoughts.

She spun to see a dark van charging down Vermont in her direction, too fast and too close.

Far too close.

She was barely able to register the figure at the wheel who wore dark shades and a watch cap pulled down low.

Her senses screamed in fright.

The van swung in toward her and she ducked in between the back of her car and the Chevy Nova parked behind it, just in time.

The van knocked her car, a crunch of metal followed by the squealing of tires.

And then it swerved off down Vermont. Hitting the zigzags that street became. Squealing off.

No plate.

Heart pounding, she stood between the cars, catching her breath, willing her pulse to calm.

After a good minute, wondering who it might have been, realizing it was connected to the anonymous phone call earlier, to determine whether she was home, she unlocked her trunk, threw her bag in, reached in, lifted the spare tire. She pulled out her copy of *Pride and Prejudice*—which contained her Bersa Piccolina in a cutout section of pages that were glued together.

She'd be doing a little reading from now on.

She took the book with her, checked both ways, got into the Torino. Deep breaths kept coming.

She started the car up and headed into work.

Her bet was that someone on the wrong side of her investigation wasn't liking the attention she was giving it. Ray's buddies up at Joshua Inn? They didn't know where she lived. Someone else? Not SFPD surely. But she was good at making enemies.

Checking the rearview mirror constantly. Checking traffic constantly.

But if it was meant to stop her, she had news. It wasn't working.

CHAPTER THIRTY

In her office that afternoon, Colleen heard footsteps headed her way. She closed the file she was working on, sat back. The wind was blowing in gusts underneath the pier, making the water slosh against the pilings.

She was a little surprised to see Detective Kikuyama standing at her door.

He wore a blue down jacket over a white shirt and the same too-big blue tie he wore the other day, and baggy grey polyester slacks. Sears loafers. Fashion wasn't his thing.

But she was glad to see him. It meant he was probably looking into her allegations.

He had his hands in the pockets of his jacket. It was cold. It was always cold in her office.

"Good to see you." She waved at a guest chair. "Please."

"I won't be here long," he said. "I just wanted to check in, since I'm in the city."

"I understand you're following up on my latest development. Any questions I can answer?" Maybe she could brownnose her way into his good graces.

He shook his head. "Detective Sanderlin in Calistoga tells me you pointed him to some potential evidence at the Joshua Inn that seems to have gone missing."

"A tin can I think was used as a fire starter. It was in the night-stand in the fire rubble. I doubt it's still there. I saw a flashlight in the cabin shortly after I was chased off. And when Detective Sanderlin asked to search the cabin, he was told to come back with a warrant."

Detective Kikuyama grimaced. "Even though I told you to back off."

"No, I think you told me not to waste your time anymore. And I didn't."

"Interfering in a murder investigation can get you into serious trouble with the California Department of Justice. You could lose your license—if you had one."

She shrugged. "Saves everyone time, then, doesn't it?"

"Why do you continue to push?"

"Because Owens didn't do it. And no one else seems too interested in proving that except for me."

"I spoke to ME Laurie."

Alistair.

Kikuyama continued: "He confirms the dental implant. Which Alice Owens apparently didn't have. Which wasn't on the autopsy dental exam. I also checked with Alice Owens' dentist—as did you. She didn't have an implant—although he hadn't seen her for about a month. She could have had one done in the meantime."

Colleen frowned. "Not so likely."

Kikuyama nodded in agreement. "But I couldn't help but notice that the date on ME Laurie's report was yesterday—a Sunday—a day after the actual autopsy review in Santa Rosa on a Saturday—one you—a civilian—were present at."

"Alistair is a busy man. He squeezed in the review as a favor."

Kikuyama rubbed his weak chin. Eyed her with a look that was much stronger.

"So," he said. "Everything checks out. I'm going to tell the Sonoma DA that there's enough new evidence to throw Owens' arrest into question. But I'm also going to tell you now—in no uncertain terms—to stay out of this case from here on out. If I find you nosing around the Joshua Inn, or anywhere in my neck of the woods, talking to Sanderlin, playing PI, then I'm going to see that charges are filed."

"*Playing PI?*" she said. "Ouch. Especially since I dug up some pretty relevant information. All for gratis."

"Did you hear what I just said?"

"Understood," she said. "And thanks for looking into the case, Detective. I really do appreciate it. Owens will even more so. Any new suspects?"

He looked at her in dismay.

"Are you planning on questioning Ray Quick again?" she said.

He shook his head, turned around, and left.

*   *   *

Colleen's level of optimism rose after Kikuyama's visit. She called Gus, up in Stinson Beach, filled him in.

"Sounds good," Gus said. "I'll put a call in to the Sonoma County DA."

"How long before you think you might know something?"

"These things can take longer than you want them to, Colleen. Weeks, sometimes. It's a lot easier to go to jail than it is to get out. But as soon as I know anything, so will you."

"Thanks, Gus."

"No, I think the thanks belong to you. But let me talk to Owens first. I don't want you to get his hopes up. And don't try to force the issue yourself. It could backfire. You should consider yourself done with this."

"Got it."

At least Owens would be out of jail at some point. Fingers crossed. Not bad.

But her work didn't feel complete, despite what everyone was telling her.

CHAPTER THIRTY-ONE

"Thanks for coming," Colleen said, her sheepskin coat buttoned against the sharp wind coming in from the Pacific.

Retired Santa Cruz homicide detective Dan Moran walked toward her along the boardwalk, past the open doors of the arcade ringing with video games. His hands were in the pockets of a blue windbreaker. Moran was a small-to-medium-sized man in his sixties, whose onetime drinking had pitted and reddened his nose. His dark mustache was greyer than the last time she'd seen him, which had been a while. There were flecks of grey in his eyebrows too. It was late morning, Colleen having driven down from SF.

"Long time, Hayes." His thick glasses were slightly misted, as if he might be fading into the leaden-grey clouds churning behind him. Colleen felt a pang of sadness. Here was another person she'd let slip away.

They stood, the arcade games at full volume competing with the waves breaking on the beach. Video games were everywhere now, filling the silence with inane tunes and sucking up every last quarter.

Not too many wet-suited souls on surfboards today. Those hopefuls that were sat on the beach alone or in small groups, waiting for the weather to change. One lone surfer paddled out on an incoming wave on a board, arching over a swell.

"I should have called sooner," Colleen said.

Moran shrugged as if it was no big deal, but it was. They had a history, going back several years to her first trip to California, when she first came out looking for Pam. Colleen had just gotten out of Denver Women's Correctional Facility and learned that Pam had taken up with a biker in Santa Cruz. Moran, a homicide detective at the time, was investigating a murder the biker gang had committed. A young woman had been murdered and Colleen had first thought it might have been Pam, but thank God, it wasn't.

Colleen's guilt lingered. She sensed there was bad news on Moran's end. She could see it in his face. Up close, she could smell it on his breath when the wind shifted. Whiskey, just a hint. Her spirits slid. Being on the wagon was important to Moran. Or had been.

"Let's go for a walk," he said.

They strolled down the long wharf, a wooden bridge to nowhere that disappeared in fog. Fishermen here and there hovered over the railing. No one seemed to be having much luck. Waves splashed and birds cawed.

"How's Daphne?" Colleen asked. Moran's spouse had never had a warm spot for Colleen, fending off her phone calls to him at every opportunity. She wanted Moran's retirement to be crime-free, and Colleen threatened that.

No answer at first. Then Moran cleared his throat, spoke, hands in his jacket pockets as he walked, looking out to sea.

"Daphne passed away. Last month. Aneurysm."

A shock wave hit Colleen. Daphne had not answered Moran's phone this morning when she had called. Now she knew why.

Colleen stopped, stood, midway along the pier. So did Moran. Their eyes met.

"I'm so sorry," she croaked.

Moran gave a tight nod and pushed his glasses up his nose.

"Thanks," he said with a slight gulp.

Colleen exhaled a sigh. "I feel like a louse. I haven't called. Until I needed a favor." With Matt gone, Owens in jail, no access to his partner Fos, and warnings to stay away from Kikuyama and Sanderlin, she'd had no other cop connections.

"You've got your own life to live, Hayes. How's Pam doing, anyway? What about that grandson? It is a grandson, am I right?"

Now it was her turn. How did one say, *I don't know? Pam lost her baby. And now she's gone too.*

"Just fine," she said.

She looked into Moran's face and saw the effects of his renewed drinking.

"How are you dealing with it?" she said. "Losing Daphne?"

"Better than she is," he said. "People always feel sorry for the survivor. Why is that? Why not the one who's gone?"

She returned a sad smile. "You've got a good point."

"We always thought it would be me to go first," he said.

"I guess that means you've got to do something meaningful with the time that's left," she said.

"Perhaps."

"I'll just go ahead and say it," she said. "You're drinking again."

He gave a dismissive shrug.

"It's not good to see," she said. Without Daphne to keep Moran on the straight and narrow, the worst could easily prevail.

"It's temporary," he said quietly. "Just to get me over the hump. I've quit before. I'll do it again."

"I hope so," she said. "I'm going to be checking in more often."

He turned as he walked, smiled. "Well, there's one good thing to come out of it already."

She gave a despondent laugh.

"I did a search on your person of interest," he said, changing the subject. "Ray Quick."

She said that she appreciated it.

"He's got a sheet," Moran said. "A prior arrest in Santa Rosa. Possession for sale. He was caught selling evidence. Heroin."

"*Evidence?*" she said, turning to look at Moran.

"Ray Quick was a property and evidence clerk for Sonoma County Sherriff's office. He got the ax two years ago."

Interesting. "Sonoma County is handling the murder of Alice Owens," Colleen said. "Ray Quick is her ex-boyfriend."

Moran squinted behind his thick lenses. "Now that's a coincidence."

"Was anyone else arrested with Ray Quick?" she asked. "Two years ago?"

"Nothing on his sheet," Moran said. "The charges were dropped, and then he was simply let go. To save the department's face most likely. But rule of thumb is that the sale of evidence usually requires cooperation. It's tough to pull that kind of thing off all by yourself."

"It also means he must have lived up there," she said. "In the same area where Alice was murdered."

Moran pushed his glasses up his nose again. "He did. He's probably got local connections."

"I'm thinking the dentist who did the flaky dental report for the autopsy," Colleen said. "Rita Zielinski. She's just Ray's type. And the people who run the Joshua Inn."

"It's not too much of a stretch of the imagination."

"Any chance I can get a copy of that rap sheet?" she asked.

Moran shook his head. "My connections aren't what they used to be. I'm retired. I made a phone call. Someone was able to look it up—under the condition of anonymity." He rustled around in his jacket pocket. "But I did get this." He removed a folded-up, torn piece of lined paper.

Colleen took it, opened it, read it as the wind blew a corner of the paper over.

An address in Calistoga.

"Ray Quick's old address," he said.

"You don't know how much I appreciate this," she said, slipping the paper in her pocket. "Let me buy you lunch."

CHAPTER THIRTY-TWO

The address Moran had given Colleen from Ray Quick's rap sheet was located within the Chateau Calistoga Mobile Home Park in Calistoga.

Interesting that Ray Quick had a prior address in the town where Alice was supposedly murdered.

The afternoon sky was grey, spots of blue breaking through windy clouds over the mountains as Colleen turned off the Silverado Trail into the northern part of Calistoga, passing wineries, mud baths, into Chateau Calistoga Mobile Homes itself, a trailer park with trimmed trees and raked gravel. Making an effort to be a notch above its siblings, of which there were several in the area to appeal to retirees, there were still trailers with deferred maintenance in this one.

Ray Quick's old address was one of them, a single-wide in the very back of the lot with overgrown weeds and dead plants, faded beige paint and a taped-up window. It was tucked away by a stack of empty propane tanks. A sun-blasted red Gremlin was parked in front.

Driver's window down, Colleen motored slowly past. Country music wafted out of an open sliding door under a battered aluminum awning that shaded a camp chair by a grouping of empty longneck beer bottles. Conway Twitty crooned about the wanting in her eyes.

She circled back up to the office where she exited the park, backed the Torino under a tree across from a Fosters Freeze, got out, walked back down to the trailer in question in her Frye boots and new jeans. Her calf was on the mend. It was cold, and the air was refreshing after the two-hour-long drive from Santa Cruz. She kept her three-quarter-length sheepskin unbuttoned.

At the trailer where Conway Twitty sang, she knocked on the open metal doorframe. The interior matched the exterior, with clutter being the dominant design theme. An empty high-ball glass sat on the dirty blue shag rug, filled with watery ice. The TV was on silently to the *$25,000 Pyramid*.

"Anyone home?"

"Just a sec!" an older man said behind a door at the back of the trailer.

She heard a toilet flush. Then a shot of air freshener. The door opened and shut.

A wide middle-aged man appeared, an older, very beat-up version of Ray Quick, somewhere in his fifties, the years hard-lived. He wore a Hawaiian shirt that clashed lime green and pink open over a long-sleeved T-shirt. He had been a looker in his day, like his son, but now sported a grey screen of hair around his crown, grown long and feathered back and sprayed stiff in an attempt to distract from his bald pate. He had a gut, a double-chin, and a multi-day growth of grey stubble. Redness flushed his cheeks and complemented a purple nose. His quick checkout of Colleen's figure and subsequent greasy smile told her what was on his mind.

She smiled innocently.

He introduced himself as Jerry.

"Jerry Quick?"

"That's right."

"Then I'm looking for your son," she said.

"Ray hasn't lived here for a couple years."

"Really?" She feigned confusion. "This is the address on the policy."

That got his interest. "What policy?"

He didn't seem to know. "He must use this for a fixed address."

"That's right. What policy?"

"Ah." She had one of her Pacific All Risk Insurance cards ready, listing her as Carol Aird, Insurance Professional. Suitably vague. Handed it to him.

"I'm working with All Indemnity Insurance of California regarding a disbursement."

"Is that so?" Jerry took the business card, read it. Looked up, his bloodshot eyes laced with suspicion. He didn't know what was going on, but he could smell money, even with his blighted nose.

"It's regarding a death benefit," she explained. "Payment on a life insurance policy. I just need to do some verification before a check is authorized."

"Check?"

"For Ray," she said. "Regarding Alice Owens."

Now he got it. Colleen saw it in his narrowed eyes.

"The gal burnt to death at the Joshua Inn."

"Yes," she said. "That *gal*."

"She knew Ray?"

Colleen divulged a conspiratorial smile, let Jerry think he was in the know. "Enough to let him insure her for a quarter million dollars."

"You don't say." He rubbed his grizzled chin. She could almost hear the gears churning in his head.

"You can send the check here," Jerry said. "I'll make sure Ray gets it."

She just bet he would.

"Your son needs to sign for it," she said. "If you have his contact information, that would be great."

"Let me get hold of him for you," Jerry said. He wasn't going to let a windfall slip away without getting a potential cut. Which was fine with her. If there was a connection, he might lead her to it.

"How can I get hold of you?" he said, looking at her fictitious business card, flipping it over to the blank side. "There's no phone number."

More astute than he looked. "I don't put it down as a rule," she said. "I prefer to work on a need-to-know basis."

He nodded, went over to a cluttered windowsill, grabbed a ballpoint resting on the sill, scribbled a couple of ovals on the back of her card until he got it working, came back, poised the tip of the pen over the back of her card. Squeezed out another oily smile, but this one was from greed, not lust.

She gave him the number of her office on Pier 26. Not her first choice but her answering machine didn't list her business, just a simple "you have reached . . ." message.

He jotted it down.

"A 415 number," he said. "Frisco."

San Franciscans hated that name. "That's right."

He tucked the card in his shirt pocket. "I'll call you as soon as I know anything."

"The sooner the better," she said. "I do hate to hold up client funds."

She let the greed dig its hooks in, wished him a good day, and left. Conway Twitty continued to warble as she walked back toward the site office, circled around a pristine double-wide with flower boxes and lace curtains, came sneaking back along the fence, out of sight and within earshot of the Quick residence. The window was open.

The music had been turned down. She heard Jerry Quick on the phone.

"What the fuck is going on with Ray?" she heard him say.

A pause.

"That girl killed in the fire. The Joshua Inn. She knew Ray."

Another pause.

"Don't give me that shit," Jerry said. "I can smell a scam a mile away. I'm coming over. Now. And you better be there."

Colleen knew what she needed to know. She spun, dashed back to the entrance of the trailer park, turned right, got into the Torino, pulled on her floppy black hat, settled low in her bucket seat.

A few minutes later, the faded Gremlin came rattling out of the trailer park, right past her on Brannan, shaking as it changed gears and picked up speed. She started up the Torino, followed at a distance. The Gremlin turned on the Silverado Trail, heading south, the mountains in the distance.

Colleen turned on the radio to get Conway Twitty out of her head. She tailed Jerry Quick.

CHAPTER THIRTY-THREE

Colleen followed the Gremlin up the Silverado Trail through wine country where it turned off and headed up into the mountains, Valley Oak trees flanking the twisting road through state forest, passing more wineries and prosperous houses where the other half spent their weekends. It grew trickier to stay behind Jerry Quick and not be spotted.

On White Cottage Road outside the town of Angwin, the Gremlin pulled off, headed up a private road. It was even tougher to follow without revealing herself.

She parked across White Cottage, tucked in a shaded layby, grabbed her camera, and set off on foot at a pace, hoping no one broke into the car. Like a bear.

Hoofing it past a mailbox and up the private road filmed her with perspiration. She reached the crest of a hill where a well-kept grand ranch–style house was bordered on one side by a riding stable, rows of grape vines on the other. She saw the Gremlin parked in front of the house next to a four-wheel-drive pickup truck with a rifle rack in the back window. The truck was caked with mud. A white late model Cadillac Seville next to it wasn't.

Wind chimes tinkled on the porch.

How close to get? She'd have a tough time trying to eavesdrop on any conversation from here. And who knew if someone might spot her on private property. She ducked behind a mature oak, of which there were several, and scoped out the house through the telephoto lens of her camera.

A large picture window revealed a living room lit up by light from windows on the far side. She focused into the living room, saw activity of some sort, people moving around. Two people, judging by the shadows.

Not long after the front door opened, and a tanned woman in her fifties with a blonde bouffant showed Jerry Quick out. He now wore a warehouseman's jacket over his Hawaiian shirt and big gut. The woman was Rita Zielinski, DDS. She wore snug white Capri pants with beige flats and a puffy white jacket with padded shoulders and sequins. She looked like she was about to go down to the gaming tables at the casino. Colleen zeroed in with the lens. Rita wasn't smiling, and it was clear she and Jerry had not had a friendly discussion as they said their goodbyes.

"You better call me, Rita!" Jerry barked as she stormed back into the house where the door slammed shut. Jerry ambled over to the Gremlin, got in, drove down the private road past Colleen's tree.

It was starting to get dark already, not even five o'clock.

Colleen waited, listening to birds protest the cold.

Twenty minutes later, Rita Zielinski came out of the house with a white handbag over a long, white leather trench coat that would have done Alex's wardrobe justice, got into the white Seville. She started it up, backed out into a three-point turn that sprayed gravel, came barreling down the private road, took a sharp turn on the paved road.

Colleen hustled back to the main road, stopping at the mailbox. She checked around, saw no one, helped herself to Rita's mail, and went on her way.

For once she was getting hungry. But there was too much to do. She'd grab something quick on the way home if she had to. But she didn't mind.

Because she had just confirmed a connection between Ray Quick and Rita Zielinski, the dentist who had fudged the dental exam on Alice Owens' autopsy.

Rita was part of the scam.

The bridges to the city were clogged with ever-increasing traffic, rush hour at its finest.

She picked up some takeout from Five Happiness and was eating Kung Pao from a container with wooden chopsticks as she sat in her home office, looking at the swirls of dark grey out the back window. She recalled with sadness the times she and Pam would order Chinese and watch trashy movies, just about the only thing they could agree on at times. How she missed her daughter. And how guilty she felt, nagging Pam to stop this, stop that, Pam drinking and smoking when she was pregnant—but when push came to shove, well, Pam lost the baby. So maybe Colleen had been in the right, but in the end, what good did it do? Pam had to be feeling the guilt too, probably more so. Colleen wished she could just talk to her, tell her she understood, that she just wanted to be there for her.

She set her unfinished Kung Pao to one side and went through Rita Zielinski's phone bill.

Multiple calls to a local number, 415 area code, SF, the day after Alice's murder.

The phone number looked familiar.

She dialed it, ready to hang up if someone answered.

A fancy answering machine picked up after six rings. More and more people were getting the machines now.

"You know what to do," a cold female voice said.

Colleen did not leave a message. But she recognized the voice on the tape. And knew why the phone number was so familiar.

It was Alice Owens.

CHAPTER THIRTY-FOUR

From Rita Zielinski's phone bill, Colleen saw that Rita had called Alice Owens' house the night after Alice had supposedly died. And several times since.

And, judging by the length of the calls, had spoken to someone.

Alice? No, she was dead too, or if not, she wouldn't have been at 41 Wawona.

But Ray would have. He came and went at 41 Wawona with impunity.

Ray was just Rita's type, and vice versa. He'd lived in the wine country. Been fired for selling evidence as a clerk with the Sonoma County Sherriff's Department. Rita had turned in at least one erroneous dental report for a dead client, so she'd quite possibly been a fixture there then too. Birds of a feather.

Colleen got up, went into Pam's old room, feeling that same pull of sadness, found Pam's old cassette player/recorder on the shelf. She pulled Pam's copy of Springsteen's *Born to Run*, a sadly ironic title for her under the circumstances, set it on the shelf, rummaged around, found a fresh cassette tape, inserted it. Checked the batteries and player with a quick "test, test." Worked.

In the living room she threw her coat back on, put the cassette recorder in her shoulder bag of tricks. Time for another visit to 41 Wawona. She grabbed her car keys, headed back out.

*   *   *

The bump key and striker were Colleen's friends yet again as she let herself into 41 Wawona one more time. She already had her plastic gloves on in preparation. It was past ten p.m. Not the least suspicious time to be invading someone's home, but probably the quietest.

She pulled the door shut gently behind her, stopped, listened. Just the ticking of a clock somewhere. Lights were off. No one home.

She found the phone in a hallway alcove and with the aid of her flashlight, she saw the message light blinking on the machine under it. Messages waiting.

She hit the REPLAY button.

"Where are you? Call me as soon as you get this. Your old man was here today, sniffing around. Seems some woman from an insurance company is following up on the check and he smells a payday. Your old man needs to understand he's not getting shit, Ray. He could mess this up big-time. You need to get a handle on him, pronto, get him to keep his big fat mouth shut. Whatever it takes."

Colleen recognized the woman's voice from her brief interaction with Rita Zielinski, DDS. Her little visit to Calistoga had generated interest after Ray Quick's father had gone round to Rita's, expecting a cut of the deal.

She rewound the message tape, listened to the older messages.

A message for Alice Owens from Macy's, how her new outfit had arrived. Another message from her doc. Her prescription for birth control pills had been called in to Long's drugstore. Then, the more recent messages, from Rita Zielinski, mentioning Ray by name. All short, all urgent. If they jived with the phone bill, they occurred when "Alice" would have been undergoing an autopsy. And a dental exam was performed by Dr. Zielinski.

"Ray," one said. "We have an issue. Call me."

What was the issue? The tooth inlay?

She rewound the messages, got her cassette player out, held it up next to the answering machine. She taped all the messages so she had a record.

Then she deleted the last phone message from Rita Zielinski on the answering machine, the one warning Ray about his father harassing Rita. What Ray didn't know about Colleen snooping around was just fine.

Then she left 41 Wawona, pulling the front door shut quietly behind her, locking it with the bump key.

And saw, over the stucco porch wall, Mr. Bucket Hat and his white frigging poodle. Looking straight up at her. Jesus H. Too late to duck down behind the wall this time. He'd seen her. The only thing to do was to act as if everything was aboveboard.

"Good evening," she said, slipping the bump key surreptitiously into her lock-pick case, the case into her leather shoulder bag, out of sight, then coming down the stairs.

He looked at her with a squint.

"Do I know you?" he said suspiciously.

"I'm Alice's sister."

"I didn't know she had a sister."

"She does—or did." Colleen feigned an appropriately solemn face, one of a woman grieving her lost sibling. "I'm in town to settle up her estate." She hefted her shoulder bag. "Just collecting some documents."

"At this time of night?"

"There's a lot to do. Funeral arrangements . . ."

"It does seem you've been here a lot. Why didn't you say you were her sister before?"

Shit. "This isn't exactly an easy time for me," she said with emphasis, hoping that might fend him off.

"My condolences," he said dutifully as his dog sniffed a tree.

"Thank you," she said with emotion, cutting the conversation short, looking down in grief, and also to hide her face from direct view. "Such a terrible thing."

"Her ex-husband, wasn't it?" he said. "The cop?"

"Not that I'm aware of," she said.

"I thought he was arrested."

"I'm not sure."

"Well, it's a terrible thing," he said.

Yes, terrible. And Bucket Hat seemed to be the neighborhood gossip.

"Well, good night," she said, turning, heading down Wawona.

* * *

She drove over to the Tenderloin, Hyde and Leavenworth, where Fia and Rhonda were braving the cold night, Fia leaning down into the window of a green Ford Maverick, talking to some guy with a hillbilly beard. The back of her legs looked blue. Rhonda was smoking a cigarette, tight with the cold.

Colleen pulled over to the curb, left the engine running, heater on full, got out.

Fia came sauntering back from the Maverick, which took off with a squeal.

"Bitch!" the guy yelled.

Fia gave him a lazy middle finger.

She joined Colleen and Rhonda.

"Rule of thumb," she said. "Guys with food in their beards are a no-go."

"Now you tell me," Colleen said.

There was silence while both women looked at her.

All three of them knew the situation by now.

"Anything on Traci?" Fia asked quietly. She'd been gone for more than two weeks.

Colleen wasn't ready for this. She shook her head. Nobody said what was on everybody's mind.

"Traci's diamond?" Colleen asked, pointing to her own canine tooth. "Know where she got that done?"

Fia spoke up. "Smile Family Dentist. Near Mission and 2-4."

Mission and 24th.

"How do you know that?" Colleen asked.

Fia grinned with perfect white teeth. "My dentist. Dr. Wu's good. Discount for cash. Tell him I sent you."

"I'll do that," Colleen said. "Know when Traci had the inlay?"

"Not that long ago."

"Last July," Rhonda said, tapping ash into the air. Some menthol drifted Colleen's way. "Some guy she spent a weekend with tipped her big. She said she wanted something to show for it."

"Well, she got it." And it might just get Traci justice, Colleen thought.

The women traded stares, everyone knowing Traci was dead.

"You ladies need to look out for yourselves," Colleen said. "Watch out for a big, good-looking guy named Ray. Drives a midnight blue Riviera. Big scratch on the right rear panel."

"You think he had something to do with Traci?" Rhonda puffed.

"I do."

More silence.

"It's not official yet," Colleen said. "But be careful—please?"

Both women nodded.

"And, as before," Colleen said, "if you two ever want to check out another line of work, I'll hook you up with COYOTE."

Rhonda took a puff on her cigarette.

"Someday maybe," she said.

She was slowly coming around.

"Good," Colleen said. "You ladies stay safe. It's freezing out here." She got into the car, threw it into first, took off, the two women watching her as she headed up Leavenworth.

CHAPTER THIRTY-FIVE

"You need to get a handle on him, pronto, get him to keep his big fat mouth shut. Whatever it takes."

Colleen reached over, punched the OFF button on the cassette player sitting on the large, empty wooden cable reel on its side that served as the outdoor table on Gus' surfside deck. Cold wind blew in from a grey Stinson Beach a hundred yards away. Winter waves crashed on the shore. Gus lived a stone's throw from his beloved surfing and ventured out even on brutal midwinter days such as today. He sat in an Adirondack chair now on the other side of the "table," decked out in a black rubber wetsuit. His wet hair was tied back in a ponytail, and for once Colleen saw him without his signature cowboy hat or aviator glasses. His brown eyes were deep-set and intelligent. His hands were folded over his trim, muscular stomach and his legs were stretched out in front of him, his big feet encased in surfer booties and comfortably splayed on the weather-beaten deck decorated with shells and ocean artifacts. His surfboard was spiked into the sand nearby.

Colleen had just finished playing Gus the answering machine messages from last night's foray into 41 Wawona.

"So that's Rita Zielinski," he said, picking up his mug of jasmine tea, taking a sip. A wisp of steam twisted from the cup.

"No doubt about it," Colleen said, picking up her mug of tea from the table with ice-cold fingers, taking a sip. The tea had been nice and hot to begin with but was quickly losing heat. She had her sheepskin coat buttoned up over her red turtleneck and a black knit watchman's cap down against the cold. Even with her bell-bottoms and Frye boots she was losing the battle, unlike Gus, who was seemingly impervious to the elements.

"So, Rita's got a direct connection to Ray," Gus said.

"Leaves him incriminating messages," Colleen said. "And more." Colleen brought Gus up to speed on the previous day's events: Ray's father's visit to Rita. Ray canned for selling evidence when he worked at Sonoma County Sherriff's.

"You been busy." Gus set his tea down, picked up a copy of the dental records Colleen had retrieved from Alice's dentist. He studied them. "No diamond inlay. Confirms what Detective Kikuyama found."

"I've got a call in to Dr. Wu in the Mission. He's the one who did Traci's diamond inlay."

Gus looked at her thoughtfully. "Well, whoever that dead woman is in the morgue, she's not Alice. The dental inlay backs that up." He scratched the side of his cheek absent-mindedly. He needed a shave. "I'll look into Rita Zielinski, DDS, myself. See if there's any dirt."

"She was contracted by Santa Rosa Coroner to do the phony dental exam, so she's got some kind of connection to Sonoma County Sheriff's office. With Ray's history as evidence clerk there, I bet that's where they might have first crossed paths. They were made for each other."

"Ray is quite the ladies' man, it seems."

"Ray gets around," Colleen said. "What's the latest on Owens? Is his release scheduled?"

"Sonoma County Prosecutors are still reviewing the case."

"Jesus. Didn't Kikuyama give them the thumbs-up?"

"He did, but, as I might have mentioned, releasing someone from jail can take a lot longer than putting them there. I've seen it take weeks."

"Have you talked to Owens?"

"Yes," Gus said. "I'll push the prosecutor again today. I'll add an addendum to the petition with these dental records. They're only going to help. Hopefully Sonoma County releases Owens from custody soon."

Colleen experienced a measurable release of tension. "Great." She set her cup down. "OK for me to stop by and see Owens on the way home?"

Gus shook his head. "Not yet. But it'll happen. Stay calm."

"I hate to see him spend more time than he already has."

"Understood. But Owens is tough. Another day or two won't kill him."

She stood up, huddled in her coat. "Let me know as soon as you know something, please. I'd like to pick him up when he's released, drive him home." She picked up her cassette player, hit the EJECT button, pulled the cassette, set it down by his teacup. "That's your copy."

"Great," Gus said, picking up the cassette, along with Alice Owens' dental records, slipping them into the manila folder that Colleen had provided, fastening the clasp. "What's next on your busy schedule?"

"Why?"

"Just make sure it's mundane detective stuff," he said, giving her a look. "Photos of cheating wives. Husbands." He waved his hand. "That sort of thing."

"I'll be able to fit those in, sure."

"Just don't fit them in with chasing down Ray Quick. Or Alice Owens, wherever the hell she might be, if she's still alive. You've done enough. You got Owens out and that's great. But it's time to stop. Kikuyama was clear."

Colleen fought the pressure building inside. "Ray killed an innocent woman, Gus. Maybe two. He tried to set Owens up for the murder."

Gus set the envelope down, crossed his hands over his midriff, gave a firm smile. "Look, Colleen, you got Owens out of pokey. If I'm ever in a jam, I hope you're in my corner. But now you have to stop. Let justice take its painfully slow path."

"Murder is still murder. Trails get cold."

Gus gave a hard sigh. "And that's not your job. Those multiple unauthorized entries into 41 Wawona?" He shook his head. "With your questionable collection techniques, the message machine tape won't ever be admitted as evidence. Ditto for your visit to the Santa Rosa morgue. Great fact-finding, but not court worthy. Especially if your friend Alistair won't testify."

She took a deep breath, let it flutter out.

"We've had this conversation before, Colleen," Gus said. "There's a process."

"Excuse me for giving a shit, but no one else was interested in proving Owens' innocence. And, however I did it, I did it. And now we know about Rita Zielinksi. And Ray. And Traci."

"What do you think I am? Chopped liver? I've got skin in this game too. And I'm telling you, now, as your lawyer, and as Owens' lawyer, to *back the hell away*. Otherwise, all your hard work might go down the tubes."

She nodded. Yes, she saw that, but she also knew what it was like to be forgotten. Like Traci.

"OK," she said. "Please let me know as soon as you know something."

Gus stood up, a big guy. "Have fun chasing down philanderers. And take satisfaction for what you did for Owens. It's huge."

She could do that. But she also knew Ray couldn't be left out there unpunished. Nobody was saying it, but if he killed Traci—and she knew he did—well, Ray was behaving a lot like Night Candy.

CHAPTER THIRTY-SIX

Next day, Owens' cell door slid open with a clatter. A Sonoma County Sheriff's Deputy in blue stood there, one hand on the handle of the baton attached to his belt.

Owens sat up from his bunk, where he'd been dozing.

He looked at the guard in surprise. The guard had nothing in his hands and Owens had already had lunch, two processed cheese and white bread sandwiches with a side of wet macaroni salad, and a carton of milk. The empty tray was on the floor of his cell. They normally didn't pick them up until the next meal round. Which wasn't for a few more hours.

"Exercise?" Owens said.

"You're out of here," the deputy said in an abrupt voice.

That made him sit up straight. "Where? Another lockup?"

"Nope. Out." The guard jerked his thumb over his shoulder. "As in home free."

Owens couldn't believe his ears or his good luck. It had finally happened. Just like Gus had said. Owens stood up in his orange jumpsuit and jailhouse flip-flops. His feet were cold, even with socks. "Did you spike my food with something? I think I'm having audio hallucinations."

"All I can say is, you've got one hell of a lawyer," the guard said.

True, but it wasn't Gus, who was worth his weight in gold, all right—it was Colleen. She was a trooper.

Damn.

"I'm not going to argue with you before you change your mind," Owens said with a smile.

"Your girlfriend's gonna pick you up later."

"Who? Colleen? Colleen Hayes?"

The guard nodded and finally divulged a smile. "Some guys have all the luck. You beat a murder rap. That should be your quota of good luck for life, right there. But no, you get a vixen too. A chump like you. You must be hung like a horse."

"I hate to disappoint you," Owens said, in a good mood, a great mood as a matter of fact, "but she's a colleague. A *respected* colleague." One who saved his life. One whom he owed everything.

"Whatever, man, your secret is safe with me. Let's go. Unless you want to stay."

Owens knew how long it took to get discharged. How long it would take Colleen to get processed. Hours. He'd be lucky to get out of there tonight.

He was scruffy, unshaven, hadn't had a shower for days. Two per week in Ad Seg—Administration Segregation—and he'd missed the last one. It wasn't easy in confinement, what they called a jail within a jail. And, to be honest, he'd been feeling pretty sorry for himself. That was about to change. But he was ripe. No way to greet Colleen, who'd saved his bacon.

"Let's go," the guard said.

"Hey," Owens said. "You and I both know this is going to take forever. Let me grab a quick shower. And a shave if you can scrounge up a disposable razor." He'd wear the suit they'd arrested him in. Shirt was rumpled, but it would work.

The guard looked at him with a smirk. "'Colleague,' huh?"

"C'mon, give me a break. I can't meet her looking like a bum."

"OK, man. Let me see what I can do."

* * *

It was late afternoon by the time Owens was shuffling into the shower in just a towel and flip-flops. The communal jail shower was noisy with profanity and water splashing. He kept his eyes to himself and headed into a corner. They didn't like him, a cop, and he didn't like them much either. He turned on the water, nice and hot after days of washing with cold water at his sink in his cell in a cell. He stood under the jets, let the hot water needle his face.

First order of business when he got home: find Ray Quick.

"Hey, pig!"

Jesus. Another asshole. Owens turned, so as to keep guard, gave the man a quick stare. The big dude shot back daggers. Covered in tattoos.

Owens ignored him, soaped up. Armpits, get the rest that needed it.

Not long now.

"He's talkin' to you, asshole," another man said.

Two guys staring him down now. Just like his first day when he got his ass kicked. *Screw this*, Owens thought. His hackles were going up high.

Quick rinse, he was done. Turned off the faucets.

Reached down, grabbed one of his shower shoes, held it by the heel.

Headed out of the shower.

The big, tattooed guy stood in his way.

"You fucking deaf, pig?"

Owens looked up at him. Tensing up.

"Out of my way," he said calmly.

"Fuck that," another man said.

"And fuck you," another said. "Fucking pig."

His exit was blocked by a wall of white flesh.

He could call for help but the guards wouldn't respond in time. And it would only make him just what these losers wanted him to be. Scared. Scared was a matter of attitude.

"Who's first?" Owens said, slapping the shower shoe against his open palm. "I can't take all of you, but someone's going to get hurt. I can guarantee that much. Hell, someone might even die. In fact, I guarantee that too. So, who's first?"

* * *

It was late evening before the guard came to get Colleen in the waiting room where the soda machine buzzed. She knew this stuff took forever, but she had been here for hours. *Hours.* It felt like they were messing with her.

Finally, one of the guards came into the waiting room. He was the one with the gruff voice, but he was actually one of the friendlier ones.

She stood up, hoisted her bag up over her shoulder.

"I thought I might be staying the night," she said as a joke.

But he wasn't responding in kind. He looked away.

Something was wrong. Her nerves startled to rattle.

"What?" she said. "What is it?"

"I've got some bad news," he said to the floor.

Her stomach sank, followed by palpitations in her chest.

"No," she said. "No."

* * *

She crossed the Golden Gate Bridge in a daze, the night fog swirling through the cables, pulled across the hood of the Torino as the windshield wipers slapped more of it away.

Owens might not make it.

He'd been jumped in the changing room, after a shower. An ambulance took him to Kaiser Santa Rosa, Critical Care. She'd followed. But she wasn't allowed to see him.

A sense of futility gripped her as she slowed down at the toll booth, got out her quarters, threw them in the basket.

How could this have happened?

Because of Ray Quick. While everybody looked the other way.

Pam gone. Matt gone. And now, maybe Owens.

Anyone who meant anything to her—gone or slipping away.

CHAPTER THIRTY-SEVEN

It was close to midnight when Colleen got home. Her flat, on the third floor, was cold with winter, dark without Pam, and silent save for the constant whir of freeway traffic in the distance. All of it suited her mood entirely. She poured herself a finger of brandy—just one this time—stood on her back deck, looking into the fog, and made a silent toast to the darkness for Owens to make it.

She drank the brandy down like medicine. It burned.

She had taken too long to save him. Been too late.

In the kitchen the phone rang.

She set the glass on the countertop, answered the phone.

"This is Detective Alvarez," a deep voice said. "Fos." There were the sounds of people chatting in the background, the noise of a busy bar. "We met the other day. At 850."

Owens' partner. Ex-partner.

"Right," she said with venom. "You walked off mid-sentence when I asked you for help with Owens. Well, keep walking." She was just about to hang up.

"Wait a minute," he said in a deep, somber voice. Then, "I heard about Owens."

There was a moment of silence.

"Yes," was all she could manage, and it was breathless, and it was lifeless.

"What happened?" he asked. There was a slight slur in his voice. He'd been drinking.

"Jumped," she said. "In the changing room up at Sonoma County. I was waiting for him to be released. The other inmates were gunning for him, an ex-cop who supposedly murdered his wife. And supposedly got away with it."

Another pause. Laughter tinkled in the background.

"I'm really sorry," Fos said, his voice nearly inaudible in the noisy bar.

"Doesn't do much good now, does it?" she said. "You and all his so-called colleagues stood on the sidelines and looked the other way while he got set up for that bullshit murder rap."

"There was nothing I could do," he said. "Not with IA." Internal Affairs.

"You didn't even lift a finger," she said. "I'm hanging up now. It's late."

"Owens vouched for me," Fos said quickly. "Got me into Homicide."

"Too bad he picked the wrong partner."

"I want to fix this."

"There's nothing to fix."

"I want the person who set him up. You mentioned a name. When we met the other day: Ray Quick."

"So, you *were* listening," she said.

"Owens' case is being handled by Sonoma County so I can't step in. Not officially. The IA investigation is still open. But you said you had someone else—someone named Traci. Is she linked to Ray?"

"I think so."

"We'll start there. You got a picture? Something I can get started with?"

"I do."

"Bring it."

"OK," she said. "Where and when?"

"Can you make it now?"

Finally, someone who wanted Ray Quick too. "Sure."

"I need to follow up on something quick. Give me an hour. Hour and a half tops."

It was about eleven p.m.

"OK," she said. "Where?"

"Bajones."

A club on Valencia. Jazz and soul music. Owens had mentioned it.

"Call me if you can't make it," she said.

"Oh, I'll make it," he said.

Maybe Fos wasn't such a lightweight after all.

CHAPTER THIRTY-EIGHT

Around eleven forty-five p.m., just before the graveyard shift change, a trio of nurses headed into the Pine Street entrance of St. Francis Memorial Hospital, white shoes and uniforms showing under their coats. Laughing at some joke, puffs of breath appeared, and one woman tossed the burning butt of a cigarette into the street behind her on the way through the glass door.

Fos Alvarez pulled up in a beige unmarked Ford Custom, a bucket, one of the older police vehicles in the garage. But he liked the old Ford, made of thick steel, a car the size of an aircraft carrier. And he wasn't paying for the gas.

Just as he got out, a security guard came out the side entrance, a gangly guy who seemed to have too many teeth, dressed in baggy grey polyester slacks and a blue polyester jacket, looking like a movie usher. Dude even had earth shoes on.

"You can't park here," the guard said, chewing something. "Unless you want to get towed."

Always assumed because he was Hispanic, Fos had no business being anywhere. He flashed his SFPD badge, along with a light-switch smile, tucked the badge back into the side pocket of his grey double-breasted suit jacket, smoothed the flap over it.

"Oh," the guard said, mouth open while he ate. "Sorry."

"I'm looking for one of your compadres," Fos said. "Officer Manuel Peña."

The guard ran long bony fingers through unruly hair. "Is this about that 187 last week? The tranny in the doctors' parking lot?"

"I said I need to talk to Peña," Fos said. "He's here, right? You guys go on at eleven." Security shifts were staged so as not to coincide with the regular hospital staff shift change.

"What's it about?"

"If I thought you should know, I'd tell you. How about you get Peña on the radio? And don't tell him who it is. Just tell him to get down here—now."

"OK." The guard unhooked his belt radio, a clunky thing the size of a brick, clicked in with a bunch of *Unit 1, Unit 2, 10-19* gibberish, telling Peña there was someone to see him at the Pine Street entrance and that it was important. He went back into the hospital without saying a word. Fos knew there was a small security office next to the entrance.

Not long after, an older guard came out the glass door. Late fifties, a dark-skinned Latino with craggy features and a full pompadour dyed jet black and Brylcreemed to a shine that caught the streetlight. He gave Fos a nod, one brother to another. "Hey. I don't know you, do I? You from the union?"

"Nothing like that," Fos said, showing his badge. Peña jumped a little. Fos put the badge away.

Peña's smile faded. "This about last week?"

"You're the one who found the body. Doctors' parking lot. It's nearby, right?"

"Just down Pine." He nodded downhill, a one-way street.

"Let's go check it out."

"I already gave my statement. Some inspector, I forget his name."

"Owens."

"You're a detective, huh?" Inspectors were higher rank. "What's this about?"

"I'm following up." Unofficially.

"Following up how?"

"Well, to be perfectly honest, your statement is a little spotty. We're talking about a murder, so the details need to be right. I was curious if you remembered anything since last week."

"No. It's all there."

"OK. Let's go take a look at the lot and you can walk me through it."

"I got my rounds to do. I don't need trouble, man."

"What trouble? You're helping out the police. That's your job."

"My job is to guard the hospital. And the staff."

"And the doctors' parking lot is part of the hospital. So, let's go."

Peña startled. "Come on, man. If the bosses know you're interrogating me when I've already given a statement, it looks bad. They don't like the publicity as is. They're gonna have questions. You're Chicano, man, you can dig that."

"I can dig you're pushing back. Like you might have a little something to hide."

"Fuck it. Let's just go, then."

They crossed Bush, walked down to the doctors' parking lot, a small lot packed with Mercedes, Porsche, and Cadillac cars, all set back in between apartment buildings made of brick. Old San Francisco.

"I found him right there," Peña said, standing at the lot entrance pointing halfway down. "In an angel position. Like Night Candy. Arms out, like Jesus."

"Let's take a closer look." Fos walked to the middle of the lot, noticed Peña reluctant, standing there.

"Come on," Fos said.

Peña followed and stopped at the spot. The white outline was still partially visible.

"Definitely an angel." Like Night Candy. Fos eyed Peña. "See anybody?"

Peña eyed him back. "It's in the report."

"I know. I read it. You saw an American sedan leaving as you were coming into the lot. Black or blue. But nothing too specific."

"It was night."

"How long you been working security?"

"Over ten years."

"So, you're trained to observe and report. I used to be a guard. What kind of car was it?"

Peña got a pack of Marlboros out, shook one loose, lit it up. Once he got it going, he gave Fos a chin flick.

"Jumpy?" Fos said.

"Not jumpy at all, Ese."

"Could have fooled me," Fos said. "And cut the *Ese* shit. I'm not your homeboy."

Peña took a deep drag, let it billow out. His eyes darted around.

"Let's just cut to the chase," Fos said. "I know you take kick-backs from the whores who use this lot for quickies. You look the other way during your pecker-checks. That's what they're called, I know. I did plenty of security myself. Most every parking lot I ever worked at night had some kind of activity going on now and then. I know what kind of money you make. Three and a half an hour, something like that. It's tough to live on. I've been there. And the hookers are gonna use this lot regardless, right? You can still keep an eye on the doctors' cars, and so can they, so no one really gets hurt."

"Not me, man."

Fos returned a wry smile. "We've got a mainframe with all sorts of interesting stuff. Comes in pretty handy. You were pulled in two years ago for questioning when a hooker got beat up in this very lot. She told SFPD she was paying you off, thought she was safe to bring her johns here. Thankfully—for you—nothing ever came of it. The police didn't care about you. You dodged a bullet. Now, I don't care either. But I know the deceased was a hooker, and she—he—used this lot. So, I figure she—he—might have paid you off too. I'm not out to screw you. I just want whoever killed the dude. Then I'll get out of your slick-backed hair."

Peña took an angry puff. He shook his head at the balls of this jumped-up Mexican cop putting on the pressure. "Just between you and me?"

"Unless you mess me around," Fos said.

Peña took a drag, blew it out into the cold night air. "Yeah, she—he—whatever he was—was a regular."

"Good. What kind of car was it? Details, man. Make and model. You know all the cars supposed to park here."

Peña flicked the filter of his cigarette with his thumb, knocking ash off. "Buick Riviera. Custom paint. Blue. Midnight blue. Wire wheels. A nice ride. Never saw it before. First time."

"See. That wasn't so damn hard. Get a license plate?"

"*¿Qué chingados?* No, man, I didn't get a plate. If I had night vision, I wouldn't be working as a fucking rent-a-cop on the graveyard shift. But it was a California plate, one of the newer ones, yellow letters on blue."

"How many in the Riviera?"

Peña puffed, making the cigarette glow as he held up one finger of his free hand. "Just a white guy, looked like a Ken doll."

"A pretty boy."

"You got it."

Fos thought about that. "See anything else?"

Peña's eyes narrowed to slits. "This comes back to me, I'm denying all of it. I don't need the attention. But I do need this job."

"You'll do what you're told. I asked you a question."

"What are you, man?" Peña shook his head. "*El coco?*"

El coco. Coconut: brown on the outside, white on the inside.

Fos' anger flashed, anger that was there much of the time. Things had risen to the surface since Owens. He might not make it.

His hand shot out, grabbed Peña by the necktie.

The clip-on tie came clean off.

Peña stepped back but Fos was on him, grabbed his collar, got his fingers hooked in, yanked him back.

Peña looked up in surprise. His burning cigarette was on the ground.

"The fuck, man?"

Fos stared into his face, inches away. "That john beat the whore to death, and you half-assed your statement to cover yourself. A good cop might die. We're not dealing with a run-of-the-mill john who's an inconvenience to you. We're talking about a murderer. We're talking Night Candy. So don't give me any of your 'El coco' shit."

"Hey, I didn't know about the cop, man."

"Well, now you do." He let the guard go. "So, let's try it again."

Peña stood back, exhaled. "Big scratch in the car's paint. Along the right rear quarter panel. Looked fresh. I think the sissy boy that got beat to death might have keyed the car. I wonder if that's why he beat him up in the first place, when he lost his temper."

"Seems like you saw a lot. You one of those guards who gets his jollies watching whores while they work?"

Peña shook his head. "I think the Ken doll didn't know what he'd picked up until she—he—started in. Thought he had himself a piece of pussy—not dick."

Fos nodded. "Another reason to lose your temper and beat the holy crap out of someone."

"Hell, man. I'd be pissed. Wouldn't you? Some of those trannies are damn convincing."

"OK," Fos said, getting out one of his business cards along with a pen. He wrote a note on the back: *Any questions, call Detective Alvarez.* "If you catch any flack, tell your jefe to call me personally," he said, handing the card to Peña. "And I'll set him straight."

Peña took the card. Fos could see he couldn't quite bring himself to thank Fos.

CHAPTER THIRTY-NINE

Just past one a.m., Colleen found Detective Fos Alvarez standing at the bar in Bajones on Valencia in the Mission, staring into a full shot glass. Fos stood tall and slender in a light grey double-breasted suit with the jacket undone. The band was playing a chunky Latin Cumbia on a low-lit stage, the accordion melody hopping effortlessly over a multilayered rhythm that swept back and forth from Africa to South America. A cross-section of San Franciscans, mostly Black and brown, but some whites too, from yuppies to the janitors who would sell them a sly lid, gyrated in a cool style that emanated from south of the equator. Cool was the word. If Colleen hadn't been so preoccupied, she would have enjoyed the ambiance.

Fos Alvarez turned as Colleen approached. His hair, parted in the middle, was swept back, a little messy as if he were agitated. His deep-set eyes were out of focus, brooding and shiny.

She'd changed into black polyester bell-bottoms and a burgundy polyester top, platforms that matched the top, along with her black leather coat. Couldn't come to a place like this in your jeans.

Fos picked up his shot, drained it, set the empty glass down next to a near empty bottle of Tecate.

"You made it," he said.

"As did you."

"Something to drink?"

"Soda water with a twist, please."

He signaled the barman, ordered her drink, ordered himself another shot and a beer.

"Owens," he said, shaking his head.

"I know," she said.

"How's he doing?"

"He might not make it." She couldn't fathom it right now. She just needed to keep pressing ahead.

The soda water arrived, and she took a sip. Fos drank off his shot and set the glass down with an unintended thump.

"You bring that pic?" he asked.

She reached into her pocket, came out with a Xerox of the photo of Traci on New Year's Eve.

He took it, studied it.

"And you think this Ray Quick picked her up?"

"And I think he killed her."

Fos lowered the photocopy, looked at Colleen inquisitively.

She told him about her theory.

"It all comes down to a dental implant?" he said, the disbelief unmasked.

"Traci disappeared the night before Alice Owens was supposedly killed. Ray Quick was Alice's ex-boyfriend. He's a bartender at The Claddagh. Out on Clement. Conveniently he's got an alibi for the night Alice was murdered."

"So where is Alice now?"

"Good question. She might well be dead too."

She saw Fos frowning. Not quite buying it. The bartender was pouring him a fresh shot.

"Ray was looking for an Alice substitute," she said. "Tall, slender, blonde. He needed a stand-in. For Alice."

"Theories are fine," Fos said, his voice a little slurred. "Facts are better."

"I'm giving you facts. The body in the Santa Rosa morgue is not Alice."

Fos took another sip, blinked in thought. Then he took another look at the photo while the Cumbia music played. Figuring something out.

"This Ray doesn't sound like Night Candy," he said.

"I don't think so either," she said. "Just a sick murderer. With a scheme to land himself a quarter of a million."

"But we need to eliminate Night Candy from the equation first."

"Why?"

"Too much overlap. Four dead prostitutes point to this Traci being another NC victim."

She could see that. That's how a cop would think. That's how Owens would think. Methodical. It made sense, although she didn't quite buy it. But cover all the bases.

"Hey, Fos," a woman said. "What are you doing here, babe?"

They both turned to see a young Latina, mid-twenties, decked out in a clingy gold and black dress, black stockings, pointy black high heels. She had long luxuriant hair feathered back over bare shoulders that shone with a hint of body glitter. Giant gold-hooped earrings. Her lips were full and painted deep red, and her lashes were long and curled. If you looked up "stunning" in the dictionary, there might be a picture of her along with the definition.

"Hey, Angie," Fos said, clearing his throat. "What are *you* doing here?"

"Just hanging out with my friends. I thought you were working tonight." She gave Colleen a curious glance.

"I am."

"So I see."

Colleen introduced herself. "It *is* work," she said, sensing Angie was a girlfriend. "I asked Fos if he could meet me tonight. Regarding a mutual friend of ours."

"Oh. Is she an older woman too? Trying to pick up younger guys?"

"It's not what it looks like," Colleen said.

"That's odd," Angie said. "Because it sure looks like what it doesn't look like."

"Angie," Fos said. "I don't have time for this right now."

"I know, Foster. You're 'working.'"

"I'm in the middle of a case."

"A *case*?" Angie laughed. "Oh, man. You can do better than that."

Fos set his glass on the bar. "Let me tell you how it works, Angie. There's a telephone. If it rings, it might be me asking you out. If it doesn't, then I don't have the time. So, you wait until it does. And you don't pull a scene on me in public. Not when I'm working. You got that, or do I need to write it down?"

Angie stepped back as if she'd been slapped. Then she raised her middle finger. It vibrated, with a long red nail to punctuate her silent anger. Her mouth bore a fierce scowl, but her eyes were glistening.

And then she turned, marched off, shoulders high.

Colleen realized her own pulse had accelerated.

"I feel awful," she said to Fos.

"Why?" he said, drinking. "You didn't do anything."

"No, and neither did she. You could have been a little nicer to her."

"Don't tell me you're going to start in too."

"Forget it. Getting back to Owens: What now?"

"I'm going to find this Ray," he said, draining his beer, looking at his watch. "He works at The Claddagh, right? Out on Clement?"

"Yes, but don't tell me you're going over there now."

"Why not?"

"Because you're just a little bit—ah—what's the word? Impaired? Half in the bag? *Drunk?*"

"Jesus. Maybe you should go hang out with Angie."

She shook her head. "Another cop who drinks too much and treats women like shit. None of my business, but if you think you're going over to The Claddagh now, I'm coming with you. And I'm driving."

Fos turned to the bar, drained his shot. Let out a deep sigh. Then he shook his head in agreement. "Yeah, you're right. We've got to finesse this."

Thank God. "Exactly."

He looked over at Angie. She was sitting in a booth with her girlfriends, wiping her eyes with the back of her hand. The girlfriends were consoling her. One stared daggers at Fos and Colleen.

"I should talk to Angie," he said.

"Not just talk," Colleen said. "*Apologize.*"

"Yeah." He shook his head up and down slowly.

Colleen patted him on the shoulder on the way out. "We'll talk tomorrow. When you've got a clear head. First thing, right?"

"Right."

"You sure you're up for this?" she said. "Ray? It might get bumpy."

"Owens was supposed to be my partner," he said, drinking beer. "Bumpy is OK."

"Go home after you tell Angie what a horse's ass you are. And take a cab."

"Right," he said, drinking. "Tomorrow, you and me. First thing."

CHAPTER FORTY

Early next morning in her office at the end of Pier 26, Colleen was typing up a report for a client on her secondhand IBM Selectric. The report included a photo of the client's wife and his father in an intimate embrace in a car down by Ocean Beach.

It took all sorts to ruin someone's happiness.

Which may not have existed in the first place.

But she needed to get paid. Working on Owens was not going to yield anything in the way of cash, and that was fine, but groceries and rent were still a priority.

She wore her black 501 straight-legs and black loafers with green wool socks, and a baggy cable stitch sweater that matched the socks over one of Matt's white T-shirts, which he had left at her place. A slummy but warm getup, perfect for a day of cold office work. She wondered how Matt was doing in Langley, and when she might hear from him.

Her office, a former maintenance room at the end of a defunct covered pier, was the size of a large garage with high ceilings, crude wood-paneled walls, with plenty of drafts. Which meant she could hear things. Like the gulls cawing on the water and the start of morning traffic droning on the Bay Bridge.

And the multiple footsteps coming down the boards of the pier toward her office. Past the storerooms and other offices, the old dock finding new life in a city with a fading waterfront. The shoes moved sprightly as they covered the thick planks milled with redwood from up the coast back when it had been plentiful. One pair of shoes had metal taps on them.

She was expecting a call from Fos. Could that be him? If so, she would have expected only one pair of footsteps.

She looked up from her beat-up green metal desk, a holdover from her time living in a warehouse she once guarded, saw two heads through the textured glass at the top of the door.

"It's open," she said, closing her report folder.

The door opened and two well-dressed young Asian men stood there, ones she recognized. Both young, one with sharp cheekbones and light skin, wearing a grey suit that draped the way expensive clothes did. His hair was a work of art, combed high with just the right amount of flick. But he still looked like a punk; no amount of money could change that. The other guy was a few years older, putting on weight, with rounder features and droopy eyes. He was the one losing his hair, who'd taken a baseball bat to the shoulder courtesy of Boom. Paper Sons. She tensed up.

"How are things at the Jade Palace?" she said, sitting back in her squeaky roller chair to force composure.

The good-looking Paper Son didn't smile.

"Is this about Billy Shen?" she asked. Billy Shen was Traci's pimp. "Traci? Do you guys talk?"

"You need to come with us."

A ship blasted out on the bay.

She picked up the phone, dialed Gus Pedersen, got his new answering machine. "I'm going with a couple of guys from the Paper

Sons to talk about something that apparently can't be dealt with here or on the phone. In case you don't hear from me."

She hung up, put her file away, locked the desk drawer, which took some fiddling since it had been broken into earlier in the year by some other punks.

She stood up, threw on her oversized leather coat.

"Let's go," she said.

They wound up at the Asian Heaven Spa in Chinatown, on a steep hill not far from the Jade Palace. It was early in the day and the "spa" was closed. They walked through a cramped waiting room with plastic chairs where the lights were up, highlighting the smudges on the lavender walls and various Far East posters and a cheap block print while a young woman in a shortie robe and high-heeled slippers vacuumed over the blare of the Chinese news on the radio. On a shelf above a requisite fish tank—Feng Shui for good luck—a ceramic cat waved a battery-operated paw in greeting.

Getting ready for the day's business.

They walked past an empty front desk where a list of services rendered was posted, from partial to "complete," along with a City of San Francisco Public Health Massage Licensing Program notice, through a beaded curtain, past rooms marked "Bliss" and "Ecstasy," down the hall past an open door leading downstairs where Colleen heard women chatting in Cantonese amidst the odor of cooking and the chugging of a washing machine. Many parlors had girls who slept on the premises, who were working off their passage to the land of opportunity. Many took years. Some didn't live long enough to see it through.

In a back room, a small office with two desks, an older woman argued on the phone as she dug through a pile of papers. A middle-aged Asian man sat at the other desk in front of a window with bars that gave out over a grim scene of pinched Chinatown backyards. He was dressed in a shapeless brown suit and wore glasses with heavy frames. His hair was thatched.

Colleen recognized him. Fan Lei. He was the owner of the restaurant she had recently served papers to. Her forty-three clients had still not been paid. Seems Fan was also involved with the Paper Sons. Not a huge surprise.

Sitting on a vinyl love seat was Rhonda, in her pink sweatpants, platform sneakers, and puffy white down coat with the fake fur collar. She looked much more attractive in casual garb, but that didn't sell on Hyde and Leavenworth.

Billy Shen sat nearby, quiet in the presence of his boss.

A full house.

Colleen remained standing. Everyone was on edge. The booming Chinese news didn't help.

"Can someone turn that down, please?" Colleen said.

The woman at the desk leaned out to the hallway, shouted. The volume dropped a good half, leaving the droning of the vacuum.

"Here we are." Colleen looked around the room.

Mr. Fan picked up a squeeze ball, gave it a squeeze. Put it down. "You and Rhonda have been talking."

Colleen glanced at Rhonda. She didn't want to get her into trouble. "I passed along a warning, that's all."

"About Traci."

"Traci's been missing for three weeks now."

Mr. Fan grimaced. "The girls sometimes take time off without notice. Some of them use drugs. I don't want you scaring my girls."

"I don't think I'm the one who scared them. Try Night Candy. Or someone similar. And you know as well as I do that Traci didn't just take off." She raised her eyebrows. "Three weeks?"

Rhonda spoke. "We want to know what happened to Traci, Mr. Fan," she said. "We don't like this."

"Billy will have someone stop by regularly. Now go. I expect you and the others to work tonight."

Rhonda took a deep breath. "You need to do more."

"I said I will take care of it."

Rhonda nodded, got up, left, patting Colleen on the arm on the way out. Colleen heard the front door open and shut. Collaborating with a man who trafficked girls and whored them out wasn't her first idea of how to proceed, but sometimes you took what you got. She could do something about Fan later.

"Traci's dead," Colleen said.

Fan's face was immobile. He rested his hands on his desk.

"You must have had an inkling," she said.

"The police? They told you?"

"No." She shook her head. "But I know."

"How do you know?"

"Don't ask."

"But you are sure?"

Colleen gave a single nod.

Mr. Fan frowned, raised his thin eyebrows above his glasses. "This Ray Quick is responsible? The one with the Buick Riviera?"

Colleen didn't need or want vigilante justice at this point.

"I don't want you going after anyone."

"I'm a businessman—one who minds his own business. And this man has apparently interfered in mine. Tell me where I can find him."

"As much as I detest Ray Quick, I don't want to hear about him floating in the bay."

Mr. Fan raised his palms to the ceiling with an expression that read, *As if things weren't difficult enough already.* "You want me to take care of my girls, but you don't want me to protect them. And now you want to tell me how to run my business."

"I want justice—visible justice—to help clear things up for some-one who's caught in the middle of all this." Owens. Still in Kaiser CCU.

Fan shrugged. "I can give you some time. But you have to give me something in return."

"Why am I not surprised?"

"We have to come to an arrangement on those papers you served me."

"The forty-three ex-employees?" she said. "I agree. We avoid court. Everybody will come out ahead."

"Fifty cents on the dollar," he said.

Colleen leaned her head back, laughed out loud. "For forty-three employees? One woman is due almost a thousand. I can't tell her fifty cents on the dollar."

"Forty-three illegals. Who have no right to be in this country?"

Most of Fan's people came into the country illegally. For which he charged hefty fees and exacted the equivalent of indentured servitude.

"They worked for you," she said. "You owe them. And don't for-get the win-win."

"We are talking over forty thousand dollars."

"Forty-one, seven hundred and five, to be exact. But with no court costs, no fine, no more headaches for you. And forty-three happy people. Well, not as pissed off."

"Thirty."

Thirty thousand. It was her turn to frown. "I can't go back to them with sixty-eight cents on the dollar. Make it seventy-five—cash—and we have a deal—but only if I get my assurance that Ray Quick won't be killed. And you do one more thing for me."

"One more thing." He actually smiled. "What 'one more thing'?"

"I need to know what there is to know about Night Candy," she said.

"How would I possibly know?"

"If anyone can find out anything about Night Candy, it's you, with all your people on the street. He targets working girls."

Fan nodded. "Why do you want to know?"

Fos had insisted they eliminate Night Candy from their search for Traci's killer. And it made some sense the more she thought about it. "There could well be a connection."

"You think Ray Quick is Night Candy?"

She shook her head side to side. "It would be easier if I did, perhaps, but no, I don't. But I need to check it out. To help my friend. Whose life is hanging in the balance."

Mr. Fan picked up his squeeze ball, squeezed it a few times. Put it down.

"I will see what I can do."

"Then we have an agreement," she said.

CHAPTER FORTY-ONE

When Colleen unlocked the door to her office on Pier 26, the red light on the answering machine was blinking across the darkened room. She flicked on the fluorescent overhead lights, took off her leather coat, hung it up, sat down at her desk, hit rewind.

While the tape rewound, she spun in her chair, looking through the window behind her desk, at a section of the Bay Bridge shining out of the water.

"Paul Oedekoven," was all the voice said. "San Quentin."

The last name was pronounced "O-Dee-Coven."

The caller hung up. The phone droned a dial tone.

Colleen hung up too, sitting back.

She knew the caller. One who worked for Mr. Fan. Billy Shen.

That was quick. She recalled her deal with Fan.

But who the hell was Paul Oedekoven? The name had been annunciated clearly enough.

And what did he have to do with San Quentin?

She called Gus. He said he would get back to her. She said it was important.

* * *

"Paul Oedekoven is years into a life sentence for stuff you don't even want to know about," Gus said, staring over the wall at Seal Rock. They were at the Cliff House by Ocean Beach, the wind picking up. Hard pellets of rain blew in sporadic time. The sun, what there had been of it that day, was slipping behind Seal Rock's white surface— courtesy of the many gulls who made it a regular target.

Gus' cowboy hat with its snakeskin brim was pulled down tight in the wind. His long tawny-colored hair was in its customary thick ponytail over the back of his suede jacket with the fringes.

Colleen hunkered down in her leather coat.

"If Mr. Oedekoven got life," she said, "then he's not a nice man."

"If there was still a death penalty in California," Gus said, "they'd still be trying to pull the switch on him. But the law changed in his favor last year."

Colleen pulled a strand of hair out of her face that the wind had blown across it.

Gus continued: "He and his accomplice raped, tortured, and murdered between eight and eleven victims—all under the age of ten—in a cabin in Truckee from '67 to '69. He was sitting on death row. Now he's sitting in Quentin for a hundred and forty."

Colleen felt a twist of revulsion inside. "Well, I did ask."

"What's the connection?" Gus said.

"Owens was working Night Candy before he got set up. Maybe there's a link."

Gus turned, looked at her. "Owens gave you the Oedekoven lead?"

"Someone else," she said.

"Paul Oedekoven can't be Night Candy. He's been in the slammer while NC has been plying his trade."

"And Night Candy is into hookers—not kids. But maybe this Paul O knows something."

"Or not," Gus said. "Just don't let it cloud your judgment."

"I want to clear this up for Owens. He's still hanging on. Barely. Santa Rosa Kaiser CCU." She sighed. "What does it take to get a visitor's pass to see Paul Oedekoven?"

Gus looked at her and she could see him repressing a frown.

"Let me look into it," he said. "But you need to start pacing yourself. You're looking tired. And Owens is where he is until he's released."

"Owens needs to catch a break," she said. She wasn't going to promise anything at this point. She didn't like the thought of all this left hanging in the air when—if—Owens got out. He might just act the wrong way.

CHAPTER FORTY-TWO

"Paul Oedekoven approved your visit," Gus said. Another late-night phone call. Some electronic music was playing in the background. "You can see him tomorrow."

She told Gus she appreciated the quick work.

"What does Paul O want from me?" she said, leaning against her tile counter. The flat was dark, but the overhead kitchen lights were on. She was ready for bed. "He must want something."

"You're not going to like it," he said. "But when he heard about you, he wanted to meet you."

"Lucky me."

"This is what you wanted, Colleen. Remember?"

"I know. And I do. But I just want to talk to him about Night Candy. *Talk.*"

"Just make sure you look right. He was specific." She heard Gus rattle a paper. "Dark plain dress, long sleeves, flat black shoes, not shiny, no heel. Fingernails clipped, no polish. No makeup or fragrance. San Quentin won't let you get away with that anyway. No skin showing above the wrists, below the neck, above the ankle. The pilgrim look."

"Our mass murderer is a prude at heart."

"He's found Jesus."

"Of course. Well, I can hit the thrift shop in the a.m."

"What's going to get you most is the hairstyle," Gus said. "Or lack of it. The woman of his dreams looks like a department store mannequin without a wig."

"I have to shave my head?"

"Only if you want to meet him."

A flurry of emotions ran through her: distrust, shock, anger, then the grim realization of what went on in some people's minds. But they said beauty was only skin deep. Hair grew back. How bad did she want Ray? Fos' help? A lead? How bad did she want Owens vindicated?

"Sounds like Paul Oedekoven is either some kind of a perv or he's testing me."

"Well, we know he's a perv."

"He wants to see how far I'll go to meet him."

"Bear in mind there are restrictions that San Quentin also stipulates: no blue or red—gang colors—no forest green or tan—guard colors—no orange—prisoner colors—no hair pins, no tight, form-fitting attire, no clothing that exposes breast, genitalia, or buttocks."

"Sounds like Paul O has already considered that," she said.

"Want me to cancel?" Gus asked, Hawkwind playing in the background.

"Not as long as there are no conjugal visits involved."

"He's not eligible."

"Thank God for her small mercies." Colleen rubbed her eyes, took a breath. "Looks like I'm going to be getting my hair cut for boot camp too."

"You're set," he said. "Three thirty. Half an hour. Don't bring anything. *Not a thing.* If he wants any kind of gift, he hasn't said so. If he brings it up, it'll have to be a credit through his prisoner account. But let's wait and see. We can use it for any future negotiation."

"Well," she said. "I'm going to call this progress. I just hope I learn something about Night Candy."

"That's the bait," Gus said. "And he knows it. So don't sell out cheap."

"I wish someone would have told me that before I met my ex," she said.

"I bet your ex wishes that too."

"If only the dead could wish," she said. "You heard anything from Fan Lei yet?"

"As you said," he said. "Seventy-five on the dollar, cash. It's in the works."

"My forty-three disenfranchised will be happy."

"*He* gave you Paul Oedekoven," Gus said. "Didn't he? Fan Lei?"

"He has eyes and ears on the street in the least reputable parts of the city. I figured if anyone might know anything, it would be him."

"Be careful what you ask for," Gus said.

"We'll see if it pans out," she said. "I can't get anything to stick to Ray Quick."

"Yet."

Yet.

CHAPTER FORTY-THREE

Saturday afternoon Colleen drove across the Golden Gate Bridge, fog blowing through 80,000 miles of wire cables that kept it in perfect suspension, wet white vapor slipping over the hood of the Torino, on into the San Francisco Bay. Past the bridge the fog lifted, and the view began to expand, the lush green of the Marin headlands to her left, Sausalito to her right. Bedroom communities for the well-to-do slipped by with Mount Tam in the backdrop. Still fogged in on top, as Colleen took Sir Francis Drake and drove out to the oldest prison in California. Built in 1852, San Quentin now sat on some very prime real estate. Over 3000 prisoners lived in the multi-tiered medieval-looking blocks by the water that shimmered in spots where the sun was breaking through. Palm trees added a surreal air to the grim institutional structure. Those on the inside called it the "Arena."

Being this close to a prison always took Colleen back to her nine-plus years in Denver Women's Correctional Facility. It was a physical memory, one that made her body tighten, hunker down, aware of everything around her, like a dog with its hackles up. Time began to slow down. She wasn't naïve enough to think that many of the 3000 were in Quentin for any fault other than their own, and society was no doubt better off without them, but she still felt a certain kinship for those behind bars.

She rolled up to the tall black iron gates, showed her letter at the guard shack, then parked and walked to the western cellblock. The wind over the water was sharp, rippling the surface, and she felt it on her bare head and neck. Alex had dropped by that morning with her clippers, and Colleen's hair had been shorn back to less than stubble per instructions, and it felt odd to say the least. No hat on her head as San Quentin wouldn't allow them. Alex said she looked dramatic as all get-out and, with the right makeup, would slay men with a stare, but Colleen wasn't so sure. She wondered what Matt would say when he saw her. *If* he saw her. She still hadn't heard from him, back east at Langley. He loved her hair. But that was the least of her worries. In her plain black wool dress from Goodwill that hung to the tops of her flat, austere shoes, with its requisite long sleeves and high collar, she felt like she was ready for questioning by the Spanish Inquisition.

After a double search, she stashed her bag in a locker before being escorted to the visitor center.

The visitor's waiting room was a long, dingy hall alongside one block called the "tube." After a wait she was finally shown into a room with stark overhead florescent lights, a linoleum floor, curling in places, and tables constructed of white metal frame with stools all bolted together into one unit. On closer inspection the table units were rusting.

Being Saturday, a number of visits were in progress. A family with a baby in a Christmas hat, wives, one visitor who wasn't female. Prisoners wore dark blue pants and light blue shirts, under the watchful eyes of guards in green and tan.

Colleen was shown to the one remaining vacant table, patted down one more time before she sat on a metal stool.

And waited. While she watched the door on the other side of the room. The conversations were the type that went on in such places and reminded her of her own incarceration: forced cheer, cloaked hostility. She remembered her mother bringing Pam to visit when Pam was young and recalled Pam's initial confusion, then later the surly teens and harsh indifference as Pam turned from Goth to punk. She remembered bracing herself for periods of stony silence and Pam telling her grandmother that she was ready to leave almost as soon as they arrived. Everyone thought prisoners loved visits when, in fact, the opposite was generally true. They didn't need reminders of what was passing them by on the outside, how people had moved on without them. Visits were a duty. You just wanted to do your time in your own mind-numbing way and get over it.

Just when she thought she might have shaved her head for grins, a guard brought in a small man in his forties. His pale face was contrasted by dark glasses and thinning brown hair. He looked like an assistant manager at a shoe store. She was a little surprised to see him not in restraints. Her visions of tattooed Charles Manson look-alike killers who had to be strapped down evaporated. Being docile and harmless-looking probably worked in his favor in getting close to his victims. But he zeroed right in on Colleen sitting by herself with her shaved head and gave her a furtive look that made her twinge. He was the real thing all right.

The guard showed Paul Oedekoven over. The man took small, precise steps. Colleen stood up, thanked him for meeting with her. He returned a curt nod before he sat on the opposite stool.

He placed his small hands on the table, clasped them together.

"Let us pray," he said.

"Pray?" He was the last person she could think of due for redemption. And with all the people around, it felt like undressing in a crowd.

"Pray." He had an unassuming voice but there was a firmness to it that might have been easy to miss. He waited, watching Colleen impatiently through his glasses. His eyes were cold and blunt and she saw the latent aggression lurking in them. He judged the world like an emperor wanting to watch it burn.

She clutched her hands together.

"Close your eyes," he said.

She wondered if he had ever uttered those words to his victims during one of his "sprees."

But she did close her eyes.

He spoke in a flat monotone:

Jesus: Wash me from my guilt
and cleanse me of my sin.
I acknowledge my offense."

He finished with an amen and she opened her eyes.

Not much of a confession for eight to eleven dead children.

"You observed my wishes," he said with satisfaction, looking at her shaved head, then her simple dress, which covered most of her skin.

"Would you have met me otherwise?"

"No."

So, it *was* a test. More than some religious pretension affected by a folksy look. How he thought a woman should look perhaps. Dismissive and humiliated? All to cull more importance for a man rotting in a cell? Or a mixture of all of the above?

"What have you heard about me?" he said.

"Not as much as you might think."

"No?" He seemed disappointed.

"The truth is, I don't want to know more than I have to."

"And why is that?"

"Because I want to believe that you and I can find some common ground. That what you did before you got here won't be a deterrent to us working together."

"Some are excited by it."

She had no doubt.

"I'm afraid I'm not one of them," she said.

"Jesus has forgiven me. Why not you?"

"I'm not Jesus."

"No, you're not. You're not even Mary."

"That's fine with me," Colleen said.

"So, what do you want from me?"

"Your help."

"You want me to *help* you?" He reared back, narrowing his eyes.

She lowered her voice. "An acquaintance gave me your name, in connection to a man—I believe it's a man—it always is, isn't it?—one who is very much in the news these days." She raised her eyebrows and their eyes connected.

"Ah," he said with a knowing look, dropping his voice as well. "*Him.*"

"Yes, *him.*" They weren't going to use Night Candy's moniker. That was fine. There were guards stationed around the room. They didn't need to know. None of them had shaved their heads to get this far.

"What about *him*?" Paul Oedekoven said, raising one eyebrow over the rim of his glasses.

"Let's start with his latest effort." That was the case Owens had initially worked before he was arrested.

"You mean the rent boy by the hospital?" The doctors' parking lot by St. Francis.

"Yes."

"Whoever did that wasn't even close."

"I did wonder."

"Oh, did you now? Tell me what you think you know, not even Mary of Nazareth."

"The attack was a beating," she said. "Not a lethal injection. Not that all of them were. But it throws it into question."

Paul O gave a single nod.

"No letter to the *Chron*," Colleen said.

"Two for two."

"No fragrance." No Night Candy Perfume on the victim.

"You get a gold star."

She could see how important it was for Paul Oedekoven to be the authority, to live his and other murders vicariously, especially as he declined in prison.

"But," she said, "whoever did it is likely to get the credit."

"He's a copycat, riding someone else's coattails," Paul O huffed. "A rank amateur."

"But even so, that's what will happen," she said. "But how do you know for sure? That it's not *him*? You've been in here for a long time."

A smirk. "What makes you think I don't know him?"

So that was it. They had communicated somehow. Was Night Candy incarcerated? Colleen cocked her head.

"He's inside?" She dropped her voice to a whisper and pointed to the tabletop with a fingertip. "Here?"

Paul Oedekoven gazed into her eyes without blinking. He was indeed pleased with himself.

Shook his head.

"So, he's not here?" she asked. "Where then?"

No response. He wasn't going to give it away.

"He's out?" she said.

"Not in the way you think."

And then it hit her. Twice as it sunk in. "He's *dead*?"

Paul O gave a casual shrug.

"He died in here?" she asked. "*Here?*"

"No, not *here*."

"Not San Quentin," she said. "Somewhere else."

A giggle.

"And spoil all my fun?" he said.

Fun. What a child. A sick child.

"So, he died somewhere else," she said. "Another prison?" It wouldn't be impossible to find out. But it wouldn't be easy either. And time was a factor.

He waved that away. "Enough of this subject."

She stifled a sigh. *Keep pushing.* "How did you two meet?" she said. "You and *him*."

"There are ways to communicate," he said. "But this subject is now closed."

She gave him a skeptical look. "How do I know you're not blowing smoke?"

"Because you *know*." He returned a sly smile. "You can sense it."

Yes, she could. But how did they communicate? Did someone pass messages for them? A third party? Who? She took a deep breath. This was overwhelming, to say the least.

She'd play his bluff.

"Or maybe *you're* the one who isn't what he says he is," she said. "Hmm?"

Instead of losing his temper, which she half expected, he adopted his supercilious attitude again. He wanted to be believed. It was important to him.

"Now why on earth would I do that?" he said.

"Because this is all you've got," she said, waving her hand around the room. "You want me to believe you. Your ego needs it."

"I couldn't care less, my dear."

She shook her head. "I call BS."

He stood up. "I've had enough."

"No, you haven't." She smiled. "Your little 'accomplishments' are ancient history. No one barely knows you anymore. When was the last time the press contacted you? You need *him*. To keep it fresh. To validate you. Just like you need me now. Without that you're just another aging prisoner, fading away, counting the minutes between meals. Bedtime. Movie night. Walks in the yard. New books in the library. Few and far between."

He eyed her with renewed interest. "And how would you know about any of that?"

"I spent close to a decade in a place like this. Nine years, four months to be exact."

He crossed his arms over his chest. "No."

"Denver Women's Correctional Facility," she said. "Got out two years ago, near enough. Still on parole."

He sat back down. "How did you earn your stripes?" Then he held up a finger and smiled. "No, no, don't tell me." It was his turn to play guessing games.

She smiled back. She had him.

He eyed her. "You don't earn a ten-year stretch for shoplifting," he said, rubbing his chin.

"No, you most certainly do not."

He scrutinized her with beady eyes. "You're no thief either. You're too drearily honest."

She shrugged. "I'm certainly not very good at it." Unless it was mail.

He looked her over one more time, then flinched. "No! You didn't!"

"I did."

His voice became a whisper. "You dealt someone the losing card!"

She smiled. "Bingo."

"Let me guess: your old man."

The accuracy hit her like a bolt of electricity.

"And here I thought I was special," she said.

He laughed. "Garden variety crime, my dear," he said. "It's always the spouse. But do tell me: *how*?"

Now *he* wanted details. To compare notes. She leaned forward. "I came home from the rubber company one Monday night. My husband was cooking eggs in a pan. I asked where our daughter was. She'd been very unhappy. For almost a year. Acting out. Crying. Tantrums. Even wetting her bed again. She was eight. 'Upstairs,' he said. Well, I could tell by the inflection of his voice that something was wrong upstairs. You know?"

He was rapt. "I do indeed."

"Call it intuition. Or the way his voice rose just a little out of pitch. Or the fact that I should have known earlier. So much for maternal instinct. Mine was in hiding. I went upstairs. My daughter was crouching in the corner of her bedroom in nothing but a T-shirt. She wouldn't even talk. But she didn't need to say a word. What he had done to her was written on her face, plain as day. It was making her tremble. It wanted to be heard, and, in its own way, it was."

Paul O's eyes were open wide in interest. He leaned forward. "He did it right under your nose. That little stinker."

She took a deep breath and nodded. "Right under my nose," she said sadly. How she beat herself up every day for that.

"You were ignorant of the facts," he said.

"I was."

"Not very motherly at all."

"No," she said, fighting the squeezing in her throat. To bare your soul to a creature like this.

"And then what?" he asked.

She took another deep breath, recovered as best she could. Why stop now? You couldn't change the past.

She looked him in the eye.

"I did the only appropriate thing at the time. I went back downstairs and asked him what the hell was wrong with our daughter." She wasn't going to tell this monster Pamela's name. "He looked away from me, slipping a spatula under his eggs as if nothing had happened. He asked me what on earth I meant. I said she told me what he did. I wasn't telling the truth, of course, but I was so close, it didn't matter. He said, 'Oh, she makes stuff up. She's insecure.'"

"Blame the victim."

"You, you took ownership for yours, found Jesus. But not Roger. He wasn't man enough. Another weakling."

"Stop stalling. Get to the climax."

Interesting word choice. "His tool bucket was next to the stove. One of those old paint buckets? With a canvas insert to hold stuff? He'd been working on the faucet. Before he raped my daughter. It was like taking a coffee break to him. He'd obviously done it before. Many times. I saw it all, right then and there, in that fraction of a second. What a fool I was. A blind fool. But not for long."

Paul Oedekoven didn't speak at first. He took a deep breath through his nose as well. "You got wise."

"I did. And then I got *even*."

"All at once," he said. "Yes. That's how it works. People don't realize the power of it."

"Screwdriver sticking out of the tool bucket. But not for long, hey? Roger flipped an egg, ignored me, fool that I was. I was nothing, like my daughter."

"Come on! Come on!"

"I grabbed the screwdriver from the side pocket of the bucket..."

"Yes, yes!"

"He didn't even see it coming. Until it was in his neck. Up to the hilt. It was easier than I thought, with all that cartilage. But I had my anger driving me. A mother's wrath. Finally! But I still had to work at it, drive it, twist it."

Paul Oedekoven's eyes were open wide, taking it all in. Then he sat back, nodded with satisfaction, pointed a cagey finger at her. "He didn't know you had it in you. But you showed him, my dear."

She forced a smile over the biggest regret of her life. "Soon he was on the floor, trying to pull the damn thing out of his neck. But I stood on his wrist. He went fast. Too fast. I wanted it to last longer. He stopped moving. A little flinch before he went still. The eggs were starting to burn. I turned off the burner, moved the pan to a cold one."

"He didn't know you had it in you," he said again, with obvious respect. "Miss dishpan hands turned into quite the dance partner."

"Just like you. I bet people underestimated you all your life."

"Yes," he said seriously, confirming with a nod. "That they did. People make assumptions."

"They don't understand. But I had the best reason. The best reason in the world—at the time."

"I had reasons," he said. "I had my reasons too."

She wondered what on earth they could be, to murder children. She didn't really want to know, though, to get into his mind that far.

"I'm sure you did," she said. "I know what it's like."

"Not many do."

"No one on the outside." She let things settle for a moment. Then she switched back to Night Candy.

"But *he* did," she said.

"He most certainly did."

"So, he died locked up?" she asked casually. "Not here? But somewhere nearby?"

He eyed her, oozed a sly smile. "Oh, you are *good*," he said, pointing again. "But I'm not that easy."

Someone killed Night Candy. "Oh, come on," she said. "We're letting our hair down. What little I have left, anyway!"

He laughed. "You are a riot!"

It was like a twisted date.

"Just tell me," she said. "When and where?"

"Oh, should I put a silver bow on it too?"

"I can find out who was killed recently in California's prisons. Trace it back." It would take forever and maybe she couldn't. "Then I don't need you. Then you're back to the big fade." She pressed the button on her Pulsar watch. She stood up. "Oh well," she said. "Thanks for nothing."

"You don't have enough to go on," he said. "You know what you know but you don't know enough. You won't be able to prove it."

He was right.

"So, help me," she said, sitting back down.

"*Help* you," he said, shaking his head. "There you go again. Everybody needs help, Mary."

"But I'm Mary. Mary needed help."

"Good point."

"What would Jesus do?"

Paul Oedekoven examined his nails. "Oh, dear Mary, I do think that's enough for now."

"No!" she said. "I need to know now. You and *him*. You were a special kind of mutual admiration society. And this other phony at St. Francis Hospital is stealing his thunder, his and *yours*, by proxy. You two are—were—the real deal."

Paul Oedekoven shook his head. Then he looked away, nonchalantly. He so wanted to talk, to be part of things again, but he wasn't going to just give it away.

"Think what it would mean," she said. "Paul Oedekoven in the papers again. You want that. Don't you? You don't want to evaporate—do you?"

For a moment she thought he was going to talk.

"Jesus has forgiven me. I have atoned for my sins."

"Sure didn't sound like it to me," she said. "That was one half-assed prayer—for how many dead children?"

He smiled, shook his head.

"You want to know who he is? *Was?* How badly?"

"Money in your commissary account," she said. "A letter to the warden? Both? Whatever I can manage."

"My mother," he said finally.

That took her by surprise. Monsters didn't have mothers.

"She lives in the Avenues," he said. "Just off Anza."

San Francisco. Now she saw where this might be going. "On her own I take it?"

For the first time his face sagged. "She loves Midnight Mass, Christmas Eve. But there's no one to take her. Everybody's gone. Her so-called friends abandoned her. I used to. But I'm in here. Even though I found Jesus. It's so ironic. It's not fair for her to suffer."

"No, it's not," Colleen said. "It's not."

"Not at all."

Their eyes met again.

"I can take her," Colleen said quietly.

"To Midnight Mass?" He squinted at her. "Yes, you could."

"It would be my pleasure. If you tell me who he is. And it's verifiable."

"I will do even better than that, dear."

It was twisted, the things that got her excited anymore. But this was one of them.

"Evidence?" she asked.

He gave a sly grin. "For a special girl like Mary? Why not?"

"Truth is," she said, "I'm a sucker for Midnight Mass too. I just never have an excuse to go anymore. Now I do."

"Mother has her pride," he said. "She won't want some jailbird doing me a favor. She'll see right through that. She will, you know."

"Give me an ounce of credit, Paul," Colleen said, using his first name. "I'll make it convincing. I'm just an old high school friend of yours. Checking up for the holidays. You fill me in on your high school years and a few key details and we're copacetic."

"Yes." He rubbed his chin, eyed her. "That might work."

"No *might* about it," she said. "It will be a Christmas Eve to remember. I'll make it so."

"Take her a present. From me. To wear to Mass. One of those nice scarves. From Macy's. Union Square. She loves that store."

"I think I know just the scarf," she said. "I'll have Macy's gift-wrap it."

"With a card, signed, 'from your loving son, Pauli.'"

"From Pauli," she said. "And then you'll tell me. *His* name."

He sat back, drummed the table, smiled with satisfaction. "Oh, I'll do better than that," he said. "I'll do much better than that."

CHAPTER FORTY-FOUR

"This is so thoughtful of you, Colleen," Mrs. Oedekoven said.

"My pleasure," Colleen said, carefully pulling Mrs. O's wheelchair backwards up the steps to St. Cecilia's, the Spanish colonial–style church on 17th Ave. Colleen was going as gently as possible so as not to impact the frail woman with the bouncing chair. Paul Oedekoven's mother was in her late seventies and not in good health. Her slender frame bordered on skeletal, and her skin was a wrinkled grey, but she maintained elegant cheekbones and a proud aquiline nose. Colleen had helped her apply makeup, giving her cheeks some color, and the woman wore a fine dress from years gone by, too big for her now, under a discerning wool coat with a mink collar that hinted of mothballs. A dark vintage hat, harkening back to the '50s, sat atop her head, with a small collection of imitation flowers around the crown. And the alpaca scarf Colleen had given her as a gift—from her son—a deep burgundy for the season, was wrapped around her neck with a touch of flourish.

Mrs. O's eyes were dark and piercing, like her son's, but, unlike her son, they blinked out of nervousness, whereas his were eerily steadfast. Hardly a surprise, Colleen thought, the woman having raised Paul—her only child—and the impact his crimes must have had on her.

"Here we are!" Colleen said as she pulled the wheelchair back up the top step and wheeled Mrs. O around so she could see St. Cecelia's in all its glory. The huge rosette of stained glass glowed with colored light. "Come All Ye Faithful" floated out of the grand open doors.

It was 11:30 p.m. and people were gathering outside for Midnight Mass.

"I haven't been here in years," Mrs. Oedekoven said, clasping her gloved hands together. "Not since . . ." She left her sentence unfinished, giving Colleen a furtive look. Colleen understood. *Since Pauli had descended into an abyss of murder.*

"Let's go in, shall we?" Colleen said. "It's chilly." And it was. Colleen wore a dark blue dress, heels and stockings, under a long tan coat, but even so winter continued to bite. And the crowning glory of her outfit, a blonde Farrah Fawcett wig Alex had leant her. With any luck, life as a blonde might improve things. As she pushed Mrs. O toward the double doors, she saw the priest, decked out in white and red and gold, giving both Mrs. Oedekoven and Colleen a look of shocked disbelief.

He blocked the door.

"Merry Christmas, Father," Mrs. O said.

"Merry Christmas, Mrs. Oedekoven," he replied in a somber tone, letting a sigh escape, which showed itself visibly in the cold air. Colleen had worried something like this might happen. Her eyes met with the priest's. He was an older man who ate well with fine white hair and liver spots.

She wasn't going to let him get away with what was coming if she could help it.

"We *are* looking forward to the service," Colleen said brightly. Around her people were halting their conversations to watch her and Mrs. O.

"I'm afraid she can't come in," the priest said quietly to Colleen.

"Don't be ridiculous," Colleen said. "It's Christmas Eve."

"It's out of my hands, I'm afraid," he said. "The parish has ruled on this."

"It's Christmas," Colleen said again. "She's an elderly woman. On her own."

"If it was up to me . . ." the priest said weakly.

Off to one side Colleen heard, *she ought to be ashamed of herself.* Along with *they never found the Sullivan's daughter.*

And all the while, Mrs. O held her head up stoically, as if nothing had transpired, although it vibrated just a little.

Colleen understood. Paul Oedekoven had struck here, members of this church.

"Very well," Colleen said, spinning the wheelchair around gently.

"Merry Christmas," the priest said. Colleen refrained from a *go to hell.*

Mrs. Oedekoven pretended to ignore the interchange.

"I imagine it'll be on the television," she said with a slight choke in her voice, trying to mask her disappointment.

Colleen checked her Pulsar watch. They'd have to move quick.

"I have an idea," she said.

* * *

Just before midnight they pulled up at St. Mary's Cathedral on Van Ness, a tall modern structure that defined the skyline with its three-dimensional cement cross roof that Herb Caen had quipped in his column resembled a giant washing machine rotor blade. Joking aside, it was striking, and the lights of the city played off the tall modern stained-glass windows.

A string quartet was playing "Joy to the World" out front and a group of carolers were carrying the tune in a soft, collective voice that soared over the wide entrance where the city's prosperous funneled in in their finery.

"This is more like it," Colleen said to Mrs. O. She had parked the Torino in a bus stop. Christmas Eve, she'd risk it. There wasn't time to find parking. Service was about to start.

"This is absolutely lovely," Mrs. Oedekoven said.

* * *

"Would you like some more tea, Colleen?"

"No, thank you," Colleen said, sipping hot tea flavored with lemon and honey.

Wee hours after Midnight Mass, the two of them were sitting in Mrs. O's flat, either side of a dining room table that showed dark patterns through lace tablecloth. The sconce lights were low, setting off a collection of crystal on the sideboard.

The flat was a once-grand Victorian on Ninth Avenue, with yellowing doilies and layers of dust on the elegant furniture. Pictures of Pauli were everywhere, through every age, a child doted upon, sent to private schools where uniforms belied his eventual nature, along with his prim, tidy appearance, and constrained composure. If you knew what was to come, you could possibly see his true character, but otherwise he was just another spoiled little boy going through the motions of trying to please a parent with aspirations of grandeur.

For all the pictures of Pauli through the years, Colleen saw none of his father. There were no masculine trappings at all in this mausoleum of an apartment.

Mrs. O sat in her wheelchair, holding a bone china cup that bore a blue and white pattern. A crochet blanket sat over her lap. The flat wasn't warm.

"I must admit I don't remember you from Pauli's high school days, Colleen," she said.

"I *am* a little surprised to hear that," Colleen said. When cornered, go for the big lie. "Paul and I were quite close for most of eleventh grade." She sipped tea. Twelfth grade was when Pauli started exhibiting problems. He was expelled from Lowell after he was caught torturing lab mice as a TA in the biology lab and leaving notes for the younger girls. Colleen and Paul had gone over his high school history.

"Yes," Mrs. O said, her eyes tightly focused on Colleen's. She probably wondered how much Colleen knew of Paul's later years.

"After that we kind of went our separate ways," Colleen said. "I started dating someone and, well, you know . . ."

"Pauli should have moved a little more quickly!" Mrs. O said. Was she thinking of the big *what-if*? What if my son had met someone and not become a serial killer? How ironic, Colleen thought, reflecting on her own trajectory.

"I *was* waiting for Pauli to make a move, Mrs. Oedekoven." Colleen shrugged. "I just assumed he wasn't interested. Or ready."

"He never mentioned you."

"Then it's just as well," Colleen said. "Anyway, that was quite some time ago."

"What happened?" Mrs. O asked. "To your beau?"

"Nothing," Colleen said. "He found someone prettier."

"I find that hard to believe."

"Someone more amenable," Colleen said with a smile.

"Ah," Mrs. O said, picking up Colleen's drift. "Well, Pauli would have been the perfect gentleman."

"I suspect he would have. And now here we are, both of us still single."

"You never married?"

"I did," Colleen said. "I'm widowed."

"Oh, I'm very sorry to hear that."

"Thank you. I'm still coming to terms with it."

"Any children?"

"A daughter."

"What's her name?"

"Pamela."

"How old is she?"

"In her teens." Colleen shaved a couple of years off Pam's age to save the issue of her own teen pregnancy.

"It's so odd to have never seen or heard from you all these years."

"I moved to Colorado with my husband. Moved back not that long ago after he died. And this year I decided to start reconnecting with old friends."

"And you found Pauli?"

There was an awkward silence. Finding Pauli meant Colleen knew he was in San Quentin.

"I did," Colleen said, sipping her tea.

Mrs. O was watching her closely. "How so?" Her voice had chilled.

"Through a mutual friend."

"And who was that?"

"Bill Hirsch," Colleen said. "The guy I dated in twelfth grade."

"Bill Hirsch? But he was killed in Vietnam."

Shit. Colleen didn't know that. Pauli probably hadn't either. "Not that I'm aware of."

"Well, obviously not if you contacted him recently." Mrs. O gave an unruffled smile. "I must have my information wrong."

Mrs. O was a little cagier than she appeared.

"To be honest," Colleen said, "it was Amy I spoke to—Bill's sister. I bumped into her at Toy Boat on Clement." Toy Boat was an eccentric ice cream parlor, with decades' worth of toys crammed on its many shelves. "Bill's name didn't even come up. Bill and I didn't exactly part as friends in twelfth grade, you see. Not after he dumped me for a cheerleader."

"I see." Mrs. O drank tea, looking at Colleen over the rim of her cup. "And Amy told you about Pauli?"

Colleen cleared her throat. "She did."

"And you decided to visit him anyway?" An air of disbelief had crept into Mrs. O's voice.

Colleen took a measured breath. "I guess I always wondered what became of Pauli. We *were* close for a time."

"And it didn't bother you?" *It* referred to Pauli's multiple murders. Mrs. O was watching Colleen closely now.

Colleen sighed. "I guess I wanted to hear what *he* had to say. I believe in giving people another chance. And, as I said, we had been very close at one time."

Mrs. Oedekoven sighed. "They made no effort to understand," she said, obviously referring to the courts and the rest of the world. "They just wanted to make an example of him."

Make an example of a man who murdered children. How extreme.

"Well," Colleen said, "I'm glad you and I finally got to meet."

"It's such a shame Pauli never brought you here after school." Colleen thought she detected the suspicion in Mrs. O's voice.

"He was always quite shy," Colleen said. She hoped that settled the subject. She checked her watch. Red digits told her it was almost two a.m. "Good Lord! I must let you get to bed."

"I do so appreciate you taking me to Midnight Mass. It's been . . . years. Pauli always used to take me."

"Again, my pleasure."

"And the beautiful scarf."

"That was a gift from Pauli."

Mrs. O returned a shrewd smile. "Oh, I think you had a little to do with it, Colleen."

"I might have helped pick it out," Colleen said standing up. "May I please use your bathroom before I leave?"

"Of course, dear. Down the hall to your left."

Colleen walked quietly to the bathroom, noting one bedroom at the end of the hall that had to be Mrs. O's. The bed, with its fluffy duvet, sat low and a makeup table was just visible.

There was a door next to that one, shut. That might well be Pauli's old room. How she would like to have a look.

She used the bathroom and, before the trip back, tiptoed to the closed door. Hand on the crystal knob, she turned, checked for any sound in the living room.

Gently she opened the door, peered in.

A guy's bedroom. In the darkness she could make out a 49ers poster, an SF Giants one, another poster of Monty Python. Just a regular guy. Who killed little boys and girls.

She blinked to focus, saw a green military-style footlocker at the foot of the single bed. Then reminded herself that the police would have been through any of Pauli's belongings with a fine-tooth comb after he'd been arrested.

But Pauli had told her he would give her evidence to move her investigation forward. Once he'd gotten a good report from his mother.

She leaned in, peering at the many sport photos on the walls. And noticed a preponderance of gymnasts, both male and female. But quite a few female. Younger females. Nadia Comăneci got a lot of wall space.

Too much wall space.

It sickened her, knowing what had transpired. Knowing what had taken place under her very own roof, with Pam.

She heard Mrs. O's wheelchair rolling into the hallway.

She quickly pulled the door shut on Pauli's room, turned around. Mrs. O was in the hallway in her wheelchair.

"Is everything all right, dear?" she said in a cool voice.

"Absolutely," Colleen said. "Just admiring your Japanese wood block." There was a print of an ocean scene in a frame on the wall.

"But you can't really see it in the dark, can you?"

"Oh, well enough," Colleen said. "And now, now I really must be on my way."

Mrs. O thanked her again for taking her to Midnight Mass, but her tone was aloof. Colleen hoped she hadn't blown her chance.

They wished each other a merry Christmas and Colleen chastised herself all the way home. She swung by Alice Owens' place in West Portal, saw no lights, no car in the driveway. Wondering where Ray had gotten to, she headed home.

*   *   *

Christmas Day she rose early, trying not to look at the dried-out tree, the gifts for Lambert and Pam that had brought so much joy in the purchasing and wrapping, but would never be unwrapped.

Enough.

She got out some folded-up grocery bags, collected the gifts together, put Pam's on her bed. You never knew. The ones for Lambert, the stuffed Paddington bear, all of the other goodies, she bagged up for Toys for Tots and Goodwill.

Then she took the tree down, scattering dry needles everywhere. She dragged the tree out on her deck, and down into her yard, next to the trash can. Then she went back upstairs, made fresh coffee, swept the living room floor. 1979 was almost over. But she wasn't.

CHAPTER FORTY-FIVE

"When are you going to finally close the IA investigation into Owens?"

Day after Christmas, Detective Fos Alvarez stood at the door to Ryan's office on the fifth floor of 850 Bryant. Ryan was about to take a bite out of a sandwich over a newspaper opened on his desk that was just as messy as he was, papers, coffee cups, you name it.

Ryan looked up mid-bite, his face heavy with jowls and irritation. He looked bleary. Christmas drinking, Fos bet. Fos knew what Ryan was thinking: the new kid, some lowly detective who didn't know his place, questioning Ryan's authority.

A splat of Russian dressing hit Herb Caen's column next to the Macy's post-Xmas ad.

Ryan set his sandwich down on the newspaper, on top of a model in her underwear.

"As soon as Sonoma County gets back to me. It is Christmas week."

Blame it on Sonoma County. "Owens was released some time ago."

Ryan wiped his hands on a paper napkin. Grimaced. "These things take time."

"Seems we could push," Fos said, an edge to his voice. He crossed his arms, leaned against the doorjamb, crossed his legs at the ankle too. He wasn't going anywhere.

"Why?" Ryan sat back in his chair. "Owens isn't coming back to work any time soon. A day or two isn't going to make any difference."

"He's not coming back to work because he's in the CCU up at Santa Rosa Kaiser," Fos said. "Because we let him sit in jail until he got beat to a pulp."

Ryan stared at Fos, his short arms on the arms of his roller chair. "So, to my point—a day or two isn't going to make any difference, is it?"

"Actually, it does, because with the IA investigation open, we can't look into who set Owens up."

Ryan narrowed his eyes. "And no one assigned you to do that."

"*Yet.* But I talked to Grimes"—the deputy chief—"and he said before we do can anything, your IA investigation has to be put to bed. That's how he put it: 'put to bed.' Owens is already in bed—a hospital bed."

"You talked to Grimes? Just like that? Did you talk to your lead?"

"Owens was my partner," Fos said, then corrected himself. "*Is.*"

"When you've been here close to thirty years, like I have, Fos, *then* you can weigh in on what should and shouldn't be done. And when."

"The charges against Owens might have been dropped," Fos said, "but no thanks to us. And now he might not make it, and we're still doing Jack about it." Everyone knew there was no love lost between Owens and Ryan, who'd had it in for Owens for years.

Ryan glowered at him, and Fos knew he had made an enemy. Fine. "And what exactly do you think your 'looking into Owens' is going to do, Fos? How are you even going to start? You're new here. Barely have your feet under the desk."

"I checked out St. Francis Memorial. Owens took the initial statement from the guard the night before he went up to Calistoga with his ex. Turns out the guard wasn't giving Owens the whole story. He's been taking kickbacks from the hookers who use the

parking lot, didn't want to implicate himself any more than he had
to. Anyway, a guy named Ray Quick sped out after the murder of
Arnold Blane—the male prostitute in drag."

There was a pause while a phone rang down the hall and Ryan
eyed Fos. "Who the hell is Ray Quick?"

"Alice Owens' ex-boyfriend. Kind of strange. Now he's looking
like a fit for Night Candy."

"How did you stumble onto that?"

"I got a tip," Fos said.

"You got a tip. A tip from *who*?"

Fos knew how Ryan felt about Colleen Hayes.

"Just a tip," he said. "Turns out it was on the money."

"So, Fos, tell me, were you assigned Night Candy? I thought the
case was given to Meyerson when Owens was arrested. And you
were put on a different one."

An old woman found strangled in her Tenderloin hotel, ten years
ago. Social Security check day. Cold. Frozen. For over for a decade.
Until Fos was sidelined on it.

"I worked the Ray Quick tip in my own time," he said.

Ryan shook his head. "Not the way it works, Fos. Not your case.
Until Owens is reinstated—*if* he's reinstated—you work cases assigned to you."

If Owens doesn't die. Has to take disability. Early retirement.

"What exactly have you got against Owens?" Fos said. "That Jasia
Salak case?" That's what he'd heard.

Ryan pursed his lips, regarded Fos with narrowed eyes. "The best
advice I can offer you, Fos, is to stay focused on the cases assigned to
you. You don't want to get yourself into trouble. Everyone wants to
see Owens resolved. But there's a procedure. Don't cowboy things.
Stay on track, and you've got a future." He raised his bushy eyebrows
to make sure Fos got the message. Then he picked up his sandwich,

took a big bite, a piece showing as he chewed. He spoke with his mouth full. "Shut the door on your way out."

Fos suppressed a snort. He left the door open.

Fos picked up Angie that night, took her to dinner at the Gold Mirror. Waiters with vests, old-school Italian. Things were still a little cool from their tiff at Bajones, despite Christmas. Which he deserved. His old man hadn't done him any favors in how he treated his mama, and Fos realized that now. This wasn't Mexico, 1950. But at least Angie hadn't told him to go take a flying jump.

He dropped her off after dinner at her parents' house in the Mission. They had relatives visiting. His 240Z rumbled, Anita Ward singing about getting her bell rung.

"Thanks for dinner," Angie said in Spanish.

"The pleasure was all mine," he replied in kind.

"You were kind of quiet, Foster," she said. "Everything OK?"

He put on a winning smile, the best he could muster up, Owens bugging the hell out of him. "It is now," he said.

She leaned in, smoochy. "You sure about that, home boy?" She looked great, smelled great. She was great. He took all of her presence in.

"Sure, I'm sure," he said.

"I thought you might try to get me back to your place after dinner," she said.

"I know you have family obligations Christmas week. And how you might need the night off," he said. "I was a little hotheaded the other night."

"You do have a temper," she said. "But hey, check out the sensitivity on Foster tonight."

"It's getting late," he said, pushing a smile. "I don't want your folks to worry."

She laughed, then got serious. "Nothing to do with work? You can always tell me, you know. You can tell me anything."

"Work is work," he said, gripping the steering wheel. "I just got to take it in stride. Yeah, it's good. And I'm just glad to see you, Angie. After Bajones."

"Me too," she said. She moved in and gave him a long kiss that made his blood simmer.

She sat back, glowing. "Don't work too hard, Foster. I got some plans for you tomorrow night."

"I'll call you tomorrow," he said. "Best to your folks."

She gave him a wink, got out, sashayed off. He watched her climb the steps to the house, plants in flower beds on the porch railings, where she turned, a little wave before she got her key out, let herself in.

He was going to put a ring on her finger. One day soon. Before she wised up.

Fos headed for home, Bernal Heights. Trying to think how lucky he was having Angie in his life.

But he just couldn't get Ray Quick out of his mind. Quick had pretty much been there the whole time, all through dinner, ever since Colleen had lit a fire really.

He found himself driving up over O'Shaughnessy, the Z's pipes throaty through Glen Park Canyon, past Twin Peaks, heading out to the avenues.

Then he was parked across the street from The Claddagh pub. The cars along Clement were beaded with shiny droplets almost crystalline in the cold, reflecting the amber streetlights. He spotted a dark Buick Riviera with chrome spoked wheels. Ray Quick's ride.

Fos got out of the 240Z, went into The Claddagh. A band were playing Celtic music on a little stage. Day after Christmas, still a crowd. Irish and their booze.

A middle-aged redhead stood behind the bar, well preserved, hair up helmet style, cigarette in the corner of her mouth.

Fos saw who he was looking for behind the other end of the bar: big white dude, creampuff muscles in a tight black T, hair sprayed like he was about to go on a model shoot. Had to be Ray Quick. Fos was the only non-white. The only dude wearing a tie, not to mention a suit. Everyone else was dressed like they were going to do yard work.

Ray had to wait his turn, people buying that black beer.

Guy who looked like Ray finally came up, didn't even talk to him. Just flicked his chin, what do *you* want?

"You're Ray," Fos said. No need to whip the badge out. Keep it low-key, since he was working on his own time, on a case that wasn't his. And Ryan was going to be watching.

The man squinted. "Who wants to know?"

"Now is that any way to talk to a customer?"

"Is that what you are?" Put his hands on the bar. "Because you haven't ordered anything yet."

"OK," Fos said. "Coke. In a bottle or a can. Not that watery stuff out of the fountain."

Ray smirked while he sprayed a glass of soda from the fountain with force, let it splash over the sides of the glass, overfilling it. More splash. "Dollar."

Fos nodded, got a buck out, crumpled it, tossed it on the bar. It rolled into the pool the drink was sitting in.

"I'm not picking that up," Ray said.

Fos got the Xerox copy of the photo of Traci out of his pocket, the one Colleen had given him. He held it up.

"You picked her up, though, right, Ray? The blonde?"

Ray did a double take before he resumed his composure, along with a smirk. "She looks kinda rough. Who is she? Your sister? No, she couldn't be, could she?"

"Oh, I get it," Fos said, nodding, putting the copy away. "She couldn't be my sister—because I'm brown. And she's white. Hey, that's funny. You're a funny guy, Ray."

"I'm glad I could bring a smile to your face. Now, run along."

Fos squinted at him. "Where is she? What did you do with her?"

Ray leaned in, dropped his voice. "Do with *who*? Your sister? I did her every which way, man, along with your mother."

"You got a thing for my mother, Ray? Sorry, but you're not really her type."

"Get the fuck out of here."

The middle-aged woman with too much lipstick came over, a look of concern on her face.

"What's the problem, Ray?"

"This guy is just about to leave." Fos went to the end of the bar, lifted the flip-up countertop, headed back to the rear of the bar. Ray saw he was going to take off.

She looked at Fos straight on. "Can I help you?" she said in a snippy voice.

"Where's he going?" Fos said.

"You know what?" the woman said to Fos. "Maybe you *should* leave." But she was rattled, Fos could see that. Saw she had some kind of thing with Ray, and there was stuff about him she might not know about. And it was bugging her.

Fos had to catch Ray before he pulled a runner. He left the bar, headed quickly to the narrow alley. The band started up again, an old Irish song of some sort.

* * *

Jesus, Ray said to himself as he pulled on his leather jacket back by the washroom, exited The Claddagh from the rear. Out behind the bar, the dark cement yard was surrounded by a high fence, crates of empty bottles, a broken jukebox, a pile of construction rubble covered by a tarp.

Half the pub was singing "Black Velvet Band" along with the band.

"Going somewhere?"

He jumped when he saw the tall Mexican standing there in the shadows in front of the trash can. Hands on his hips. Casual. *Damn.*

Some friend of the woman Traci or whatever her name was. Long gone. Her pimp?

Ray reached into his jacket pockets with both hands, casual, gripped his Stanley knife with his right. Pushed the short blade out with his thumb in his pocket. Ready.

"Oh, it's you," Ray said. "How you doing, amigo?"

"I wasn't done talking to you—*amigo.* Traci—the girl you picked up, Bush and Leavenworth. Ring a bell? And that tranny at St. Francis Memorial. And get your hands out of your damn pockets." He reached inside his jacket. Going for a gun?

"Wanna talk about this?"

Ray whipped the knife out, slashed him across the neck in a quick swipe he was pleased with. Blood spurting before he even got the knife back for another swing.

"Well, go ahead, Speedy Gonzales—talk! The floor is all yours."

The guy stumbled back, choking, and grabbed his neck while he tried to reach inside his jacket. But Ray had one mother of a head start. Nothing like a sucker punch to put you on top of the fray. Ray came in again with the knife, but the guy had a gun out now, a snub-nose revolver, which he pointed at Ray while the shine of blood ran through the fingers he pressed on his neck. Blood running down his collar. Ray danced around in the narrow space, whipping the Stanley knife around Kung Fu style. Moments like this made it worthwhile. The Mexican guy squeezed off a shot, gritting his teeth, consumed by his wound. The crack of the gun was lost in the music in the bar. The bullet went wild. Staggering, the guy tried to raise the gun on him again, but it was sloppy.

Ray had done a good job on him. A good job. "Black Velvet Band" was hitting a crescendo in the bar, loud and heartfelt voices singing along.

Ray lunged in, split the guy's left cheek open with the Stanley knife. His face became a river.

The guy grunted, eyes bleary, the gun wobbling. Ray kept at him with the knife, didn't let up until the man was on the ground, still, and all he could hear was "Black Velvet Band" in the bar, coming to an end, voices wailing. Fools.

But helpful fools. Noise cover.

The man lay still.

Ray retracted the knife, put it away, reached down, grabbed the guy by his lapels, dragged him back by the broken jukebox. Puffing.

He went through the guy's pockets.

Found an ID in a leather wallet. What?

Pulled it out, opened it.

SFPD. Homicide.

A cop after all. Ray's head went sideways for a moment, before he gathered his wits. He was definitely earning his 250K.

What to do?

Move him somewhere.

Here we go again.

He pulled an old tarp off the pile of construction trash.

With any luck he'd have that insurance money soon. Then he'd have to scoot. Mexico, where this cop probably came from. Life was a circle.

CHAPTER FORTY-SIX

Next afternoon Colleen tried to call Fos again at 850 Bryant.

Nothing. She left another message. She thought Fos was on board helping her nail Ray Quick. He had seemed committed. Was he busy on a case?

She called Santa Rosa Kaiser, checked in on Owens. She'd been calling every day. He was still in the CCU. Still in and out of consciousness.

"Can he have a visitor?"

"I've told you," the nurse said. "Immediate family only."

"That would be me, near enough." Colleen said that Owens had no immediate family, and she was his closest friend.

The nurse checked, came back.

"OK. A brief visit."

She thanked her, wondered where Ray was hiding. Where Fos was hiding.

It would take an hour and a half to get up to Santa Rosa. She put her paid work to one side, used the restroom, startled herself again when she saw the blonde staring at her from the mirror, went out, tanked up the Torino one more time, headed up to see Owens.

She didn't want to call it a wasted trip, but Owens wasn't even conscious when she arrived. A man on tubes propped up in a bed in a darkened room with machines making noises in his place. The dim light hid his bruises, of which there were many more of now. A leg was in traction, along with an arm in a cast.

Her head sunk and she caught herself. At least he was alive. The last person she had known to wind up in a situation like this hadn't been so fortunate.

She pushed that thought to one side.

She left a bag of a black licorice from See's Candy on Owens' nightstand.

"He won't be able to have those for some time," the nurse said.

"But he'll know who they're from," Colleen said. Apart from wanting to see him, she had questions about Night Candy. "I'll check in tomorrow."

"Call first."

She squeezed Owens' hand. Cold but a hint of warmth. "Hang in there," she whispered.

As she was coming home late that night through the back door on her third-floor deck, she heard the phone ring. She set her shoulder bag on the kitchen counter, rushed to grab the phone off the wall. Always hoping it might be Pam.

"Would you accept a collect call from Paul Oedekoven?" the operator said.

But, if not Pam, he would do.

"Of course," Colleen said.

The operator put Pauli through.

"I caught you at home," he said.

"Yes," she said, pulling off her blonde wig, rubbing her bristly head. She couldn't wait for her hair to grow out. If Matt came back from Langley any time soon, he was going to get a shock and a half.

She waited. The man had the personality of a child, with his games.

"Well?" she said. "Here I am."

"Mother enjoyed Christmas Eve," Pauli said.

Colleen experienced the equivalence of relief. "That's nice," she said. She didn't want to go overboard and say she had enjoyed herself, because she didn't want to lie.

"I thought I might call her and check up on her," she said to Pauli.

"You have my permission," he said.

"You said you'd have something for me," Colleen said, tacitly reminding him of their agreement to divulge Night Candy's identity once she had taken Mrs. O to Midnight Mass. He said he would provide her with even more.

"All in good time," he said, hanging up.

God damn it! His passive-aggressive behavior, hanging onto what little leverage he had. But then she reminded herself that prison calls were monitored. He had a reason for secrecy although he was basking in his role. She wondered what the evidence was. She didn't think Mrs. O would have any idea.

Next morning, she called Mrs. O.

"It's almost 1980," Colleen said. "Are you ready for a new decade?"

"Do we have any choice, dear?" Mrs. O said.

"It's such a nice day," Colleen said. "I thought we might get some fresh air."

"What time should I expect you?" Mrs. O said. Colleen's visit sounded nothing like two friends, more an expectation of a bitter old woman who needed to negotiate social interactions.

Colleen arranged to pick her up.

They passed the morning with a walk—Colleen pushing Mrs. O in her wheelchair along the bumpy path to Baker Beach past the ruins of the old Sutro Baths, with views of the Marin Headlands and the Golden Gate Bridge.

Back at Mrs. O's apartment building in the avenues, Colleen helped the woman into the first-floor apartment. They finished the morning with lemon tea. Colleen kept surreptitiously checking her watch. Waiting for some mention of a package from Pauli, a gift, something.

She had dawdled for as long as she could. If she drank any more tea, she'd float away. Mrs. O was stifling yawns, and they were infectious.

"I don't want to keep you," Colleen said, standing.

"Oh," Mrs. O said. "Pauli said perhaps you could take him a package from me."

News to Colleen. But she'd play along.

"I'd be more than happy to," she said. There were rules about taking items to prisoners. But Mrs. O might not know that. "But I'm curious. Why can't you take it yourself?"

Mrs. O looked at Colleen as if she'd lost her mind. "I never go *there*, dear," she said in a haughty voice.

Mrs. O had never visited her son in prison. She wouldn't be caught dead in such a shameful place. Which meant she hadn't seen him in years and would never see him again.

"It arrived some time ago," Mrs. O said. "He said he would like you to bring it. It's in the hallway, by the phone."

Colleen went into the hallway where the phone was nestled in an old phone alcove. Letters and bills were leaning on one side next to a small brown package.

She picked it up.

A small parcel, wrapped in brown paper. Addressed to Mr. P. Oedekoven. From a PO box with a San Francisco zip code. The mailing date was in September. Months ago.

"This must be it," she shouted. "By the phone?" Mrs. O was still in the living room. "Addressed to Pauli?"

"That's it, dear. If it's not too much trouble."

"None at all," Colleen said, hefting the lightweight box. "None at all."

CHAPTER FORTY-SEVEN

The moment Colleen got into her car she was tempted to rip open the package addressed to Paul Oedekoven then and there. But she resisted that impulse. Whatever was inside might well contain fingerprints.

She drove down to her office on Pier 26.

At her desk she donned gloves, unwrapped the package, cut the tape sealing the box inside with her open scissors. Opened the box.

Wrapped in a partial sheet of wrinkled newspaper she found a baggie.

Which contained a hypodermic needle and a lock of blonde hair.

A chill ran through her, one that manifested itself in a cold sweat.

Night Candy had murdered some of his victims by lethal injection. And the lock of hair had to be a trophy.

She set the baggie down without opening it.

Paul Oedekoven had delivered on his promise. But no name. More games.

She went through her Rolodex, found Alistair Laurie's number at SF Morgue.

* * *

Alistair was halfway through a pint of bitter in the Edinburgh Castle, the bar filling up with a spirited after-work crowd. The jukebox was playing "Sultans of Swing."

Colleen went up to Alistair, still in his black ME uniform. She was wearing her jeans and black leather car coat over a blue turtleneck. It went well with the wig.

"Hey, blondie," Alistair said, giving her a look of surprise. "Whatever did you do with Colleen?"

"Long story."

"What are you drinking?"

"Nothing right now," she said. "I was hoping you could take a look at something."

Alistair sipped his pint. "Ready when you are."

"Not here," she said.

"Ah." Alistair drained his beer in one long draught, set the empty glass down on a coaster. He pushed his change toward the bar well. "Lead on, Macduff."

Then they were sitting in her Torino, parked on Geary half a block down from the bar, Colleen behind the wheel, Alistair in the passenger seat, examining the contents of the baggie through the unopened plastic under the car dome light. The sun had gone down.

"Is this what I think it is?" he asked.

"You got it."

"Bloody hell." He turned in his seat, looked at her. "Where on earth did you get it, Colleen?"

"Best if I don't say, right now, but the source is about as genuine as can be."

"I need to know."

"Fair enough." She told him about Paul Oedekoven.

"That explains the wig." He reached into his pocket, extracted a folding pocket magnifying glass in a square case, pulled out the lens, zeroed in on the syringe.

"There appears to be some sort of residue in the tip of this syringe," he said.

"Too much to hope for?"

He switched to the lock of hair. "If this isn't bloody creepy."

"Tell me about it," she said. "Do you have any way to see if it's genuine?"

"I can try. Night Candy has four victims."

"Number four is still being investigated." The transvestite hooker at St. Francis Memorial.

"I'll start with the first three." He held up the baggie. "I'll need to hang onto this," he said.

Colleen nodded. "I'm hoping this is between you and me."

"For now," Alistair said.

"I appreciate it," Colleen said. "Now, how about that next drink?"

"If you insist," Alistair said.

*   *   *

Before she went home that night, Colleen swung by her office on Pier 26, parked out front on Embarcadero. The chain was up over the entrance, blocking the way, and she wasn't going to be that long anyway. The last of December blew with a vengeance through the covered pier as she walked the thick planks back to Hayes Confidential.

She called Fos to tell him what she'd found. Still no answer.

What had happened to him?

It would take a while before Alistair could analyze the evidence and get back to Colleen.

In the meantime, she was stuck on Night Candy's identity. Paul O was being coy, and she wasn't sure she'd get a truthful answer if he told her anything anyway.

Good due diligence meant using multiple sources.

She slipped a sheet of 24-pound bond with its Hayes Confidential letterhead into her Selectric, typed up a letter to the post office, inquiring about the PO Box on Paul O's package. People thought post office boxes were anonymous, but anyone wanting to do business with one was entitled to inquire about the box holder's name and address. A written request worked best, even if it took longer.

When she finished, she stuck a fifteen-cent stamp on the envelope.

She mailed it on the way home in front of the liquor store, where she picked up a bottle of Chardonnay and a pack of Virginia Slims. Her emergency pack had been sitting in her junk drawer for months and the cigs tasted like burning sticks.

*　*　*

At home she kicked off her shoes, poured a glass of wine. Late. She dimmed the lights, sat back on the sleek leather sofa with the chrome arms, lit up an illicit smoke, put her feet on the glass coffee table, pulled off her wig, tossed it on the sofa, scratched her head, twiddled her toes in her socks, tried to blow a smoke ring while she swirled Chardonnay.

A long day.

But to her credit she hadn't gone into Pam's room tonight. She'd call that progress. She'd put 1979 behind her. And say it never happened.

She still hadn't heard from Matt.

She needed to check in on Owens.

The only good thing about being in emergency care was that one could call at any hour. Colleen called Santa Rosa Kaiser. Owens was still in the CCU, still unconscious. Touch and go. She hung up with sadness.

Owens *had* to pull through.

The doorbell rang.

She was up by the front window, looking down at Vermont from behind the curtain she held an inch or so away from the glass.

An SFPD black-and-white sat in the middle of the street.

Good news didn't come at this hour.

Cigarette in hand, she padded to the intercom.

"It's almost midnight," she said.

"SFPD, ma'am. Inspector Stoll has a few questions for you. If you'd come down to the station. We can take you. And bring you back."

Inspector Stoll was Ryan's toadie.

"It's the bring-me-back part I question," she said. "What is this about anyway?" Something to do with Owens? Traci? Fos?

"Inspector Stoll can fill you in, ma'am."

"I bet. Am I under arrest?"

"No, ma'am. Just a few questions."

"Then it can wait until tomorrow."

"This is an emergency."

"Now it's an emergency. How much of one? On a scale from one to ten?"

"It's in regard to a homicide," the officer said.

Just a few questions. In regard to a homicide. At close to midnight. With Inspector Stoll, who loved her not, in the mix. Whenever the police had just a few questions on something like a homicide at an hour like this, they might not have an arrest in mind, but they had suspicions and were looking to confirm them. An arrest was always hovering. And for an ex-felon, even more so. She'd fallen prey to Ryan and Stoll's "questions" last year and ended up walking home at 3:00 a.m. from the farmers market. She was lucky to have gotten away.

But there was always the possibility there might be something in it for her, too, something she could use. And a homicide? They had her attention. It didn't work to avoid the cops for too long anyway. They always got their way in the end.

"850 Bryant?" she said.

"Yes."

"Wait just a minute."

She left the intercom, went into the kitchen, called Gus Pedersen on the wall phone. Pink Floyd's "The Wall" was in the background at low volume up at Stinson Beach.

"Do you ever listen to show tunes?" she asked.

"Can't say that I ever have," Gus said in a smoky voice.

She explained the situation.

"With your history," Gus said, "complying with the police is wise. And who knows what they might have? I suggest you go. With your lawyer present, of course."

"When can you make it down to 850?" she asked.

"An hour."

"See you there. Thanks."

Back at the intercom she resumed her conversation with the police officer.

"Tell Inspector Stoll I'll come down for a *voluntary* interview in one hour. With my lawyer present."

CHAPTER FORTY-EIGHT

"So," Colleen said, "why are we here in the middle of the night?"

Two a.m., she was sitting in a familiar interview room on the fifth floor at 850 Bryant, the Hall of Justice. The overhead fluorescents hummed with no office noise to compete for their attention.

Sitting next to her was Gus Pedersen, uncharacteristically not wearing his signature cowboy hat, no doubt due to the late—or early—hour. He did have his tinted aviator shades on, and his long hair was pulled back in a thick ponytail over his fringed suede jacket.

Across from her sat Inspector Stoll, a small, furtive man in a too-big shirt and a tie with a huge knot, his round glasses amplifying a look of wariness. His thinning hair was pasted over his narrow skull.

What made this interview noteworthy—apart from the hour—was the presence of Inspector Ryan, rumpled and terse, in a suit just as ill-fitting as his apparent mood. His five o'clock shadow was well past midnight.

If he was here, something was going on. Something serious.

So much so that no one, except Gus, seemed to notice Colleen's blonde wig, which helped keep her warm in the unheated building, along with her jeans and heavy V-neck cable stitch sweater she wore over a turtleneck under her leather coat.

She had been in this room many times, mostly being interviewed by Owens, once an adversary, now friend and ally, and someone she was more than worried about. How things changed.

Stoll spoke: "What kind of dealings have you had with Detective Alvarez?"

Fos. She hadn't heard from him since their meeting at Bajones almost a week ago. She'd given him a picture of Traci. Christmas had happened in that time, too, but she'd wondered if he'd gotten cold feet. Now she didn't know what to think. Had he run afoul of the IA investigation Ryan was heading up?

"Why?" she said.

"Just answer the question," Ryan said in a gruff voice, coarse hands clasped together on the Formica table. It had coffee stains, chips, ink marks, years' worth of stories to tell.

Gus broke in. "Let me remind you that my client is here on her own volition, purely as a courtesy. Not as part of any interrogation."

Ryan shot Gus a hot look.

"Detective Alvarez is dead," he said.

A bolt hit Colleen. She wasn't sure she'd heard correctly. But that would explain why she hadn't been able to get hold of Fos.

"Dead?" she said. "As in . . ."

"Stabbed to death," Stoll said. "He was found by Sutro Baths."

Sutro Baths was once a large public saltwater swimming pool complex by Ocean Beach. Built in the late nineteenth century, the grand baths were a major attraction in their time. Now they were ruins, a shell of their former grandeur.

"When?" Colleen asked.

"He was found yesterday. The autopsy will tell us how long he's been dead. But his fiancée saw him last two nights ago."

A few days after Colleen last saw Fos at Bajones.

"I met him twice," she said. "Once about two weeks ago on the steps of 850 Bryant. And again about a week ago."

Both Ryan and Stoll we're watching her.

"And how did that come about?" Stoll said, his voice loaded with suspicion. "With the IA investigation, Detective Alvarez shouldn't have met with you, seeing as you're an acquaintance of Owens." The word "acquaintance" had a derogatory ring to it.

"I was looking into who set Owens up for murder."

"How well did you know Detective Alvarez?"

"Like I said, I met him just those two times."

"You sure about that?" Ryan said.

Gus spoke: "She just said so."

"Was Detective Alvarez a homosexual?" Ryan asked Colleen.

Colleen screwed her face up in dismay. "How in the world would I know that? And why would I care?"

"Seems there are a few things you're not telling us."

"I'm not going to keep telling you," Gus said. "My client is here as a courtesy."

"I have no idea," Colleen said. "But it seems your thinking is that Fos wandered down to Sutro Baths to make some sort of anony-mous acquaintance?" Sutro Baths had that reputation.

"We're not ruling it out."

Have at it, she thought. She was going to help them about as much as they'd helped Owens. She'd get to the bottom of things herself.

"I guess anything is possible," she said.

Stoll squinted. "So, you don't know anything?"

She shook her head. "I wish I did. Got any leads?"

"Cut the shit!" Ryan pounded the table. "Stop holding out on us. You and Fos had something going on—about Owens. We're going to find out, one way or another."

"This interview is over," Gus said, standing up.

Colleen did the same. She was still numbed by the news.

"We're not done here," Ryan said between his teeth.

"Well, we are," Gus said, taking Colleen's arm.

* * *

Outside, on the steps to 850, Colleen and Gus hunkered down, shoulders up, hands in pockets, muscles tightened by the early morning December cold.

Colleen thanked Gus for making the trip in the middle of the night.

He looked down at her with a wry frown. "Feel like telling *me* what you know about Detective Alvarez, Colleen?"

She dug out a cigarette to steady her nerves. Lit it up. It still didn't seem real: Fos gone. She had pushed Mrs. O in her wheelchair past Sutro Baths just yesterday, where Fos might have been lying dead at the time. A young guy with his whole life ahead of him. Cops seemed as if they should be exempt from the kind of mayhem they pursued. But there was Owens, barely hanging on. And Fos, who wasn't. No one was immune.

"First time I met Fos was before Owens was released, and he pretty much told me to go take a flying leap." She dragged on her cig, blew crystalline smoke into the night air. "After Owens was jumped in Santa Rita, sent to the CCU, Fos changed his tune. We met at Bajones. I told him about Traci, the hooker who disappeared from the Tenderloin, an awful lot like the stand-in for Alice in the morgue up at Santa Rosa." She took another drag. "Fos didn't buy my theory that Ray might have killed Traci to set Owens up, and then we lost contact." Another drag. "He wanted to set things right for Owens. It seemed on the level. But when I didn't hear from him, I thought he might have had second thoughts."

"Any idea who might have killed him?"

"Same as before." She smoked.

"Ray Quick."

"I don't have any proof. But if it's Ray, I'll find out."

"Why didn't you share any of that with Ryan and Stoll?"

She took another puff, blew it out. "Because Ryan has it in for Owens. Hasn't done one thing to help him out. Just the opposite. I don't trust him to do anything on Owens' behalf. Or Fos', if Owens is involved."

"If they find out, it's going to look fishy."

"I know. But Ryan wants Owens so bad he can taste it. If I gave him anything, he'll screw it up, accidentally on purpose."

Gus took in a deep breath, let it out. "You know my feelings about you continuing to do this on the sly."

"I do believe you've made your position clear."

"You need to hand over what you know to Ryan and Stoll."

"When I've nailed this last piece: who killed Fos. I'm responsible. I laid a guilt trip on him so he'd help me. Now he's dead."

"If Ryan catches you withholding evidence on a murder, with everything else you've been doing, you could be in some serious trouble, Colleen."

"That's why I have a good lawyer." She smoked, let it drift out of a tight smile.

He shook his head. "It's time to put my foot down," he said.

"And do what? You can't tell anybody, dude. Not without my OK. Attorney-client privilege, right? You think I'm not listening?"

Now it was his turn to smile, but it wasn't a warm one. "It's time to bring this to a close, Colleen."

"Not just yet, Gus," she said. She flicked her cigarette into the street where it spit embers against the glistening asphalt. "Not just yet."

CHAPTER FORTY-NINE

Four a.m. She couldn't sleep. Not after Fos. Colleen grabbed a hot-hot shower, made coffee in the French press, extra scoops to get her heart started. Drank it black while she dressed warm, called Santa Rosa Kaiser.

"Mr. Owens is speaking a few words," the nurse said. "Not out of the woods by any stretch. But coherent."

If there was anything that could improve her outlook, that was it.

She donned her blonde wig and drove down to Pier 26 for a couple of hours before she set off for Santa Rosa.

* * *

When she got to Owens' room in Santa Rosa Kaiser, late morning, he was sleeping, mouth open, snoring at the ceiling. She went and got a cardboard cup of coffee out of the vending machine, killed more time, checking in on him periodically. The nurse told her she was probably wasting her time. It was hers to waste.

Around lunchtime Owens started to wake up, blinking in apparent wonderment at his leg in traction.

She stood at the foot of his bed.

"Welcome back, stranger."

He fought himself up on his pillow, looked up with a bruised, bleary face.

"Colleen?" he croaked, blinking in obvious confusion for a moment, looking at her wig.

"It's a long story," she said. She went over, stood by the bedside, poured him a glass of water from a plastic jug. Positioned the straw. Held it to his lips. He sipped as if in pain.

Frail wasn't the word. It was all she could do not to shake her head.

He caught her looking.

"You should see the other guy," he gasped, nodding for her to take the cup and straw away. "*Guys.*"

"Looks more like you were hit by a bus."

"That must have been it."

"Thank God you're still here," she whispered, taking his hand. Something she had never done before. "Small mercies."

He leaned back, closed his eyes. "I'll take all I can get."

"What happened?"

"I can't remember," he said, his eyes still shut. "I was in the shower—getting ready for you to bring me home. I didn't want to come out smelling like a bum. I got some flak from the other inmates in the shower, but it blew over. I thought I was golden. I went to the lockers to change. And that's the last I remember."

"Sounds like you were jumped in the locker room."

"Feels like it."

They stood there for a moment, saying nothing, doing nothing. She squeezed his hand. It wasn't romantic in any way, but it meant more to her than any other hand squeeze she could remember.

"What day is it?" he asked, opening his eyes.

She told him. "Two days before 1980."

"Wow," he said. "I've missed a few days. Quite a few. What's the latest?"

He was determined to be positive, and she appreciated that. It might make the next part easier. She hoped so.

She took a deep breath, looked him in the eye.

"Just tell me, Colleen."

"It's Fos," she said. "He's dead."

CHAPTER FIFTY

Propped up in his hospital bed, a look of dismay and shock traveled across Owens' discolored face.

"Any idea what Fos could have done?" Colleen asked, once the news had sunk in.

Owens took a deep breath, wincing at some unseen pain.

"What were you working on before your arrest?" she said.

"Night Candy number four," Owens said. "I interviewed the security guard at St. Francis Memorial. He found the body . . ." Owens stopped to catch his breath. "Scared off the alleged perp. Guy driving out of the lot."

Owens closed his eyes, settled back again.

She didn't like pressing him for answers, but he was awake. And she needed to know.

"Maybe that was why there was no fragrance," she said. Night Candy earned his moniker by using a cheap fragrance of the same name that he sprayed his victims with. "He didn't have time."

Eyes shut, Owens nodded, winced again. "Could be."

"Did you get any kind of description when you went out there?"

"A guy in an American sedan. The car was dark in color."

"Not much to go on."

"It was late, and the perp took off in a hurry. But I did wonder if the guard was giving me the whole story."

"Why?"

Owens took a deep breath. "Vice had interviewed him a couple of years ago after a prostitute was beaten up by a john. There was a strong rumor he was taking kickbacks to let her use the parking lot."

"Did you write up a report?"

"I did."

"Did Fos have access to that?"

"He was my partner at the time, so yes. But the case would have been reassigned once I was arrested. And he would have been pulled off."

"But he'd still have it on his radar."

"If I know Fos, yes. He is—*was*, I should say—a good detective, but he tended to fly off the handle. But Ryan's IA investigation should have blocked him."

Maybe Fos looked into the guard before she met with Fos at Bajones. He'd said he had something to do beforehand. And, as Owens said, Fos was headstrong. She'd seen evidence of that herself.

It was about the only lead she had to go on.

"How would I get to Fos' files?" she said.

Owens opened an eye, smiled. "Without me? Good luck. Ask your beau."

She frowned. "Matt's in Langley. Three-week extensive interview and background check for the CIA."

There was a moment of silence. "I didn't know that."

"I didn't either," she said with a scoop to her voice. "He was keeping it under wraps until it happened."

Another moment of silence.

"You can do better," Owens said.

Owens and Matt were never friends.

"He was kind of growing on me," she said.

"He's a good cop," Owens said. "But you can do better."

"You know something I don't?"

"I know you're worth a lot more than you think."

"That's sweet," she said, patting his hand. "But you forgot to factor in the part about killing my husband."

"Details. She kills one husband, and no one ever lets her forget it."

"I know. You'd think it was a big deal or something."

"People are assholes."

She squeezed his hand one more time, let it go. "So, no way to find out what Fos might have written down?"

Owens took another deep breath. "I don't see how. I'm not sure he would have had that much time. If he did, it was probably off the record."

"Who was the security guard you talked to at St. Francis?"

Owens stared at her. "Forget it, Colleen."

"I'm just going to find out anyway."

Owens sighed. "Some guy on the midnight shift—Peña? Yeah, that was it: Peña."

A nurse came into the room with a tray of meds. Not just a pill in a cup. Several cups.

"Visiting time is over, hon," she said to Colleen. "I've let you slide longer than I should. This guy needs his rest."

Colleen thanked her, stood aside.

The nurse went to Owens, set the tray on the nightstand. She started racking the back of his bed up, much to his displeasure.

"If I don't see you," Colleen said to Owens. "Happy New Year."

"I know you want to chase down what happened to Fos," Owens said with a gasp. "But I'm going to ask you—respectfully—to let sleeping dogs lie. Hopefully, I'm going to get out of here one of these days and I can take it from there. I plan to."

Maybe, she thought. But he might take it the wrong way. Owens didn't need to be hunting down Ray Quick.

"I'll take your request into consideration," she said.

Owens shook his head, winced again. "Sure you will."

CHAPTER FIFTY-ONE

Late that evening Colleen entered Bajones, dressed up one more time, flared black pants over black platform shoes. Soft tangerine cashmere sweater under her black leather coat. Saturday night, the place was full, people dancing to a four-piece playing an edgy pop-reggae number, full of jangly reverb. The lights were soft blues and oranges.

She saw what she was looking for sitting in a plush booth by the bandstand: several young women who'd been keeping Angie company the other night when Angie and Fos had had their blowout. Colleen went over, earning a ration of dirty looks.

"I'm an acquaintance of Fos Alvarez," she said.

"Yeah, we know who you are," a woman with jet black hair sheened and straightened said. She wore a dark big-print floral blouse with puffy shoulders that were in fashion. "And it's a little more than 'acquaintance.'"

Colleen shook her head. "I'm a private investigator. Fos and I were working a case, trying to set things right for his partner. I'm so sorry for your loss," she said. "I feel responsible."

She let that sink in, stood there while the band took a trippy guitar break that seemed to make things float away. If only.

"What do you want?" the woman with the hair said.

"Angie to start with. Or anyone who saw Fos before he was killed. I've pieced some of it together, but not everything. I'm going to get the guy who did this."

The woman looked at Colleen, blinking heavily mascaraed eyes. "Let me call Angie, see how she feels about talking to you."

Colleen thanked her.

The woman got up. "You may as well sit down."

"I'll stand, thanks. I can't stay."

The woman headed off to the pay phone in a hall by the restroom. Made a call with a finger in one ear to block the music.

Came back. Got a ballpoint pen out of her purse and wrote a number on a Bajones matchbook. Handed it to Colleen.

Colleen thanked her, left the club. She'd find a pay phone where noise wasn't an issue.

The liquor store one block away had a pay phone outside. Colleen inserted a dime and called Angie's house, shivering in the biting wind.

Angie answered.

"I'm sorry to be calling so late." Colleen expressed her sympathies, explained her situation.

"Are you saying this thing you and Foster were working on is the reason he's dead?" Angie said harshly.

Colleen sucked in cold air. "I think so, yes."

There was a pause while a car on Mission blasted its horn.

"And what do you plan to do now?" Angie said.

"Find the person that killed him," Colleen said.

"SFPD has already talked to me."

"They don't know everything I know. And I don't think they'll be able to get the guy. I can."

"So, what do you want from me?"

"I'm putting together Fos' last hours. Trying to find where he went. Who he met. You saw him the night before he was found dead at Sutro Baths."

"Last I saw him was Wednesday. We went to dinner. He didn't call the next day like he said he would. We had a date set for that night. His work said he didn't go in either."

So that was the night Fos disappeared.

"Do you have a key to his place?" Colleen asked.

"Why?"

"I'm wondering if he might have left some notes on the case we were working on."

"Wouldn't those notes be with SFPD? Down at 850 Bryant?"

"Not necessarily," Colleen said. "There might not have been time, and what we were doing was under the radar, if you know what I mean."

"So, now you're telling me Fos got killed because you had him working on something he shouldn't have been working on?"

"Owens was his partner. Fos was doing what he thought he should in order to help him."

"Seems he should have been doing what his boss told him to do—not you."

"If I could go back in time and change things, believe me, I would. But I'm not sure it would make any difference."

Angie sighed, gave Colleen an address in Bernal Heights. "I'll meet you there. I'm going to be there while you look around. And you don't touch a thing without asking me first."

"I'm going to see that Fos gets his due," Colleen said.

CHAPTER FIFTY-TWO

They met in front of a small turn-of-the-century two-unit Victorian on Banks. The steep narrow street was packed with cars perched up on the sidewalk. Colleen had to park up on Cortland and walk down.

Angie was waiting out front in a dark coat with a high collar turned up against the cold and high heels even this late at night. Her hair was up and stylish. Colleen suspected she never left the house without being presentable, under any circumstances.

Colleen thanked her and they went into the upstairs flat, a comfortable, roomy place where guy stuff prevailed: sparse mismatched furniture, a Marantz stereo with huge speakers, bare walls save for a poster of Joe Montana mid-throw and an 8x10 of Fos and Angie in a silver frame on the mantelpiece, dressed to the nines and smiling in a fancy restaurant somewhere, next to another picture of Fos in uniform with his graduating class at SFPD.

"He always wanted to be a cop," Angie said softly.

"I can't imagine what you must be going through."

Colleen noticed the table in the small dining area was cluttered with files and books. *Rising Through the Ranks: Leadership Tools and Techniques for Law Enforcement* had been a recent perusal, judging by its prominent position on top of a file folder.

"He was moving up," Angie said with a sigh. "But he knew he had to work on his temper."

Colleen nodded in sympathy: if Fos hadn't been so headstrong.

"Cops live by their own rules," she said, moving the book to one side to examine the file folder underneath, with "NC" underlined in ballpoint on the front. Had to be Night Candy. Her sense of anticipation grew.

She looked at Angie questioningly before she opened it.

"Go ahead," Angie said.

Colleen did. Sheets of lined paper, with notes scribbled on Night Candy.

There was even a sheet on her: Colleen H, with her phone numbers. One note said: *agresiva.* Spanish for "pushy." Well, she could be. What of it?

Another said "Traci." A note had "Traci—Ray Q? NC?" Ray Q was circled. Fos was thinking Ray was a candidate for Night Candy.

His interview with Officer Peña at St. Francis Memorial Hospital came next, the evening he'd met with Colleen and had the fight with Angie at Bajones. She remembered Fos had said he had to do something before he met her that night. The doctors' parking lot was mentioned. Arnold Blane was the male prostitute who'd been murdered. Owens had done the initial interview, and Colleen recalled he'd said the guard seemed to be holding back on something.

"Not forthcoming" was written in English. "Lied to Owens."

Then a note on a new line, underlined, caught her eye.

"Dark Blue Buick Riviera."

A virtual gut punch hit Colleen.

Ray Quick's car.

If so, that was huge. It meant Ray was the guy who had taken off.

It meant Ray killed Arnold Blane, the transvestite sex worker.

Was *that* what Fos had discovered?

And then he was killed.

She kept going.

Two photos: one, a black-and-white photocopy she had given Fos at Bajones, of Traci, last New Year's Eve, with Rhonda and Fia. Almost a year to the day.

And another one, a composite mug shot, also black and white. A slender man in drag. In the left shot, full frame, he wore a short dark dress, white flats on his long, toned legs, long arms limp by his side. A smirk, no stranger to mug shots. You could see the defiance, even with the eye makeup. His blonde hair was teased up. It looked real. The next two shots were from the side and front. Same hairdo, same dress. Full lips, painted. Wearing a sign around his neck. ND 28206.

Arnold Blane.

She kept studying the photo.

Arnold Blane, as a woman, was tall, slender, blonde.

Just like Traci.

Just like Alice.

She went back to the notes on Arnold Blane. His body had been found on December 1. He'd been beaten to death the night before.

Colleen got out her notebook, flipped back pages.

Traci had disappeared that same night.

She looked up, blinking in realization.

Now it made sense.

CHAPTER FIFTY-THREE

"What kind of car did Fos drive?" Colleen asked Angie. She had almost said "does."

"240Z," Angie said. "Gold. He loved that car."

"Any chance you might know the plate?"

"That's an easy one," Angie said gloomily. "A-N-G-I-E."

Colleen felt terrible. "I'm so sorry, Angie. No sign of the Z anywhere that you know of?"

Angie shook her head. "It would be in the driveway with a car cover on it if he'd parked it here."

"Got it," Colleen said. "I think we're done here." She was holding the file folder. "I'd like to borrow this. I'll make copies, get it back to you."

Angie shook her head. "No, I don't think that's a good idea."

Colleen nodded. She'd pushed enough. She knew what she needed to know. Ray Quick had picked up Arnold Blane as a stand-in for Alice, then discovered she was a he, and that wouldn't work. So, he killed Arnold Blane, either out of anger, or simply because he was a cold-blooded killer and that's what came naturally. He must have picked up Traci shortly thereafter, another stand-in, and female, a better fit. Colleen set the file folder back on the table. "I just need to use the phone real quick, then we can leave."

She called City and County of San Francisco Impound, asked about a Datsun 240Z registered to Fos Alvarez, license plate ANGIE.

"It's here," the clerk said. "Tickets, towing charge, and impound fees brings your total to $184.50."

"Where was it towed from?"

"You don't remember?"

"It was a night to remember—or not remember—as the case may be. My memory is a little hazy."

"Just a minute," the clerk said. Then, "Twenty-fourth and Clement. Tell your friend he better pick it up first thing to avoid another day's impound fee."

Colleen thanked him, hung up.

Twenty-fourth and Clement.

Right by The Claddagh.

Fos had gone to see Ray the night he was murdered.

CHAPTER FIFTY-FOUR

Colleen caught security officer Peña about to do his patrol of the hospital perimeter on Pine Street. It was after midnight. The night air was sharp and cold and didn't feel like it was ever going to change.

Officer Peña was an older Hispanic guy, with a '50s hairdo Brylcreemed back in a slight ducktail, probably as much as he could get away with at a security guard job. He had a Detex clock—a big round clock on a black leather strap—over his shoulder. You inserted and twisted keys hanging on chains at various patrol points to mark the paper tape inside the clock to verify when you'd done your rounds.

Owens had said he thought Peña was holding back when he interviewed him after the dead transvestite was found. Fos' notes said the same.

And Peña didn't seem big on eye contact.

But, to his credit, he'd agreed to talk with Colleen. He lit up a Marlboro, tossed the spent paper match, which was caught by the wind and swept away.

"I take it you've heard the news," she said. "About Detective Alvarez?"

Peña took a drag, the cigarette between thumb and forefinger. Smoke was pulled from the side of his mouth down Pine. He nodded.

"You met with him right before he was killed," she said.

"Who told you that?" he said cautiously.

"You just did. But, if it makes you feel any better, he wrote up some notes about that meeting."

"Damn." He shrugged. "Yeah, last Wednesday. Start of shift."

"You discussed Arnold Blane, the sex worker you found beaten to death in the doctors' parking lot first of the month."

"If you think I had anything to do with the death of that detective, you've got rocks in your head. I've been working double shifts all week. *All week.* Go ahead and check." He took a defiant puff.

"I don't think anything of the kind. And I couldn't care less about your prior association with hookers who use the parking lot. I just need to know the details of what you and Detective Alvarez talked about."

Peña looked at her guardedly while he smoked. "You a friend of his?"

"I was just getting to know him. But I am close with his ex-partner, the man who interviewed you right after the sex worker was killed. Both Owens and Alvarez seemed to think you weren't telling the whole story. About what you saw the night you found the body."

Peña eyed her.

"Dark Blue Buick Riviera," he said. "Custom paint. Wire wheels. Big scratch down the rear passenger side. Big, good-looking guy driving. Sped out as I came into the lot. Is that what you wanted to know?"

Ray Quick. Confirmed. "That answers my question."

"If there's any way you can keep my name out of this," Peña said. "I've got a family, four kids. My mother lives with us. I'm not whining but I'm fifty-three, no high school diploma, and I don't need to be looking for a job with everybody else and his brother right now."

Inflation was over ten percent. The economy was hemorrhaging jobs.

"I've no reason to mention it," she said. "But the cops might come looking once they review the case. And there's nothing I can do about that. I just wanted to confirm the vehicle. And the perp. It helps me find who did it."

"I hope you do." Peña gave a sigh of regret, dropped his cigarette, stepped it out. "I should have just told that older cop what I knew in the first place."

"Better late than never," she said.

"I've got my rounds to do," Peña said, looking down, shifting the clock up on his shoulder.

He took off then, headed down Pine, head down, shoulders hunched. She almost felt sorry for him.

CHAPTER FIFTY-FIVE

The phone call came after Colleen got home, feet up on the glass coffee table, swirling a freshly poured glass of white wine. Lights low. No music. No TV. She didn't think she had turned the thing on since Pam left. Never cared for it. And silence, especially now, silence was better. Even without Pam.

Colleen set her glass down on a coaster, answered.

Alistair's Scottish accent was subdued.

"I've been trying to call you." She heard him drink. In the background muted bar chatter filled the gap.

"I've been here, there, and everywhere," she said. "You should have left a message on my work machine. I always check." And he hadn't left one.

"Kitty Bliss," he said. "Night Candy victim number three."

"You're sure about that?"

"There's a trace of blood on that syringe you gave me. Just enough. Type O negative. Not the rarest but only about six and a half percent of the population falls under O negative. With the sex female, half that."

Colleen didn't know sex could be ascertained from blood and hair samples. Forensic science was making leaps and bounds. "So, we're down to just over three percent of the population who could match that sample," Colleen said. "That's still a lot of women. Several million, no?"

"Right," Alistair said. "But add in the fact that Kitty Bliss had hepatitis—probably through drug use—also present. She used heroin. Plus, her racial group: Caucasian. Plus, two more protein matches that sync up with her postmortem. It's dead on, Colleen. The sample you gave me is *her*."

"So that needle belonged to Night Candy? To kill his victims?"

"I'd lay my paycheck on it."

That was darkly satisfying. "I'm just amazed what you guys can figure out."

"Electrophoresis," he said. "The latest technology. It's the bee's knees."

"But is it admissible?"

"In my book it is. But who knows what a jury will think. Or some sleazy lawyer in a three-hundred-dollar suit. I'm happy to be an expert witness. Provided it gets logged in as evidence."

"It's good enough for now," Colleen said. "I owe you a month's worth of pints."

"That might set you back a few bob."

"I'm not worried," she said. "Any fingerprints on the syringe?"

"None."

A swell of disappointment flowed through her.

"None? Are you sure?"

"Wiped clean," he said. "No prints."

Damn. It couldn't be pinned to anyone easily. Not until she went up to Sacramento, combed the databases for prisoners killed around the time Paul Oedekoven said Night Candy died. She could ask him, but she was weary of his games. And he probably wouldn't tell her the truth anyway. He wanted her to sweat for it.

"I'll need to open a file on this, Colleen."

"Can't you keep it under wraps for a day or two?" she said. "I didn't exactly come by it through regular channels, and I need to collect some more info."

There was a long pause. "Why not make it official?"

"Because Owens has enemies in high places. One in particular."

"Is it who I think it is?"

Ryan. "And I'm worried he'll intervene. He's done nothing to help so far. Only hinder. He'll sideline it like everything else." She also didn't want to see a botched investigation that would alert Ray Quick, make him take off.

"I'll give it one more day. But that's it. So, take care of whatever you need to take care of."

Someone had to pay for the crimes committed.

Traci. Fos. Arnold Blane. All the others.

She would have to make it so.

"Call you tomorrow," she said.

CHAPTER FIFTY-SIX

An early start and another tankful of gas saw Colleen on I-80, on her way to Sacramento, hitting morning rush-hour traffic around Berkeley. But a lead foot and lane changes that channeled Mario Andretti got Colleen to California Department of Corrections and Rehabilitation Headquarters on S Street in Sacto just before nine a.m. The trees around the grey five-story facility were winter bare, but there was still some street parking to be had. They were just opening. She'd call that luck. She needed it. If CDCR didn't pan out, she'd have to hit the Federal Bureau of Prisons to continue her search and she was running out of time. She needed a match of some sort today. Early today. It was New Year's Eve, and they'd be closing early. If Night Candy was still alive, she had to know.

If he wasn't, the world could bask in blissful ignorance. And she could plan accordingly.

She spent much of the day in the research center, filling out Public Record Requests for the last year, looking for unnatural deaths in the California prison system.

Four hits.

The first was a man beaten to death in a yard fight at Chico, over a year ago. Too far back. Night Candy's last victim—not including Arnold Blane—was September. She wasn't counting Arnold, regardless of what Fos might have thought about Ray Quick being Night Candy.

She perused the next one. A Black prisoner stuck with a home-made knife more recently in a workshop in Bakersfield by members of Aryan Brotherhood. He was in for burglary.

The time frame fit. But the burglary charge didn't. And serial kill-ers tended to be white.

That left two more.

One was a man smothered to death in his cell at Vacaville.

Paul Oedekoven said Night Candy was stabbed.

Could she believe him?

Not one hundred percent. But he'd been right about most of what he said. When he felt like being forthcoming.

The last one was a man named Richard Hellman, stabbed in the yard at Santa Rita. He was being held for trial on attempted statu-tory rape when the prostitute he'd picked up turned out to be sev-enteen. They were caught by SFPD patrolling a parking lot by Candlestick Park. Hellman had been a hospital janitor who'd had a prior arrest for possession of child pornography. The hospital job would explain his access to needles and such.

That seventeen-year-old didn't know how lucky she was to have been busted.

"Bingo," Colleen said out loud, earning a look of rebuke from a librarian. She put Richard Hellman's info to one side.

She'd found Night Candy. Now she needed the copycat who killed Arnold Blane.

She already knew who that was.

CHAPTER FIFTY-SEVEN

Colleen called San Quentin from a pay phone, asked for prisoner Paul Oedekoven. She knew there was no way they'd roust him to the phone for a personal phone call.

"Who's calling?" the SQ operator said.

"I'm a friend of Richard Hellman's," she said. "Settling up his estate." Paul O would love it. Game playing was his thing.

"We'll leave a message."

Good enough.

On her way back to the Bay Area, she had to fill up again. Another twenty dollars out of the tailpipe. She made a stop at Santa Rosa Kaiser. Owens was still in the CCU. But they let her in to see him.

Owens was lying in bed, listless. He blinked himself awake as she came into the room. His leg was no longer suspended. One good thing.

"I still can't get used to that wig," he said, raspy.

She took his hand. His pulse wasn't strong, but it was a pulse. He wasn't on oxygen, another plus.

"How much longer are you planning to milk this?" she asked.

"I'm hooked on the hospital Jell-O," his voice scraped. "The nurse throws in an extra one now and again. I'm livin' the life."

"Five bucks says she wants to jump your bones."

"Probably."

"I'll tell you what: get your ass out of here and I'll make you all the Jell-O you want. I'm not talking the hospital crap either. I mean the kind with the little marshmallows."

His eyebrows raised in interest. "And pineapple chunks?"

"Canned cherry pie filling, too."

"Deal."

They looked at each other for a moment.

"I got him," she said quietly.

Owens looked at her, his bleary eyes coming into focus. "Night Candy?"

"Yeah. Now for the guy who killed whoever was burnt up in the fire. The one who set you up. He's the one who counts as far as I'm concerned."

"Is he who I think it is?"

She gave a single nod. "I got him where I want him. Not long now."

"Leave him be," he said.

"What?"

"You've done enough," Owens said. "I'll take it from here, when I get out of here."

Revenge. Her man of integrity was descending into lowly revenge.

"I don't like it," she said. "It's not you."

Owens' face grew dark. He went silent, sullen. His eyelids fell shut. And then he was out.

She just stood there for a while, the sounds of the CCU making the floor the unrelaxed place that it was. Until Owens was head back, snoring, his mouth open.

"Sweet dreams," she said. She could wish. But she knew his dreams were anything but. People changed. Even Owens.

* * *

When she got home that night, she poured a glass of Chardonnay and called her answering machine at Pier 26 for messages. There was one from Paul Oedekoven. She recognized his voice.

"Hello, Richard," he said. "So nice to hear from you from the great beyond. I do miss our little chats. Oh, and Happy New Year." Then he chuckled and hung up.

Richard Hellman. Night Candy. Right on the money. Night Candy was no more.

She called Gus.

"You're not out celebrating," she said.

"New Year's Eve is just another day."

She told him the good news. What passed for good news anymore.

There was music in the background, as always, The Youngbloods singing "Pride of Man."

"Nothing to say?" Colleen asked Gus.

"I've got some news, too," Gus said. "Not so good."

"OK," she said, sitting down in her roller chair, bracing herself. "Lay it on me."

"Alice Owens' remains have been cremated."

Pow. A left hook out of nowhere. Her ears were ringing.

"How could that possibly be?" she said.

"Ray Quick is the executor of the will. He ordered it."

"You've *got* to be kidding." A flurry of thoughts raced through her head.

"I wish I was."

"So," she said to Gus. "No hard evidence. Finding that dental implant in a few pounds of ash is going to be impossible. No real way to prove Alice wasn't Alice."

"We've always got Alistair's testimony."

Colleen sighed. "He did the examination on the condition we keep everything off the books. As a favor. A fact-finding mission. I promised not to land him in deep yoghurt."

"Well, that will have to change if he's going to testify."

"He could lose his job," she said.

Gus sighed too, something he didn't often do. The Youngbloods sang in the background. "Maybe this is a sign, Colleen," he said. "For you to hang it up. You got Owens out of jail. That's what counts."

She couldn't deny his sentiment. She thanked him, hung up, lit an illicit cig.

But she wasn't giving up. Ray wasn't going to get away with it.

And her sense of playing fair was going up in smoke, like the stuff she exhaled.

CHAPTER FIFTY-EIGHT

The next step was locating Ray. Colleen prayed he hadn't run. But she figured he wasn't going to ditch that check.

She headed back out, over to 41 Wawona.

On Wawona, the odd New Year's Eve party erupted into merriment. In the distance, fireworks popped as San Franciscans celebrated the end of the '70s. No one noticed a lone woman with a bump key. Soon she was inside.

The mailbox in the garage had no mail piled up and the trash can contained several new additions. So, Ray'd been by that morning checking the mail. Waiting for that quarter-million-dollar check.

Colleen stopped in West Portal, used a pay phone by the Muni tunnel to call The Claddagh.

New Year's Eve was in full swing, and she had to shout. She asked for Ray.

"He called in sick," Mary said suspiciously. "Who is this?"

Colleen hung up.

Ray must be awfully sick to call in New Year's Eve. Since she was nearby, Colleen checked Mary the redhead's place on Sloat, made sure a dark Buick Riviera with wire wheels and a scratch down the side wasn't parked in the driveway. It wasn't.

She was near the beach. She'd check The Shorebird Motel south on Highway 1. Ray might be celebrating New Year's with the skank of the day. Or night.

Fifteen minutes later she was parked down from The Shorebird, on the sandy shoulder, whitecaps breaking to her right on a winter night ocean.

Sand blew across the road as she got out. She headed up to The Shorebird, hugging herself in the knifelike wind.

Most of the cabins in the run-down motel were vacant and there were few cars.

She walked around the back.

Ray's Riviera was parked in front of Room 7. Lights shone around the curtain.

And two people were going at it like gangbusters. Ray sounded like he might be passing a kidney stone. She had to hand it to him. He was a man committed to what he was.

His partner was a woman with a shrill nasal voice, calling out his name in the throes of passion in a slice of acting that was just that: acting. It was amazing what men believed. Or wanted to believe.

And it made Colleen freeze in her tracks. And not from the cold.

The woman's voice was one Colleen had heard before.

One that had once been married to Owens.

One that was supposedly dead.

Alice Owens.

CHAPTER FIFTY-NINE

Colleen shouldn't have been that surprised. Ray Quick was due to collect the 250,000 dollars in the event of the death of Alice Owens. He'd killed a stand-in and set the fire up at Joshua Inn or had help.

What she hadn't figured on was that Alice was part of the scam as well. Colleen had thought Alice might be well and truly dead herself by now. Ray was a killer. He'd want all of the insurance money to himself. If anything, bring her in on the swindle at first, but why keep her around?

And it hadn't bothered Colleen too much.

But Alice wasn't dead.

Bold wasn't the word for it. What Alice did to Owens was beyond criminal. She and Ray were made for each other.

But Colleen needed proof.

She headed back to the car to get her camera. She really didn't need to listen to two murderers getting their rocks off.

Back at The Shorebird with her SLR, Colleen snuck around the back again. Calm had finally descended over Room 7. She ducked behind a clump of tall grass where the sound of the camera's shutter wouldn't carry, hoping the high-speed film would be enough to catch a shot or two.

Then, out of the serene night came drops of rain, scattered at first, then big and persistent.

She wasn't going back to the car now and miss her potential photo op. Her divorce work had taught her that the best shots happened when you ducked out for just a second.

She sat down and bore it out.

After what seemed like an age, she pressed the button on her Pulsar watch. Red digits told her it was close to two in the morning. The rain let up. The top of her head was good and wet.

Eventually the door to Room 7 opened and Ray Quick appeared, face shiny and hair mussed in the ambient motel room light. Slimy grin on his face.

Behind him stood a tall blonde woman in a white robe.

Alice Owens. Partially obscured by Ray, but it was her all right. Colleen had seen her pic at 41 Wawona.

Colleen got a snap, the two of them together, Alice behind Ray, arm around his neck, nuzzling his ear. Colleen's heart thumped along with the camera clicks. Anger rising. Thinking of Owens. Fos. Traci.

Got them as they kissed goodnight.

She watched Alice shut the door, winking at Ray, Ray strutting to his Riviera, getting in, firing it up, backing out, snaking around to the front of the motel. He probably wanted to get back to Mary's before she came home from The Claddagh.

Colleen recalled a week or so back, overhearing a similar scene at The Shorebird, no idea at the time that the woman had probably been Alice Owens.

Right under her nose.

Bold wasn't the word for it.

CHAPTER SIXTY

The day after New Year's, lunchtime, Colleen sat on a stool at Rudy's, the cop bar near the Hall of Justice, turning a bottle of Calistoga water on the ringed, beat-up bar top. The place was half empty, unlike the last time she was here with Matt. People were still sobering up, on break for the holidays. The jukebox was playing "Baker Street," another song that just gave her the blues, even more so under the current circumstances. On top of it she hadn't heard from Matt yet, still in Langley. He'd been gone long enough that he'd gotten the job. Oh well.

Right before noon a familiar face entered, one she'd been waiting for.

Inspector Ryan, in a rumpled herringbone check sport coat that looked like he slept in it. Like clockwork, coming in for his bourbon lunch.

Staring straight ahead, he walked right by her, down to the end of the bar where he stood in front of the serving hatch. The bartender arrived, poured him a shot of Jim Beam and Ryan downed it like medicine, held one finger up, got a refill. The bartender went to the register, made an entry in a book.

Colleen waited a few minutes while Ryan stared into his second shot, letting the first one take hold. Then she got off her stool and ambled down. Forced a smile.

He turned, saw her, expressed his displeasure with a grimace.

"What do you want?" he said coldly.

"To buy you a drink," she said. "A peace offering. My New Year's resolution. Happy 1980." She pushed a smile.

Ryan grimaced at her. "Forget it."

"How about a minute of your time?"

Shook his head again. "Nothing to talk about."

It was going to be like that.

"OK," she said. She pulled the photo she'd had developed of Ray and Alice cozy in the doorway of Room 7 from the pocket of her leather coat.

She held it up.

He eyed it.

"Ray Quick with Alice Owens," she said. "Taken two nights ago at The Shorebird Motel down Highway 1."

"If that's her."

"It is. Ray and Alice plotted to pin her 'murder' on Owens. But as you can see, she's very much alive. Because a sex worker named Traci was substituted for Alice. By Ray. Her remains were cremated so it's a pretty tight scam."

"Owens was released."

She feigned confusion. "Oh, so drop the whole thing?"

"You've been told to, on more than one occasion."

"Ray Quick, with the help of others, murdered Traci," she said. "And Ray killed Fos Alvarez."

Now he looked at her. "How do you know that?"

"Fos and I were working on Ray. Before Fos was killed. His car was towed from The Claddagh the day after he was last seen. He went to see Ray, and that was the last anyone saw of him. Until he turned up dead at Sutro Baths."

"What's that got to do with Ray Quick spending the night with some broad?"

"*Alice*," she said. "Alice Owens. I just told you: they're in this together."

He crinkled his thick brow. "Have you got some kind of thing going on with Owens?"

She set the photo down next to his untouched shot. "Do the right thing for once."

He pursed his lips, nodded, picked up the photo, looking at her the whole time, tore it in half, tore the two halves in half, dropped the four sections. They fluttered to the rough floor.

"Does that answer your question?" he said. Then he picked up his shot, downed it.

Colleen shook her head, left.

* * *

On the way to Santa Rosa Kaiser, she stopped at the Sonoma County Sherriff's office, asked for Detective Kikuyama. He was still out on leave for the holidays, not back until next week. She put a copy of the photograph, along with a note and her business card, in an envelope, asked for it to be given to him. The desk sergeant said he would see that Kikuyama got it.

But it wouldn't be until next week at least. And that might be too late.

Next stop: Owens at Kaiser CCU.

Owens was asleep in bed, an oxygen tube hissing under his nose. One step back.

She sat on a chair in his room, deciding what to tell him when he woke. He deserved to know about Alice. And then he didn't. He didn't need the madness. His weak constitution didn't need the stress.

She heard him stir.

"Hey, there you are," she said with a smile.

He blinked his eyes open and shut several times.

"I feel like I've been here since the dawn of time," he said.

"Just since last year," she said. "Happy 1980."

They chatted for a while, until he looked at her, said, "OK, something's up. Out with it."

She took a deep breath, found herself averting his gaze.

"Out with it," he said again, getting impatient. His tone of voice was dark today, had been getting worse, ever since this episode had begun.

"No easy way to say it," she said. "I saw Alice."

There was relative silence while the oxygen hissed. She could feel his eyes drilling into her, not at her per se, but the world at large.

"Did I mishear you, Colleen?"

She met his gaze, frowned, shook her head.

"Tell me," he said with a tone of forced patience that was anything but.

She told him she saw Alice with Ray. She didn't tell him the juicy details.

He sat up in bed and she could practically hear his teeth grit.

She sighed. "Now I wish I hadn't told you," she said.

"No," he said. "I'm glad you did. To keep it from me would have been wrong."

True.

"Who have you told?" he said. "Besides me?"

"Ryan and Kikuyama."

"And Ryan couldn't care less," he said.

She confirmed with a nod. "And Kikuyama is still out on vacation."

Owens clamped his jaw. "Well, if nothing else, it's given me the motivation to get the hell out of this damn hospital."

That's what she was worried about: Owens going off the deep end. Who could blame him?

But she couldn't let that happen.

She couldn't.

She had started this thing off. It was up to her to finish it. Before anyone else got hurt. Before Owens ruined things for himself.

CHAPTER SIXTY-ONE

The next morning Colleen parked as close to 850 Bryant as she could get with workday traffic and walked under a changing grey sky to the Sixth Street entrance where the Department of Public Health trucks entered the morgue. Her brown leather bag swung over one shoulder of her leather coat. The Medical Examiner-Coroner's Office comprised the northeast end of the building's first floor.

"Alistair's tied up in the lab," the desk clerk said, recognizing Colleen. She was a Black woman in green scrubs and thick glasses. "You can wait out here and read old magazines or go on in."

Colleen was on a meter outside and knew Alistair was frequently too busy to interrupt his current tasks.

She found Alistair bent over the corpse of a young boy on a stainless-steel autopsy table. The boy's face was ashen, drained of life, and his whitish lips were parted as if he might have had one more thing to say before he left this world. But he hadn't had the time. It was chilling, the swiftness of death, not the kind of thing you saw on *Quincy*. But to Alistair, it was all in a day's work. He looked up, grey beard and mustache poking out of a blue face mask.

Then he stood back, leaned against a counter, pulled his mask down, lit up a cigarette.

She noticed a baggie with the lock of blonde hair, which had been transferred to a smaller plastic evidence bag inside, sealed in a larger bag, with the hypodermic she had given him. A case number was written neatly on a label stuck to the side of the baggie.

She had hoped for a little more time.

He noticed her looking at it.

"You opened a case file," she said.

"I can't let it go undocumented, Colleen," he said. "Once something like this comes into my lab, it's my responsibility. I've already crossed a couple of lines for you." He raised his eyebrows. "Detective Kikuyama ring any bells? I vouched for you when he stopped by. I'm risking my bloody job."

"I totally understand, Alistair."

But she was running out of time. Sooner or later, Ray Quick was going to get that check, take off. And then where would she be? No perps, no fingerprints. Traci's death would go unpunished. Fos' death might well go the same way. Owens, although technically cleared, would remain under a cloud.

Alistair exhaled smoke across the room, avoiding the child's corpse, as if out of respect.

"You haven't logged it in yet, have you?" she asked casually.

"Just about to," he said. "I wanted to talk to you first."

"I know you've bent rules, Alistair, and I'm more than grateful. I'm asking for one more."

He shook his head. "That's not the way this is done, Colleen." He took a drag on his cigarette, let smoke billow away from her as he exhaled. Smoke floated over the extended hand of the child, and she saw grass stains on a small arm, and, in her mind, she saw mist rolling over a grave site.

"I'm the one that gave you the damn evidence in the first place," she said.

"Because you knew it was the right thing to do, Colleen."

"'The dead have rights.' Isn't that what you've told me on more than one occasion?"

"And that they do. And the way to do that is to show respect for how the job is done." He tapped ash from his cigarette into a metal sink. "I'm sorry, Colleen, but when it came into my lab, that evidence became my responsibility."

She sighed. "You're right, of course."

"No idea who NC is?" he said. "Your source couldn't tell you ... ?"

She shook her head.

"Your research didn't lead anywhere?" he asked.

"Dead end," she said with a straight face. What she'd learned in Sacto wasn't for sharing now.

She had a scheme of her own.

But not a lot of time.

The Black tech in the green scrubs poked her head in. "The director is waiting for us, Alistair," she said. "The Miller file?"

Alistair looked at his watch in shock. "Oh, right, Phyllis!" He leaned over the metal sink, ran the faucet, extinguished his cigarette under it, turned off the water, tossed the wet butt into a waste bin.

"Let me get that file." He picked up the evidence bag, with its syringe and lock of hair, took it into an adjoining room.

Colleen watched him come back out a moment later with a three-ring binder under his arm. The assistant in the green scrubs was waiting by the door.

"Let's go," Alistair said to her. Then he looked at Colleen. "Anything else, Colleen?"

"No. Not at all."

"We best go, then," he said, waiting by the door.

They left the boy on the table, and Alistair turned the lights off as the three of them exited the room.

"Thanks again, Alistair," Colleen said as Alistair and the assistant rushed down the hall in the opposite direction. "I'll see you at the Castle."

She ambled toward the small lobby, taking her time. At the end of the hall she stopped, turned around.

Watched Alistair and the tech hurry around the corner. Gone.

She waited a moment, walked slowly back to the lab. Checked the door. Unlocked. Alistair had been in a hurry.

Did she feel good about what she was about to do? No. But she didn't feel good about most things these days. How Owens might go off the deep end. How Fos didn't make it. How Traci didn't make it. Had been treated like garbage.

She checked the hallway one more time. Empty.

She went in quietly, came back out not long after, adjusting her brown shoulder bag.

CHAPTER SIXTY-TWO

That evening Colleen stopped by the corner of Hyde and Leavenworth.

"No sign of Traci," Rhonda said, burrowed down in the fake fur collar of her coat. Streetlight made her Afro look like a black halo. Fia was up by the curb, leaning on the windowsill of a TransAm, negotiating with a guy in a mullet.

But Colleen knew Traci was no more. They all did.

Two days after New Year's. It was still cold as hell.

"You know something about Traci?" Rhonda said, eyeing her curiously. She had her hands in her pockets and was down in her coat as far as she could go.

Colleen gave a nod.

Rhonda squinted. "Just spill it."

Colleen let out a visible breath of exasperation. "About the worst news you could expect."

Rhonda's face dropped. She let out a sigh as well. "I shouldn't be surprised," she said with a frog in her throat.

"It's not official yet," Colleen said. "So please don't share it. Fia is the one exception."

"Night Candy?"

"All I can say is that if you see that good-looking guy in a midnight blue Riviera, with a deep scratch along the rear right panel, stay well away."

"Uh-huh. And what do you plan to do about him?"

"I've got something in mind," she said ominously.

"Something like what?"

Colleen shook her head. "The less you know and all that."

"I see," Rhonda said. "Why not tell Billy and Mr. Fan where to find this character with the scratched-up Riviera? They'll take care of him."

By the curb, Fia strutted around to the passenger door of the TransAm, got in. It took off, thundering up Leavenworth.

"Because *I'm* taking care of it," Colleen said.

"OK," Rhonda said doubtfully. "But if I don't hear back in a few days, I'm gonna sic Billy on him."

"Billy Shen? Do you think he really gives a shit? You guys are just business assets. And not valued ones."

"I can hope."

Colleen looked around theatrically. "When are you two going to wise up?"

"I got my father to look after, who's got emphysema. My boy, going to a private school. You tell me how to pay for all that working some shit job at minimum wage? If I'm lucky enough to find one?"

"I hear you," Colleen said.

"Sure you do. Got big ideas for everybody else. Maybe you should look after yourself."

"Ouch. But that's what I'm doing, believe it or not."

"All right then." Rhonda shrugged in her coat. "Anything we can do to help, you let us know."

"There is one thing."

"What's that?" Rhonda said.

"I need something to ease the pressure," she said, pressing her forehead. "You know anybody?"

Rhonda gave her head a shake. "This the time you pick to zone out? With all of your 'big plans'?"

"Why don't you let me worry about that?"

Rhonda shook her head again. She nodded down Leavenworth. "Orlando's the guy you want. Corner of Ellis. Bushy sideburns. Wears a newsboy cap. Tell him I sent you and he won't rip you off too much."

"Will he be there now?"

"Saw him earlier."

"Good enough," Colleen said.

"Beginning to wonder about you, girl."

She found a guy in a slouchy blue denim newsboy tilted to one size, long dark fuzzy sideburns, sunglasses at night, down on Leavenworth. Not standing on the corner but inside the corner convenience store, where it was warmer, chatting with the owner. Colleen went in. On the radio, the news announcer was talking about the Russian invasion of Afghanistan. Colleen bought a pack of Juicy Fruit, caught Orlando's eye, gave him raised eyebrows, nodded that she was going outside.

He joined her.

"I'm a friend of Rhonda's," she said on the corner.

"And what does Rhonda's friend need?"

"Something to put my boyfriend in the mood," she said.

"Fresh out of 'ludes, babe. People cleaned me out for New Year's."

"I don't want Quaaludes," she said. Quaaludes were bitter tasting.

"Uh-huh." He eyed her closely. "So, you want him to *know* he's in the mood? Or you want to *surprise* him?" He gave a sly smile.

"He just loves surprises," she said. "Got any roofies?" Rohypnol, the latest thing from Europe.

"I can get my hands on a few. But they don't come cheap. Even with the Rhonda discount."

She asked how much. He told her.

"I'm good with that," she said.

"OK, then." He put his hand out. "Up front."

She peeled off a couple of twenties.

"See you back here in an hour," he said.

"An *hour*? Jesus H."

"'First thing you learn is that you always gotta wait,'" he said. He pocketed her money, walked down Leavenworth into the heart of the Tenderloin, singing to himself.

CHAPTER SIXTY-THREE

The band was playing "Mull of Kintyre" when Colleen pushed through the double doors into The Claddagh. It was late and there was a goodly crowd, drinking the night and their wages away. Colleen didn't see Ray behind the bar, but she did spot Mary of the red mane and undone upper blouse buttons.

Colleen went up to the bar. A wiry construction worker, covered in plaster dust, no doubt here since quitting time, hopped off his barstool, swiped it off with a hanky from his back pocket, proffered Colleen a seat. The fact that she was wearing her red minidress under her black leather coat, blonde wig, and black platform boots might have had something to do with it. She was cold, yes, but she was on a mission. She thanked him.

It took a moment to get Mary's attention. She had done a double take when Colleen entered and was ignoring her, but eventually curiosity got the better of her.

She came over, wiped the bar down with a rag.

"I'll take a Miller Lite," Colleen said. "I just can't get into that heavy Irish stuff."

"You've got some nerve."

"That's what I've been told," Colleen said. "Is Ray here?"

"Unbelievable," Mary said. "You come in here asking for him the other night, like you knew him. And he didn't have a clue who you were. So, I don't know what you think you're up to."

She squinted. "You sure you don't have a little idea?"

She had Mary's interest. Any woman involved with Ray had to keep one eye open for competition.

"When Ray doesn't come home until the wee hours?" Colleen said. "You know what I'm talking about?"

Mary tilted her head to one side, gave Colleen a stare.

"Yeah," Colleen said. "I bet there's nights Ray doesn't come home at all. Guess that's the price you pay, hooking up with a guy who plays the field."

Mary placed both hands on the bar, showing quite the collection of jewelry and rings.

"If you got something to say, spit it out."

"I'll just let this say a thousand words for me." Colleen pulled the photo of Ray and Alice kissing in the doorway at The Shorebird, held it up.

Mary looked at the photo, her mouth twisting into a frown.

Colleen shrugged. "It's not a very good picture. Got any idea who it is? I sure do. But you wouldn't believe me. Ray will though."

Mary took the photo, studied it, her grimace turning into a look of hurt and anger, emotions she was trying to cover up. Colleen actually felt sorry for her. It was obvious Mary didn't know what Ray was up to—really up to—as far as Alice, murder, and insurance fraud were concerned.

"You can keep that," Colleen said, nodding at the photo. She stood up. "Give it to Ray. Tell him I said 'hi.'" Colleen put a business card on the counter. "If it's any consolation, I was married to a louse who could have been drinking buddies with Ray. And, if I were you, I'd change the locks before Ray gets home. And write him off. The guy is bad news. Really bad news. You should be worried for your own safety."

Their eyes connected for a moment as the band finished up "Mull of Kintyre."

"Such a great song," Colleen said. "Schmaltzy as all get-out, but it gets you right there." She tapped her chest above her heart. "Take care of yourself, Mary."

CHAPTER SIXTY-FOUR

Mary examined the business card the woman had left on the bar, a corner of it in a puddle of beer.

Hayes Confidential. Colleen Hayes.

A private detective.

Then the photo of Ray and whoever his latest sleazebag was.

Steam was coming out of her ears.

She called Anthony over, who was working the other end of the bar.

"Anthony," she said. "Man the fort for the rest of the night. I think I'm coming down with a stomach bug."

"Sure, Mary, you're the boss. Feel better."

Mary drove home to her house on Sloat, murder in her heart.

No sign of Ray's car. Probably off with his latest piece of ass.

Ray the dirtbag.

Whatever, Mary collected Ray's clothes, his Members Only jacket reeking of Brut, dumped everything unceremoniously in a pile on the front doorstep. Left the photo of Ray and his slut on top of the heap, along with the PI's business card. Shut the door, locked it, put the latch on, went and got into her fluffy nightgown, robe, got her 45 automatic out, checked if it had a full clip, got her ciggies and a glass, and the bottle of Old Bushmills for Dutch courage, turned up the heat, turned on the TV, sat in the living room with the gun on the coffee table next to the whiskey, with a view of the front door.

Johnny Carson was just beginning his monologue.

*   *   *

Mary had nodded off when she heard Ray trying to come in. The front door stopped against the chain. The TV was braying with some late-night rerun.

"Mary? Let me in. I can explain."

She rubbed her eyes. The bottle of Old Bushmills was down an inch or so. The cap sat on the coffee table.

The chain rattled as the door pushed back and forth.

"Mary? Let me in, for Chrissake."

She sat up, coming awake. She grabbed a Pall Mall, lit it up, took a puff. Her heart was beating. Ray scared her, and she realized he had always scared her, but now more than ever.

"Just leave, Ray. I don't want to hear it."

There was a pause.

"Mary? I can explain."

"That photo says it all."

"C'mon, baby."

"Fuck you, *baby*."

A pause.

"Let me in, Mary. I'm freezing my ass off out here."

"Go get your piece of puss to warm you up."

His voice shifted down. Getting angry. "I said let me in this fucking house—*now*."

Heart thumping, she picked up the Taurus 45, flipped off the safety, held the gun up, racked it by grabbing the slide, the way her ex had showed her, with her weak hands, held it in both hands, pointed it at the front door. Cigarette hanging from the corner of her mouth, she squinted around the smoke curling up, her vision a little bleary, not to mention she was more than a little upset.

Fired. Loud in the house. The gun jumped in her hands, making them buzz.

But a hole appeared in the back of the front door, near the lock. Not bad.

She heard Ray scramble back.

"Jesus fuck, Mary!"

"I'm not gonna tell you again, Ray," she said, puffing on the Pall Mall, taking the cigarette out of her mouth with a shaky hand. "After that gunshot, the cops might show up any minute. I wouldn't want to be you when they do. I'd have to tell them what I know."

She poured herself another belt, just a small one, while she heard Ray collect his shit from the front step, muttering what a bitch she was. Her hands were beginning to steady as he got into his car, started it, backed out of her driveway.

CHAPTER SIXTY-FIVE

It was only a matter of time, but it was time that had slowed to a crawl. The next evening, in her darkened office at the end of Pier 26, Colleen was trying to concentrate, waiting. Waiting for Ray to make a move. Finally, around seven thirty p.m., the phone rang.

"Hayes Confidential."

"So, you're a private dick," Ray Quick said. "And you don't even have one."

"Don't need one," Colleen said, sitting back. "I've got the other thing and I can get as many dicks as I want."

"Hilarious."

"But true," she said. "How's Alice?"

"What are you talking about?" Ray said.

"And here I thought you might have wasted her too, so you wouldn't have to split the quarter mil with her."

"Let's just cut to the chase."

"I'm onto you, dude," she said, putting her feet up on the desk. "So, Mary must have shown you the photo of you and Alice at The Shorebird and given you my business card. Did she just slap your face or throw you out?"

"This is harassment."

Colleen laughed. "So, sue me. I'm curious what the judge will say when I show him how you killed Traci, tried to pass her off as Alice. Don't forget Arnold Blane, the dead transvestite. And while we're at it, there's Fos. Not to mention Owens, who started this whole thing off. Put it all together, oh man—you got problems if I go to anybody."

"You're a good bluffer."

"You think so? There's that photo of you and Alice. I've got one of Traci at Calistoga morgue with a diamond tooth implant Alice doesn't have."

"So why don't *you* go to the cops? Hmm?"

"Because there's no reason you and I can't work together," she said.

There was a pause. "You got balls, lady."

"I've definitely got yours—in a vise. But let's not be enemies, Ray. This could be what they call a win-win situation."

"Uh-huh," Ray said. "I was wondering what your angle was. Now I see it. How much?"

"Let me see: quarter of a million split two ways? You do the math, Ray."

There was a pause. Ray laughed.

"You still walk with a lot of cash," she said. "Think of the alternative. I'm actually being pretty generous when you think about it."

Another pause. She thought she heard a familiar clock ticking in the background. The grandfather clock at Alice's house in West Portal?

"Not all of that 250 is free and clear," Ray said. "I've got plenty of expenses."

"Like Alice? And your dentist pal? Rita Zielinski?"

"You don't miss much. I'll give you that."

"Don't forget the manager at Joshua Inn—Donna? Her mainte-nance man, too—Anders. You got them to lie to the cops about Owens being in the cabin, and some bogus argument, before it went up in flames. Oh, and to hide the evidence I found. The tin can used as a fire starter."

"And they all get a cut," he said. "So, half of what's left comes down to a little less than one hundred thou. And that's me being generous."

"Well, your expenses just went up, Ray. Because I get half of the gross. One twenty-five."

There was a long pause. "Jesus."

"Take it or leave it," Colleen said. "I bet a good-looking guy like you can make a lot of friends in Quentin."

There was another silence.

"You drive a hard bargain," Ray Quick said.

"Ah, come on. You're still sitting on a pretty pile of cash."

"Only problem is, I don't have it yet."

"Well, that's certainly not what I wanted to hear."

"You think insurance companies just hand out checks that size without an investigation?"

"Then what have you got to show good faith, Ray?"

"I can lay my hands on a few grand."

Good, he was scared enough and desperate enough to keep her from spilling the beans.

"That works," she said. "But let's make it five."

Another pause. He sighed, then said, "OK."

"Good," she said. "When? Here's a hint: make it soon. Here's an-other hint: make it tonight."

"I'll need some time to raise the cash. Midnight."

"I like the sound of that. I'll be there."

"You know where?"

"Of course. 41 Wawona."

He actually chuckled. What a freaking psycho. "I have to hand it to you. You do your homework." There was even a modicum of admiration in his voice.

"See you at midnight, sport. Oh, and just you and me. No need for anyone else to be there. Like Alice. If I get a sniff of her, or anybody else, I'm gone. Straight to the cops. I'll be leaving a trail in case anything happens too."

"I don't need Alice in the way."

Ray and Colleen were best of friends now. What a world.

CHAPTER SIXTY-SIX

Eleven fifty-five p.m. Colleen's friend Alex Copeland parked down the street from 41 Wawona in her white Jag. The streetlights sparkled in the dark crystal night.

She turned to Colleen in the passenger seat. Alex's blonde hair was tousled, half of it up in a black bow. Her blue eyes were clear. Her face was smooth and relaxed, not puffy from drinking and drugging. She'd been sober throughout the holidays. Impressive. But she still bore a look of concern.

"If you're not out in thirty, Coll, I'm calling the cops."

"I'll flash the lights when I'm ready," Colleen said.

Alex frowned. "You know how I feel about this, right?"

"And your concern is appreciated," Colleen said. "But it's what needs to be done."

Alex forced a smile. "I'm getting used to that wig."

"Good," Colleen said. "I'm going to have to wear it for a while longer."

Alex winked, squeezed Colleen's knee in its white pantyhose. "Knock 'em dead, killer."

"Interesting choice of words."

"Later."

Colleen got out of the Jag, legs shivering in her red mini-dress, just her boots and her sheepskin coat and white pantyhose to keep the rest of her warm. The blonde Farrah wig continued to help in that respect too. She whiffed nicely of Opium, a dab be-hind each ear.

Little Bersalina of 22 caliber fame was nestled in her coat pocket and her hand was wrapped around it. She had a few other goodies in her pockets besides.

Up to the house, the lights were on but no car in the driveway.

She stepped up to the porch, thinking about how all the times she had been here before, she had let herself in. This time would be legit but ironically more dangerous. She was just about to press the door-bell, her finger poised, when the front door opened. She had sensed someone was on the other side.

And he was. Ray stood there, dressed in blue flared polyester pants and a wild shiny floral shirt that was mostly blue, unbuttoned down to his midriff. He was firm, his hair was short and coiffed, and, for a despicable human being, nature had been more than kind in the packaging.

He obviously thought the same of the way she looked, giving her a once-over with a sly leer before letting her in, shutting the door behind her. The gravity air furnace did double time, wafting out of the old register vent by the door.

"Sexy wig," he said.

"Just having some fun," she said.

"Nothing wrong with that," he said, raising his eyebrows, obviously liking the idea.

"Where's my cash?" she asked.

"Whoa," he said. "What's your hurry? Like you say, we might as well be friends. Stay for a drink."

"You *do* have my money, right?"

"Of course, I have your money. In the living room."

He had nothing in his hands and his pants were tight. He wasn't carrying a weapon. She let go of the Bersa in her pocket, brought her hands out of her coat. Her nails were painted red to match the dress. She put her hands on her hips.

"Let's see it," she said.

"Before we do anything," he said, "I need to pat you down."

She raised her arms and her coat parted open. "Just don't get any ideas."

He raised his eyebrows again at the glimpse of her dress. "Kind of hard not to with you dolled up like that but, hey, I'm a professional."

He patted her down, nothing too excessive, she had to admit.

"Keep your arms up," he said. "I need to check your pockets."

Her blood pressure raised at that. "I've got a piece," she admitted. "Right pocket."

He nodded as he went in, came out with the Bersa, her shiny little Argentine gun that fit in the palm of his hand like a toy. It had been worth a try.

"Cute."

"I want that back."

"Of course you do." He popped the clip, handed her the empty gun. He stuck the clip in his shirt pocket.

"People know where I am," she said. "My lawyer has a copy of the photo of you and Alice at The Shorebird. So don't even think of trying anything."

"Smart," he said. "I'll have to meet this lawyer of yours. He sounds like my kind of guy." He went through her other coat pocket, came out with her car keys and a box of Virginia Slims.

"'You've come a long way, baby,'" he said, opening the box, poking around the cigarettes, came out with a loose joint.

"Colleen, Colleen," he said.

"The pause that refreshes," she said.

"My type of girl too." He tucked the joint back in the box, handed her the box back, along with her car keys.

"Shall we?" He waved her into the living room, an elegant affair designed by Alice Owens, paid for by her ex, still up at Kaiser CCU in Santa Rosa. The lights were low, and Herbie Hancock was oozing out of the stereo at a volume to match the lighting.

On the coffee table lay a white envelope, thick with cash. A bottle of champagne sat in a bucket of ice to one side of a silk-embroidered sofa. Two champagne flutes were lined up on the coffee table.

"Little sure of yourself, aren't you?" she said.

"Like you said on the phone, we should be friends. Go on, take off your coat. Grab a seat." He sat down.

She did as well, draping her coat over one arm of the sofa.

He gave her figure an approving nod, pulled the bottle from the bucket, dripping, along with a white dish towel, which he used to wipe the bottom, set the bottle on the towel in his lap.

"You're as smart as a fox and pretty foxy to boot," he said, peeling the foil back off the cap. "We can definitely work together."

She watched him, thinking, if the bottle hadn't been opened, it was OK to drink.

"We *are* working together," she said. "We have a deal."

"Oh, sure," he said, working the cork out slowly with his thumbs. "You're getting half of the settlement. A little steep, yeah, but I like a woman who knows what she wants. No, I mean, we can work together on future projects too. I've got plenty of ideas."

She just bet he did. "I'll be honest," she said. "I'm surprised you're not a little more upset. I tattled to Mary and you're splitting your insurance money with me."

He sat back, away from the cork between his thumbs. "Oh, Mary'll come around. Trust me. I know how women like her work.

But there's a lot of room for more upside with you and me. With your brains and talent, and my opportunities, we can clean up."

Everything he said sounded like an innuendo. "What opportunities?"

"Patience, grasshopper," he said. "All will be revealed."

Was he for real, or putting on an act to lure her into a false sense of security? Maybe both. A true psychopath could be both friend and enemy at the same time.

The cork popped, hit the chandelier, the crystal dangles tinkling in response. Champagne frothed as Ray leaned forward quickly to fill the two flutes. He set the bottle in the bucket, picked up the glasses, handed her one with the most charming of smiles.

"To friends," he said.

"Not so fast," she said, setting her glass down on the coffee table. She reached over, picked up the envelope. Started thumbing through it, the cash still inside.

Fifty Benjamins, near enough.

"Looks like it's all there," she said.

"Of course it is," he said. "You can trust me." He leaned over, grabbed the envelope, threw it on the coffee table near him, not her. "But it's not quite yours yet."

"How do you figure that?" she said.

"I gave you the five Gs to show good faith."

"You gave me five Gs to keep me from ratting you out. And I don't have it yet."

He shrugged. "OK, but now that you see what a team we can make, I'm gonna go ahead and call my side 'good faith.'"

"Is that what you told Alice Owens?"

He returned another smile, easy, friendly, confident. "You've got Alice beat by a mile. Beauty- and brains-wise. And she's no slouch."

But he was still prepared to throw Alice under the bus.

"OK," she said, sitting back, crossing her arms over her bosom. "Better tell me what you have in mind then."

His smile stretched wide as his eyes went to her legs. "They say business and pleasure don't mix. I, however, say 'not so fast.' Especially in our case. In our case, they're the glue that binds."

She wasn't too surprised at that either.

"You want to seal our arrangement with a kiss," she said.

"I can't think of a better way to cement an alliance like ours. We have to trust each other, Colleen. Have to. And there's no better way than showing we've got nothing to hide than you and me getting it on. And come on, look at us. The way you look, and the way I look, and what you are, and what I am, you know it's gonna be a night to remember." He picked up her glass along with his—handed hers to her.

That's for sure, she thought. "What makes you think I'm going to sleep with you?"

"Because you don't have any qualms about doing what's best for Colleen. Here I thought you were setting me up for a fall with the cops, but you were really in it for yourself."

"That doesn't mean I'm going to ball you."

"Oh, come on. You aren't totally repulsed."

She grinned. "That's your 'come on' line? I'm not 'totally repulsed.' Well, it is original. I'll give you that."

"Once we get started, you're gonna want more. I've got plenty of happy customers."

"Not sure that's a selling point, dude."

"Well, it's the way it's gonna have to be. Trust me on this."

Trust him. Ha. But she had him. She just had to play it right. She set her glass back down. "Tell me about these other opportunities," she said.

He set his glass down too.

"OK," he said, rubbing his hands together. "Alice, for one."

"What about Alice?"

"This house," he said. "Is hers. Or *was*." He smiled a crafty smile.

"It was hers until she 'died.' But you and I know different."

"She left it to me. She couldn't let her thieving family grab it. Or the state."

Colleen hadn't considered that. Alice "dead," no house. She'd need a proxy to keep it. So, she left it to Ray. To be split later. Colleen questioned Alice's sense of trust.

"And if I throw in with you in the way you suggest," Colleen said. "She's dead again."

"Bingo. The house is all mine. But we still have a teensy problem."

"The real Alice is still alive. And we kind of need her to be the opposite. That helps with the money split too."

He shook his head in admiration. "Quick as a whip. Where have you been all my life?"

"So, you split the insurance with me, which you were going to have to share with Alice, but now you won't have to, because Alice is going bye-bye. So that's pretty much a wash for you now. And the house you don't have to share with her anymore." A house like this was worth over a hundred K. "Talk about a bonus. And all I have to do is help you get rid of Alice."

"Like you say, 'win-win.'"

"For you."

"Oh, come on, Colleen! I'm not quibbling about what you asked for. One hundred and twenty-five K—it's all yours. And that's just the start."

"What do I get of what else you got coming? Especially if I help you get rid of Alice?"

"We negotiate that."

"Fifty-fifty."

"Why not?" He reached over, stroked her shoulder. "You wear that just for me?"

She smiled demurely. "What if I did?"

"I think this is the beginning of a beautiful friendship." He handed her the glass again.

She took it. "You watch too many old movies."

"And I have other opportunities," he said, raising his glass. "Plenty. Come on. To success."

Opportunities. He was about to swindle Alice, get rid of her, which seemed kind of fitting, but still. And there were others. Rita Zielinski, the dentist up in Calistoga who fudged dental records for him. And Donna, manager at the Joshua Inn. Hiding a fire for Ray. But probably carrying a torch. She owned a nice little place. And Mary, out in the avenues. Another property. Yes, opportunities for Ray abounded.

She smiled wonderfully, leaned over, clinked glasses. Drank.

So did Ray.

They both savored the moment, each for different reasons. Hers one of justice that had become shaded by revenge. For Owens. For Traci. Fos.

CHAPTER SIXTY-SEVEN

Colleen and Ray sat there for a moment, listening to Herbie Hancock, while they sipped champagne.

"Well?" Ray said. "It's not every day a girl lays her hands on 125,000 bucks. And half of what's to come."

She returned a come-hither look, along with a little smirk. "True."

He gazed at her body in the slim dress, her legs in white pantyhose. "I'm going to lick every inch of you."

She tried not to think about it.

"If that's what it takes to get you to trust me," she said.

She set her champagne down on the coffee table, stood up, unzipped her platform boots, the sound carrying across the living room. Not taking her eyes off him, she reached under her dress, pulled down her white pantyhose, stepped out of them, tossing them to one side. And then she pulled down her undies, slowly, black lace things that cost a fortune but didn't do much to keep her warm. She did it slowly, letting the material drag over her goose-bumped thighs, making a show of it, not taking her eyes off his.

He was eating it up. His eyes glistened.

"Oh my," he said in a husky voice.

Then: "What's that?" he said, looking at her wounded leg.

"Your buddy's dog up at Joshua Inn."

"Let me see."

She turned her leg around to one side. The stitches had been removed but it was still red and ugly. "So much for my career as a leg model."

"I kind of dig it," he said.

Sick bastard.

With a sly grin, she tossed the panties at him. He caught them on the fly.

Closed his eyes and pressed them up to his face.

Ugh.

"I knew it," he whispered, breathing in through the fabric. "Perfect."

She sat back down on the sofa, straightened her dress, reached into the pocket of her coat laying over the arm, came out with her cigarettes, slid one out, put it between her lips.

"Why did you stop the striptease?" Ray said. "I was enjoying that."

"All in good time, grasshopper," she said.

She leaned forward to grab the lighter from the table.

"Allow me," Ray said, feasting his eyes on Colleen's bare legs. He leaned forward too, grabbed the lighter, lit it up, held the flame under her cigarette. Making goo-goo eyes up close, particularly repulsive when you considered what he was.

She took a puff, leaned over to tap into the ashtray on the coffee table.

Knocked over her champagne flute, accidentally on purpose.

The fragile glass shattered, champagne splashing onto the table, the floor, the stem of the broken flute rolling off, breaking into even more pieces on the hardwood. Just what she wanted.

"Ay yi yi!" she said. "You can't take me anywhere."

"No sweat." He hopped up, darted around the coffee table.

He dashed into the kitchen, came out with a dish towel, mopping up the table and hardwood floor. There was broken glass, so Colleen had scooted her bare feet on to one side. "Any way you can clean that up some more?"

"You betcha," he said. Trust a man in the throes of lust not to think clearly. Or not to think about what he should be thinking about. "I'll need another cloth anyway."

"You'll need a brush and dustpan to get all that glass."

He was back in the kitchen, opening a door downstairs, rummaging around in the pantry.

While he was doing that, she set her lit cigarette down in the ashtray, got her pack of Slims, pulled the joint out of the pack. Leaned forward, peeked into the kitchen. Ray was tramping down the stairs now to the garage. She set the joint down on the coffee table, tore it open carefully.

There, amidst the loose tobacco, were three small blue pills.

One roofie would be enough to take him down but three would have him in the ozone.

She tore off a piece of foil from the cigarette pack, wrapped the pills in it, put the foil packet on the floor, crushed it quietly with the heel of her loose boot, grinding the contents into powder.

He was coming up the stairs to the kitchen.

Hurry.

Colleen picked up his glass, dumped the champagne down the back of the cushion behind her. She quickly poured the contents of her foil packet into the champagne flute, set it back to where it had been, filled it up from the champagne bottle.

The swirling liquid and bubbles dissolved the mixture. Tasteless. Odorless. Roche's finest.

But as the eddying drink began to settle, a tiny chunk of blue pill swirled in the bottom of his glass. Hadn't quite dissolved.

Shit on a shingle.

He came back into the room, wiped up the remaining champagne on the floor, swept up the broken glass.

"I'm going to have to spank you for that," he said.

She could still see the tiny piece of blue pill. But could he? Would he?

"Promises, promises," she said. "I'll need a fresh glass first."

"Oh. Right." Back into the kitchen.

While he clattered around in the cabinets she reached over, one eye in his direction, stuck her finger into his champagne glass, fished out the tiny blue speck. Wiped it off on the sofa cushion.

He came back in and put an empty glass in front of her, filled it up, went around, sat down next to her.

"So," he said in a dreamy voice. "Where were we?"

She reached over and got her full glass, and he got his.

"To friends," she said. "Down the hatch."

Both of them drained their glasses, and he refilled them.

Not long now, she said to herself. *Not long now.*

"Things are about to get interesting," she said, giving him a wink.

"Just what I love to hear a hot woman say."

He was grinning ear to ear. He had about ten minutes of sanity left.

CHAPTER SIXTY-EIGHT

Hand on Ray's elbow, Colleen guided him to the bedroom, the man stumbling in front of her, blinking in a drug-induced stupor.

"This way, stud," she said.

"Are we going . . . where I think we're going?" he slurred.

"We are indeed," Colleen said, directing him to the bed.

"I'm wiped out," he said.

"You are, indeed," she said, leading him over.

"What was in that . . . ?"

She turned him around, pushed him onto the bed. He went down easily, falling in slow motion.

"Don't go anywhere," she said. She left him there, went out into the hall, stopping in the living room to turn the lights on and off three times.

She donned underwear, pantyhose, and boots. Then out the front door.

Down on the first step was her shoulder bag, thanks to Alex.

Back upstairs, Ray had managed to get off the bed and was now curled up on the floor.

"Up you get," she said, laying her bag down on the foot of the bed, getting Ray back up with a struggle. He wasn't light. "Clothes off, buddy."

"Now . . . you're talking," he mumbled as he sat on the bed. He'd gotten his pants undone, down to his thighs before he fell over. "Man, I'm wasted."

It was not her favorite experience as she got him down to his underpants and socks. With a fair amount of effort, she got the big man up against the headboard.

"What in the hell"—he blinked in confusion as he sat up—"is going on?"

She reached into the bag, came out with a pair of plastic medical gloves. Slipped them on.

He watched in bleary interest. "What . . . ?" he said dumbly.

"Party time," she said.

Then she retrieved two pairs of handcuffs. Held them up with a grin.

"Who's your buddy?" she said.

He returned a smile that shone with drool.

Soon his hands were manacled to the headboard, and he was smiling like a fool.

"I . . . like . . . you," he said.

"Answer me one question, Ray. Was 'Alice'—the pretend Alice—already dead when you shot her with Owens' gun?"

He squeezed his eyes in thought, opened them.

"She . . . was. I did her . . ."

"Did her *how*?"

"My hands." He made a strangling motion with his open hands. "Old school. While we were . . . fucking. In the cabin. She was . . . *God*, she was . . . hot. It was . . . *incredibly hot*."

Revulsion filled Colleen's guts.

"But she wasn't dead, Ray. The fire killed her. There were particles of soot in her throat. So, you didn't kill her. The fire did."

"Oh . . . well," he said, trying to shrug with his hands in the cuffs on the bedpost. "Whatever." Then he laughed. *Actually laughed.*

She retrieved the evidence bag she had liberated from Alistair's office, containing the syringe and lock of hair.

"What . . ." he said, "is that?"

"You'll find out, sweetheart."

". . . sweetheart . . ."

Syringe in hand, she went over, reached for his hand hanging in the handcuff off the bedpost, pushed the hypodermic into it. Wrapped his hand around it tight. Pressed his fingers onto the shaft, getting good impressions.

He looked at her in squinted confusion.

"What . . . is going on?" His voice rose as if he suspected something.

"Your demise," she said. "Sweet dreams."

She retrieved a roll of duct tape from her bag, tore off a six-inch piece, placed it over his mouth as he tried to turn his face away.

He looked at Colleen with bulging eyes, coming to some sort of stoned conclusion.

Tried to scream. It came out as a muffled howl.

"Oh well," she said with a shrug. "*Whatever.*" She gave him a beautiful smile.

Then, "Her name was Traci, you sick bastard."

Downstairs, in the basement, she found a coffee can full of nuts and bolts on the workbench. She tucked Night Candy's syringe in it, fresh with Ray's fingerprints. Back upstairs she found a copy of the bible in the bookcase. Trust this household to have a bible. She turned to Deuteronomy. All that Sunday school as a girl had to be good for something.

She found the appropriate passage, 5:1–33, inserted the lock of hair.

Pressed the book shut, slid the book back into the rack. The stereo had gone off, the LP finished. She left the power on.

She checked in on Ray one last time, collapsed over in the restraints of his handcuffs.

In the living room she picked up the envelope full of cash. Tucked it in her pocket. Let herself out.

And then she was gone. Alex was waiting down the street in her white Jag.

CHAPTER SIXTY-NINE

Early next morning Colleen called the SFPD Anonymous Tip line.

"Night Candy," she said. "41 Wawona. West Portal."

"How did you come by that information, ma'am?"

"Have Homicide search the place. Thoroughly. You'll find what you're looking for."

"And how did you come by this information?"

Colleen hung up.

She sat there for a moment, pondering her deception. She had fallen and she knew it. But the person who killed Traci, Fos, the transvestite prostitute, Alice when he got the chance, and God knows who else was going to be stopped. And pay. In spades.

* * *

About that time Alice Owens got out of a yellow Chevette down the street from her house at 41, wearing a headscarf, sunglasses, and a beige raincoat with the belt cinched around her narrow waist. She headed down to 41. Morning grey was seeping into another cold winter day.

She spotted Ray's Riviera parked, with that big gouge in the rear panel, wondering what the hell Ray was up to. He was supposed to come back after he had dealt with the woman who was blackmailing them. Her high heels clicked down the street until she got to 41, her house, a house she hadn't entered since she had 'died.'

She checked in either direction before taking the stairs up to the porch, getting her key out. On the porch she looked around one more time, unlocked the front door, let herself in.

The living room was untidy, a half-empty bottle of champagne in a silver bucket, which had left a wet ring on the antique table. Two empty glasses.

The stereo had been left on. She went over and checked the turntable. Herbie Hancock. Ray's seduction music. She shook her head, her temper rising.

Ray, she thought, *you ass. You supreme ass.* Here they were, on their way to a fortune, one that was tricky enough to start with, and had gotten much trickier, finding that look-alike, getting rid of her ex, all sorts of juggling, and *then* to have it diverted by that Hayes woman, and Ray had to pull *this*. His little head thinking for the big head. *Jerk.*

Anger and jealousy, but mostly anger, coursed through her.

A muffled groan from the bedroom yanked her out of her thoughts.

More grunting. Ray?

She clacked into the bedroom, saw him handcuffed to the bed in just his underpants and socks. Duct tape over his mouth.

Found herself shaking her head again.

Ray, for his part, tried to communicate, grunting through the tape over his mouth. Eyes bulging.

She went over, still in her headscarf, sunglasses, raincoat, ripped the duct tape off his face with maximum force.

Ray gasped.

"Alice . . ."

She slapped his face. Hard.

"I can explain!"

Slapped him again. Back and forth. And again.

"You damn fool, Ray," she said between gritted teeth. "You damn fool."

"Give me a fucking minute, will you?"

"You thought you'd sneak a quick piece of ass before you got rid of her? You moron. You louse."

"Alice," he panted. "Just go downstairs, get the bolt cutters, get me out of these fucking things!" He shook his hands, constrained by the cuffs on the bedposts.

She slapped his face again. "Give me one good reason I should do anything for you, Ray?"

"Quarter of a million bucks?" he wheezed, smiling, shaking the cuffs on his wrists. "Bolt cutters?" Shook the cuffs again. "Please?"

Alice laughed, hard and nasal, nodding at his underwear, handcuffs. "Yes, you really came out on top of things, didn't you? Now she gets half our money. If not all of it."

"Alice," he said. "Please understand that I've got a handle on this. She's not getting a damn thing out of us—except a trip to the bottom of the bay. That was the whole point. Get her on my side. It just went sideways. But not next time. I paid her the 5K. She's on the hook. She wants the big payoff. She'll be back. And we'll take care of her then."

Alice thought about that. He'd already gotten rid of one person, two if you counted the transvestite, who was an accident, three if you counted that Mexican cop. And there was Owens, of course, but he didn't count. He was still alive. What was one more? And it wasn't like Alice had much choice. She couldn't walk away from the

money now. And her house. She had come this far. She could walk
away from Ray. Later. But that had been the plan all along once she
got her house back.

She'd just have to ride it out. Trust him.

And then stick it to him.

"When?" she said. "When are you going to get rid of her?"

He rattled his cuffs. "As soon as you get these fucking things off,
dear."

"You better mean it."

"You can come with me."

She thought about that too. She didn't want to be so close to a
murder, but she had to keep an eye on him.

"OK," she said. "But if you mess this one up, I'm turning you in
myself."

Ray smiled his winning smile. "I love you, baby."

She slapped his face again. "Shut up!"

"That's my girl." He shook his wrists and raised his eyebrows.
"Any time you're ready."

There was no turning back now. After all, she was dead.

She went through the kitchen, scarfed, sunglassed and raincoated,
out to the pantry, high heels clacking downstairs to the garage. The
bolt cutters were hanging up over the workbench.

CHAPTER SEVENTY

"Open her up," Inspector Meyerson said, standing to one side by the front door of 41 Wawona.

There had been no answer.

The locksmith moved in, set his bag of tools down. Two SFPD officers in blue waited behind him at the top of the stairs. A crime scene investigator stood by. Late afternoon was quickly fading to the west, another cold night ahead.

Soon enough they were inside.

On the draining board in the kitchen, he found two champagne flutes, upside down. One had a bead or two of water on it. The trash contained an empty champagne bottle. A silver champagne bucket sat on the pink Formica kitchen table.

The master bedroom had a poorly made bed. Examination of the posts revealed heavy scratches, and if he was any judge, they were recent, the wood scrapes bare and light in color. On the floor by the bed, he noticed a small metal oval ring that had been cut. He bent down, picked it up with the tip of a ballpoint pen. Looked like a link in a chain.

From a set of chain-link handcuffs?

He examined the bed posts again. *OK.* He got it now. He instructed the evidence tech to bag the link.

Downstairs, the officers were going through everything.

"Check this out, Inspector," one said, lifting the garbage can lid.

He went over, while the officer pointed his flashlight into a nearly empty trash can full of unopened mail.

Two pair of handcuffs sat on top, both cut. That's where the link came from.

"Looks like someone had themselves a little party," the officer said.

"Bag those and get prints off of them."

Meyerson went to the workbench. The person had once been a neatnik, tools hung in order of size at one time on the pegboard. But now a pile of tools and junk lay on the workbench.

Including a pair of bolt cutters, open, lying next to a vise.

The vise, likewise, was open. He examined the blades of the bolt cutters. Silver residue, shavings.

And another silver link, next to the vise.

Party indeed. He turned to the tech. "Make sure we get prints off that champagne bottle. Glasses too."

"They've been washed."

"Do it anyway." He nodded at the bolt cutters. "And these."

The evidence tech blinked. "Isn't Night Candy smarter than that?"

He turned, glared at him. "You running this case?"

The tech complied.

Someone had been cuffed to the bed and had to be cut free. It took a second person to do that.

Something odd had taken place. Very odd. Very recently.

This was the house owned by Alice Owens, the ex of the guy in the CCU up in Santa Rosa. She had been murdered, so they said, Alice. Ryan was sidelining any real investigation.

He'd been through the house once. Time to go through it again, in more detail. And again, if necessary.

*   *   *

"Check this out," one of the uniforms said on the second pass.

Inspector Meyerson came in from the bedroom where he'd been looking at the scratched-up bedposts again.

The officer was holding open a copy of the bible.

There was a lock of blonde hair.

"Deuteronomy," Meyerson said, reading the passage under the lock of hair. "The Ten Commandments."

"How do you know that?" the officer said.

"Try growing up in my house and *not* know it," Meyerson said. "Bag the hair. And the bible."

He'd keep looking. Something about that workbench.

By the end of the night, he poured a Hills Brothers can full of nuts and bolts onto a sheet of newspaper.

Then he saw it.

A hypodermic syringe.

Night Candy's signature in three out of four murders.

Bingo.

He called the evidence tech over. The man looked at where he pointed.

"Still think I'm on the wrong track?" he said.

The tech nodded in admiration. "Looks like you hit the jackpot, Inspector."

CHAPTER SEVENTY-ONE

Next evening, working on a Sunday, Colleen's phone rang.

It was Alistair.

"We need to talk, Colleen," he said curtly. In the background she heard the usual bar chatter, tinkling of glasses. Someone laughed.

The guilt hit her, although it was never distant. Ever since the day she killed her ex, all those years ago. And recently, these last few days, it was like a river.

"I'm on my way, Alistair."

She drove over to the Edinburgh Castle on Geary, parked down the street.

She found Alistair in corduroy pants and a plaid shirt, standing in front of a glass of whiskey. No beer tonight. He'd gone straight to the hard stuff. She walked over, stood by him. He didn't look at her.

"SFPD got an anonymous call," he said, twisting his glass on the bar in front of him. "An anonymous tip."

She didn't respond at first.

But she didn't want to lie anymore.

"I know," she finally said with a sigh.

"Of course you do," he said, taking a sip of whiskey.

"I'm sorry for what I did to you, Alistair. Truly I am. But not what happens to the guilty."

Alistair turned, looked at her sharply. "I went to bat for you, Colleen. The trip to Santa Rosa morgue. Nothing would have come to light without my help."

"I know that," she said. "And you don't know how much it meant. But I had to do this."

"If Owens means anything to you, you'll know he always played it by the book."

"And it was coming to an end, Alistair. Owens had changed. I sensed it. I didn't want him getting out, going after the people who set him up. I need him to stay the way he was."

There was momentary silence.

"So, you beat him to it?" Alistair said.

She shrugged. "Fos is dead. So is Traci. How is Owens supposed to live with that?"

"SFPD searched 41 Wawona," Alistair said. "And guess what they found?"

"You know I don't have to guess."

"That evidence was stolen from my lab. I was waiting for you to come to your senses, return it. Realize the enormity of your mistake. But no. *This!* Frame Ray Quick for Night Candy!" He turned to her for the first time, stared. "What do you think I should do?"

She took a deep breath. "Whatever your conscience tells you, Alistair. I won't fight you."

"My *conscience*," he said. "What would you know about such a thing?"

"It's not black and white, Alistair. It never is. But Owens is shut off from revenge. I'm tired of losing people. Traci. Fos." She almost said *Pam.* "I won't lose Owens. Not while people like Ryan ignore justice for the sake of a grudge."

Alistair turned back, sipped his shot. "Trying to talk yourself into something, Colleen. Trying to talk me into it as well."

"I don't expect you to understand, Alistair," she said. "But if you care about Owens . . . well, I just hope someday you'll forgive me."

"Owens might not," he said.

"Owens doesn't get a vote," she said. "This is on me."

"So, you're saying you'll simply stand by if I shop you? Turn you in? You'll accept that?"

"I'm hoping you'll at least give me a running start." She actually smiled. "I can run pretty fast when I have to."

He downed his shot. "Good thing for you that I think highly of Owens. But this isn't a victory. Don't think that."

She didn't feel a victory, but she did feel a surge of relief.

It was easier to ask forgiveness than permission.

"It's justice," she said. "Or what passes for it these days."

She got the barman's attention, ordered two shots, a refill for Alistair, one for her.

"To Owens," she said, lifting her glass.

Alistair frowned, blinked, finally picked up his shot. "To Owens."

They clinked glasses.

CHAPTER SEVENTY-TWO

"So, you admit to planting the syringe? And the lock of hair?"

There was still an element of shock in Inspector Meyerson's reedy voice, despite the fact that Colleen had been questioned for several hours now, with Gus in attendance. The inspector's weary expression, which seemed to arrive on all homicide officers' faces at some point in their careers, had etched deep lines in his not-yet-middle-aged boyish features. His thinning dark hair flecked grey at the temples.

Colleen and Gus sat opposite him.

The stuffy interrogation room where she had spent many hours, often across from Owens, felt as if it were closing in on her once again, the flickering fluorescent bulb overhead about to fail, buzzing along with the demise of her private war against Ray Quick. Windows that hadn't been opened since early fall were coated in frost.

But she had done the right thing, she told herself, even if Ray—and quite possibly Alice—had gotten away with murder.

There was an APB out for Ray. But he had yet to be found. Alice, well Alice was dead. Technically.

"It's all in my statement," she said.

Colleen had come clean to SFPD, despite Alistair's eventual willingness to hide her "mistake." When push came to shove, she simply couldn't abide by her deceit. But whatever happened now, Owens, still languishing in Santa Rosa Kaiser, would not be part of any retribution.

If nothing else, the whole process had highlighted the end of Night Candy's reign. And put a hold on Ray's death benefit.

"Then we're done here—for now." Inspector Meyerson collected his papers, stood up. "Don't leave town. Be where we can find you."

Colleen and Gus stood up as well.

"I want to stress my client's spirit of cooperation," Gus said. "And her tireless work to identify Night Candy."

"She's a busy woman," Inspector Meyerson said, nodding. "But it's not going to be enough to start a fan club for her here."

"You have what you need to go after Ray Quick," Colleen said. Even Ryan couldn't sidestep killing Fos. With Colleen's testimony and the file in Fos' apartment, SFPD were able to connect Ray Quick to Fos.

Outside, on the front steps to 850, the wind blew sharp. Colleen had her wig to keep her warm. No hat required. Underneath, the hair was growing out itchy.

"I don't need to tell you you're now persona non grata at SFPD," Gus said, donning his aviator shades.

"So, what else is new?" she said.

"Just between you and me," Gus said. "Impressive work. But enough. This is a good time to hunker down with your divorce work. Keep your nose clean."

"I can certainly use the income," Colleen said.

She parted with Gus, went to work, a hollowness taking up the center of her being.

She worked late at Pier 26, got into the Torino parked on the covered pier, the car taking a couple of starts with the ongoing cold.

She headed up the hill on Twentieth to her flat on Potrero Hill, pondering what came next.

A violation of parole. Gus had his work cut out for him there.

She thought she saw a pair of headlights in the rearview mirror.

Colleen squinted in the mirror.

A car appeared to be following.

Without signaling, she turned off on De Haro, quick, a couple of blocks before her street.

Lo and behold the headlights did the same.

She drove past the International High School, turned right, and the vehicle behind her did too, and the driver didn't seem to care if she noticed.

OK, she thought. OK.

She didn't have her gun, and she wasn't in the mood to shoot anyone anyway, but she needed to know what was going on.

She pulled over, engine running, waited, watching the rearview, her heartbeat picking up. The radio was playing the Bee Gees in a Saturday night fever, and she turned it down.

The car stopped behind her.

The long nose of a white Monte Carlo.

Two people behind the glass. She peered into the rearview mirror.

Ray Quick at the wheel. Alice Owens in sunglasses and headscarf in the passenger seat.

Ray staring at her. Staring. Waiting.

Alice Owens took a puff on a cigarette, blew smoke out the open window.

Colleen wasn't about to get out of the car. They could well be armed. They could run her over.

She rolled down her window. Bitter night air wafted in, blending with the tension holding her in its grasp.

"It's over!" she said, loud enough to carry. "For the both of you. It's over. No money. It's only a matter of time."

In the mirror she saw Ray barely shake his head from side to side, then grip the steering wheel with both hands.

She rolled the window back up, put the Torino into gear, headed back home.

The Monte Carlo followed.

Up the hill toward her flat.

Going home would expose where she lived, if they didn't already know, which could prove fatal.

At the top of Vermont, she stomped the gas, cut a hard right, tires squealing. And set off.

She'd lose them, take it from there. Pray the Torino had one last chase in her.

Late night, this time of year, she could get away with running stop signs at high speed, and she did.

Potrero came and went. South Van Ness turned into Van Ness, which turned into Lombard. And the Monte Carlo stayed right behind.

She threw the car into higher gear, bumped onto the Golden Gate Bridge, swimming with fog split across the cables like soft cheese through a giant slicer. It all seemed to tear by so fast.

She eyed the rearview mirror.

Familiar headlights. Coming up fast.

Too fast.

Her heart pounded as the Monte Carlo rammed her from behind with a heavy crunch, sending her into a skid on the bridge. She grabbed the steering wheel and righted herself, the tires slippery on the wet grates, losing traction with the bounce.

With a deep breath to steady herself, she looked over, saw Alice's window down alongside her.

The barrel of a pistol resting on the windowsill sent her nerves skyward.

Not too much traffic, thank God. Colleen hit the brakes, let the Monte Carlo rip by, then she yanked the Torino over into the oncoming lane for a moment to get on the driver's side of Ray's car in a skid that tested her skill and tires. A scream of horns as an oncoming van veered out of the way, but then she was back behind Ray's door, her passenger side kitty corner to his driver's side. He turned, looked at her with surprise, and that was OK. Her hands were tight with tension as she clung onto the steering wheel.

She dropped to second gear, stomped the gas, shot past the Monte Carlo across what was left of the bridge into the Marin Headlands. Shifted up as the engine screamed.

And then it was another blur. Up the Waldo Grade, through the tunnel, the speedometer needle leaning far to the right, touching three digits. The car shuddered with the speed, and a road limited at a good fifty miles per hour slower. In a car that was long in the tooth.

And somehow, somehow, the Monte Carlo managed to stay behind.

It was tough to do battle with a psychopath. Make that two.

She had less than a quarter tank of gas left. At these speeds it evaporated.

Down the steep hill into Marin, she snaked off toward Mt. Tam at the very last moment, swerving onto the narrow road. The corners up the mountain would be rough on the Monte Carlo. She knew the Torino like an old friend and had been here before. And she was heading toward Stinson Beach, where Gus lived. Possible sanctuary if she still had Ray and Alice on her tail then.

Taking the mountain curves on less than four wheels at times, she was able to lose the Monte Carlo, but not without incident. On one hairpin turn, she spun out, heart thumping, righted herself, continued up and over Mt. Tam in a spray of dirt and leaves.

Out of the last of the trees over the top of Mt. Tam, the sky cleared as the moon shone over the ocean and the beach far below on her left, the sea reflecting a freezing cold iridescent winter.

Down Highway 1, two lanes with enough turns to burn the brakes to the point of fadeout.

And behind her, with alarm, she saw the Monte Carlo's headlights pop out of the darkness again from around a corner.

They had already rammed her once.

She sped up. But downhill, the Monte Carlo's big engine was a locomotive on steroids.

Here they came. Right up behind her, slipping alongside now, getting close, too close, ready to push her off the cliff down a rocky slope into the ocean.

She wrenched the car to the right just in time. Fishtailed on the narrow two-lane blacktop. But not without another crash of metal that left her nerves in rags.

She caught Ray's grimace as they came in toward her from the left. She fought to recover the steering.

Again. The smash of metal pushed her off the road temporarily, up against a wall of dirt that collided, knocking her senseless, but the car righted itself just as she bounced it back into the narrow road. A scrape of fender on wheel tightened her nerves even more.

And over on the left, here they came again. The pop of the gun from the open window as the car swung toward her, heavier than her, two against one.

She bit down, heaved the Torino into them—not what they were expecting. Her arms were burning as she pitched the car into the Monte Carlo's nose and kept it there, pushing them over to the ocean side as both cars approached a hairpin curve.

Tires screaming, she pressed them to the edge of the asphalt. To the cliff. The water shimmering.

She caught a glimpse of the fear on Alice's face, masked by scarf and sunglasses, the shock, two open mouths now, as she pushed, their car wobbling, unsteady, the corner fast approaching. And she swerved to the right, swung what was left of her car squarely back into the Monte Carlo like a battering ram. Heard a scream as their car failed to stay on the road, went sailing over the side, rocks and dirt flying.

And she was next. Bouncing on dirt. Right after them.

She slammed on her brakes, heaved the Torino into reverse as she headed for the edge of nothingness, pulling the wheel hard. Her head hitting the roof of her car. Her senses jumbled. A smear of vision. Was this it? Her life, over?

The Torino finally skidded to a stop. She couldn't recall when she'd ever been quite so grateful.

One wheel hanging over the edge of oblivion as she heard a succession of crashes below, the Monte Carlo bouncing down the tall bluff.

Then she saw the flash of orange from down below, which reflected off her windshield, cracked and broken. Twin flames, the second more wild than the first.

She gunned her car in reverse, was able to pull herself back onto a lip of mountain road.

The engine thundered roughly in protest as she sat there, breathing deeply, wondering if she was alive or dead, whether this was some kind of hell she had entered, one she had justly earned. The entire day had felt like this, ever since the interrogation.

She got out. Walked over. Looked down.

Flames licked the twisted metal of the Monte Carlo on the rocks. Screams burst out of the burning vehicle.

The screams of a woman who had already died in another fire, weeks ago. Screams no one else would hear. Or ever know of. A woman finally facing the flames.

And, against what she knew was right, Colleen stood, listened, putting those screams in a dark place in her heart. As they grew less forceful, she wished that Traci and Fos might hear them too.

CHAPTER SEVENTY-THREE

Colleen pulled up on Hyde and Leavenworth in Alex's white Jag. It was still relatively early in the evening. It was still bitterly cold. Past New Years, it had to change at some point. But it felt like it would never end.

She got out of the Jag, left it running, a purr where the Torino had been a growl. The Torino was a write-off.

She walked over to Rhonda and Fia, both women huddled down in the cold.

"That detective business must pay pretty well," Rhonda said, puffing on a Kool.

"I wish," Colleen said. "It's a loaner."

Just the three of them standing there on a cold slow weeknight.

"Where's the gas guzzler?" Rhonda said.

"In the junkyard," Colleen said.

"How'd that happen?"

"Careless driving."

"Hmmm," Rhonda said. "Seems I heard Ray Quick had a little mishap too. Highway 1 up by Stinson Beach."

"Went off the road," Fia said, making a little sailing motion with her hand. "Like a bird. Couldn't happen to a nicer guy."

Rhonda tapped ash into the air. "They figure out who the woman was, who was with him?"

"Who knows?" Colleen said. "One of his floozies. Both of them were burnt up. She was beyond recognition."

"Huh," Rhonda said, giving Colleen a squint. "And your car wrecked too. Funny how that works."

Colleen shrugged.

"I've got something for you two ladies," she said. She reached into her pocket, came out with the white envelope Ray Quick had given her the night she put him in handcuffs. She dug through it while the two women watched her intently, and she took twenty-five of the hundred-dollar bills, handed them to Fia. The other twenty-five she handed to Rhonda.

"Merry Christmas," she said. "Sorry I'm a little late."

"Whoa," Fia said, looking at the money open mouthed. "Thanks, Santa Colleen. But this is an awful lot of cash. I don't think I've been that good. In fact, I know I haven't."

"Enough to last you a couple months if you don't blow it," Colleen said. "But it comes with conditions."

Rhonda gave Colleen a sly smile. "I figured as much."

"Each of you takes two months off this street. While you look for another line of work. I'm buying your time. Two months of it. Starting now."

Fia folded her money. "No strange dick for two months? I can handle that."

"Nice," Rhonda said, folding her wad, tucking it into her coat. "I always wanted to work with kids. My son's school is looking for someone."

"There you go," Colleen said. "Now you got time to catch your breath and plan for your futures."

"Thanks, Detective," Fia said.

"De nada."

"And what about you?" Rhonda said to Colleen, flicking her cigarette out to the street.

"Going to take a break," Colleen said. "Drive up the coast for a few days with a friend." She and Alex had talked about it once. Something they kicked around at one time, but it had never materialized. Now it would. After she took care of a couple of things. See Owens out of the hospital for one.

"I heard that," Rhonda said.

"I'm going to check with Traci's old man and little brother too. In Modesto."

"You found out where she lived?"

"Guy from Traci's apartment building saw some mail for her about to be returned. Was nice enough to clue me in on the return address." Do-Rag.

Rhonda nodded. "You got news for Traci's old man?"

She did. Not the best news. But closure.

"Traci didn't die unnoticed," she said. Justice had been served. In its own twisted way.

"Well, Happy New Year, Detective," Rhonda said. "It's a whole new decade."

"Yeah," Fia said. "Happy New Year. Thanks for all the cool cash!" She gave a big grin.

"Happy New Year, girls," Colleen said. She pulled the photo that Rhonda had given her from her pocket—Rhonda, Fia and Traci celebrating New Year's 1979. "Thought you might like this back."

She handed the Polaroid to Rhonda.

Rhonda took it, looked at it for a moment, her face turning to sadness.

"Thanks," she said quietly, clearing her throat.

"Make 1980 a fresh start."

A car pulled up behind the idling Jag, a red Cadillac, two middle-aged guys leering at the women. The men spoke to each other for a moment, then the window rolled down.

The driver did a come-hither with his finger at Colleen in her blonde wig.

"Hey, blondie. I think I'm in love."

"That's nice," Colleen said. "But I'm not on the menu."

"Too bad." He shrugged, gave Fia the same curled finger. "Hey, Suzy Wong. Let's party. Bring your friend." He made a fist. "Black is beautiful, babe!" he said to Rhonda. His friend started singing "Brown Sugar."

Rhonda returned a hand gesture, but it wasn't a nice one.

"Sorry, guys," Fia said, tucking her money in her pocket. "We're out of business."

CHAPTER SEVENTY-FOUR

Traci's family lived out in the part of California people didn't think of when they thought of the Golden State. Modesto, where it was warmer, even in winter, a world away from the city and its pretentions. People here voted on the right if they weren't illegal transplants from south of the border, up here for farm work. Los Angeles and its little sister, San Francisco, were islands, as foreign as could be to much of California. The air smelled of cow manure and earth as Colleen drove down Highway 99, where the turns to Los Angeles could practically be counted on one hand.

The family lived on the outskirts of town near a spanking new gas stop that dwarfed the small, modest houses scattered here and there. Theirs was a sunbaked shotgun house defined by deferred maintenance. Once-blue paint now was flaking, and a tarp flapped over a section of roof. An old fridge rested on the stoop by an open window where an air conditioner sat silent.

Colleen parked, walked past a broken gate, through a weed-strewn lawn, past a power mower that seemed to be purely ornamental. She was comfortable for once, not cold, in her denim flares and a crinkled tribal print blouse with deep red flowers. No coat required. A floppy hat over the soft short curls growing back, where the wig had been. In the distance the whir of Highway 99 added to the thrum.

In the driveway a man was bent under the open hood of a pickup truck that was a good twenty years old and looked every year of it.

A tall boy, six or so, with strawberry blonde hair and freckles stood by in baggy cutoffs, wearing a new A-Team T-shirt and black Keds. He watched Colleen with a sun-impaired squint as she approached. He was clearly Traci's little brother. Next to him lay an open toolbox.

Colleen announced herself with a "hello," and waited while the man clanked around and muttered at a particular part that apparently wasn't cooperating in the repair effort.

Something scraped.

"God damn it!" the man under the hood said.

"Dad," the boy said when it was clear he wasn't aware of Colleen's presence.

"Nine-sixteenths!" the man said. A big grease-smeared hand stuck out, waiting.

The boy rummaged around in the tool tray, came up with a wrench, placed it in the man's waiting hand.

The man went back to work with a squeak of metal.

"Excuse me," Colleen said.

"God damn thing," the man under the hood muttered. "WD-40." His hand stuck out again.

The boy picked up a can of WD-40, although his eyes were on Colleen, who was wondering if she should come back later.

"Dad."

"WD-40!"

"Dad!"

The man rose up from under the hood, his head missing a jagged latch by an inch.

He was a tall older version of the boy, but with dark hair and a grown man's weight and thickness. His face was darkened with five o'clock shadow and more darkness around his brooding eyes. A man with a load to bear.

Unlike the boy, he wasn't a spitting image of Traci, but the skin tone was there, and the face was long like hers had been.

He looked at Colleen with questioning eyes.

"Can I help you?" he said gruffly but not unkindly.

She got out a business card, handed it to him.

He took it, frowned. "This about Traci?"

She said that it was.

"James," he said to the boy. "Go wait inside until I call you."

Colleen wondered where Mom was.

"OK, Dad." The boy marched inside the house.

The man turned to Colleen. "If she's in trouble again, I'm not sure how I can help. I've tried just about everything."

"Can I ask where Traci's mother is?" Colleen said.

"Gone," he said. He didn't elaborate. He pulled a shop rag from the fender of the truck, wiped his hands, looked at her with his eyebrows raised. "Last I heard Traci went to Frisco. Lowlifes. Drugs. The whole thing. I keep writing to an address but never hear back. Don't expect to, really. She wrote us off long ago."

Colleen weighed up her words, words that had changed since her initial mission, one to provide closure. There really was no such thing.

"It's a long story," she said. "But I just wanted you to know: Traci got married, moved to Alberta. A guy in the Canadian Air Force. But she was clear she doesn't want to be contacted. She just wanted you to know she's doing OK."

A taut grimace formed over his mouth, nowhere near a smile, but perhaps a sense of relief.

He nodded.

"I guess that'll work," he said. "As long as she's OK."

Traci was as OK as she was ever going to be. Justice had been served.

"She is," Colleen said. "She's OK now."

EPILOGUE

"Come on, slow poke," Colleen said, holding the elevator door that opened up onto the outdoor walkway to Owens' motel on Lombard, where traffic whirred by on three lanes in and three lanes out of the city to the north bay.

"Hey!" Owens said, hobbling out of the elevator on crutches, "a little respect, if you please." He wore grey sweatpants and his red 49ers sweatshirt, number 16. Colleen carried his suit on a hanger and the bag with the few effects he'd collected during his jail stint and weeks in Santa Rosa Kaiser.

She shepherded him along the exterior walkway to his room facing Lombard.

She unlocked the door, stood back, let him shuffle in.

Despite the fact that the room had been freshly cleaned, and a new Monstera in a bright white pot sat on the table with a "get well" sign sticking up, alongside a bottle of scotch, the place still felt like a motel room. One Owens had been living in since divorce proceedings began with Alice almost two years ago. Colleen had pushed him to move into a permanent place more than once, but he just couldn't seem to do it. Always hoping for that reunion. Now maybe things would change.

"Welcome home," she said, shutting the door.

He stood, propped up on his crutches, looking around the room, then at her. He'd lost weight and although his bruises were long gone, a waxy ashen look had settled on a face that looked weary, exhausted. He needed a haircut.

"I laid in some groceries," she said. "Hold you for a few days." She nodded at the dorm fridge. "There's homemade Jell-O in there. Pineapple chunks. Mini marshmallows."

His eyes shone. On the edge of tears. "How do I ever begin to thank you, Colleen?"

"You already did. Just by being here."

"It's not enough."

She nodded, feeling emotional too. "It was a pleasure and an honor."

He looked at the bottle of Cutty Sark on the table, then at her. It was late afternoon. He raised his eyebrows. "The sun is over the yardarm," he said.

"Not for me, thanks. I've got a wily contractor I'm trying to track down before Alex and I head to Mendocino. But knock yourself out."

"I better hold off," he said. "It feels good just to clear my head after weeks of painkillers."

"I can imagine."

He gestured at the door. "Can you open that, please? I've been locked up for so long, even traffic noise is welcome."

She did. He ended up heading back out on the walkway, working the crutches gingerly but getting the hang of it quickly.

He stood at the oxidized metal railing; afternoon traffic headed toward the Golden Gate Bridge.

She joined him. It was cold but for once it didn't matter. The air was fresh.

"What's next?" she said.

"They're going to try to retire me off," he said, looking across Lombard. "But it's not going to work."

"I'm glad to hear it."

"And you?"

"I don't know," she said. "With Pam gone . . ." She had brought him up to speed on Pam on the way back from Santa Rosa. "I just don't know."

He turned on his crutches, looked at her, turned back to the flowing traffic.

"I can understand you've probably had enough of the life you've been living in 'Baghdad by the Bay.' Pam was the reason you came out here. Started up your PI business. To get by. Find her. But, you know, it suits you, somehow. And you're damn good at it. And God knows where I'd be without you, Colleen."

"It's not for everybody," she said. "But it's kind of grown on me." She found herself shrugging. "This is a good town for misfits."

"You got that right."

There was a pause. "I'm only going to say this once and then we're never going to talk about it again," she said. "I know you're not happy with the way things played out—with Ray and Alice. But I had to finish what I started. I couldn't have you coming out of the hospital, going after Ray. Or Alice. Or both of them."

There was another pause, a long pause.

"You probably did me a favor, Colleen," he said. "The anger is gone. I don't feel it anymore." He took a deep breath. "All I feel now is empty inside."

She understood. Because that's how she had felt ever since she had put an end to her husband, all those years ago.

ACKNOWLEDGMENTS

Thanks, as always, are due my stalwart writing group who keep me on the straight and narrow (as much as they possibly can). They are, in no particular order: Barbara McHugh, Dot Edwards, Heather King, and Eric Seder, all talented writers whose input is invaluable to my work.

Thanks as well to Graham Cowley, former investigator with the SF Medical Examiner's Office, for insight into how the job was done back when Colleen was doing her thing, and Adam Chin, filmmaker, whose documentary *Graham's Tales* details much of what it was like.

Others who helped me flesh out *Night Candy* with details:

Kim Marie Thorburn, MD, MPH—*San Francisco Coroner's Office: A History*

Patrick O'Donnell, retired Milwaukee PD.

But most of all, thank you, dear reader, for reading *Night Candy*. It was a pleasure to write and I hope you enjoyed it. You are the reason I do this.

BOOK CLUB
DISCUSSION QUESTIONS

1. How do you think Colleen's life as an ex-con, unlicensed female PI in the late '70s would compare to her life in those circumstances in the present day?

2. Many of the characters in *Night Candy* struggle with the textbook version of right and wrong. How much do you think the absolutism of these views affects law enforcement? And justice?

3. Why do you think the three "working girls" Colleen befriends are important to her?

4. Were you surprised when Colleen disclosed the most emotionally vulnerable piece of her life to the serial killer Paul Oedekoven?

5. Judging by what Colleen discloses in *Night Candy*, do you think she was justified in killing her ex?

6. Colleen ultimately reneges on her plan to frame Ray Quick as Night Candy, but she comes close. What would you have decided to do?

7. Do you think Colleen is justified in letting Alice's "death" at the Joshua Inn persist as the death on record?

8. Colleen suffers many losses in *Night Candy*: Pam, Matt, and nearly Owens. She loses Alistair's respect. Does she lose her way?

9. How important is Owens' friendship to Colleen? Why?

10. Do you see the end of the novel as an ending for Colleen as the 1980s approach? Or a new beginning?

PUBLISHER'S NOTE

We hope that you enjoyed *Night Candy*, the fifth in Max Tomlinson's Colleen Hayes Mystery Series.

While the other four novels stand on their own and can be read in any order, the publication sequence is as follows:

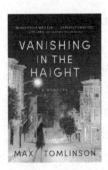

VANISHING IN THE HAIGHT

It's 1978 and Colleen Hayes sets off to solve the decade-old murder of a wealthy man's daughter. She is an ex-con, recently out of prison after nine years for killing her abusive husband, now trying to make ends meet as an unofficial PI. She has little to go on in this case, but fearlessly searches the underbelly of San Francisco for a link to that brutal murder of a child ten years ago at Golden Gate Park.

"*Vanishing in the Haight* makes for a classic detective tale: a postmodern noir featuring period perfect San Francisco settings that wondrously carve a slice out of time. Max Tomlinson's new series launch takes us into the waning days of the counter culture where private eye Colleen Hayes picks up the trail of a decade-old murder."

—Jon Land, *USA Today* best-selling author

TIE DIE

Colleen Hayes is hired by a 1960s rock star to find his kidnapped teenaged daughter. This search takes her to 1970s London, where she discovers a thread that traces to the death of a forgotten fan, connected not only to a music industry rife with corruption and crime, but to the missing teen.

"Tomlinson deepens the character of his multi-layered lead, Colleen Hayes, an unlicensed PI and ex-con who's still on parole. Readers will want to learn more about this surprising and pragmatic woman."   —*Publishers Weekly* (Starred Review)

BAD SCENE

San Francisco, 1978. While investigating a suspected plot to kill the mayor, PI and ex-con Colleen Hayes learns that her runaway daughter has joined a shadowy church. The cult is now building a settlement in South America near a volcano about to erupt. Death is the path to perfection—and the day is fast approaching for her daughter and hundreds of others.

"The fast-paced action, colorful setting, and realistic mother-daughter dynamic help make this entry a winner. Readers will look forward to Colleen's further exploits."   —*Publishers Weekly*

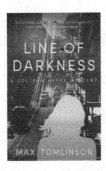

LINE OF DARKNESS

Postwar darkness may be the darkest of them all—Nazi-hunters reach deep into 1979 San Francisco and Colleen discovers an international vigilante group, which leads her to Italy and a secret project hatched in a concentration camp.

"*Line of Darkness* is an engrossing noir novel that grows darker and more complex under the lingering pall of Nazism."

—*Foreword Reviews*

We hope that you will read the entire Colleen Hayes Mystery Series and will look forward to more to come.

If you liked *Night Candy*, we would be very appreciative if you would consider leaving a review. As you probably already know, book reviews are important to authors and they are very grateful when a reader makes the special effort to write a review, however brief.

For more information, please visit the author's website: www.maxtomlinson.wordpress.com.

Happy Reading,
Oceanview Publishing
Your Home for Mystery, Thriller, and Suspense